DATE DUE

	JAN 28 2002
	OCT 15 2002
MAY 03 2001	
	MAY 08 '03
MAY 09 2001	SEP 02 '03
	FEB 16 2005
MAY 21 2001	
MAY 29 2001	
JUN 12 2001	
JUN 26 2001	
JUL 09 2001	
JUL 30 2002	
MAY 23 '03	

This Large Print Book carries the
Seal of Approval of N.A.V.H.

Harper's Moon

Harper's Moon

Suzanne Judson

G.K. Hall & Co. • Thorndike, Maine

Published in 2001 by arrangement with The Berkley Publishing Group, a member of Penguin Putnam Inc.

G.K. Hall Large Print Core Series.

The text of this Large Print edition is unabridged.
Other aspects of the book may vary from the original edition.

Set in 16 pt. Plantin by Christina S. Huff.

Printed in the United States on permanent paper.

Library of Congress Cataloging-in-Publication Data

Judson, Suzanne.
    Harper's moon / Suzanne Judson.
      p. cm.
      ISBN 0-7838-9390-6 (lg. print : hc : alk. paper)
     1. Runaway wives — Fiction. 2. Travel writing — Fiction.
     3. North Carolina — Fiction. 4. Large type books. I. Title.
PS3560.U4 H37   2001
813'.6—dc21   00-054022

Harper's

Moon

Prologue

New York City

It was a stranger's hands that hurt her, a stranger's hot liquory breath that rasped in her ear. Annabel Mahoney pivoted on the toes of her evening sandals, struggling to duck under the arms that were pinning her to the silk-lined wall of the foyer.

One heel slipped on the glossy parquet floor just as his hand grabbed at her long, dark hair, scattering the clips that held her chignon and making her gasp. Her slender body twisted helplessly against his big, burly one. A white-hot jolt of pain burst inside her as he yanked her hair again, pulling at her until her hip collided with the sharp corner of the hallway's antique console table. The lamp on the table rocked and crashed to the floor. Porcelain exploded at the impact, the shards as delicate and colorful as fireworks. She stepped on one sharp fragment and slipped, falling against his body. His strong hands grabbed her bare upper arms, and her legs kicked uselessly as he pulled her farther into the apartment.

"Don't," she breathed, terrified, hurting, knowing it was useless but gasping the word out anyway. "Don't."

"Bitch," he grunted, grabbing for her arm. "You don't tell *me* what to do."

It was a stranger's voice, harsh and low-pitched, thick with anger and heat.

A stranger's strength that slammed the bedroom door open, shoved her toward the bed.

A stranger's eyes that stared down at her, deep brown and drunken. A stranger's wild eyes above a stranger's set, handsome mouth.

A stranger's hand, ripping the silk of her dress as though it were tissue, grasping her shoulder with agonizing tightness.

A stranger's hand.

Wearing her husband's simple gold wedding ring.

Her husband. A stranger. When exactly was it that the charming man she'd tried so hard to please had become a monster she didn't even know?

Staring into his eyes, breathing raggedly, she twisted until she sat upright on the bed, defying him, only to feel his hand yank at her hair again. The force of it bent her neck and brought tears to her eyes. As he raised his hand to slap her, she moved first, punching at his chest with both arms. Her hands glanced off his shoulders. He shook his head like an angry bull.

It was a mistake; she could see that at once. The weak, useless blow had only enraged him further. Fighting would only make it worse. Annabel Taylor Mahoney turned her head, squeezed her eyes shut, and tried to brace herself for whatever would come next.

Twenty floors below, the Park Avenue traffic rumbled softly, but the penthouse echoed with silence.

Annie — she always thought of herself that way, though Tom hated the nickname — lay motionless in the thin city sun, her tangled black hair streaming across the expensive Pratesi linens she'd never liked. She kept her eyes closed and her breathing steady. Feigning sleep was one of the skills she'd mastered perfectly in the four years of her marriage. And feigning agreement, feigning apology, feigning confidence. No one had ever told her how crucial deception could be to a marriage, she thought with the dark, bitter amusement that was the only kind of humor she could muster these days. They should teach it to young brides. Elementary Wedlock: How to Lie to Your Husband, Your Family, and Yourself.

The huge ivory room smelled so civilized, of furniture polish and lavender sachets and potpourri. Heavy chintz drapes filtered the light and muffled the raucous city sounds below. On the top of Tom's obsessively neat bureau a small gold clock chimed eight. Her body's inborn rhythms always woke her at dawn, but Annie had learned to lie still until Tom left for work each day. He was tense in the mornings, and cutting when any part of his routine was disturbed. Something as small as too-strong coffee could enrage him, and when it did, he nursed the anger all day. If she pretended to sleep late, she could usually stave off conflict, start the morning with at least the illusion that the day would be clean, fresh, and innocent.

Today she needed that illusion desperately. She couldn't bear more of his rage this morning. She wasn't even sure how she would face him tonight, how she could meet the deep brown eyes that were so handsome and so deceptive and so dangerous.

Not after last night.

At the memory, a wave of revulsion shuddered through her. Disgust rose like bile in her throat and nausea roiled in her stomach. Squeezing her eyes shut, hugging her aching torso with her arms, she forced herself to remain still and strained her ears for any hint of sound.

Nothing. He was gone.

The peaceful hours without him were too precious to be wasted. She rose heavily from the king-sized bed, pulled the worn chenille robe Tom hated so much around her slender body, and padded toward the bathroom.

She rarely looked closely at herself anymore. She had learned to put on the elaborate makeup and clothes Tom liked with barely a glance, concentrating on the hair she was styling or the cheekbones she was dusting with blusher, never taking in her whole image at once.

But this morning, numbed by the events of the evening before, she finally looked, and looked hard.

What she saw shocked her. Try as she might, she could not recognize the woman who looked back.

The long, black hair she'd once been shyly proud of hung dry and lifeless. Her skin, always pale, had a greenish cast. Slowly, she'd been losing weight, precious pounds her slender frame could ill afford. Dark circles ringed her pearly gray eyes, blue purple arcs that matched the fresh bruises on the skin under her collarbones.

But it was the expression in her eyes that most disturbed her. She'd never realized it was so visible, so plain to see. The defeat. The indecision. The despair. The fear. And above all, the dreadful, paralyzing shame.

Like everyone else, young Annie Taylor had read newspaper stories about battered women. Like everyone else, she'd shaken her head, mystified. It could never happen to her. She had intelligence, strength, pride, talent, common sense. She was going to get a good job, become a good artist, choose a good man, have good kids. Surely the attractive, capable, often well-educated women in the newspaper reports she read could do the same. How could they allow men to abuse them time after time, year after year? Why didn't they just get help?

Well, now she knew.

Women like her didn't get help because they began by loving their husbands and wanting to be good wives. Because they'd been trained, as young girls, to please rather than confront. Because they assumed the problems were their fault, not his. Because it all started so gradually, with criticisms first, and then rages, and only then blows. Because — at least at the beginning — the bad times always passed, letting them believe that each would be the last.

They didn't get help because the people around them saw only the attentive public man, the good provider, the charming spouse. Because their husband helped keep their family in comfort. Because their mothers told them to try harder or their friends dropped away.

They didn't get help because by the time they accepted the abuse for what it was, it was too late. By then it had gone on for years, and they knew no one would ever understand.

Staring at her image in the mirror, she didn't understand it herself. Where had the old Annie Taylor gone? Where was the girl who had aced every subject in school, fought to defend the class nerds from the school bully, sang lustily along with rock anthems, and sat with her girlfriends in the long, fragrant grass of Central Park, hooting with laughter and making endless plans about love and travel and children and life? Where was the young woman who had gone to art school over her mother's protests, who had no trouble at all fending off overamorous boy-friends, who had saved for a beat-up Toyota and driven it like an Indy racer? How could she be so much less confident at thirty-five than she'd been at twenty-five? How had the simple act of falling in love with a handsome, successful man replaced that funny, feisty girl with this cowering waif?

She didn't know; the transition had been so gradual, so seamless, that she'd barely noticed it was happening.

But suddenly she realized that it didn't really matter. She could — would — sort it out later. What mattered was that she had to make a choice, and make it now. She had to choose the known or the unknown.

The past or the future.

The lies or the truth.

Death or life. Because if she didn't, this se-cret, shameful hell would continue. No, it would get worse. Once he crossed a boundary — the first crude insult, the first push, the first slap — Tom never went back. Until last night, he had never forced her sexually. But he had been excited by the struggle; she had seen it in his eyes. He would do it again. A year from now, if she stayed, the woman in the mirror would only be more haunted, more fearful, more ashamed.

Somewhere in the apartment the central air-conditioning clicked on. The rush of cool air and the vision of her future made Annie shiver.

She pulled the robe tighter around her body, careful not to jostle the aching places under her ribs.

Tom had told her he would never let her go a hundred times, and she believed him. The statistics she read bore the threat out. Battered women were at the highest risk of all when they tried to escape. She had little money of her own and no friends she could turn to; they'd all slowly drifted away over the last few years, baffled by her unease and evasiveness. As for her mother, her only family, Matilda had always been quick to argue that Tom's was normal male behavior and insist that he wouldn't get so angry if Annie just tried harder. It was one of Annie's deepest griefs, her mother's unremitting refusal to reach out, to help, even to see.

It wouldn't be easy. But somehow, despite the odds stacked against her, something deep and hidden and defiant inside her — some ghost of the gutsy woman she used to be — chose truth.

And the future.

And life.

Swiftly, Annie stepped under the shower, wincing as jets of hot water hit the fresh bruises. She pulled on the warm robe again, then padded into the kitchen to turn on the fancy coffee machine.

With its stark granite countertops and top-of-the-line stainless steel appliances, it was a beautiful room. But it wasn't her idea of a kitchen and never had been. She'd dreamed of pretty curtains, little pots of herbs, a round oak table, a comfortable scattering of homey old things. Not a kitchen as sterile as an operating theater, or a dining room large and formal enough to entertain the whole diplomatic corps, or a study that was too carefully decorated to hold the worn, motley books she actually read. She had always been grateful for the financial security Tom's job as an investment manager brought her and her mother. She knew that thousands, millions of others had nothing; she had grown up with nothing herself. Yet it wasn't the luxury that had kept her here. Nothing in this glamorous lifestyle touched her, comforted her, nurtured her soul.

She sat at the glass-and-iron kitchen table in the grayish New York sunlight, twirling her empty coffee mug in her hands. Galvanized by the decision, her mind worked swiftly, clearly, calmly. The daze of weariness and confusion she'd lived in for months suddenly lifted. Plans and decisions seemed to make themselves. It was as if some secret part of her had already mapped out an escape route, ready to be used the moment she finally made a choice.

The city had places a woman could be safe. But the thought of living half imprisoned terrified her, and so did the idea of being anywhere within Tom's reach. She needed to get away, far away. Annie had a sudden memory of herself at ten or eleven, curled on the Indian bedspread in her tiny bedroom, making rebellious plans to run away from the claustrophobic apartment and her mother's endless, carping criticisms. She'd never gone, of course. She was too good a girl for that, too responsible, too anxious to please. And maybe these dreams of flight were just as impractical as her old ones had been. But she was going to try.

Her only chance of getting away was to go as far as possible before he started looking. Tom had a Racquet Club dinner tonight, an all-male brandy-and-billiards affair that would last past midnight. She would leave a note saying that she'd gone to stay with her mother for a day or two — a move that wouldn't surprise him, after last night. May Williams wouldn't be in to clean until next week, so that would be no problem. And when Tom called her mother, he'd get no answer; Matilda always spent Tuesdays shopping with her friends, and Wednesday was her standing appointment at the hairdresser. If Annie left now, he wouldn't be suspicious until Wednesday afternoon, maybe even Wednesday night. It wasn't much of a lead, but it would have to be enough.

She wouldn't have much money. Tom controlled their finances, all but the money she earned from her quilts. He resented her fabric work and sneered at what he called the pathetic proceeds from it. They weren't so pathetic anymore, though. Over on Madison Avenue, the little shop called Pleasures was selling her quilts for almost a thousand dollars each these days.

Even with her last quilt still unsold in the store, there must be more than five thousand in the account.

She could use that and withdraw some cash from their checking account before she left the city and maybe sell one of the pieces of jewelry Tom had given her over the years. Once she left Manhattan, she wouldn't be able to use her bank and credit cards; they would be a sure trace to her whereabouts. But she would have enough, at least, to start, and she was lucky to have even that. Annie thought of that fresh start, of the chance to be in a world not filled with fear and rage and pretending. A small tendril of hope curled deep inside her, as delicate and tentative as the tiniest shoot of new spring growth after a long, cold winter.

Automatically, still thinking hard, she rinsed her cup in the sink. Tom had an almost obsessive interest in what she wore. If she took too much, he'd know at once that she was gone. Back in the bedroom, she rifled through what she thought of as "her" clothes, not the stylish garments — uniforms, really — she wore as a Wall Street wife.

Her old jeans, she decided, a couple of sweaters, a comfortable cotton turtleneck. Sneakers, her sturdy little hiking boots, a pair of simple leather flats that she could wear today. On impulse she fished out a pretty vintage dress she'd bought at a thrift shop and cached away unworn in the back of her closet. She'd risk taking her trench coat but not her robe or heels or an extra handbag.

She sorted dispassionately through the jewelry in her top drawer and chose a single pair of earrings, diamonds that she knew she could sell easily. Putting the small velvet box on the bed with the clothing, she carefully shut the drawer. Then, on impulse, she opened it again and tucked her Tiffany wedding band inconspicuously amid a tray full of costume jewelry.

Back in the bathroom, she took a few favorite toiletries, abandoning most of the expensive products without regret. Wherever she was going, she thought with rueful humor, she certainly wouldn't need eyelash curlers and brown contour stick and hair sculpting gel. She zipped the travel case and dropped it on the pile of clothing. She would pack her things in paper shopping bags, leaving untouched the stack of Vuitton suitcases that were the first thing Tom would check.

With the two bags packed and placed near the front door, she took a deep breath and started toward the back of the penthouse. Her step made no sound on the thick Oriental runner. This was the hard part, the only loss that would ache, she thought. She turned the knob of the last door in the hallway and braced herself for regret.

It had been a maid's room originally, small and narrow and with only a single window. Annie had brightened it with deep marigold paint, inexpensive white wood furniture, and a colorful hooked rug. The back wall was a nest of cubbyholes, each filled to bursting with folded lengths of fabric. Her cutting table sat with a tall stool near the doorway, her sewing machine was angled into the corner, while her quilting frame took pride of place along the long wall. She'd filled an interior window box with geraniums, tacked favorite postcards and swatches and quotes to the walls, made a stack of her favorite books next to a shabby, comfortable armchair. Novels by writers from Jane Austen to Joanna Trollope. Biographies of artists. Travel books, by everyone from J. M. Bell to John McPhee, that brought the world to life in her imagination. Each well-thumbed book was a friend, a companion for lonely hours.

Tom thought her studio was childish, but he left it alone. He said he didn't give a damn about her silly hobbies, as long as they didn't interfere with her duties as a wife. Annie had tried to make sure they never did. Her studio and her quilts held the whole of her heart these days, as though the entire meaning of her life had concentrated itself in these few colorful square feet. If there was any place in which the old Annie Taylor still lived, it was here. But she would have to leave it behind her now.

She drifted to the side of the room and ran her hand gently over her latest quilt. Years of learning and looking and practice glowed in the six-foot patchworked square. She'd always loved fabric and fibers, even though her art school teachers had dismissed sewing as a mere craft. Her first quilts had been traditional ones, sewn of repeated blocks. Later, she'd begun branching out, abandoning regular patterns, using fabric as inventively as an artist might use paint. Her newer quilts were all free-form, one-of-a-kind pieces, each with its own theme, name, and meaning.

In her own mind she'd called this new one *Fortress* and based it loosely on the traditional log cabin quilting block beloved by generations of American women. Her own version transformed the simple cabin pattern into something contemporary, urban, disturbing. The fabrics she'd chosen were all variations of silvery gray — the glimmery, subtle gray of mist and metal. The bottom section of the quilt held recognizable log cabin shapes, but as the eye moved upward, they grew and splintered into forms that might be skyscrapers, fountains, ice crystals, even bars. By the top of the quilt, you could no longer tell whether the fragmented cabin shapes were solid or broken, prisons or retreats.

Annie always lavished her heart and soul onto these fabric artworks; they were the one place she didn't pretend, didn't deceive, didn't lie. Looking at it now, she saw that she had poured all her yearning for a stable, happy home into this quilt. All her longing for a loving family and a safe haven, and all her brokenhearted fear that no such thing existed.

Abandoning the painstaking work made her heartsick, but try as she might, she could think of no way to bring it with her. It was huge and bulky and still peppered with pins; the doorman would surely notice if she carried it out of the building. No, she needed to travel light. Numbly she gave the soft fabric a final caress, then turned toward her worktable to think.

There was so much here, beloved mementos, sewing tools, papers, much-thumbed books. But in the end she took only her bulging notebook of sketches and ideas, the sterling thimble her grandmother had once used, and a few cherished photos. As she bent to replace the photograph album, a beloved book on Appalachian fiber arts caught her eye. Maybe she could head there, she thought, pausing for a moment in the warm, cheerful room. Drive down to the Appalachian Mountains, to North Carolina or Georgia or Tennessee. She had never been to that part of the country, but it was remote and probably cheap to live in. As good a place as any, when she had no-where in particular to go. But she would get on the road before she decided for sure.

God, she was going to miss this room, miss this small, bright, private world. Her eyes stinging with tears, she took one last glance around. Then she gathered up the small handful of things she'd chosen and forced herself to shut the door.

In the foyer, she cleaned up the Chinese lamp that had broken the night before. She slung her satchel handbag over one shoulder, balanced the shopping bags that held her clothing in her hands, and tossed her trench coat casually over one arm.

The bags were so light, she thought wonderingly, to contain a whole new life.

She pushed her car key into a pocket and left the rest of the ring in the console table's narrow drawer. The apartment door swung soundlessly shut behind her, locking her out. When the polished brass elevator slid open, she stepped inside swiftly. She pushed the lobby button hard, breathing in the clear, frightening air of freedom, never looking back.

One

Burnsville, North Carolina

He'd had his family home razed to the ground ten years before, making half the tongues in Burnsville wag. That was nothing new. The local matriarchs had shaken their heads over him way back when he was just the youngest member of that white-trash Harper clan. They'd clucked even harder when he'd confounded their dire predictions and made a success of himself. They'd probably say he was no damn good even if he invented the cure for cancer, won the Nobel Peace Prize, and ascended into heaven on the very same day.

That was small-town life; it branded you right from the start, and you could never quite escape the label you started with. Jed Harper had learned not to let it bother him, most of the time at least. Standing on the spot where his family's house — shack, really — had been, he'd just grinned at their dark mutterings and made sure that every single plank and brick of the old structure was carted away. Then he'd built his own kind of house on the empty site on the mountainside. A big log building that was simple but almost sinfully comfortable. A home filled with light and silence, order and peace. An eligible man living alone in a nice, clean house and ignoring the town's marriageable maidens: That irritated the hell out of the local ladies, too.

Almost no evidence of his parents remained amid the sturdy old Mission furniture he'd bought himself, the books and musical instruments and artifacts he'd collected over the years. Yet a hint of the chaos they'd created seemed to tremble over the place sometimes, especially when he'd been away awhile. For an instant the memories flooded back, echoes of cold and dirt and shame and endless fighting. His father always angry, his mother always disappointed or withdrawn, both of them drunk half the time, or more. And a skinny kid, edging around them, wanting nothing more than not to be noticed.

The visions hung in the bright mountain air for a moment, then vanished, just as the reality had vanished ten years before. He was almost forty, and the past was gone, except when he was stupid or self-pitying enough to resurrect it. Shaking his head at his own overactive imagination, Jed dropped his duffel bag on the wide wooden porch, anchored the case for his precious laptop computer more securely under his arm, and turned the key in the lock of his front door.

Rooster was untroubled by Jed's complicated human woes. With canine simplicity, he was just glad to be home after five months' absence, even if he'd only gone as far as Meg Thorn's house right off the Burnsville town square. As soon as Jed pushed the front door open, Rooster was off in a burst of flying fur, loping through the big, spare rooms, skidding a little on the well-worn Navajo rugs that dotted the polished floors. No sooner had he made sure that no other retriever had taken over his turf during his absence than he was thumping against the kitchen door, eager to complete the same inspection in the back-yard.

Rooster's exuberance banished the last traces of Jed's sour memories. Grinning, he dumped his gear in the hallway, let the dog out again, and leaned back against a counter to say hello to his home.

Jed had been in Hong Kong for five long months, five months of heat and humidity and hundreds of conversations with everyone from fish vendors to financial wizards. Even in a place as opulent as the thriving British colony, he lived rough on the road. He worked hard, trav-eled light, and moved around often. The easy comforts of his house looked good to him now. The firm king-sized bed upstairs, designed to accommodate a six-foot-two frame in comfort. A shower with really hot water, his beloved dul-cimer, a couple of thousand books. His study, complete with a big leather chair and a computer with a decent-sized monitor. Absently, Jed reached up to rub the nape of his neck, where the muscles still ached under the thick bronze hair he'd cut short in the Hong Kong heat. Laptops were definitely a blessing for roving writers, but after months of hunching over a finicky little portable computer, he was looking forward to working upright again.

Meg Thorn, Jed's oldest friend, had aired the house for him, and dour but rigidly reliable Moira McTeague, who came in to clean every few weeks, had kept the place spotless. The rooms smelled of lemon oil and the faint hint of wood smoke that always hung over the mountains in the autumn. Here in the kitchen, John and Susie Addamson had stuffed his refrigerator with food. Jed laughed out loud at the wild array, everything from a big T-bone steak to a jar of salsa, all crammed untidily on the wire shelves. Warmed by their thoughtfulness, he snagged a beer from the rack on the door. It was an Irish ale, he noticed, scrutinizing the bottle with the same curiosity that kept his fans intrigued, his publisher happy, and his bank accounts full. Where the hell had John gotten a bottle of Harp in the middle of Burnsville, a small Southern town in a dry county better known for its Baptist churches than its beer? He twisted the cap and drank straight from the bottle, letting a trickle of liquid slip down his chin. Wherever it had come from, it was damned good. Amused, Jed dropped into one of the old Windsor chairs to tug off his dusty boots, took another hefty swig of the ice-cold beer, then ambled out onto the small back porch.

His house was built into the hillside above Jack's Creek, one of the hundreds of small brooks that wound through the hilly terrain of western North Carolina's Black Mountains. From the front of the house he could see the creek, the valley, and the scattering of houses that dotted the slopes above it. But from the back, few signs of humanity were visible. Just the edge of the Wellmans' farm, a couple of vacation chalets that were mostly empty, and Alma Honeycutt's cottage, now deserted, too.

It was a landscape of wooded peaks, mountain after mountain as far as the eye could see. Now, near the end of September, the hills were still green, though a few maples flamed crimson against the dense foliage. A pocket of thick white mist drifted along the nearest ridge, but the sky above was cloudlessly blue. The September air was so clear and crisp it almost sparkled. Pine needles and oak leaves rustled gently in the breeze, and Jed could just about hear the rushing tumble of the creek farther down the mountain. One of the Wellman farm's horses was wandering near the fence again, in the same exact place one Wellman horse or another had wandered for nigh on thirty years of autumn Tuesdays.

It was home. Jed leaned lazily back against the

sun-kissed clapboard and propped one bare foot on the stoop. Home. And he was glad to be here. Even with the old ghosts barely kept at bay and the town gossips sitting down in the Cupboard Café at this very moment, sharpening their knives. Even with the jangle of Hong Kong and the daze of jet lag still fogging his mind. Even knowing that in three or four or six months, the restlessness would hit him again, making him itch to be away on his next trip — this time to Newfoundland, the subject he'd already chosen for his next book. Burnsville was an essential part of Jed Harper's soul, but never in his whole adult life had he been able to stay there for more than six months at a time, and he expected he never would.

Rooster glimpsed him on the stoop and streaked back across the yard's steep slope, abandoning the rabbit he'd been stalking out beyond a stand of maples. Racing up the steps, he cannoned full force into Jed's blue-jeaned thighs, panting and barking and writhing with welcome. Wanting to make sure, Jed figured as he set his beer safely on the wooden railing, that his master would actually be around for a while. And, in fact, he would. There were friends to see, business to attend to, and hundreds of pages of Hong Kong notes to write up before the need to escape would begin to burn like fire in his belly once again.

Jed squatted down onto the stoop, liking the feel of the sun-warmed wood under his feet, the bittersweet aftertaste of the ale, the kiss of the breeze that made his denim shirt flap around his spine, the dog's uncomplicated greeting.

"That's right, boy," he said aloud as Rooster pushed against him, nuzzling his cool black nose into Jed's bare, tanned neck, welcoming the way Jed's big hand gently ruffled his silky fur. "We're home." He knew there was just the faintest tinge of irony in his voice. Luckily, Rooster didn't seem to care.

"Pick up the goddamn phone, you stupid broad," Tom Mahoney muttered, his perfectly manicured fingertips drumming angrily on the equally perfect surface of his desk. It was almost five o'clock on Tuesday afternoon. There'd been no answer at the apartment all day, and no one at his mother-in-law's, either. Matilda was out shopping, probably. She'd gotten damn good at shopping ever since Tom had started paying her rent. As for Annabel, she was probably drifting around some museum with her head in the bloody clouds. Someone else might have let him know where she was, what she was doing. But not Annabel. Why was he surprised?

He was due at a Racquet Club dinner at eight. The event just happened to be organized by one of his most important clients, not that his wife gave a damn. Well, wherever she was, Annabel had better have picked up his tux, and for that matter gotten herself something decent to wear for the gala benefit ball they were due to attend later that week. When you were at Tom's professional level — successful, but not quite at the top of the heap, not yet, at least — the pressure was intense, and everything counted. Your clothes. Your club memberships. Your accent: Tom, who'd grown up working-class Irish, had labored hard on that. Where you spent your vacations. And who your wife was. A wife who didn't fit in could sink your career.

The top men of the firm always pretended things like that didn't matter. But it wasn't true, not unless you wanted to stay down there among the meek little middle managers, which Tom definitely didn't. He had plans, and at forty-three not much more time to achieve them. Men who didn't make it by forty-five or so started to be spoken of as over the hill. His career was an intensive, all-out war, a war in which a poor Irish kid from New Jersey was going to defeat an army of overbred WASPs. He was determined about that, and no artsy, ditsy foible of Annabel's was going to get in his way.

Goddamn women, he thought, staring at the figures flashing on his computer monitor as he listened to the apartment's answering machine click on. *Lazy bitches. They loved to spend a man's money, but they didn't lift a finger to help him while he earned it.* His own mother had been the worst of all, a useless broad who'd resisted his father every day of the poor pathetic sonovabitch's life.

Tom had chosen shy, beautiful, struggling

little Annabel Taylor, thinking she'd be different. He'd figured she would appreciate the financial comfort he brought her, not just her but her shrew of a mother, too. He'd thought she'd be grateful for the chance to learn the social ropes. But she never quite came through when it counted; she found a million petty ways to resist. Tom could remember his father's bitter complaints that when it came to women, none of them were different under the skin. Annabel was living proof. They were all bloodsuckers, out for everything they could get.

"Thomas." Stretch McNaughten stood in the office doorway, six foot five inches of silver hair, patrician bones, custom tailoring, and implacable will. "You're busy?"

It was high time for the crabby old bastard to retire, but until that happy day finally came, he was a force — *the* force — to be reckoned with at Finch McNaughten. Tom straightened his back and stilled his drumming fingers. "No, Stretch," he said pleasantly, clicking the speaker-phone off. "Of course not. Come on in."

"I've been lunching with Miller," McNaughten said, stepping a grudging foot or so into Tom's office. Tom's work space was elegantly appointed. But McNaughten ignored the damask love seat as though it was too common for his aristocratic ass. The old bastard didn't want to imply approval by actually sitting down, Tom thought resentfully. Or give up the advantage of looming three feet above Tom's own seated form.

"We were wondering if you'd heard from SafeCo," the old man continued.

"Not yet." Tom kept his voice even, smiling over the anger that surged through him at the question. He was a senior vice president of a major investment management firm, not some fucking toddler who had to be checked on every five minutes. But he was also dependent on the goodwill of Miller and Stretch for his annual bonus, which made up most of his income. "I'm sure they'll be in touch shortly, Stretch. You know how it is. They're working on end-of-the-quarter financials, and I understand that the firm is gearing up for their annual meeting, too."

"Do you understand that? I'm surprised. What I understand is that they're unhappy with Finch McNaughten, and that they're looking around for another firm to manage their pension money."

Where the hell had McNaughten heard that? "My wife and I had dinner with Jim Perry just last night," Tom said sharply. "We went to dinner, saw a show. I can assure you, Stretch, Jim was perfectly happy with our work."

"Mr. Perry is an underling." *Just like you,* McNaughten's tone implied. "He doesn't run SafeCo or make the final decision on the management of their pension funds. We've had a relationship with the firm for ten years, Thomas, and we'd be very unhappy to lose a two hundred million dollar account. Especially after — what shall I call it? — the defection of Manchester Industries last month."

The Manchester debacle hadn't been Tom's fault; he'd explained that a million times. How the hell was he supposed to stop the pension manager there from turning the business over to an old buddy from Yale? In the end, WASPS always stuck together. McNaughten had scapegoated him for it, though, and Miller Finch did, too. "Stretch, I really don't think —"

"You'll keep on top of it," McNaughten interrupted. "Keep me personally advised."

"Of course." Tom forced himself to unclench his back teeth and smile. "I'll do some checking tomorrow. How are the grandchildren, Stretch? And Dora?"

"Well, thank you." McNaughten didn't unbend, but he was too polite to refuse a social gesture. "And your wife?"

"Annabel is fine," Tom lied. *Wherever the goddamn hell she is.*

"Dora noticed one of Annabel's artworks in a shop the other day. She was very impressed."

Annabel's artworks. Bundles of rags his wife stitched together like some immigrant seamstress. *Christ.* "That's very sweet of Dora, Stretch. Of course, it's just a hobby."

"Really? From what Dora said, it sounded like much more than that. Well, we're hoping you'll be able to persuade Annabel to donate a piece, even a small one, to the firm's benefit auction," McNaughten continued. "Dora would be most grateful. And it's for a good cause, of course. The East Side Shelter is doing excellent work

33

for those unfortunate women. Terrible thing, domestic violence."

McNaughten's voice was cool, his face stony. Was there a glimmer of judgment in those hooded gray eyes? No, Tom thought, it couldn't be; it was just the old man's usual coldness.

"We'd be honored to donate something, Stretch," Tom said, sincerity ringing in his tone. "Of course, Annabel barely has time for that kind of thing now, what with her volunteer work and all of our entertaining."

"That's a pity. It's a shame to waste that kind of talent. But speak to her about it, Tom, and let me know. As you know, the auction is in December, so time is of the essence. And, of course, you'll stay on top of the SafeCo situation."

"Naturally, Stretch." Tom sat still as McNaughten stepped back into the hushed, thick-carpeted corridor, leaving Tom alone with his fury.

Just what he needed, one of his wife's tacky little creations held up for the entire firm to see. Why couldn't she stick to lunching, shopping, museum visits, and volunteer work like a normal Park Avenue wife? She had a penthouse apartment, a part-time housekeeper, all the money and clothes she ever wanted. Was what he asked from her in return so goddamn difficult?

The rage crested inside him like a wave, pushing aside the SafeCo mess and jolting him with an almost sexual rush. As he jabbed at the memory-dial button on his phone again, his thoughts flashed to the night before. Sitting there soaking up the escargots and the Scotch. Watching that asshole Jim Perry put his hands all over the blond bimbo he'd picked up for the evening. Annabel sitting at his side, watching Jim with that quiet, reserved scrutiny that always ticked Tom off. Jim had caught it, too, winking at Tom as though to emphasize the comparison between his own giggling, sexy date and Tom's cold little wife, making sly little digs that fueled the rage the Scotch and another difficult day at the office had sparked.

She was such a bore, his apparently oh-so-meek little Annabel. But she hadn't been a bore later that night. Her body had struggled against his, turning him on. Desperate gray eyes, soft, parted mouth, heaving body amid the ruins of her oh-so-perfect, oh-so-boring little dress. Usually she just lay there like a corpse. He'd gotten carried away, sure. He'd have to buy her some flowers, jolly her along. But he was only taking what was his. They wouldn't have to get into these goddamn brawls if she was a better wife, tried a little harder to please.

For the first time that day, Tom's lips curved into a genuine smile. He couldn't do anything about McNaughten, the disaster with Manchester Industries, the handicap of his own wrong-side-of-the-tracks roots. But Annabel was a problem he could always solve.

Let her disappear for a day if she wanted. She'd be back tonight. She'd get what was coming to her in the end, he thought, hanging up the phone before the apartment's answering machine picked up yet again.

And he'd damn well enjoy handing it out.

Annie's car gave out on Wednesday, twenty-six hours from New York City.
She'd waved a casual good-bye to the doorman, picked up her car from the garage, cashed a check on the joint checking account, withdrawn everything in her small personal savings, and stopped in New York's bustling jewelry district to sell the diamond earrings. Once she got through the hellish grime of the Lincoln Tunnel, she'd driven like a woman possessed, fueled by panic and purpose and that tiny glimmering of hope. She'd started on the turnpike, risking the big, busy highway to get as far as possible away from New York before Tom began looking, then branched onto smaller roads where traffic was sparser, below Delaware. She'd slept long and late in an anonymous motel, eaten from the drive-in lanes at fast-food restaurants, and paid for everything in cash.

As she wound her way into North Carolina, the highways grew narrower, the terrain steeper, the land greener. Outside her rolled-down window, the breeze was fresh and crisp, and her small car — the same old Toyota she'd had in college, saved as her own little runabout, much against Tom's will — strained in the thin mountain air. West of Winston-Salem, towns grew fewer and farther apart. Billboards for tourist resorts and fancy developments vanished, replaced by signs for mills and feed stores. The small highways she followed as she swung westward rolled past small farms, auto repair yards full of dented trucks, immaculate Baptist churches.

It was hardworking, hardscrabble country, she could see, but ringed on all sides by the majesty of the deep green peaks. The very roughness of it spoke to her. As hard as it might be, life was real here, nothing like the gleaming illusion that had been her existence in Manhattan. And the secrecy of the landscape comforted her, too; the small houses tucked far apart on the pine-filled hillsides, the promise of privacy and rest.

By noon on Wednesday, her eyes burned and her muscles — already sore from the fight with Tom — ached with strain. She would have to stop soon, she thought, glancing at her watch. She'd slept like the dead in a cheap motel the night before, but she hadn't eaten since dawn. She needed some food, some coffee, and a chance to stretch.

To the north of the highway, the neat, clustered roofs of a small town caught her eye. Impulsively, she turned the car in their direction.

Though it was only a block from the highway, the town — Burnsville, the sign said — might have been in another world, another more innocent time. On one side of a flower- and tree-filled square, an old white clapboard inn sprawled, its long porch dotted with rocking chairs. On the other, a hardware store, a post office, a tiny storefront realtor's, and something called the Cupboard Café coexisted cheerfully side by side.

Watching from her car as a laughing couple pushed through the café's big green door into the sunlight, Annie battled her own longing. Fast-food places were safer, she knew. Strangers with New York license plates were all too memorable to small-town residents and small-town police. But the beauty of the town, its sparkling restfulness, held her fast. She pulled the dusty Toyota into a spot in front of the café, promising herself that she'd have a single quick meal and move on.

The tuna sandwich she ordered was spiced with relish and dill, the coffee that accompanied it rich and fragrant. Annie leaned back in her wooden chair and savored its warmth, feeling the terrible strain ease for the first time in hours.

Outside the café's big window, a maple glowed as red as fire in the September sunlight, the color sharp against the soft hues of the town. Her family had lived in a small Connecticut town once, when she was very small. Annie had vague but happy memories of a shady yard with big trees and a swing set, a yellow bedroom bright with sunlight, a smiling grandmotherly neighbor next door. Then her father had died, and her mother had moved them to the city, where it was easier to get work. Annie had grown up in a dark, cramped, painfully neat apartment in a deteriorating building on the East Side, surrounded by the sounds of car horns and human voices. It wouldn't have been a bad life if it hadn't been for the incessant drumming of Matilda's bitter complaints. "I deserve better than this," she had told Annie over and over. "I've done the best I can. Now it's your turn. You owe it to me to do what you can." Dutifully, always anxious to do the right thing, Annie had tried. Tom had been the result.

Annie finished the last sip of coffee and gave her head a brisk shake. It was in the past. And it was over, at least for now.

But maybe it was the reason this small town appealed to her so much. It was like returning to the peacefulness of her early childhood, erasing the anxious years with her mother, the frightening ones with Tom.

If only she could stop here, settle into this small, sweet place, root herself into the secretive mountains. Watch the maple leaves outside the café fall, the snow drift, the buds of spring blossom. Make friends. Find some kind of job. Heal. Start a new life. It was probably an unrealistic dream. How could she start a safe new life when the old one was still raging, unfinished, at her back? And did someone like her, someone who had made such a drastic mistake in her marriage, even have what it took to manage a fresh beginning? Yet she had to stop somewhere, and maybe Burnsville was as good as anywhere else. Annie worried over the decision as she exchanged a tentative smile with the stocky, red-headed cashier and trudged out of the café.

Wearily, she slid back into the car, every muscle protesting. But when she turned the key in the ignition, she was met with silence. She tried again, and then a third time, but the car stayed as silent as a statue, and as still.

The bearded mechanic at the repair yard down the road told her it would take an hour to replace her battery. Annie drifted back to the grassy square and lowered herself gently onto the shady brick edging around the statue in the center of the square. The breeze danced gently around her, making the dahlias bob and the maple leaves flutter, lifting the ends of her long, fine hair. As she watched the life of the town eddy around her, she seemed to become part of its ordinary, cheerful routine. She listened to the church clock ring two and knew, suddenly but surely, that she could go no farther. Whether Burnsville was safe or dangerous, far or not far enough, it would have to do.

She combed her fingers through her wind-blown hair, took a deep breath, and walked to-ward the real estate office she'd glimpsed at one edge of the square.

The realtor, who introduced himself as John Addamson, was a big square man with a soft voice, prematurely silvery hair, and a capable manner. He looked to be only a few years older than Annie, but there was something easy and almost paternal about him. Annie used her maiden name, Taylor, and told him only that she was an artist from up North, looking for a quiet, solitary place to work. She knew it sounded odd, but it was the best she could do. He quirked an eyebrow at the story, but he asked no questions and sat patiently as she paged through his rental listings. When she winced at the prices, he gave her another shrewd glance.

"Well," he said slowly, leaning back in his creaking desk chair, "there's the old Honeycutt place, up past Jack's Creek. It's out of the way, and it's more than a mite dilapidated. But it's furnished and about the size it sounds like you're needing. I'll show it to you, if you want me to."

"It's much cheaper than the rest," Annie said, glancing at the Xeroxed information sheet.

He nodded. "It's old-fashioned, and like I said, it's out of the way. Plus the owner wanted to price it so that she could get the right kind of person in it." At Annie's raised brow, John Addamson grinned. " 'No good ole boys, no hot-dog skiers, and no stuck-up city folk with those dad-blamed little phones.' Those were her exact words. I think it's safe to say you probably qualify."

"I think so." Annie smiled at him. The rent he quoted was within her price range. She could manage four months at that rate, and if the place wasn't utterly terrible . . . Her mind worked, calculating, assessing. "That's fine," she said firmly. "I'd love to see it, if you have the time."

"Sure do. Alma's living down in Tampa with her son, now. Broke her hip this June, and didn't have much choice. She should really sell the place, but she's still clinging a little. They'd be tickled to get it rented."

As John Addamson guided his gleaming black Cherokee out of town and onto a narrow and winding road, he told Annie about the cottage's owner, a local girl who had married a local boy and taught at the Burnsville school for almost fifty years. "Alma taught most of the county our times tables and our manners, too. Say her name, and half the folks in Burnsville sit up straight in their chairs," he said, grinning. "We'll be turning off onto a gravel road soon. Hold on; it gets bumpy."

Annie let the conversation lapse as she took in the landscape around her. Except for a few vacation chalets, the houses they passed were simple white farmhouses and cottages, neat and unpretentious. The homes, the trucks in their gravel drives, the barns, the fences — everything seemed battered yet sturdy, made for work rather than for show. The houses thinned out even more as they drove, the truck winding up along the road's gentle curves.

"This is the turnoff," John said, breaking into her reverie. Annie grabbed the door handle as they bumped onto the gravel of the smaller lane. "The Honeycutt place is the only one on this road," he continued, " 'cept for the Harper place down the hill to the south. You can just see his house from up here, but he's gone a lot, anyway. Alma's is just around this stand of trees, now, over to the right, inside that fence."

The truck passed the fencing, took a final curve, and pulled into a tilted gravel drive. Braced for serious business, Annie took one look at the cottage and fell in love.

It was a small building, square and sturdy, made of soft gray brown fieldstone. In the front, a long porch with four dirty white pillars supported the second story. Under the sharp angle of the roof, two dormer windows peeked out. A tangle of bramble, shrub, and wildflowers rioted around the foundation, wildly overgrown but bursting with color. On one side of the house, a battered trellis held a tangle of morning glories as vividly blue as the cerulean sky.

It was probably awful inside, Annie warned herself as she followed John up the short flight of front stairs. Dark and dirty and unlivable. She couldn't afford a renovation project, she added silently, trying to restrain the hopes that were soaring like a runaway helium balloon. John Addamson pushed the old oak door open, and she stepped inside.

Dark, more or less, and certainly dusty, she conceded. The absence of a live-in owner showed. But not unlivable, no. The amount of space was right: a kitchen, small dining room, and living room downstairs, a bath and a pair of bedrooms above. There was too much furniture covered in too many shades of brown and about four thousand knickknacks, but the old chairs were comfortable and the mattresses surprisingly new and firm. Alma Honeycutt had left brooms and mops, ample stocks of linens, china, and cookware — everything Annie would need. Both the front and back doors had strong, new-looking locks. In the kitchen, old-fashioned Mason jars stood on top of a new refrigerator, and what looked liked modern electrical outlets stood out from the faded yellow of the walls.

"Bobby used to come up twice, three times a year, once his daddy died, fix things up for his mama," John said, answering her raised brow. "There's a new well, too, and an almost-new furnace, if you want to look." Annie did. In the end, she scrutinized every inch of the cottage from basement to attic, peppering John Addamson with questions as she went. None of his answers — about the house, the property, the small shed out back, the town, the safety of the area — diminished the instinctual sense that this was the right place. She knew logic demanded that she look around more before deciding. But she'd ignored her instincts for years, and look where that had gotten her. Maybe it was high time she gave them a chance.

"Well, that's it, signed and sealed," John said, *back in his sunny little office, handing her a pair of keys.* To her gratitude, he hadn't pushed the question of references, just accepted a bigger than usual security deposit instead. "The gas

44

and electric are on, like I said, and the plumbing is in good shape. I'll have them turn on the phone again. You can do anything you want to the place except throw things away or make permanent changes. If you have any questions, just ask."

"I really appreciate your time," Annie said. "It can't be much of a commission."

"No problem," he said, walking with her to the door. "Don't hesitate to call if you have any questions about the house or even the area. I'm glad to help. You're sure you'll be all right up there?"

"Fine," Annie said.

"Well . . . if you're ever lonely, my wife Susie and I would be glad to cook you a dinner, introduce you to some of the folks in town."

"Thank you, John." Annie could see that he was uneasy. Maybe the thinness of her story was bothering him, or maybe his Southern gallantry just didn't take easily to the idea of a woman living alone. She liked him, liked his sensible, sun-creased face and his warm eyes and his quick laughter. It was hard not to relax around him, and even harder not to accept his offer of help. It had been too long since she'd enjoyed the simple pleasures of friendship.

But it just wasn't safe. The more she spoke to people, the harder it would be to keep her real story and her false story straight; the more people she met, the easier it would be for Tom to track her down. Her own small house, freedom from Tom's rages . . . that would have to be enough.

"I'll call if I get lonely, John," she said lightly, smiling at him from the sidewalk to take any sting out of her refusal. "I'm here to work, though, and I tend to get pretty preoccupied. I probably won't go out much. But I'll see you around town, I'm sure."

"All right. 'Bye, then, Annie."

" 'Bye, John." Annie made a small, sketchy wave and turned to walk down to the garage to pick up her car, uncomfortably aware of his puzzled gaze following her.

Meg Thorn's kitchen, John Addamson thought at ten-thirty that evening, was just about the best place to be in Burnsville on a cool September night. Even better than his own kitchen, which was pretty damned good.

He tilted his chair back and polished off his serving of Meg's wild raspberry pie. Meg's house was a sturdy old Victorian, big and lacy with gingerbread. It sat only a half block away from the Cupboard Café, which Meg owned and cooked for and fussed over like a broody hen. In her kitchen at home, professional-quality appliances coexisted cheerfully with mellow oak furniture, warm yellow curtains and cushions, knotted bunches of herbs hanging to dry. Meg was a widow who lived alone now that her only daughter, Tilly, had married and moved away. But her home was still a family place, John thought, the kind of home he and his wife Susie were trying to make for themselves, a place that embraced you with warmth and stability and love.

And then there were the delights of Meg's cooking, he added silently, sipping his coffee and listening with one ear to the women's lazy conversation. He was a lousy cook, and Susie was getting too big to be standing in front of the stove, so meals like this were an especially welcome treat.

Creations from Meg's own kitchen appeared regularly in the Cupboard, and overflows from the restaurant found their way back to Meg's home. Tonight, along with their chicken, green salad, and raspberry pie, John and Susie had eaten some of the pureed soup Meg had made for the café's lunch menu. With its savory autumn flavor and sprinklings of fresh herbs, it was delicious, they all agreed, but it hadn't gone over big at the Cupboard. It looked like the good folks of Burnsville just weren't ready for liquid squash.

"I'd take another slice of pie if there's one going, Meggie," John said lazily, putting down his fork and letting the front legs of his chair thump onto the hardwood floor.

"Don't you dare, Meg." Susie wagged a warning finger at her husband. "He's getting as big as I am." Susie was six months pregnant with twins, a glowing blond Madonna in a roomy print dress. "He gained ten pounds this summer. We can't afford to buy him all new pants, not with these babies coming."

John winked at Meg, who reached for the pie plate despite Susie's protests. "It's not my fault you decided to have two," he teased. "One would have been more economical."

"And more comfortable," Susie grumbled. "I swear, these are the busiest darned babies this side of Asheville. They spend at least half their time kicking, and they know just where to aim."

John and Meg smiled at each other over Susie's head as she put both hands on her belly. Susie Fields had been five years behind them in elementary school, and even back then she'd been a fiercely maternal little girl. Whatever Susie's protests, Meg and John knew that she was going to be a helplessly adoring, blindly devoted mom.

Susie looked up, catching their affectionate glances. "Stop looking at me, you two," she said, blushing a little over the light dusting of freckles on her cheeks. "I feel like the blue-ribbon sow at the county fair. Let's talk about something else. And go ahead, Meg, give him his darned pie. Just a small slice, though, okay?"

Laughing, John reached to touch Susie's cheek with one hand while accepting the replenished dessert plate with the other.

"All right, Suse," he said obligingly. "On to a new topic. There's a new woman in town, Meg, did you know? Rented the Honeycutt place today."

"Well, that's going to make Bobby Honeycutt's day. He's had ants in his pants about that place ever since he dragged poor Alma down to Tampa. Is she nice?"

"Alma?"

Grinning, Meg swatted his arm. "The tenant, you fool."

"Mmm. Quiet, and intelligent. She says she's an artist, needs a quiet place to work."

Meg leaned back in her chair, waiting. She'd known John Addamson her entire life, ever since they'd fought over who would put the baby Jesus in the crèche, way back in Sunday school. She knew the things he left unsaid, and she could hear the doubt in his voice now. She forked up a last bite of pie and quirked an eyebrow upward. "But you don't think so."

"He's so suspicious," Susie grouched. "It's all those espionage novels he reads. Makes him think everyone's got something to hide. What do you think, honey, that she's part of some kind of conspiracy? A criminal on the lam? Maybe a foreign spy?"

John rose to pour them all more coffee, a special decaf blend that Susie liked. "No, of course not. But think about it. People don't just show up in Burnsville looking for a place to rent and move into the same day, with no family and no real luggage. Artists on retreat plan ahead. And there was something odd about her. Frightened, maybe, or at least wary."

Intrigued, Meg sat upright again in her chair.

"I think I've seen her," she said. "Tall, slender, with long, dark hair?"

At John's nod, she continued. "She came into the café while I was watching the register. Lizibet was out yet again, so I had to fill in. She was sitting over in the far corner. I only noticed her because her face was so unusual. Pretty, and old-fashioned, and sort of sad looking. And tired. I got the feeling she could have sat there all day, but she finally got herself together and left."

Susie shook her head in amusement. "Your imagination is as wild as his is, Meg."

"Probably. But you'd be curious, too, if you saw her," Meg said, smiling. "She looks like a character from one of those ghost stories we used to tell when we were little. Remember, John? There was one about a dead girl who went to a dance. What was her name?"

"Rowena," John said promptly. "You're right. Did you ever hear that one, honey? Rowena had long, black hair and a sad, beautiful face, and she showed up at a local dance wearing a pretty but outdated dress. One of the boys danced with her, loaned her his sweater to ward off the cold, walked her home to a lonely cottage and fell in love. When he went back the next day to talk with her again, the man in the cottage said she'd been dead for ten years . . . and the boy found his sweater in the cemetery, folded neatly on her grave."

"Ugh." Susie wrinkled her small nose. "I can

barely sleep as it is, what with this belly and having to run to the bathroom every five minutes. Don't give me nightmares, John."

"Sorry, sweetheart. Gave me the shivers, too, when I was a kid. Still, Meg's right, this woman was an unusual type. It sort of makes you wonder."

"Not me." Emphatically, Susie shook her blond curls. "I'm having enough trouble trying to figure out how to fit myself into the car, what to name these babies, and how to get my husband to assemble two cribs, two high chairs, two car seats, and who knows what all else."

"Oops," John said, laughing, and the conversation moved on to baby names, a puzzle made ever more complicated by the fierce and divergent opinions of his parents, Susie's family, and half the folks in town.

A half hour later, Meg walked John to the car while Susie made a last stop at the bathroom. Over on the mountain, an owl called, and moonlight gleamed silver on the shining white paint of Meg's picket fence. "So what's your mystery lady's name, friend?" she said as John unlocked the Cherokee and slung Susie's handbag inside.

"Annie," John answered. "Annie Taylor, I think."

"You think? Surely her name's on her check. And her references must know."

"She paid in cash, and I didn't ask for references." Meg frowned, and John shrugged. "I just didn't think she would give any, and she needed that house, Meg. I can't explain it, but I just knew. She was hunted, or scared . . . or something. She needed help."

"I saw it, too. But she could still steal the silver."

"No silver to steal, not in Alma Honeycutt's place. I got a security deposit and an extra month's rent in advance, and I checked it with Alma, who informed me that, I quote, 'the poor young woman probably needed a haven,' and she was glad to oblige, so I should get on with it and stop bothering her, she had things to do. She's feeling a little more settled in Tampa, I gather. She sent her regards to you and said to tell you to comb your hair."

Meg laughed out loud. The constantly tangled red pigtails of her youth were now a cap of short curls dusted with silver, but they were still untidy. "That sounds just like Alma."

"Mmm. Watch out for her if you see her, Meg, will you?" John asked, his tone a little sheepish. "Annie Taylor, I mean."

"You're going to make a good daddy, John," Meg said, her voice dry. "You always did love to meddle. But I'll look out for Annie maybe-Taylor, if you want. Offer some neighborly help if she needs it."

"Great. I invited her to have dinner with us, but she looked terrified, and I backed off. Maybe she'd be more open with you. And maybe Jed could keep a friendly eye on her."

Meg snorted. "Great idea. If we sic young Jed

on her, by next Friday, she won't have a secret left. He's the most inquisitive soul I've ever met. If he wasn't also the least meddlesome one, we'd all be in trouble."

"He'll kill you if he hears you calling him young Jed."

"I can't help it, it's a habit by now. A habit you'd have, too, if you'd had to live with my mother. 'Margaret Mary, you're not going anywhere with young Jed Harper and his friends, and that's final.' 'Young Jed Harper, you get your feet off my sofa.' 'You tell that young Jed Harper to get his hands out of my cookies.' "

John smiled at Meg's perfect mimicry. Meg's mother was seventy now and living outside of Fort Lauderdale, but the last time he'd seen her, she had still sounded exactly the same. "He always was trouble," John said. "Good trouble, not the kind of trouble his daddy was, God knows, but trouble just the same."

"And he wrapped my mother right around his little finger anyway, just like he did every other woman within miles."

John propped one elbow on the Cherokee's roof and laughed. "Well," he said, "maybe that's all the more reason he should meet Annie Taylor. Truth is, they'd make a nice couple, and he needs a woman."

"We talking about the same man, Johnny-boy? I have the feeling Jed gets all the women he needs. He just doesn't get 'em in Burnsville."

"I didn't mean a woman for sex. I meant a

real woman, a wife. Someone to share that nice house of his, give him a couple of kids."

Meg gave something close to a snort. "Jed's not going to settle down with a wife, not as long as he's haring halfway across the world every five minutes. And probably not as long as he remembers Big Jed and his mama snarling at each other, either. Those two were enough to put any man off the idea of holy wedlock. I've never heard Jed say a good word about marriage, and I've known him my whole life. I know you've been in heaven ever since you gave up your bachelor ways, and I'm pleased as punch about it, but there's no point trying to convert the likes of young Jed Harper to wedded bliss."

"Why are we talking about Jed?" Susie asked plaintively, coming to join them on the sidewalk. "I love him and all, but I'm sleepy, and it's cold out here, and he's probably sitting next to his fire with a brandy, counting his money or reading James Joyce or something, not standing in the dark talking about us."

Grinning, John gave her shoulders a squeeze and bent to help her get settled into the Cherokee's passenger seat. "You're probably right, both of you. I wasn't cut out to be a matchmaker. And what does a man know about what another man needs, anyway? Thanks for the dinner, Meggie. I'll see you tomorrow, at the café, for lunch."

"You can have some more squash soup, I have to use it up somehow. 'Night, John. 'Night,

Susie, honey. Take care of those babies, and call me if you need anything."

Meg watched the Cherokee's taillights disappear and strolled contentedly back into the house. In her warm, golden kitchen, she rolled up the sleeves of her cotton shirt and started to fill one side of the double sink with sudsy water. Despite her scoffing to John, the images of her old pal Jed Harper and Burnsville's newest resident stayed in her mind. Her wide, capable mouth curved into a smile as she plunged a stack of pottery dishes into the hot suds.

They made a nice contrast, she decided. Jed's rampant curiosity and Annie Whatever's mystery. His warmth and her cool reserve. Her air of sadness and his easy good cheer. Jed was a surprisingly sunny soul, given what he'd grown up with.

Meg stuck the final plate in the dish rack and gave her head a brisk shake. What was she doing? She was as bad as John, or worse. For all they knew, Annie Taylor could be a first-class bitch trailing a long line of troubles behind her. And surely Jed Harper, charming enough to seduce a nun out of a convent without half trying, could choose his own women. With the deft gestures of habit, Meg shut off the tap, drained the sink, and hung the damp dish towel over the spigot to dry.

She was getting sentimental in her old age, she decided as she blew out the candles that still flickered on the round table. And a little lonely.

She was missing Tilly, and Abe. Her husband had died in the fall five years before, tingeing each autumn since with bittersweet memories. She still loved him, but she'd moved on. She'd like to meet a nice new man one day, not that there were many possibilities in Burnsville. But she still felt a little odd — sad, yearning, restless — each year when the leaves started to turn.

That was her problem, though, not Jed Harper's and certainly not Annie Taylor's. Still, it wouldn't hurt to introduce them, see what happened. Change — new blood, new relation-ships — were good for a small town, kept things fresh and lively. Yawning comfortably, Meg turned off the downstairs lights and made sure the front door was locked. Upstairs in her bed-room, she chose a good complicated British mystery to take her mind off foolish romantic connivings and settled herself to rest.

Two

Annie slid into the unfamiliar bed nervously on Wednesday night. She was afraid her first night in the cottage would bring insomnia or dreams of Tom. But instead, she fell asleep easily. Something about the small, old-fashioned bedroom with its faded floral paper and high iron bed soothed her, gentled her to sleep.

And then there was a man in her dreams, after all. Not Tom; nothing like him. A man she had never met before, a *kind* of man she had never met before, easy and confident, strong and yet tender. In her dream they were in this same small house, but now it was clean, bright, filled with friends. Music played somewhere outside, lanterns bobbed in the darkness.

The man pulled her gently into his arms, led her body into a dance step, twirled her in a turn. She was wearing her pretty vintage dress, and when he spun her to face him again, she could feel her breasts pressing against his chest, their curves and tender points achingly sensitive under the layer of thin fabric. His warm hand rested on the curve of her rear, his breath stirred her hair, and in her dream Annie looked up into his face and felt herself consumed by longing. They were going to make love; he knew it, she could tell from his face, and so did she. And it was going to be urgent and primal and yet somehow utterly safe. Dreaming, Annie felt her body melt into readiness, her nipples stiffen, her hips rocking gently to his rhythm, everything in her open, a woman — any woman — with a beloved man.

A night bird called from the rooftop, its mournful screech rousing Annie from the dream. She woke suddenly, sitting bolt upright, her heart pounding from fear and something that wasn't fear. She could remember only fragments of the dream: a clean male scent, the sound of soft music, the press of a man's thighs against hers. But the feeling of it lingered, a sweet ache in her body, a vision of being cherished in her mind.

She shook her head at herself as she lay back down and pulled the quilt around her shoulders again. She was in a strange house, in a strange town, exhausted to the bone and sick at heart. And yet she was dreaming of lovemaking, as eager and innocent as a teenager. Maybe Alma Honeycutt's lingering presence had some kind of power, she thought drowsily, smiling a little in the darkness. Maybe there was a sweet spell over this room. Whatever it was, she was grateful for it. She fell asleep again in moments, but the man in her dreams was gone.

The haunting sound of a ballad drew her down the hill.

58

Annie had awakened that morning to a dazzle of sunlight. She blinked at its glare, sitting stiffly up on the bed's worn quilt. Her eyes were gritty and her mouth dry. Light streamed through the pair of dormer windows, splashing the bare wooden floor and the old-fashioned white-painted furniture with sun. No room could have been more different from her huge, elegant bedroom in New York. But an almost tangible air of peace and security seemed to hover in the musty bedroom air, as warming as her dream.

Annie dug out her toothbrush and gave her tangled hair a cursory combing. Down in the kitchen, she boiled water for tea in the dented copper kettle. Porcelain teacup and a slice of bread in hand, she pulled the stiff front door open and padded barefoot onto her porch, drawing in a quick delighted breath at the beauty spread out below her. No landscape painter could have asked for a more beautiful vista. She leaned out over the porch railing, drinking in the landscape, the sparkling air, the silence.

Even if she failed, she thought, even if Tom found her or she could figure out no way to make a living or some other disaster struck, she was right to have come.

Annie finished her tea and bread on the porch, then went inside to inspect her new home. The first order of business was a good, thorough housecleaning, she decided. She would air out the stale, musty rooms, make the place her own.

Pleased with the thought, she reached for the first of the living room's heavy drapes.

Hours later, hunger forced her to stop. The living room looked like a cyclone had hit it, but it was a good start. She made herself a cup of tea and a quick sandwich, using the end of the few foodstuffs she'd bought the day before, then perched on a dusty armchair to eat them. It was then that she heard the lilting of music, soft and distant, drifting up to her house as pretty and insubstantial as mist. The song was half familiar, a plaintive melody with an undercurrent of sadness. It tugged at her somehow, a beckoning, an invitation. Impulsively, she put her tea down, found a roomy jacket that had been left in the hall closet, slipped on the shoes she'd kicked off the day before, and stepped out onto the porch.

There was a small square of overgrown lawn around the cottage, ringed by a thick band of trees. At one corner of the yard, a path opened in the undergrowth. Annie strolled toward the opening, instinctively followed the sound of the music. The narrow path led her gently down the slope of the mountain below her house. She walked along it slowly, surveying the thicket of leaf and branch that surrounded her and enjoying the fresh coolness of the air. Then the trail curved sharply around a slender maple, and the mountain spread out before her again.

She hadn't realized that the other house was so

near or that she'd walked so close to it. Her neighbor — neighbors? — were rarely home, John Addamson had said, if she recalled his words correctly. Obviously, though, they were in residence now.

The house sat a hundred yards below her, a sturdy log structure gone silver with weather, much bigger than her own small cottage. Annie's artist's eye took it in, appreciating the simplicity of its design. No rustic shack, this, yet it was pleasing and somehow modest. Nestling gently in the hill, echoing the mountain's colors, it fit itself perfectly into the land.

It took a moment for her to notice the man. He slouched at the head of the wide steps, his back propped comfortably against the wooden balustrade and one booted foot braced on a lower stair. A dog reclined by his side, its muzzle resting near the angle of his blue-jeaned knee. She couldn't see his face, which was half hidden by a lock of bronzy hair and bent over the instrument he played.

A mandolin, she thought, or a dulcimer. She didn't even know the difference.

She was close enough to notice the glinting of golden hair on his nape, the way the muscles of his forearms corded as he played, even a frayed spot on one rolled-up sleeve. Some female instinct noted the strong masculine shape of him, too: the width of the shoulders under the soft denim shirt, the way the jeans, worn almost white, fit the strength of the narrow hips and thighs. The quick jolt of awareness made her wary. So did whatever force it was that seemed to root her to the spot, keeping her standing as still as a startled deer in the thick bracken, watching and listening to him play.

He looked familiar, she thought, but she couldn't understand why. Blue-jeaned mandolin players had no part in her experience. As she puzzled over it, he played on, easy and intent. Each clear, metallic note seemed to tremble delicately in the soft air. His deft, long-fingered hands worked the frets with unselfconscious pleasure, flashing above the silver chasing. As she stood on the path, frozen, the notes slowed and his hands went still.

The silence brought Annie to herself. Suddenly she felt foolish, standing in the grass on what was almost certainly someone else's property and gawking like a voyeur. But as she turned back toward the cottage, a fallen branch cracked like a gunshot under her heel, making the dog lift his head and growl. The growl turned into a bark as she shifted on the path's thatch of leaf again. Suddenly, the animal rose from the man's side to race toward her, past the small garden and up through the long grass of the hill. Annie froze again, this time from fear. Country dogs were guard dogs, she remembered, not the tame status symbols they were in the city. She should have thought of that before she went wandering off into the woods.

"Cut it out, boy," the man called from the

porch, his deep voice commanding and unworried. "Sit. *Now*." He put the instrument down and started up the hill in the dog's wake. His voice calmed Annie's pounding heart a little. Surely that was amusement rather than alarm in his tone. Unless her musical neighbor was a sadist, the dog must be less frightening than he seemed.

To her surprise, the animal sat at his command, though the big ears still quivered with excitement and a whine of eagerness still sounded in his throat. Instinctively, Annie put out a tentative hand an inch or two, flinching a little when the dog nosed its head toward her. She felt his cold, wet nose nuzzle her palm, and saw the feathery tail lift in greeting.

"Sorry. You must have been scared half out of your mind. Don't worry, he's harmless," the man said, smiling at her as he strode up the hill. Feeling more foolish than ever, she stepped onto the grass to meet him, the dog hovering at her side.

"I'm the one who should be sorry. I didn't mean to trespass," Annie said hesitantly.

"No trespass. You're welcome to the mountain." His eyes were the same deep, soft blue as his chambray work shirt, with a fan of fine lines in the golden skin at the corners. Instinctively, the artist in her studied him. His face was lean and strong-boned, with a well-shaped mouth and a strong jaw that glinted with the lightest of stubble. It was an intensely masculine face, but a sensitive one as well. Despite the openness of his expression, there was some contradiction in it: not quite a rogue's and not quite a dreamer's, but with a little of each mixed in. It was the kind of face an artist would itch to paint and a woman would long to kiss. The thought startled her, astonished her, but for a moment she couldn't let it go. She could almost feel his mouth, tender and yet insistent, warm on her own.

He was the man in her dream. The thought came to her suddenly, indisputably right and infinitely embarrassing. He was the man who had guided her through the dance, held her against his chest, kissed the side of her face. He was the man she had been longing to make love with, the man she had wanted to lie over her, his strong body heavy yet graceful on hers, her legs opening around him, her hands frantic on his back.

His gaze, startled and curious, met hers before she glanced away. *Damn Alma Honeycutt,* she thought ruefully, *or whoever — whatever — it was.* Something had cast a spell on her, indeed. Making her dream, last night, of making love to a total stranger. Making her aware, now, that her hair was barely combed and her hands were covered with furniture polish. She'd thought she was over that kind of female longing and that kind of female coyness. God knew, she needed to be.

Flustered, she brought her attention back to the man, who was regarding her with something in between a primal male scrutiny and the inquisitive stare of a child. She'd counted on having some placid hillbilly for a neighbor: no one too astute, too worldly, too inquiring. But this was no yokel. Even if his worn jeans and boots, the dog, his music said country, this man had cleverness and, it was clear, curiosity to spare. The thought made her feel even warier. Instinctively, she reached up to brush a strand of long, black hair from her cheek, then wrapped her arms around her waist under the loose corduroy jacket. Her heart was pounding, and her legs felt unsteady.

"I was walking, just following the path. I've rented the cottage, the old Honeycutt place," she said belatedly, aware that her cheeks were flushing a little but unable to stop them.

"I know. I've been noticing you up there, cleaning." The handsome mouth widened into a grin. "Reckoned I might do some neatening up for myself," he continued, his eyes steady on hers, "but sitting on the porch picking out a song appealed to me more in the end."

"It appealed to me, too," Annie admitted, grateful for the neutral subject. She couldn't seem to get her emotional balance, and she needed it badly. A quick, forgettable little neighborly exchange, she thought; that was what this situation called for. Then she could escape back to her house . . . but not if she stood here stammering and blushing like a schoolgirl. "I don't know the instrument. But you play it well."

"It's a dulcimer. Most of us here are practically born with one in our hand. Or a fiddle, or a banjo, or a psaltery. I'm used to sitting on the porch with it, but I can move inside if it troubles you."

"No. It's pretty." She flinched a little as the dog nuzzled gently at her thigh again. "Your dog is friendlier than he looks. When he started running up the hill like the Hound of the Baskervilles, I thought I was done for."

"Mmm. He might have licked you to death. He's a lamb in wolf's clothing, Rooster is."

"Rooster?" Despite her unease, her mouth quirked upward. "That's . . . unexpected."

"Damned animal wakes me up at dawn." His grin flashed again, teeth white against the golden skin. Unlike Annie, he seemed utterly at ease. "That's enough, boy. Leave the poor woman alone. You're not from the country," he added to Annie.

"No. City. Up North." Lifting her chin, Annie felt her face stiffen, her voice go cold. Like a cloud obscuring the sun, the easiness that had flowed between them for one brief moment was just as suddenly gone. She felt a pang of regret, much sharper than she wanted to admit, but it just couldn't be helped. She needed peace, quiet, privacy and some hard, healing work on her house. She didn't need a neighbor with a male model's body, the face of a gentleman-thief, and the piercing gaze of a private eye.

She was sure he'd ask another question, and

she braced herself to fend it off. But once again he surprised her. When she glanced at him, there was nothing but a shrewd, tolerant mildness in his eyes.

"The city," he repeated simply. "That's a different world, for sure. Well, you're welcome to walk here, as I said. Rooster will be friendly now, too friendly maybe. Send him off home if he wanders up your way. And holler if the music ever bothers you." His blue eyes held hers for a moment, their expression oddly gentle. Then, with a quick nod and a small, final smile, he walked away, Rooster trotting happily behind him. Annie was halfway up the path, and the man was back on his porch, before she realized that she hadn't asked his name.

A thick drift of cloud obscured the sun, making the day seem suddenly chilly. Jed called Rooster inside, then replaced his dulcimer absently on its shelf.

His new neighbor was as pretty as a doe, he thought as he headed for the kitchen. And as timid. Shyness had fought with curiosity on her face as she'd spoken, and fear with friendliness, and caution with a fledgling trust. But trust had lost out when he'd asked where she'd come from. Wherever it was, it had hurt. The rush of protectiveness he felt at the thought surprised him. Damsels in distress had never been his style.

It was only six or so, but he was hungry; his

stomach still hadn't adjusted to eastern standard time. He got his dinner started, the motions automatic after decades of making do for himself, usually in places a damn sight rougher than his house. The steak John and Susie had left him was readied for the grill, a juicy ripe tomato sliced to go with it. As he opened the bin of Rooster's food, he thought again about the woman.

He'd been aware of her all afternoon. He'd glimpsed her spreading the drapes and linens on her porch. Raised his brows at the obsessive thoroughness of her spring — well, fall — cleaning. Smiled a little at the feminine foolishness of it, the scraps of lace curtains fluttering in the breeze, the rugs she beat as if they were the devil himself.

The light began to die as the coals on the grill heated. He stood in the blue twilight above them, poking idly at the pulsing crimson embers and watching a trio of deer as they loped up the ridge near Wellman's farm.

She'd looked like a boy from the distance, tall and slender and willowy. But she was definitely a woman close up. A man would have to be half blind, half dead, or totally addled not to notice the fall of her long, black hair, the rosiness of her mouth, the gentle curves her loose clothes half hid, the wide opalescent eyes that were unmistakably female. The rough jeans and jacket she wore emphasized her femininity in a way no amount of makeup or frills ever could. Made a man want to use his thumb to wipe the smudge of dirt from the angle of that pretty jaw, brush the soft, black hair back with his fingers, unwrap the layers of clothing to discover the delicate body beneath.

A picture rose in his mind, a slender woman lying on a big white bed, her black hair spread out over the snowy pillow, her eyes wide, her breasts high and firm and warm, her legs as long and graceful as a Thoroughbred's. She'd be shy first, wild after. He could almost taste the sweetness of her mouth, feel the strength of her legs clasping him.

A drop of fat made the charcoal sizzle, bringing him back to himself. The light had gone while he was standing here daydreaming, and he'd charred the hell out of John and Susie's expensive steak.

You got too much imagination when they handed out brains, bubba, he admonished himself silently, echoing the opinion — rarely stated even that kindly — of year after year of frustrated grade-school teachers. The pictures his imagination drew had often been more vivid than real life, especially back when real life meant a daddy who spent half his time in jail, a mama who spent half her time in a stupor, and a cold, dirty, falling-down house.

But he was too damned old for daydreams, except those that made him his living. And this little fantasy was even more foolish than most. He'd had his first tumble with curvy little Bobbie

Jean Nystrom from over on East Main Street way back in tenth grade, but ever since then, he'd avoided local women. His months here at home were for work and friends and peace, not for entanglement. He didn't want the complications he'd get if a romance here went wrong or the guilt he'd feel if it went right and he left anyway, as he certainly would in the end. The last thing he needed was to get involved with his wary, vulnerable, beautiful new neighbor. Even if she'd wanted to, and his instinct told him that she very definitely didn't. He couldn't quite figure out why she'd come to live in Alma Honeycutt's cottage, but he was certain a hope for male company had nothing to do with it.

And yet the vision of her hovered in his mind's eye.

Long, soft hair, with a widow's peak, and the faintest glimmering of silver strands amid the darkness.

A haunting, haunted face, the face of a beautiful princess trapped in an evil spell.

Eyes pearly and cautious. A mouth made for kissing.

Enough, he said silently. He shook his head.

"Come on, Rooster. Dinner," he said aloud, and carried his meal indoors.

He was still irritated with himself after the meal was eaten and the dishes were done. Rooster went to sleep near the living room sofa as Jed clicked off the big kitchen light. He'd made no plans with friends, thinking to sleep off his lingering jet lag, but suddenly his own company didn't appeal. He prowled through the silent rooms, picked up and put down a book, fingered the dulcimer. For once there was no peace to be found in any of them.

"What the hell's your problem, Harper?" he said aloud, drumming his fingers on the living room's smooth oak mantelpiece. Maybe he was still geared up for the seething bustle of Hong Kong, where a man couldn't so much as spit without hitting twenty people. He felt restless, edgy. It reminded him of being a teenager, careening around town full of frustration and hormones and energy crying out to be used. Too bad he was too old for a little innocent vandalism. He needed some good sex, maybe. Or maybe a good rough fight.

Now, that was a thought. Stepping over Rooster's slumbering form, Jed dropped another log on the low fire. He flopped onto his deep leather couch and picked up the cordless phone. It rang thirteen times before a gravelly voice answered.

"What the hell do you want?" it said.

Jed grinned, immediately cheered. "You're such a charmer, Rasmussen."

"Bloody Harper. That bloody nag told you I was drinking again," Sven Rasmussen said truculently, his voice rough with grievance and bourbon.

Sven was a fellow writer, a burly blond mountaineer who wrote surprisingly elegant accounts

71

of life and death at high altitude. "That bloody nag" was their mutual agent, Dana Wilensky, who clucked over their personal lives almost as vigorously as she nurtured their careers. Jed laughed. Drunk or sober, Sven was sharp.

"She did," he said easily. "As I recall, your tendency to fall into the bottle since your divorce worries her."

"And you, being my true chum, were *worried,* too." Sven's voice dripped with scorn.

"Nope. You know me. I reckon that if you survived the Eiger you'll probably survive a little Jack Daniel's. I told Dana not to waste her energy on a useless thug like you. And reminded her that she has the careers of civilized, talented, sober folks like me to think about."

"She's thought about your bloody career, all right. If I see your name splashed all over one more issue of the *New Yorker,* I'm going to puke."

"Thanks. But you'll probably puke anyway, from the sounds of it."

"Damn right. So if you're not checking up on me, why the hell are you calling?"

"Beats the shit out of me." Jed propped his neck more comfortably against the arm of the sofa and grinned at the phone. "I felt restless, and then I felt like I wanted to get into a good old-fashioned brawl, and then I thought of you."

"Restless? You've been home a day, two days, and you're restless?" Jed could hear Sven swig-

72

ging a mouthful of something, probably straight from the bottle. "So who is she?"

Jed scowled at the phone. Jesus, the sonovabitch was smart. If he wasn't a surly loner already half dead from high-altitude oxygen deprivation, he'd probably be out in a lab someplace inventing the cure for cancer. "Who is who?" he said aloud, stalling.

"Must be a local lass, seeing as you told me Oriental ladies weren't really your cup of tea." There was silence, then another swig.

"Now, I'd like to meet the lady who's making the great Jed Harper restless. In fact," Sven continued, the gleeful malice in his voice audible all the way from New York, "I'd like to meet her so much I might just haul my ass down to a backwater filled with a bunch of illiterate rednecks in the middle of — 'scuse me — effing nowhere. It'd sure beat sitting around getting plastered, arguing with Dana, and reading your damn reviews."

"Forget it. There is no lady, for Christ's sake." And it wasn't a lie. Except in his own damned mind, he had only the most casual of connections with his neighbor. But the words didn't sound convincing, even to Jed. "And I'm working. On deadline. Galleys of the last book, draft of this one. I don't need you and your crazy fantasies screwing up my life."

"There must be a hotel in that godforsaken town you live in," Sven said.

"Yeah. A very nice inn. And an even nicer bed-and-breakfast. Not your kind of places."

" 'Fraid your lady won't appreciate your taste in friends?"

"You're no friend if you come down here, Rasmussen. And there is no lady," Jed repeated, knowing it was useless.

If there was anything worse than having inappropriate adolescent fantasies about your neighbor, it was having inappropriate adolescent fantasies about your neighbor while knowing that one of your burly, beery, utterly tactless pals could show up on your doorstep at any moment, soaked to the gills and out for trouble. But if Jed was lucky, he figured, tomorrow's hangover would obliterate the whole discussion from Sven's mind. Jed shook his head as he turned off the cordless phone. He shut off the halogen lamp next to the sofa and nudged Rooster awake for a final trip outside. Early or not, it was definitely time to call it a night.

The big gray quilt was the first thing to go. The gleaming Fiskars shears he grabbed from the sewing table caught at its seams as though protesting against the task, but Tom jabbed harder with the points and eventually the fabric began to give. Fueled by Scotch and fury, he slashed fiercely at the intricate material until it hung in thready tatters on the quilting frame.

So much for one more useless piece of crap, he thought, breathing hard as he stood back to survey the ruins. So much for that useless bitch, Annabel Mahoney.

It was past eleven o'clock on Thursday night. Annabel hadn't been at her mother's, he'd discovered when he finally reached Matilda the evening before. Matilda hadn't so much as heard from her daughter in days. Tom was suspicious by then, and he found the signs he'd missed before.

A pair of diamond earrings, too fancy for day wear, were missing from her drawer. Her wedding band was there, stuck in a pile of costume crap just as though it wasn't worth thousands. Her key ring was lying in the drawer of the hallway table. Ike, the building's parking attendant, told him that Mrs. Mahoney had taken out her car yesterday morning and never brought it back.

Even with his mind racing, Tom took a moment to banter with Ike, covering up the oddity of his questions. The car was being serviced, he explained. Mrs. Mahoney wasn't home yet, and he just wanted to make sure she hadn't returned the vehicle before he called the mechanic to check on its progress. You could never be sure, with women; they did the darndest things. Had Ike heard the one about the golfer with the jealous wife? Ike hung up, chuckling, and Tom put down the receiver in a rage. His wife had been gone for what, more than two days? And he hadn't known a fucking thing.

Tonight he'd put on his tux and go to the Century Club for the benefit gala. After twenty years on Wall Street, he could handle a party like this one in his sleep. He knew what half lies to tell to cover up his wife's absence, what stories to exchange with the husbands, and just how long he could hold the wives' gaze before risking comment.

But the need to cover up for Annabel rankled. By now, the rage that had been building felt as though it was going to explode. This little runaway stunt would make him a laughingstock if it ever got out. Or worse. Tom could imagine the censure in McNaughten's eyes if he heard about it, what with the old bastard's bleeding-heart pity for all the poor women out there, all those poor, sweet victims.

She'd come crawling back, Tom was sure of that, assuming he didn't catch up with her first. She had no money, no friends, no brains, no guts. She'd never stick it out on her own. But if she thought he was going to store her tacky shit in the meantime, she was in for one hell of a surprise. Shears still in one hand, he reached unsteadily up to loosen the silk tie he wore. Then he turned to the wall. The place looked like a college dorm room, for Christ's sake. One by one, the clippings and photos and swatches came down, yielded to the shears' sharp blades, fluttered like vivid confetti onto the bright hooked rug.

Annabel was more clever than he'd given her credit for, he thought as he went to work on her books, yanking sheaves of pages roughly from each before tossing it onto the floor. Smarter than she looked, under that meek little waiflike face and flower-child hair. But now that he knew she was gone, the playing field was level. More than level, in fact. He would block the bank accounts and watch the credit card transactions. He would pay a little visit to Matilda, make it clear that her ride on the Tom Mahoney gravy train was about to end unless she helped get her daughter back. Maybe he'd speak to a detective, begin to figure out where the hell Annabel had gone. Or maybe not. No point in creating unnecessary trouble when she'd probably be back in a couple of days. He'd have to think about that, weigh his options.

Its pages torn, its spine broken, the last of the books dropped onto the pile of debris on Annabel's flowered rug. Tom rocked on his heels as he looked down at the wreckage, his smile widening at the sight. All of poor little Annabel's tacky little things, gone.

"Poor Annabel," he said aloud, liking the sound of it, even though his voice was a little thick with the Scotch he'd gulped. "Poor little Annabel."

The next time she got it in her fucking head to run away from home, he thought as he walked across the penthouse to the bedroom, poor little Annabel Mahoney would definitely think twice.

It was Wednesday, a week to the day after Annie had moved into Alma Honeycutt's cottage. The bright sun of her first days in town had given way to mist and shadow. Clouds hung on the mountain, white fleecy shapes drifting below her house like huge, soft, slow-moving animals. When she stood with her coffee on the porch each morning, leaning against one of the weathered columns and looking at the patchwork of cloud below, she could feel the sting of a cool wind on her cheeks. Even shrouded by mist, the beauties of the mountain beckoned, waiting to be explored. But Annie didn't care. She was busy working on her house.

Her house. Happy words, unfamiliar ones. Not her mother's house, not Tom's house. Her own house, however modest, however temporary, however eccentric. The freedom of it made all the hard work worthwhile.

And hard work it was. She tackled the rooms one by one, scrubbing the white woodwork and the robin's-egg-blue walls, wiping the windows with vinegar, damp-mopping the wooden floors. She washed linens and curtains and slipcovers, hanging them over her porch railing to dry slowly in the soft, damp breeze. She found the trapdoor to the attic and half-filled the dusty space with extra furniture, pictures, knick-knacks. She polished each doorknob and drawer pull, rubbed all the furniture with lemon oil, beat the rag rugs with her broom until the dust of decades flew from the soft, worn fabric. The small transformations pleased her, and the tiredness they created helped keep the dreams — whether frightening or sweetly sensual — at least partly at bay.

Finally the interior was sparkling, and the only project left to worry about was the riot of weeds around the house. Now she sat contentedly in the Cupboard Café, treating herself to an inexpensive lunch. After a week of solitude, it felt good to sit among the babble of human voices again, even if she wasn't joining in. She didn't belong here, not really. But the doubts couldn't overwhelm her today. Not with her little house sparkling, good food in her stomach, and the warmth of the small town wrapped around her like a blanket against a winter chill.

She just felt good; that was the simple truth of it. No, she felt wonderful. Happy. Free. Annie left a tip, pulled her handbag over her shoulder, and went to pay her check.

"Everything okay?" the woman at the register asked cheerfully.

"Delicious," Annie said sincerely. "You have wonderful cooking here."

"It's not hard, just simple food. You're new in town, aren't you? I'm Meg Thorn."

"I'm Annie." Annie smiled at the woman, liking her blunt face, the tousle of curly red hair glinting gently with gray, the calm, confident eyes. A difficult woman to distrust. "Annie Taylor," she amended. "And yes, I'm new. I'm renting a place here, for a while."

"Mmm." Meg handed over Annie's change with a nod, and Annie suspected she had known Annie's location already. "Well, I've lived here since I was born. Let me know if there's anything I can do to help you get settled. And stop by at teatime some afternoon. It's quiet then, and we could get acquainted."

"Thanks. Actually," Annie said, "there is something you could help me with. The nights are getting chilly, but I'm afraid to use my fireplace. John Addamson wasn't sure it was in working order. Who could I call to have it checked?"

"Young Jed could do it," Meg said consideringly, propping her elbows on the scarred wooden counter. "He's a good person to know, being close to your place. He'd probably be glad to help."

Annie's mouth quirked into a smile. Was young Jed sixteen or sixty? She suspected that you couldn't tell in these mountains. But it would be impolite to quibble. "He would be fine, then. How can I reach him?"

"He was off to Asheville for the day, business and such. But he'll be stopping for dinner here tonight. I'll tell him for you, if you'd like, and he'll call."

Annie's brow furrowed. It was so casual; what if young Jed, whoever that might be, had no time, or no interest, or charged a fortune? "I don't want to impose or put him out. And to be honest, my budget's a little tight. Are his fees reasonable?"

"Very. Don't worry about it, Annie. And if he can't do it, I'll let you know."

"Okay." Annie abandoned her doubts to the

relief of having the problem taken care of. "I'll expect to hear one way or the other, then. You made it very easy."

"My pleasure. Do stop by some day, Annie. I'm always glad to visit."

"Thanks, Meg," Annie said. Walking back to her car, she felt warmed by the invitation. Even if she never took advantage of it, she had a relationship with Meg Thorn now. She had young Jed, whoever he might be, coming to help with her chimney. And she had a neighbor, however unsettling, who welcomed her listening to his music and walking on his land, and who never needed to know that she was still dreaming about dancing close in his arms. Not a very comfortable connection, but at least she wasn't entirely alone. There were three narrow, tenuous bridges off of the isolation of her new life. Smiling a little, she started up the Toyota and turned her attention to the more urgent problem of her wildflowers and her weeds.

Three

Late that evening, the mist cleared. A glow as bright as a flashlight's beam shone on the mountains. Through the parlor window of her aunt Moira's house, Lucinda Byrne could see the moonlight gleaming on the dim shapes of bushes and trees, touching them with silver.

If she was home, Cindy thought longingly, maybe she and Billy would be sitting together on the little wooden deck behind their house. Well, double-wide trailer, really, and the deck wasn't much bigger than a back stoop. Still, it was a place to sit, watch the moon or stars, enjoy the cool air of a pretty night. The kids would be asleep, and the ten o'clock news that Billy loved would still be a half hour away and maybe, if she told him she was cold and sat on his lap to wrap his sheepskin jacket around her, he'd forget about the news altogether for once. The thought of Billy's big, strong body against hers made Cindy smile. The pale, blush-prone skin that had been the curse of her childhood flushed a little, and she felt a tiny spasm between her legs. Even after six years of marriage, Billy Byrne still made her tingle.

From the other side of the circle of chairs, Moira McTeague coughed sharply, giving Cindy a look as cutting as a rebuke. Her blush darkening, Cindy brought her attention back to the meeting.

The Burnsville Daughters of Britain met monthly to share genealogical and historical notes, lore about the old country, and information on the varied history of the many Irish, Scottish, and English families that populated the mountains. Tonight, twelve women perched uncomfortably on Moira's stiff chairs. There had been lots more members in the club once, but Cindy suspected her aunt's prickly personality had driven them away. Now it was just eleven older ladies and Cindy, sitting around, eating apple cake and coffee, and blabbing on about ancestors and the Empire and who knew what.

Dottie Barclay was giving tonight's talk. Cindy liked Dottie, whose cheerfulness never failed despite crippling arthritis. Still, she felt her attention begin to wander again. Surreptitiously she wiggled a foot that was starting to fall asleep. It was hard to sit still when you were used to moving around all the time. And her chair — one of the cushionless straight-backs from Moira's never-used dining room — was miserably uncomfortable. So was everything else in her aunt's house, for that matter. Rigid chairs, tables and dressers with knobs bristling out all over the place, sofas with barely a hint of stuffing, twin beds in every bedroom. Cindy stifled a giggle. The furniture in Moira's house, she decided, was as mean and sexless as Moira herself.

It wasn't fair, she thought rebelliously as her inner laughter died. She barely had the time to do her job, handle her housework, be a good wife, and raise her kids, much less come to these silly monthly meetings about something that she didn't even understand. Who cared whether a Scottish regiment from Spruce Pine fought in the Civil War? Who cared what long-dead McTeagues or Barclays had accomplished? Who cared whether anybody was British or Dutch or Greek or Chinese, for that matter? They were all Americans now.

But Moira insisted on the honor of the McTeague name, pooh-poohing the fact that, since her marriage, Cindy was just an undistinguished Irish Byrne. The McTeagues' long lineage, Moira lectured stridently, was a valuable heritage. An honor. A legacy that held them apart from all the riffraff and white trash of America. It was the least Cindy could do — that was a phrase Moira used a lot — to help her aunt with the family genealogy. And years of dealing with her aunt had taught Cindy that it was easier just to go along than to fight.

Cindy was a little afraid of Moira; that was the truth. Or maybe more than a little. There was something extreme about her aunt, despite Moira's obvious respectability. Something weird about the hands scrubbed so often they were red, the pills Moira took for a thousand vague ailments, the glitter in the eyes behind the unflattering bifocal glasses, the gray hair pulled back so tight you could almost see the veins of Moira's temples pop, and the body that was so severely dressed you could see no hint of hips or breasts at all. Cindy loved little denim miniskirts, cute tops, things that showed off her curvy body just a little. Moira disapproved loudly of such flirtatious frippery. She looked sort of like a nun, and not one of those friendly sisters at that.

Billy, usually so steady, was different about Moira. He said she was crazy in private and disagreed with her to her face, but he was one of the few to do it. Cindy's mother Jean had always been intimidated by her older sister. Even Moira's husband had felt the scourge of his wife's strong will. Uncle Arthur had been dead for years now, but Cindy remembered him well, a mousy, balding little man who'd sneaked her Milk Duds from his general store when she was little. He'd seemed so sweet, but that didn't stop Moira from scolding him for a million different faults, from giving little discounts to some of the town's poorer folks to smiling too much at Alma Honeycutt. He never did enough, it seemed. No wonder he'd cracked up in the end.

Poor Uncle Arthur. Cindy had never seen him and Moira touch, not even when Arthur and Moira were working together in the narrow space behind the counter at the store. Not one single time. And back when she was a teenager, Cindy had watched like a hawk for evidence of people's sex lives, for proof that other ordinary people felt the same embarrassing, exhilarating, totally distracting stirrings she did. But no hint of sex ever touched Moira. No wonder Arthur had sometimes looked a little tenderly at Mrs. Honeycutt. No wonder he had killed himself. Sure as shooting, part of the blame for that could be laid at Moira's door.

Dottie kept her talk short. The meeting broke up a little after nine, much to Cindy's relief. She helped her aunt tidy up the parlor, move the extra chairs back to their positions, and rinse the dishes. Nothing sloppy or soiled was tolerated in Moira's home, with its plastic-encased sofas and bathrooms so spotless you felt afraid to pee.

Moira had promised her a ride home after the meeting. Out in the cool air of Moira's driveway, the two women climbed silently into Moira's ancient but immaculate Chevy. Moira backed down the sharply angled gravel drive, guiding the car along the treacherous slope with the deftness only mountain-born folk commanded. She paused at the junction of drive and roadway, then turned decisively to the left.

"What . . ." Cindy glanced at her in the dim greenish light from the dash, surprised. "Aunt Moira, I'm over the other way. You know that. The other side of Nineteen."

"It's a fine night, and a bright one." Moira's voice was even but implacable, her profile as sharp as a hawk's in the shadowy car. The streetlights on this well-traveled stretch of road shone on her glasses, turning the lenses into opaque white ovals. "We'll go up to the cottage, Honeycutt's cottage. I've been wanting to see those books and papers of Alma's ever since she moved, but I had those heart flutters so bad until just yesterday, and next week Patsy is coming to visit. This is the perfect chance."

Cindy opened her mouth to protest, then closed it again. Moira's speech was rough with a hillbilly's rural burr, but she was sharp as a tack, and Cindy could tell from her tone that Moira meant business. The force of her seemed to engulf Cindy suddenly, to blot all her own strength out, like the moon eclipsing the sun. The Cindy that was thirty-three, ran a house, kept two rambunctious preschoolers in line, dealt with even the Cupboard Café's rowdiest customers with an iron hand — that Cindy didn't exist here in the moonlit darkness. Someone else, someone more timid and much more eager to please, took her place.

"Alma's cottage?" she asked, her voice a little shaky. The energy of the long and busy day was gone now, leaving tiredness behind it. The last thing she wanted to do now was start hunting around abandoned houses in the dark. There would probably be bugs and disgusting snakes, and if anyone caught them, there'd be hell to pay. She was anxious to check on little LuAnne, too, see if the child's earache had calmed down. "Aunt Moira, it's going to be cold up there, and pitch dark, and I'm sure the house is locked. What are we going to be able to see?"

"I have a flashlight." Moira smiled her thin, sharp smile. "And a key. Alma gave young Jed Harper one a couple of years ago, in case there was ever an emergency."

"And he lent it to you?"

" 'Course not, Lucinda." Moira never used the bouncy nickname Cindy preferred. It was common, she said. "Why in tarnation would Jed Harper give me the key to someone else's house?" the older woman continued. "I borrowed it, that's all. Man never noticed a thing. Too busy with all them rich boy's toys. He'll never even see it's gone."

"Jed isn't rich. Wasn't always, anyhow."

Cindy had nursed an almighty crush on young Jed Harper for years. He'd been her first real love, the source of those first mind-numbing moments of desire; his was the face she'd seen as she made her first tentative explorations of her own budding body. And she would have done something about it, too, that year she was sixteen and suddenly pretty, would have walked right up and asked him out, even if he was seven years older and way out of her league.

Only Billy had started to make calf eyes at her that year, and her mama had insisted that the Harpers were nothing but lousy white trash, and then she'd started in with Dr. Andrews, anyway. Cindy's pale face flushed at the thought. Even now, the memory filled her with shame. When the nightmare was all over and she'd gotten her life back on track, she'd bumped into Billy again, back from ag school and ready to settle down. Blond, lumbering William Byrne didn't have young Jed's narrow hips or wide shoulders or those flashing, electric-blue eyes that pierced a girl right to her spine. But he was sweet and safe and sexy, and he made her mama happy, and she knew he'd forgive her for the shame of Dr. Andrews if she ever got up the nerve to tell him.

"Huh. Well, boy's rich now," Moira said, breaking into Cindy's memories. "Fancy kitchen with more gadgets than a space station, computer, fax machine, who knows what all. Never think he grew up eatin' his dinners right out of the can."

"But . . ." Dogged, Cindy returned to the point. "We'll be breaking in."

"Who's going to see us? 'Sides, no one knows that Alma didn't give me the key herself."

A deaf, dumb, and blind person wouldn't have missed the fact that the two women had been chalk and cheese, oil and water. Or that Arthur's yearning glances at Alma hadn't gone over any too well with Arthur's wife. The thought of darkness and bugs and being arrested for burglary made Cindy unusually willing to fight. "I don't see the point, Aunt Moira. And what good will Alma's books do you?"

"Honeycutts were thick as thieves with those Historical Society people for years. And Alma was such a pack rat, who knows what papers she has stuck away? It's none of your business, anyway, Lucinda. Respect your elders, I've always said. Jean always was too soft on you. There, now, your lip is giving me that pain in my side again. Should have taken one more of those little pills. You can never be too safe. So don't you argue with me, girl. It's enough for you to know that I just want to look around there, is all. No harm in that."

Cindy frowned. It didn't make sense. "Maybe she brought the stuff, the books and papers, to Tampa with her," Cindy said. Despite the defiant words, she felt herself giving in, and she sensed that Moira knew it, too.

"Huh. You think she had time to pack up those things, with a broken hip? It's still there, all right. It's my right, after all the hard work I've done in my life, and all I've suffered. The least you can do. You wouldn't deny me, such a little thing."

"Of course not, Aunt Moira," Cindy sighed, leaning back against the car's hard seat. No moldy old papers could possibly warrant wandering around some tacky old cottage in the middle of the night. There was something urgent and excited in Moira's voice, anyway, something the wish to see Alma's papers didn't quite explain. Suddenly Cindy felt not just reluctance but also a pang of danger. She knew better than to voice it, though. She'd tested

90

Moira enough for one night, and the edge in Moira's voice was a clear warning.

"Okay, then," she said. "But let's hurry, okay? Billy wants me home by ten. Ten-thirty, at the latest, when the news gets done."

"I'll just bet he wants you, girl." Moira's chuckle was sharp and suggestive, making Cindy flush in the darkness. The older woman concentrated on the drive for a few minutes, peering into the dark night as they left the empty main road for an even narrower gravel one. "You see that?"

"What?"

"Up there." Moira angled the car onto the rutted roadside. Leaving the engine idling and Cindy inside, she yanked on the parking brake and got out into the night. She stood for a moment, a ramrod-straight figure in the silvery light, then muttered something Cindy didn't catch as she climbed back into the car. "That's Alma's place up there, through those trees. And there's someone up there. Lights on in every window. Car in the drive."

"Oh, Aunt Moira. That's too bad." Cindy rubbed her arms as the chill night air hit her, trying to project a regret she didn't feel. "I guess we should have gone before. Maybe Alma's back. Maybe she's not going to stay with Bobby and Judy in Florida anymore."

"If Alma came back, I'd of known. And I want to look at them things."

Moira's tone was angry, and Cindy recognized the finality in it. If Moira wanted something that bad, Moira would get it. But if she was lucky, Cindy would be busy next time, and Moira would do whatever she was going to do at Alma's on her own.

Relaxing against the hard seat, Cindy turned her mind to nicer things: Billy and the kids and the shabby, cheerful double-wide — no plastic sofas there, thank goodness — waiting for her on the other side of Highway 19. Suddenly, fervently, she wanted nothing to do with Moira. She wanted that leftover wedge of Cupboard Café apple pie that would still be sitting on the kitchen counter, and the low, familiar drone of the news on the old TV, and Billy's sweet smile welcoming her back. Silently, dreaming of his big, musky body warming hers in their wide, sagging bed, Cindy looked out at the starry heavens and let her aunt bring her home.

Annie was half buried in the weed-choked shrubbery that surrounded her house when she heard the crunching of wheels on gravel. Peering past a juniper branch, she could make out the shape of a dusty blue Chevrolet truck making its way up the drive, what looked to be tools heaped in its flatbed.

"Damn," she said, yanking a final misplaced maple sapling out of the ground and squatting back on her haunches.

This must be the mysterious young Jed, come to check her chimney. She'd been half expecting to hear from him in the two days since she'd spoken to Meg Thorn, but used to the formality of the city, it hadn't occurred to her that he might just stop by. Irritated, she blew out a long breath.

Fixing this garden was war, and she was losing. Much as she wanted her fireplace checked, it was a lousy time for anyone to show up. Her face was filthy and her flimsy white T-shirt was full of burrs and good old young Jed was probably going to drive back down the mountain and tell everyone that the Honeycutt place had been rented by a witch, and not a white one at that. She wiped one forearm across her sweaty forehead, then blinked in astonishment as her dulcimer-playing neighbor slid out of the Chevy's door.

"Howdy," he said cheerfully, ambling over to the house. "You look frazzled."

"I am." Annie felt her face flush. Why did she blush like a schoolgirl every time she bumped into this man? Because he always caught her off guard, that was why. Because he appeared in her dreams and there was nothing she could do to stop it. Because she had tangled hair and dirt on her face every time she met him in real life. The fact that his own white T-shirt was as clean as new snow, not to mention that it showed off a torso worthy of Michelangelo's David, didn't do anything to mend her self-consciousness.

For someone who John Addamson said was rarely in Burnsville, she thought irritably, this man certainly seemed to pop up a lot. Briefly she closed her eyes, wishing she could chant a magic spell and send him back to wherever it was he went when he wasn't here. "I'm sorry," she said edgily, swatting a fly away from her ear. "I'm up to my neck in weeds and mosquitoes. It's not a great time for visiting."

"I'm not a visitor," he said easily. "Meg said you wanted your fireplace looked at, and I'm here to do it."

"You're young Jed?"

"Oh, Christ. She'll be calling me young Jed till I have my first stroke. But yes, to answer your question, I'm Jed. Jed Harper." He grinned, and she could have sworn he was enjoying her discomfiture. "You didn't expect it to be me."

"No. I'm not sure what I expected, but it definitely wasn't you." Annie thought of his beautiful house, the silver-chased dulcimer, the boots that had obviously been expensive before he'd worn them to death. Even his truck must have cost a pretty penny; under the light coating of gravel dust it looked like something out of an auto museum. "You can't possibly do this for a living," she said.

"I don't. But I grew up without central heating. Been fiddling around with chimneys my whole life."

This was her own fault, Annie thought. She should have queried Meg more carefully. "I'm sorry, Mr. Harper," she said resolutely. "But I was looking for a business transaction, not a favor. I couldn't impose on you."

"Can you brush dogs?"

Annie gaped at him. She couldn't keep up with him; his mind seemed to dance around hers, fast where she was slow, easy where she was anxious. "What?"

"Or mend china? Or maybe you could stick some flowers in vases for me, seeing as you seem to like gardening so much. I'm giving myself a birthday party next Saturday, and I've been thinking the place looks kind of bare."

Annie blew out a long, frustrated breath. "I'm not being clear, somehow. I don't want to feel beholden. I can't afford to be beholden."

He put his hands on his narrow hips and considered her face with those blazing blue eyes. "Annie. If someone you seem to want to call Mr. Harper can call you that." She could hear the effort at patience in his voice. "There's no favor here. This is a small town. I do fireplaces, Meg bakes pies, old Miz Honeycutt used to read kids' college essays and help folks trace their family trees. We help each other out. We don't have the luxury, here, of hunting up some fancy expert every time we have a problem."

Annie glared at him. "Right. You're telling me there are no professional chimney cleaners in Burnsville."

He hooked one thumb through his belt loop and stared right back, clearly unfazed by her rudeness. "I'm telling you that old Dick Hend-

rickson will pinch your pretty little ass, spit tobacco on your rugs, and charge you a fucking
fortune, excuse my French, for a job that would
take ten minutes if you'd ever stop arguing and
let me look at the damn thing."

"Oh . . . fine." Shaking her head so hard her
hair bounced on her shoulders, Annie pivoted
on her heel and headed for the steps. She knew
she was being ungrateful and making a mountain of a molehill to boot. But it scared her, this
interdependency. And he scared her. Scowling,
she pushed open her front door, gestured to the
living room. "In here. You probably know that
already."

"I do." He strolled to the hearth, surveying
the room unabashedly as he went. "Place looks
great. Clean, pretty. Alma always was a pack rat.
What happened to the dying stag?"

"The . . ." There'd been a hideous bronze
statue of a stag at bay on the table under the back
window; Annie had carted it off to the attic, along
with about a hundred other eccentric artifacts.
But he was already leaning into the fireplace, absorbed.

Needing a moment to regain her composure,
Annie headed for the kitchen to pour some iced
tea, pausing for one moment to tuck a sprig of
mint in each glass. By the time she returned, he
was perched on a footstool on her hearth, his
head hidden up the chimney and his long legs
braced wide. She put the tea down on a side
table and tried to avoid staring at his narrow

hips, the muscular thighs that pulled against his jeans, the places where the denim was worn almost white. Tom was strong but burly, with a squarish build made bulkier by daily workouts in the gym. This man was lean, rangy, almost elegant despite his toughness. An ache rose deep inside her.

Stop acting like an adolescent, she ordered herself.

Annie Mahoney — Annie Taylor — had a house to organize, a living to find, and a husband to hide out from. Annie Taylor had made one disastrous choice already. Fantasies about handsome males were for teenagers, innocents with no bruises and no scars and their whole shining lives ahead of them. Fantasies weren't for Annie Taylor. Particularly when they came attached to utterly unpredictable men.

"What's up there?" she said, keeping her voice businesslike.

"Flue's open, but the chimney's blocked. Alma liked her central heating, didn't clean it much, I guess. Bird's nest, probably, and about fifty years of soot." To her relief, he ducked his head, now speckled with black dust, out of the chimney. "Towel?"

She fetched one, trailed back to stand at his side, knotted her hand into a fist against the impulse to brush off the smudge of soot that still darkened one side of his jaw. "What needs to be done?"

"I'll look from the roof. Then probably blow

off a shotgun blast up the chimney."

"A gun?" She frowned.

"Don't worry. I'm not violent." He grinned at her. "I'm probably the only man in the county that never kills a thing. Used to irritate my daddy something fierce. Shotgun pellets will break up the soot that's hardened up the chimney. Makes a holy hell of a mess, though. You'll want to move all these things away a little and cover them up."

"I should have done this before I cleaned. Another lesson learned." She sighed. "I don't even know if I have a ladder."

"You do." He grinned at her, the smudges of soot on his face making his teeth seem blindingly white, his eyes electric blue. "Out back, in the shed. Well, unless Alma brought it to Tampa with her. But I've got one too, if we need it."

Glad to have something to do, she shoved her furniture away from the hearth and found a couple of old sheets to cover it in. While she worked, she could hear Jed Harper thumping up and down on the roof. She returned to her flower bed while he drove down the hill for a gun and kept weeding as the muffled boom went off inside. Brushing her hands off again, she peeked anxiously at her living room. A cloud of black dust mushroomed in the hearth, matching the one that had already settled over half of Jed Harper's snowy white shirt.

"That should do it," he said, breaking the shotgun barrel and tucking the empty shells into one pocket. His hands, big and tanned and long-fingered, moved as deftly over the gun as they did on his dulcimer. "Let's give it a few minutes to settle, then we'll clean it up."

"*I'll* clean it up," Annie corrected.

"My mess, my responsibility. And in the meantime," he added, clattering down her front steps and propping the shotgun against the stoop, "I'll do the weeds on that side."

"Get out of my garden." Seriously irritated now, Annie stamped off the porch in his wake. He was gorgeous and he was uncontrollable and he was also, apparently, deaf.

"Make me." Gracefully, he bent to tug at the thickets of asparagus fern that ran wild along the south side of the cottage. The white shirt pulled tight over the rippling muscles of his back, emphasizing the strength of the muscles that narrowed to his waist. He looked like a damned Calvin Klein model, she thought. Except that he was way too smart and way too annoying and he never stood still.

Well, she'd just run away from one controlling, unmanageable man. The last thing she needed was another one, trampling all over her life and telling her what to do.

"Mr. Harper." Annie gritted her teeth. "*Jed.* I'm serious. They're my weeds. And quite frankly, I don't need your damned help."

"You do need my damn help. You're just afraid to take it, in case it makes you even more obligated. Well, it doesn't. And I'm either going to occupy myself with the weeds, or I'm going to sit on your porch and ask you questions about where you came from and why." He looked over his shoulder at her, eyes narrowed against the sun and one straight brow lifted. "Take your choice."

Glaring at him, Annie knelt beside the other flower bed. She took out her fury on the weeds, yanking them much more efficiently than she had that morning. Her annoyance was not soothed by noticing that Jed Harper uprooted more weeds in ten minutes, than she'd managed to do in an hour. After fifteen minutes, he jerked his head at the house and they went inside to move the furniture back.

"Thank you," Annie said stiffly when they finished. "I know that I'm not being gracious, but I do appreciate the help."

"It's nothing." Back out on the porch, he propped his hands on his hips and stared broodingly at her, his expression unreadable. When he spoke, his voice was gruff. "Look around you. You can just about see the Wellman farm from your kitchen window, and we can both catch glimpses of a couple of vacation places. That's it, Annie Taylor. Someday, when your car breaks down or your water heater bursts, you might need me. Someday, when I wake up too sick with the flu to move, I might need you. We don't have to be confidants, or even friends," he finished. "We just don't have to be strangers." The blue eyes burned at hers for a moment, then he was gone.

"Damn it," Annie said aloud, then followed him outside. "Mr. Harper. Jed," she called from the porch. He stopped with one booted foot already propped inside the open door of his truck. Standing at the porch railing, she struggled to find the words. "I don't really like it, but I do understand what you're saying," she said finally. "And I'll try."

"Good," he said mildly, turning to slide the end of the ladder into the back of the truck.

"Fine, then. So what do I owe you?"

"Oh, hell." He propped one elbow on the truck door as he looked at her. "I suppose you just have to be payin' me something."

"I do."

"Ten bucks, then. That do you?"

"Ten dollars." Annie folded her arms across her chest and stared at him. "For almost an hour of work, thorns all over your hands, and a shirt that's probably ruined."

He shrugged, his face alight with laughter, his shoulders rippling. "Christ, woman, you're as stubborn as a mule. Twenty, then. Forty. Two hundred. Whatever will let you hold your head up high, Annie Taylor, that'll be fine with me."

His grin was infectious, damn it. And she was acting like an idiot. She couldn't help but smile as she headed back into the house, then leaned over the porch railing to hand the folded bills down to him. "I can afford twenty-five, actually."

"Thank you," he said, one corner of his

mobile mouth still twitching with amusement.

"You're welcome. May I ask why I'm so funny?"

"Oh, I wouldn't exactly say you're funny." His blue eyes took her in with one swift glance, head to chest to hips to toes, and she had to resist the impulse to fold her hands over herself like some Victorian maiden. "Interesting, maybe. So. You goin' to help out with those flowers?"

When she didn't answer, he held her gaze and smiled. "Chicken," he added softly.

"Don't be ridiculous," Annie said, trying to hold on to her dignity. "I'll be happy to help with the flowers, if you like. And then we'll be even."

"Mmm." Jed gestured at the bright yellow plumes that lined her road. "Don't use ragweed."

Annie's jaw clenched again. He was like a roller coaster, sending her from fury to pleasure back to annoyance again. "Why ask me to do the damned flowers if you think I don't even know ragweed when I see it?"

"Well, now, you said you're a city girl, Annie," he said, stretching his slight Carolina burr into an outright drawl. He swung into the cab side of the truck and pulled the door shut after him. The ignition fired, and he leaned out from the open window, his bronzy hair gleaming in the sun and his grin flashing white against the soot that still smudged his jaw. "Ain't no telling what-all you might not know about plants," he continued. "Man could end up with deadly nightshade fallin' all over his birthday cake. But I didn't want you to lose any of your beauty sleep bein' beholden to me."

Annie stared at him. "Oh . . . just go away," she spluttered, shocking herself. His face dancing with laughter, Jed Harper tipped an imaginary cap at her and drove off down the hill.

Annie Taylor was trouble. Capital T trouble. And the worst kind of trouble there was, the kind so sweet, a man lost the wits to run away.

She was smart, Jed thought as he drove down the mountain. And feisty. And warm, he suspected, underneath the gruffness she struggled to muster. Folks who were cold by nature didn't have to work so hard at keeping their distance. He could actually see it happen, watch the jolt of something painful shutter her eyes and make her face go still. Always curious, Jed couldn't help wonder. What had driven Annie Taylor — who seemed to know nothing about the country, who looked as elegant as a debutante even in filthy jeans — to live in a dowdy little house in the middle of nowhere? What memory made her flinch away from simple kindness like a whipped dog?

The writer in him was caught by the mystery of it. But the man in him was caught by something else. *Jesus,* he thought, whistling softly as he pulled the truck in front of his house, *she was pretty.* Her face had looked less haunted, more peaceful this time. The sun — and her indignation — had kissed that luminous skin, made it glow bright against the tangle of black hair. Her body was delicate and sweet under the little T-shirt, and she had a world-class rear. The sight of her on all fours in her garden as he drove up made him ache even in retrospect. This time his imagination ignored the possibilities of feminine bedrooms, black hair against white lace, slow seductions. It zoomed straight to hot, frantic screwing right there on her little front lawn, both of them sweaty, still clothed in everything except what needed to be ripped aside to let them take each other. It would be hard and fast. Mindless. Primal. And then he'd carry her upstairs and lock the door and keep her safe from whatever it was that scared her.

Right, he jeered at himself, braking the truck and his imagination at the same time. *You'll keep her safe. And then you'll run off to Newfoundland for six or seven months.*

Shit. He muttered it aloud as he clattered up his steps. Getting a little dazed by a sexy woman was one thing. But acting like an starry-eyed adolescent, letting some weird white knight fantasies run away with him, that was just plain stupid. His whole damned career, not to mention his sanity, demanded that he be able to forget about Burnsville the minute he left it. And whatever her problem was, Annie Taylor clearly didn't need some here-today, gone-tomorrow son of a bitch messing with her body or her mind. It was all so clear. So why the hell was he mooning over her like an infatuated seventh-grader?

He was losing his mind. Or, at least, thinking with something other than his brains.

There was a cure for that problem, and he was too experienced not to know what it was. After dinner, he tucked some money in his pocket, tossed his leather bomber jacket over a flannel shirt and a pair of old jeans, and drove his truck down the mountain. Lulu's was just on the other side of the Tennessee border, a ramshackle old-style bar with a rowdy, old-style clientele. The parking lot was crowded with pickups, the barroom was crowded with good old boys, and the whole place smelled of tobacco, whiskey, and sweat.

You could find cheap booze at Lulu's. You could find a fight, if you wanted one. And you could find a woman who wanted it just as quick and anonymous as you did.

Jed locked his truck and walked from the night's coolness into the barroom, his nose twitching at the smell of stale beer. Beer had been his old man's cologne. By eleven each and every night he had reeked of it. In fact, Big Jed had brought him to Lulu's for his first taste of liquor, back when Jed was a teenager and his daddy still thought he could teach him to appreciate the manly arts of hunting, boozing, breaking the law, and tomcatting around.

Jed tossed down some bills and picked up the

glass of bourbon the bartender slid across the scarred bar. With the fire of the first swallow in his throat, he scanned the room. Amid the jostling crowd he saw her immediately. A small, curvy woman, young but not as young as she wanted to look, pretty but probably not as pretty as she used to be. Pretty enough, though, and she met his steady, dispassionate gaze with one of her own. He let his eyes drift down her body, making no attempt to hide his scrutiny. Long, blond, teased hair, from a bottle probably, and a foxy little face with full red lips. Heavy, round breasts with no bra, the nipples obvious under her cheap satin cowgirl shirt. Heeled lizard-skin boots. Jeans stretched tight over her hips, which swayed a little with the jukebox's blare. When he lifted his eyes, she held his stare again.

She would do just fine. Slowly, taking his glass, he sauntered in her direction. He put the glass down and leaned one elbow casually on the bar next to where she stood. This close up, he could smell her perfume: cheap violet toilet water, the kind little girls bought in dime stores. The vulnerability of it, the toughened woman still wearing the innocent scent, made him wince for a minute, but he pushed the thought away. She took a swig from her beer, then licked the foam from her lips while she held his eyes. In the dim light a small diamond sparkled on her left hand. "Where's your husband?" He let his voice go lazy, almost cruel. She wouldn't respond to need, he judged, and she didn't want kindness.

"Mill. Overtime," she said carelessly, flicking back her mane of hair. "Out of sight, like they say. I'm Missy."

"Jed."

"Like your belt buckle, Jed." Her fingernails were red, unnaturally long and shiny. She looked down at his crotch as she ran one gleaming talon slowly and teasingly over the silver buckle, never letting her finger touch his body. She knew what she was doing, this one. Good. "Want to dance?" she said.

That wasn't what he wanted, but he led her out onto the sawdust-scattered square that passed for a dance floor and took her in his arms. An old Patsy Cline song played scratchily on the jukebox, mournful and ironic, about the foolishness of men. Perfect, Jed thought as he put his arms around Missy, settled his chin against the teased blond hair. Letting her breasts rub against his chest and dangling one hand off his hip, she expertly followed his lead.

She was warm and small, and the feminine softness of her was as genuine as the blond mane and the red fingertips were false. It always moved him, the sweet liquid mystery of a woman's body, and it aroused him now, though her closeness felt claustrophobic, cloying. He ignored the feeling and moved her slowly around the floor, trying to concentrate on the sexual promise of her knowing eyes, her seductive hips.

She'd be just what he needed, he told himself, sliding his hand down onto her rear, a quick, mindless, undemanding release, a woman who asked even less from him than he did from her.

The song ended, and she pulled lazily away. "That was nice," she said.

"It gets nicer." Jed narrowed his eyes as he tossed back the rest of his bourbon.

"You got a truck here, sugar?" she asked. He nodded and led her outside.

He'd parked toward the back of the lot, where a big tree shaded the orange glare of the streetlight. The truck felt cold after the smoky closeness of the bar. Missy slid across the seat toward him immediately, tilted her head for his kiss, splayed one hand on the denim over his thigh, long fingernails almost brushing his crotch. Yeah, she knew what to do. Well, so did he. He nudged his leg closer to her, making the fingernails move again, and put his hand on her breast before reaching to kiss her, knowing the direct gesture would arouse them both.

It did. She made a little mewing sound as his lips met hers and arched her back so that her nipple pressed into his cupped hand. His body responded, hot and urgent, but then the confined, crowded feeling returned.

It felt wrong, he thought dazedly. Flesh as giving as marshmallow, cheap, scented, cloying. Too easy, too soft, too much. Stubbornly, he shut his eyes and kissed her harder, trying to push the unwelcome sensation away, fighting to shut down his mind. He could feel Missy shift her legs upward, feel her deepen the kiss as she swung them up onto the seat.

She was eager, and he was hard, and it was wrong. His mind wouldn't shut down, the thought wouldn't go away. *Wrong, wrong, wrong.*

Because he wanted Annie Taylor, not just some quick, anonymous screwing. He wanted Annie Taylor's fierce shyness, and her reluctant warmth, and her slim, delicate body. Wanted it, wanted her, even if they both fought like tigers against it and it made no sense at all and it screwed up both their lives something royal. He probably wasn't going to do anything about it, no matter how bad the wanting got, and Annie Taylor had no claim on him at all, but that still didn't make what he was doing anything but cheap.

That's right, Annie, his mind jeered. *You're so damned attractive, I just had to screw someone else.* The thought jolted him into stillness as the heat in him died.

"Jesus." Missy pushed Jed off her body and sat up. "What's wrong with you?"

He righted himself with a quick, disgusted shake of his head. "I can't do this," he said shortly. "My fault, not yours."

"What's the problem, baby?" Her voice was scornful. "Seems to me I turned you on."

"It's not that," he lied. "I have someone else. I shouldn't cheat on her."

In the dim light of the truck, Missy gave him

the withering look he knew his words deserved. She tilted the rearview mirror to check her reflection, poked at her hair, and opened the truck door. "You should have thought of her earlier, you stupid prick," she said before she slammed it shut.

"You're one hundred percent right," he said aloud as her boots crunched back over the gravel toward the bar. He made sure she was safely inside the door again before he fired the ignition, slid the truck into gear, and started driving back up the mountain, where he belonged.

Four

Annie had no intentions of going to Jed Harper's party, but somehow the party came to her.

On Saturday afternoon, armed with one of Alma Honeycutt's big wicker baskets and a sharp pair of scissors, she gathered a whole armful of flowers from the verge of the road leading to her house. September weed and Queen Anne's lace, yarrow and thistle, some wild breed of black-eyed Susans, and scores of flowers she couldn't even name grew wild there, standing yellow and pink and lavender and white against the green grass and deep blue sky. Annie's artist's eye rejoiced in the riot of color, almost as much as her city-bred soul savored the warm, fragrant abundance that was here just for the picking. *Gorgeous flowers for nothing,* she thought as she bent to cut the first stem. *Clean, crisp air. The heavens full of stars and the big, beautiful moon. Silence. Peace.* Country folk took for granted things even city millionaires didn't have.

It was almost five when she arrived at Jed Harper's house with the flowers. When she emerged from the path, he was bending over the flatbed of his pickup with Rooster capering happily at his feet, hauling out the first of what looked to be twenty boxes of bottles. The wind rippled his T-shirt — navy this time — as he propped the heavy crate on his hip, his forearm cording with the weight. When he caught sight of Annie on the path, he waved.

"Kitchen's to the left of the front door," he called, flashing that gleaming grin at her. "See you in a minute. I've got to get this on ice."

Good, Annie thought, carrying her basket toward his kitchen. He was treating this as work. In the days since she'd seen him, she'd had time to regret her impulsive agreement to do the flowers. He'd half dared her, and she hadn't been able to resist the challenge. Well, he was confident and comfortable. Whatever in the world he did for a living, he obviously didn't have a care in the world. He could afford to play games. But she couldn't. And she'd better stop letting him goad her into them, she thought as she stepped into his kitchen.

A tall pottery jar with a gleaming green glaze stood on the Mexican tile countertop. She dumped the flowers beside it and glanced curiously around.

Like the exterior of his house, this room was simple — almost spare — and yet somehow luxurious. Sunlight streamed through a line of high, clerestory windows onto oak cabinets, a deep window seat, a warm tile floor. Jed Harper's kitchen was a plain, masculine room, but it wasn't unsophisticated, and it hadn't come cheap. In fact, it was probably almost as costly as her kitchen in New York, though the pleasing warmth here couldn't have been more different from that high-tech sterility. It made her wonder again what he did for a living, what it was that left him free to wander around cleaning people's chimneys but kept him in Stickley tables, hand-woven fabrics, and Navajo rugs. Or maybe he didn't work at all. Maybe he'd been born rich. Yet another reason to keep away from him. She hadn't much liked most of the wealthy folks Tom loved to socialize with in New York. She certainly didn't need that kind of arrogance or attitude now.

Meanwhile, though, she'd promised to help. She could hear the thump of Jed's feet and the thudding of the crates on the porch, but he didn't come anywhere near the kitchen. She began to strip the bottom leaves from each branch, then cut each stem before putting it into the water. Within minutes, the vase was bursting with flowers. It looked good, she thought, stepping back. Vibrant, colorful. Better than any of the expensive bouquets she used to order from fancy florists.

"That looks great," Jed said from behind her.

Annie turned, startled, as she always was by him. His arms gleamed a little with sweat, and he smelled good, like sun and clean denim and soap. He smiled at her and propped one lazy shoulder against the doorjamb. Even though he didn't enter the room, the kitchen seemed sud-

113

denly small to Annie.

"Did it look to you like I have enough drinks for forty or so people?" he asked.

"It looked like enough drinks for the entire state of North Carolina," she said. "You must have thirsty friends. Do you have another vase or two?"

"Vase?"

"Container." She gestured at the countertop. "I picked too many flowers, I guess, and I'd hate to just throw them away."

"I'm not big on frills," he said, stepping beside her. "I've only got this pot, or vase or whatever you call it, because Meg gave it to me as a housewarming present. But we can probably find something."

"It's all right," she said hastily. She'd forgotten how big he was and how energy radiated from him in waves she could almost see. "Look, I'll just run up and get one from my house, let you go back to your work." She edged carefully past him and headed for the door.

"Whoa, girl," he drawled. "Don't give up on this place so fast. I'm sure there's something here, let's just see. . . . " He reached out one long arm and hooked a finger under the back of the pale pink cotton sweater she'd worn with her jeans, letting his knuckles brush gently against the nape of her neck.

It was Jed Harper's touch, casual and light, and his hand was warm against her skin. But suddenly it was Tom's touch, too. The cheerful kitchen blurred in front of her, turned dark and narrow like her New York foyer. It was Tom's touch, slamming her against the wall. Pulling her into the bedroom. Ready to slap her, drag her, hurt her again . . . *hurt* her. And she couldn't bear to be hurt again.

Her reaction was automatic, an avalanche of fear. Adrenaline jolted through her veins. The air left her lungs with a gasp. She wheeled around, knocking Jed's hand aside with her shoulder, throwing her own hands up over her breasts, stumbling backward until her hips hit the counter hard.

"Don't." Her own voice hung in the air, half a whimper and half a muffled scream, shocking her with her own panic. It rang in the room like an explosion.

Jed stood frozen, his hand still lifted, his body motionless. His eyes held hers, and his face was white under the golden tan. "Jesus, Annie, what . . ."

"I'm sorry." Her voice was jerky. She breathed in, trying to fill her lungs again, feeling sickened and startled and regretful. He'd made a small, innocent gesture, and she'd turned on him like a fury, and she couldn't even explain why without telling him much, much more than she could possibly get into, much more than she wanted him to know. God, it was so stupid, stupid and unfair.

"Jed . . ." she said haltingly. "I'm just . . . God, Jed, I'm sorry."

"I'm sorry, too." He shook his head, helpless. "Annie, I didn't mean to scare you."

"You didn't. Well, not really. It's . . . not you."

"No. It's *not* me." His voice was fierce, as if he was arguing some crucial cause. He stood regarding her, big and handsome and already familiar, and yet suddenly she barely recognized him. It took her a moment to realize that it was because his face was so still; the quick play of expression she'd grown used to after only a couple of meetings was gone, replaced by intent concentration.

"It's not me, Annie," he repeated finally, quietly, his eyes still fixed on hers. "I've hurt plenty of women in my time, and I'll probably hurt more. But I don't do it with my fists."

"I know." And she did, probably. Annie closed her eyes against the sudden sting of tears. There was something in his tone: compassion or respect or tenderness. Why did it fill her with pain? She shook her head, willed the moisture in her eyes to go away, prayed that he wouldn't reach out to her.

"Jesus," he said. "I'd like to kill whoever it was that scared you like this."

"Don't, Jed. Please. . . . I can't talk about it. I should go," she said raggedly.

"Annie . . . no."

"I'm almost done." She turned to the flowers again, pushed the extra stems clumsily into a pile. Her pulse still raced, and her hands still trembled with tension. One of the long, graceful bunches of Queen Anne's lace fell to the floor at her feet. "You don't need me anymore. The big vase will be enough. You can put these in a pitcher or something, or even a glass. They'll be fine."

"I didn't ask you here just to work. That wasn't the deal."

"Yes, it was." She kept her eyes averted. "I said I'd do the flowers, Jed. I didn't say I'd stay for the party. As a matter of fact, you didn't ask."

"Annie . . ." he said again. He leaned back against the opposite counter, frowning as he folded his arms. "I took it for granted."

Annie gave a sharp shake of her head. Whether or not he'd invited her to a party she didn't want to attend wasn't the point. It was a foolish argument, though she was grateful for the way it had distracted them both from her outburst a moment before.

"Jed, I'm sorry. God, I keep saying that. Look . . . I didn't think about it. I offered to help you because you'd helped me, that's all, just to repay a debt. I don't know anyone here. I barely even know you." She took a deep breath, rolled the discarded leaves and stems into a paper towel, forced herself to go on. "And that's not going to change."

"Annie." He put out his hands, then before they touched her, lifted them in the air. "Stay."

First terror, then tears, now anger. For years she'd lived in hell without so much as cracking, and now here she was, a whirlwind of hurt and fury just because a man brushed his hand against her neck.

"I'm sorry I overreacted," she said fiercely, "but I'm not taking orders, Jed, from you or anyone else. I'll go if I want to go. Don't tell me what to do."

"Oh, hell. Annie, please. Would you just look at me for one second? Please?"

Grudgingly, defiantly, she raised her eyes to his, lifting her chin so that she wouldn't look as fragile as she felt, clutching the armful of discarded greenery in front of her waist like a shield.

"I didn't mean it to come out that way," he said carefully. *How could someone so big and virile look so gentle?* she wondered.

"I'm not telling, I'm asking. Annie, I won't bother you. I promise that. And no one else will, either. They're good people. Kind, easy. You can sit on the porch, listen to the music, eat Meg's food, watch all the kids run around like hooligans. If you won't do it for yourself, do it as a favor to me, Annie, just for a little while? Because someone's going to come up that road in about ten seconds, and I'm not going to even be able to talk to you." He paused for a moment, and when he continued, his voice was quiet and rough. "It's going to drive me crazy all night, Annie, if I have to think about you sitting up there in your house, all by yourself, after . . . this."

As if responding to his words, a car door

slammed in the drive and a woman's voice called his name. *"Hell,"* he said again.

"It's all right, Jed." It was so unfair to him, she thought wearily; he was just trying to be kind. "Really. Go ahead."

"It's your decision, Annie," he said softly from the doorway. "But I want — I'd like — you to stay."

Her decision. Great. She didn't know how she felt or what she wanted: to run or stay, to rage or scream, or just to dissolve into helpless tears.

"Hey, Meggie-girl," she could hear Jed saying on the porch. His voice sounded cheerful, though she could hear the undercurrent of strain. "Hope you brought lots of desserts. Buffet table's in the dining room, and the bar's here. You know Annie Taylor, don't you?" he added as they came into the kitchen. "She's not sure she can stay for the party, had some earlier plans. But she was neighborly enough to come over and do some flowers for a poor bachelor man."

"Sure. Poor, pathetic, bachelor man," Meg scoffed, smiling at Annie, her silvered red curls bright over the stack of pie boxes in her arms. "Nice to see you, Annie. I don't suppose you could spare just a couple of minutes to help me with these? The poor bachelor man here would probably crush them with those huge, macho hands of his." She slid the cartons onto the counter and fixed Jed with a look.

"Get out of here, Harper," she said. "John and Susie were right behind me. Go help John unload the stuff, and let Susie get herself settled somewhere comfortable. I think she's feeling a little frail."

"Yes'm," Jed said, but he kept his eyes on Annie as he turned to go through the door.

"Annie?" Meg handed her the last of the cartons with a shrewd look. "You okay?"

"Yes, basically," Annie said sheepishly, straightening up. "A little distracted."

"Mmm. Young Jed can do that to a person." Meg's voice was dry, but to Annie's relief, she didn't pursue it.

Instead, she stuck her hands on her solid hips and squinted at the kitchen. "What do you think the odds are that the man has a pie server?"

"Slim to none," Annie answered.

"You're probably right. Well, the pair I brought will have to be enough. Are you rushing off, or could I possibly wheedle you into helping me with the salad? I'm not above bribing you with a free lunch or two at the café if that would persuade you."

"It's okay, Meg, I'd be glad to help. Let me just get these flowers out of the way. Where do you think he wants them?"

Annie had almost forgotten how comforting the friendly, undemanding presence of another woman could be. The two women filled huge bowls with salad, stacked fragrant, just-baked sourdough in long baskets, and laid out cutlery and flatware. The familiar tasks were soothing, and so was the simplicity of Meg's presence, the

120

easy way the two of them worked side by side. By the time they'd finished, Annie felt calm again, as though some poison had been drained from her. Whatever it was, she no longer wanted to go home.

She wanted to sit with John and Susie Addamson and talk about innocent things like babies. To watch the children racing around with Rooster in the yard, maybe even to pretend one of the flushed little toddlers was her own. She wanted to sing over the birthday cake, as raucously off tune as everyone else. To stand, swaying with rhythm, a few feet away from the place where Jed played reels and ballads on his dulcimer. The harmonious sounds of the dulcimer mingled with the notes of John Addamson's banjo and a couple of other instruments, the music filling the air, rich and lively. Some of the songs were funny and some were sad, but she liked them all. She liked the unselfconscious way the people gathered on the porch sang along and the ease with which the musicians played together, laughing when one of them hit a sour note or wandered off into the wrong key.

In the end, there were forty or fifty people wandering happily around Jed's house, porch, and yard. Jed was everywhere, it seemed to Annie, a born host. Telling jokes, asking questions, opening the silly little gifts guests brought. Busy as he was, Annie could sense him keeping an eye on her. She would swear she could hear him laughing with the clusters of people on the porch, yet suddenly he'd be at her side, refilling her glass or introducing her to a friend. As the air cooled, he appeared with a denim jacket, which he handed to Annie with a quick smile before bending to scoop somebody's laughing toddler into the air.

Tired of talk for the moment, Annie wandered onto the porch a couple of hours later. The night was cool and clear, the sky thickly salted with stars. The flames of torches and candle-filled hurricane lamps flickered in the breeze. Behind her, the house rang with laughter, conversation, more music. She wrapped Jed's jacket around her shoulders, liking the roughness of the fabric and the faint echo of his scent, and leaned her elbows on the porch railing, gazing up at the velvety sky.

She sensed his presence behind her even before he spoke. "Everything all right?" he asked.

"Fine." Annie was surprised at how peaceful it was to stand next to him. Mysteriously, the encounter in the kitchen had exorcised some demons. And simplified things, too. He might not know her story, but at least he knew her fear. "It's a nice party, Jed."

"I'm glad you think so." The words were simple, but she knew he meant it. "Look up, Annie. Out there, over to your left."

Annie obeyed, bending over the porch rail to follow his gesturing hand, then drew in a breath of pleasure. The full moon was bisected by shadow, as though a giant hand were blocking its source of light. "What is it?"

"Lunar eclipse. Last one this century. The shadow will keep moving across the moon's surface, and then at the full eclipse, the whole moon will turn a sort of dusky red. Pretty spectacular, really." She could hear the grin in his voice. "I'd like to think it was Mother Nature's fortieth birthday present to me."

"Such an ego," she scoffed gently, her eyes still on the sky.

"Yeah." They gazed upward in silence for a moment before he spoke again. "When I was a kid, I used to watch the moon from my bedroom window, up in the attic. Not this house. In the old shack I grew up in, right on this spot. You know the way the moon hangs low over the mountain, in the early part of the night, low and yellow and really big? I used to lie there and pretend I'd discovered it, that they'd named it after me. Harper's Moon. Stupid, really. But it always made me feel better. And when I first started traveling, damned if it didn't make me feel less homesick, finding out that my own personal moon had followed me so far." He gave a small laugh. "Guess you never had a moon like that, in the city."

"No. Not like that," Annie said. "You couldn't see the moon from our apartment, or the sky, just the buildings across the street. I had a lamp, though."

He waited beside her. Dreamily, Annie gathered the rough denim jacket more tightly around her, lost in the memory.

"My bedroom was tiny, but it had a little window. That was a luxury in apartments like ours. Right across the street there was a row house with an arched window I used to look at. It had a lace curtain on it, and a table that always had some kind of flowers next to this pretty lamp, a little brass one with a frosted glass shade. It always looked so warm and peaceful and secure. I thought I'd get a lamp like that when I grew up. I thought I'd have some peaceful little house, and I'd leave one little light burning, when my husband or one of my kids was out late, so they'd know they were welcomed — missed, wanted — at home."

Beside her, Jed nodded. No part of his body touched hers, but she could feel his warmth, his solid presence close to her, and for some reason it comforted rather than scared her now.

"Did you ever get a lamp like that, Annie?" he asked gently.

She looked up at him. "No," she said, thinking of the shattered porcelain lamp in the New York apartment and wondering at herself, at how far she'd let her life stray from those simple, tender dreams. "No, I never did."

"There's time yet," he said simply. "Annie . . . would you dance with me? Right here, just for a minute?"

After her overreaction in his kitchen, she owed it to him. Or maybe, she thought, she owed it to herself.

Whatever the reason, she couldn't refuse. There

in the darkness of the porch, with the music playing faintly beyond them, she lifted her hand to his and let him take her in his arms.

It was just like her dream, and it wasn't like her dream at all. His height, his strength were just as she'd imagined them; they made her feel small, cherished, feminine. Her breasts pressed against his chest just as they had in her dream, and the sweet heaviness that filled her was just the same.

And yet there was so much more to notice, so much to learn. The particular angle of his shoulder, where she rested her head. The feeling of his breath stirring the hair over her ear. The way he moved, in a slow, ghostly step that barely lifted their feet from the porch's rough fieldstone floor. The rough callus on two of the fingers that clasped hers, the shivery delicacy of the way his other hand brushed her spine.

He wasn't a fantasy, now. He was a man, particular, unknowable and yet known. The feeling he called up in her was more powerful than she'd dreamed, more primal. Something in her claimed him, woman to man. She raised her head and answered his gaze with hers, bent her head, and waited for him to kiss her.

But then footsteps thudded at the other end of the porch, and someone called Jed's name. Annie pulled away. The eddy of air around her body, so much cooler than his warmth, made her feel lonely and bereft. And foolish, too.

"God, Annie. This is our day for interruptions," he said, his voice reluctant. "I probably need to say good-bye to someone."

"I know. It's all right. I . . . shouldn't have done this, Jed. I — can't. And I'll need to go myself, soon."

"I think John and Susie are leaving, too. Susie's tired these days. Let them drive you home, okay?"

Annie opened her mouth to refuse, then changed her mind. She was tired of fighting his help. She could be wary and solitary again tomorrow. "Yes. All right," she said. "Thanks, Jed."

"No, keep the jacket, I'll get it back later. Thank you for staying, Annie."

His voice was charged with some emotion she couldn't read.

"You're welcome, Jed. You were right. It . . . helped," she said. There was silence between them for a moment, then some impulse made her stand on tiptoe for a moment and brush his mouth with the lightest of kisses.

Her lips barely touched him, but the kiss stayed in her mind as she said good-bye to John and Susie, locked up her house, got ready for bed. His skin had felt warm, and despite the lightness of her touch, the brush of her mouth had discovered the contrast between the smoothness of his cheekbone, the rougher skin below, the warmth of his lips. He had held her eyes again after she'd kissed him, and one corner of that shapely mouth had quirked upward with pleasure. She could tell he desired her, and she could tell he would do nothing about it unless she asked.

She trusted him, she thought in the silence of her bedroom. It occurred to her that she'd never consciously trusted Tom; she simply hadn't believed that any man she loved could want to hurt her. She believed it now, and yet her instincts told her that Jed Harper would never deliberately do her harm.

Not that he couldn't hurt her. He could. In some way, he already had.

He was making her feel at home in a place that wasn't her home.

He was making her feel hopeful and clean again, as though she didn't carry a trail of wreckage and bad choices and unresolved problems in her wake.

He was making her want things she couldn't have. A husband, kids, a normal life.

He was making her want *him*. Want him with something that was an ache, a physical need, and yet more than a physical need.

And how could she afford to want anyone?

Standing in the warm light of the little bedside lamp, Annie ran a finger gently over her lips. The scent and touch of Jed Harper stayed with her as she turned off her light, slid into her bed. She lay, sleepless, in the cool, moonlit dark.

May Williams let herself quietly into the Mahoney apartment and paused in the foyer to change her shoes. The yellow cotton uniform she always wore to clean in rustled with starch as she bent, a little creakily, to tie her soft-soled white shoes. The first thing she noticed as she straightened was the silence of the house. Miz Mahoney always tried to be home on May's day, Monday, so she and May could review any entertaining Mr. Mahoney had planned for the week. She must be in that study of hers. Lord, the woman loved that little room.

The second thing May noticed was the empty space on the hallway table, where the Chinese porcelain lamp had stood. May's broad forehead creased in puzzlement. Miz Mahoney had loved that lamp, too. Her fingers had caressed it as she'd lifted it out of its bag, and she'd told May about finding it — for pennies, in a thrift shop — with the enthusiasm of a child. May rarely saw Annabel Mahoney's face light up like that. It was hard to imagine her removing that lamp, especially when nothing had been put in its place.

But that wasn't May's business. Maybe they'd bought something new, something that hadn't been delivered yet. She hung her sweater neatly in the hall closet and placed her handbag carefully on the closet floor, below the neat shapes of the Mahoneys' coats. Mr. Mahoney had come home early one rainy day and been furious when he found May's bag and umbrella propped in one corner of the hall. May didn't like Thomas Mahoney or his blustery, domineering, self-satisfied type. But she needed the job, and she did like Thomas Mahoney's wife, whom she suspected didn't need any extra worries. Since that day, the two women had kept all evidence of May's presence strictly out of sight.

May walked quietly to the kitchen, frowning again. The coffeemaker was empty, the lights shut off even though the day was drearily dark and gray. Miz Mahoney always made sure there was hot coffee in the pot for May's arrival, and a snack or pastry as well. Perhaps she had forgotten it was Monday. May ground the fresh beans and set the pot going, then padded down the hallway to let her employer know she was here.

But there was no Miz Mahoney in the little room. No signs of her, or even her work. No quilt rested on the wooden rack, no pictures fluttered from the yellow walls, not a single book stood on the once-crowded shelves. Nothing was left but the battered furniture and a not-very-clean hooked rug. Even the little wooden window box was empty of anything but soil.

Frowning, May bent to look more closely at the debris on the rug. Scraps of paper, she thought, puzzled, and shreds of fabric. Snippets of thread. Not neatly cut, like the ones May vacuumed up sometimes. No, these were roughly, randomly, violently torn.

May's children always teased her about being an unimaginative woman. That was fine with her. Life had brought her enough trouble, and she wasn't one to go inventing more.

But there was trouble here. Suddenly she was

sure of it. Bad trouble.

What kind of trouble it was, exactly, and what to do about it, that was a horse of a different color. It might not be what it looked like. Maybe Miz Mahoney had left on her own. May wouldn't blame her.

But maybe something else had happened. Something that wasn't Miz Mahoney's choice.

May was a sensible woman, and not one to interfere without reason. She was just the maid here, and if one thing was certain, it was that Mr. Thomas Mahoney wouldn't welcome questions from his cleaning lady. And beyond Mr. Mahoney, well, she could just picture a policeman's face when an old colored woman came in with some tale of suspected mayhem on Park Avenue.

But she wasn't going to abandon Miz Mahoney, either. She was a good lady, kind and honest and hardworking. You couldn't say that about many of May's clients. If May could give her even a little bit of help, well, the woman deserved it. Sometimes you had to stand up for what was right, even if people didn't like it. She would have to think on it for a bit, figure out what was best, talk it over with Joe tonight.

Thoughtfully, as though they held some kind of answer, May curled her hand around the bright scraps she was holding, then put them carefully into the pocket of her yellow uniform. She closed the door behind her and went off to clean the house.

"Have some more wine, gorgeous," Tom Mahoney said to the redhead across from him on the banquette at La Maison. She giggled a little, then shook her head, her glossy auburn hair bouncing on her shoulders, her eyes hesitant under the makeup that was just a little too heavy.

"I shouldn't," she said. "It's only Tuesday, you know. A work night."

"Maybe. But it's not just any work night." Tom held her eyes as he gestured for the waiter to pour. "We're celebrating, aren't we?"

"Celebrating what?" she asked, her long fingernails grasping the wineglass awkwardly.

Christ, she was young, Tom thought. Young, and creamy, and nubile, with endless legs and big bouncy tits that would overflow his hands when he cupped them. The thought sent a jolt of excitement to his groin. But there was time for all that.

Timing, boy, he admonished himself. *Timing is all.*

He flashed her a reassuring smile. "We're celebrating anything you want, honey," he said, still holding her eyes, keeping his voice silky. "Anything you want."

It was more than a week since Tom had seen his wife, and he was discovering, to his surprise, that he really didn't give a good goddamn that she was gone. After the anger had passed, he'd started to wonder why the hell he even wanted her back. Oh, she'd come crawling at some

131

point, sorry little bitch that she was. He was still sure of that. And he'd have the pleasure of making her pay. But why go out of his way to end his newfound freedom? Why even bother to look for a broad he was happier without?

It made him laugh, how easy it all was. Obviously, no one else cared about Annabel, either; her absence had rated little more than a passing question or two. He had told colleagues at work, guests at the gala, and the building staff that she was off ministering to a terminally ill cousin. He had told Matilda the truth, that her daughter had run away. Well, he'd implied that Annabel had left a note saying she needed some time alone, but so what? The details of his marriage weren't her business, anyway, and besides, underneath the superficial cluckings of concern he could see the calculation in her eyes. Matilda Taylor wouldn't truly worry unless Tom stopped paying for her apartment, her hairdresser, and her Saks Fifth Avenue charge. It was one of the few things that Tom and Annabel had agreed upon, that her mother was a self-absorbed cunt. Not that Annabel would ever use that particular phrase, of course. Not his proper, fussy little Annabel.

To hell with them all, Tom decided as he clicked the base of his wineglass neatly against the girl's. It was a goddamn thrill to be single again, even temporarily. It had been too long since he'd enjoyed the pleasure of the hunt, savored the kick of seduction, had the freedom to think about having sex when and where and how he wanted it. Over the years of his marriage, he'd forgotten just how many ripe, willing women there were in Manhattan.

Like Jenni here, he thought, only half listening to her chatter. He'd barely had to ask her out; she was all over him five minutes after they'd met at some corporate reception. Chicks like Jenni weren't just available, they were desperate — ecstatic just to be lifted, for an hour or two, out of the jobs that would never become "careers," the desperately cluttered West Side apartments shared with three or four other girls just like themselves, the dutiful monthly visits to parents in Patchogue or Tom's River. They almost shone with the thrill of going to a classy restaurant like this one, having a sophisticated older man like Tom order them steak *au poivre* and listen to their stories. Most of the so-called men they dated still had pimples.

Yes, he'd forgotten it, the rush he got from seeing some nubile young girl flush with excitement when he turned his attention to her. Or maybe not forgotten it — he'd done his share of flirting over the years, and even had a casual lay or two, if truth be told. But at least set the knowledge aside. He'd been focusing on the respectability and steadiness Finch McNaughten demanded of its top-level executives instead. And where had it gotten him? His so-called perfect wife gone God knew where. His perfect boss on his back twenty-four hours a day. His worthless clients giving their business to their asshole buddies. His annual bonus spent before it was paid. Not that he was going to throw it all away. But for now, Thomas Mahoney deserved a goddamn vacation.

He brought his attention back to the table as the waiter flourished a dessert menu. He'd definitely have some dessert, all right, he thought sardonically. Crème brûlée, and then cute little Jenni. Jenni was twenty-four, maybe, or twenty-five. A baby, still unformed, pathetically eager to move up in the world, pathetically grateful for instruction.

"What about a sorbet? Or do you like chocolate mousse?" he said, letting every bit of his confidence and power wash over her.

"I don't think I've ever had it," she confessed, and Tom smiled. She was so eager to please, he thought again. He was eager, too. Eager to lick chocolate mousse from those generous boobs. He smiled at her and ordered the dessert.

The long, rich dinner over, Tom reclaimed their coats, overtipping the coat-check girl, just for show. Then he led Jenni out onto Madison Avenue. "We'll walk a few blocks," he said, taking her elbow. "Work off a little of that mousse."

That was another thing about these young ones; they'd not only agree with whatever you suggested, they'd be grateful. Sure enough, Jenni didn't resist. As they walked up the darkened street, between the sporadic lighting of the streetlamps and store windows, she wobbled a bit on her high heels, lurched just a little against his side. Her cloth coat flapped open, teasing him with glimpses of the big breasts, the swaying young hips under the imitation designer dress.

He let his hand touch her shoulder for a moment, then moved it to her hip. She giggled a little but let it stay there, let his fingers remain curved over her ass. *Bingo,* he thought, and squeezed the soft flesh there. She made a little sound in her throat. It was half whimper of pleasure, half protest. But he knew — they both knew — that the protest was rote.

At nearly ten o'clock, Madison Avenue was quiet but far from deserted. Couples got in and out of cabs in front of restaurants and clubs. Behind their metal security grilles the shop windows were brilliantly lit. Prada, Givenchy, Pratesi, Manolo Blahnik. Dresses, linens, shoes — a world of expensive luxuries, each more enticing than the last. LaCroix, Armani, Calvin Klein.

The stupid little shop where Annabel sold those quilts of hers was somewhere around here, he thought. Pleasures, it was called, or some such horse shit. Tom wondered for a moment if he should look for it. Maybe they knew where his fucking wife was. On the other hand, he could always call them tomorrow, on Finch McNaughten's time. He dismissed the idea from his mind and scanned the row of shops. Not far from where they were walking, he glimpsed a break in the glass-fronted line, an indentation with a darkened door and small, half-hidden vestibule. Swiveling, he pulled Jenni inside it, pressed her up against the door, and lowered his mouth to hers.

After a moment's pause — as though the stupid little fool was pretending she had to think about it — she opened her mouth to his kiss. He held the back of her head and kissed her roughly, his tongue laving her lips and teeth, his breath shortening. She tasted good, so fucking good, like chocolate and toothpaste and lipstick and young girl. And she was getting into it, pushing her face against his, tasting him with her tongue in return. She arched her back, pushing that fantastic chest against him. His hand dropped, cupping the curve of one breast under the layers of blouse, jacket, trench coat. He could feel her big, stiff nipple right through all that cloth. God, she turned him on.

Thank Christ the fashion was for shorter skirts again. The half-remembered midi skirts from his adolescence had been a real drag. He pulled his hand from her chest and slid it along her thigh, feeling the hot skin and tight young muscle underneath the slippery casing of her panty hose. She parted her legs ever so slightly to his touch, moaned lightly into her mouth, bucked her hips forward a little, giving him a little promise of things to come.

"Your roommates home?" His voice, half muffled against her mouth, was rough, urgent.

"Mmm," she said.

Goddamn it. That was the one problem with

these girls, he thought. Not one of them could afford to live alone. He was tempted, for one wild moment, to bring her home. He wanted to have her, have her now, wanted it so bad he was ready to explode. But it wasn't wise. Sly Ike in the garage and Dan, their dumb-ass doorman, were thick as thieves. They'd notice in a minute if he brought a bimbo home while Annabel was gone, and it'd be all over the building by morning. Fucking Annabel. She wasn't even around, and she was still holding him back.

Tom pulled his mouth reluctantly from Jenni's but kept his hand on her leg, stroking the inside of one thigh possessively. "Check the schedule," he said, half growling. Breathless. "Find a night no one's gonna be home but us. And that night . . . don't wear goddamned panty hose."

She raised a brow, but she didn't argue. "Yes, master," she said, giggling.

"That's right. Master. And don't forget it," Tom Mahoney said and kissed Jennifer Stern again.

Five

Suddenly, he couldn't write worth a damn.

Jed swore to himself softly and saved his current file onto the computer hard drive. Sighing, he leaned back in his old swivel chair. Rooster was at his usual post, asleep at the side of Jed's desk. The dog's ears twitched at the creak of the chair, but he didn't wake. He was used to the many noises his master made at work, the shiftings and pacings and dulcimer strummings, even the not-so-occasional curse when a tough sentence wouldn't come right.

Today was worth a whole string of curses. The Hong Kong book just wouldn't jell. He'd worked doggedly through sheaves of notes, accumulated new pages, typed stubbornly away, kept up the iron discipline he'd honed over the years. Eventually, he knew, the mass of facts and impressions he'd gathered would find their proper form.

Be nice if it would happen sometime this century, he thought. Especially since he had a deadline to meet.

He pushed the chair away from the desk, rose to stand at the window. At nine in the morning the mist still hung like smoke on the mountain, a muffling gray white presence. The sun was visible only as a faint, diffused glimmer of light amid the blanket of fog. He could barely make out the edge of the trees behind his yard. The Wellman farm, the road that wound around the hill's slope, the scattering of vacation chalets, Annie's house — the whole world of the mountain might not have existed at all.

He stood unseeing at the window as he pulled his mind back to the task at hand. A few months was usually plenty of time to pull a book together from the thorough notes and drafts, both taped and typed, that he kept while he was on the road. The Hong Kong material alone filled ten folders and thirty microcassettes, each a dense testament to some facet of life in one of the world's most complex places as it adjusted to Chinese rule and dealt with a new millennium. It was all there, but the image that would connect all the disparate impressions into a vivid, coherent book just wouldn't come. Without that central thread, he couldn't tell whether the pages he was forcing himself to draft now were usable work or just useless crap.

He wanted to think the problem was exhaustion, the lingering aftereffects of hot, disorienting travel. Only tiredness had never bothered him before, and he'd been in tougher places than Hong Kong.

Or maybe some kind of flu bug coming on. Only he felt totally healthy. A little sexually frustrated, maybe, he thought wryly, remembering his abortive encounter at Lulu's. But basically fine.

Or maybe . . . His mind cast about for excuses. Maybe it was some kind of astrological disruption.

Something in the water.

A witches' curse.

Demonic possession.

He laughed at himself, then blinked in surprise as sunlight bathed his face. While he'd been lost in mental gymnastics, the breeze had pushed the mist down the mountain. Suddenly the windowsill he was leaning against, the yard, the hill, the whole world gleamed with light. He could see Annie's front porch with its weathered, once-white columns and the pair of old terra-cotta pots she'd filled with chrysanthemums. What time, he wondered, did she get up? Maybe he could drop by later. He hadn't seen her in the almost ten days since the party. He'd sure thought of her, though. Wondered if she'd been avoiding him after that impulsive, intimate kiss.

He shook his head. *Demonic possession,* he thought. *Sure. Angelic possession, more like.*

He was possessed, all right.

By Annie Taylor.

He wasn't writing well because, for the first time in his whole adult life, he suddenly didn't want to write. Much less want to be a famous travel writer who was writing about Hong Kong today and would be writing about Newfoundland tomorrow.

He wanted to be an ordinary man with an ordinary job who came home to Annie Taylor. A man who talked to Annie, made love with Annie, cooked and laughed and relaxed with Annie. He wanted to explore Annie's soul, not some new land. He wanted to plumb her mysteries, not listen to the tales of a hundred strangers.

He shook his head, suddenly angry at himself. Annie Taylor did have mysteries, and he suspected they'd take her far away from the mountain before long. And Jed himself. . . . Even in the unlikely event that she had any interest in him, how long would he last in the kind of domestic bliss he was mooning about? How long before this wild infatuation — he was too honest to pretend that what gripped him was anything else — died down into the same resentful, never-ending battle of wills he'd grown to know all too well as a child? How long before Annie Taylor, or any woman for that matter, got frustrated with his travel or the bouts of twenty-hour days he sometimes put in when a book really got going or his resistance to the whole idea of children? How long before his own restlessness would start: the boredom, the need to see new people and places, the need just to be alone? And how long would a woman tolerate that? A few months? A year? Two?

He didn't know. All he knew for sure was that happily ever after was a pipe dream. He could barely think of a marriage he respected. Ted and Alma Honeycutt's, maybe. Meg's, way back when. John and Susie had a chance, although it was early days yet. It didn't even matter, really. The fact was that his whole identity — the career he'd built up so painstakingly, the orderly and comfortable life he loved — depended on the freedom to move. Dana had suggested once that he write a book about his home, about the mountains and the lives they shaped. But Jed didn't want to stir up such bittersweet and very private memories. He wanted to write about Morocco, about Finland, about Hong Kong, about Newfoundland. And he couldn't do that when he was mooning around in some self-indulgent white-picket-fence fantasy.

The sun disappeared again. Suddenly his office seemed cold, cheerless despite the built-in bookcases overflowing with books, the warm kilim rug, the golden wood — a tight, confining cage, not the haven it had always been. Impulsively, he stabbed a number onto the keypad of his portable phone. "Is Dana in yet, please? Yeah, Matt, it's Jed Harper. Fine, thanks. I'll hold."

He dropped into his chair, propped one bare foot on the edge of the desk. "Dana? Yeah. Fine, how about you?"

"Can't complain," Dana Wilensky said cheerfully from the other end of the line. Jed could picture her, plump and attractively lined, her frosted hair pulled back in a neat French braid, sitting in her untidy New York office among stacks of manuscripts and a litter of pink phone message slips. "I just got the cover art for the

Scotland book. I'm express mailing it tonight, so don't get antsy. No glitz, no gold, no author photo — just your style. It looks great."

"I'd forgotten all about it, actually," Jed said truthfully.

At Dana's snort, he laughed and went on. "I was calling about something else. I'm thinking of finishing up the Hong Kong book on the road if I need to, moving on to Newfoundland earlier than I'd planned. I wanted to let you know."

"That's fine." He could hear the surprise in Dana's throaty New York voice. "I'm a little startled, though. You've only been home a couple of weeks. It's not like you to start planning so soon."

"I'm restless." Jed didn't elaborate, and he knew Dana wouldn't pry. They'd had a terrific working relationship for twenty years and a warm friendship for ten, partly because she knew when to probe and when not to.

He told her most things, in the end. He just didn't like to be rushed.

"I'll get talking with the travel people, start making the arrangements," he added. "I'll let you know how it develops. But plan on seeing me in New York right after New Year's, say. I'll go on to Canada after that."

"You'll do some signings while you're in the city? Readings?"

He sighed. The inevitable grind of publicity events wasn't his favorite part of being a writer, to say the least. "Of course, slave mistress. If I have to."

"You have to. That's great, Jed. And Livy will be thrilled to see her uncle Jed. Especially around Christmas." Dana's ten-year-old daughter was Jed's godchild, and he spoiled her shamelessly.

"Give her a hug for me. Tell her I'll bring presents."

"I'll do that. You'd better bring long johns, too. Canada's going to be a bitch in January."

"No point writing about a cold place in the heat of summer, darlin'. And cold's no problem. I could use some cooling down right now," he concluded dryly.

"Mmm?" When Jed didn't explain, Dana went on. "Sven said he wanted to come down and see you. Wanted to meet some woman you've got down there."

"Jesus, Dana. If I had some woman, as you put it, would I be rushing off to Canada?"

Her grin was almost audible. "Yes," she said promptly.

Jed winced as he laughed. "Touché. You know, the worst thing about your friends is how well they know you. But there is no woman, not really. And if Rasmussen comes down here, I'll never get the Hong Kong book done." Not that he was getting it done now. But Sven's amiable, obnoxious, totally distracting presence would really put the final nail in the coffin.

"It would be good for him." Dana's tone turned coaxing, almost flutelike. "It's that damned divorce that's the problem," she continued. "He's in trouble, kiddo. I'm not asking

144

you to be his baby-sitter. Just let him come down, get his mind off it, and talk with you. You'll be able to get through to him."

Jed frowned. He hated getting involved in other people's messes, and a wild, macho mountaineer mourning for his money-grubbing, dumb-as-dirt ex-wife was pretty damn messy, indeed. The very thought of making Sven's problems his own made him queasy, and he was pretty certain Sven would fiercely resent the so-called help. But, Jed thought, sighing, he'd never forgive himself if something happened to the man while he sat back doing nothing.

"Oh, hell. You win, as always. I'll give him another call, let him come if he wants. Which, I warn you, he probably doesn't."

"We can both keep on telling him not to. That'll get him there in a flash."

Jed laughed. "You're right, probably; he's a contrary son of a bitch. Just like me, I guess. Well, when I send you a few hundred pages of incomprehensible bourbon-splashed gobbledygook and call it my final draft, remember that it's your own fault."

"I'm not worried." She had every reason to trust him; he was always meticulous about his work. "And thanks, Jed. I'll talk to the publicity people, have them get in touch to schedule the New York events."

"Good. Give Livy that kiss, okay?"

He leaned back in his deep, leather chair, his spirits suddenly lightened. It was October 7.

145

Less than three months, he calculated, looking at his calendar, and he'd be gone again.

He had always loved travel. Bad weather, weird food, seedy hotels, exhausting plane or train or boat connections, even loneliness never fazed him. He never felt more alive than at the start of each new trip, with the puzzle pieces of a whole new world waiting to be assembled in his mind.

And this time around, getting on the road would be even more welcome than usual, because it would solve the problem of Annie Taylor. How much trouble could a man get into in less than three months?

He reached for his Rolodex, dialed the number of his travel agent, and began to make his plans.

Jesus, did he have indigestion.

Not that heartburn was anything unusual. When you were a cop in a city where smack-addicted mothers stuffing their babies into trash cans was an everyday thing, a sour stomach was only to be expected. But it usually didn't start until after lunch. He was probably just tired. If there was any justice in the world, which he would swear on oath there wasn't, it would have been him off for a week using up his accumulated sick leave, not Rozetti. Detective Pietri Rybczinski popped another antacid and tried to concentrate on his woefully piled-up desk.

"Pete." His partner dropped a grease-spotted white bag on one of the stacks of papers in front of him. "Want a donut?"

"Christ, Rozetti. Spare me." If anything was guaranteed to blow a hole in his aching gut, it would be one of Rozetti's beloved Italian pastries. Where the guy even found the damn things was a mystery. They worked on Manhattan's Upper East Side, for God's sake, not in Little Italy. It was easier to find caviar up here than cannoli. Pete stifled a belch and shoved the bag away. "Welcome back. We missed ya. *I* missed ya, 'cause there was nobody to help me with this crap."

"Anything new?"

Rozetti didn't sound any too interested, and Pete couldn't blame him. The guy had been a good cop in his day, but with thirty years under his belt and retirement ten seconds away, he couldn't really be expected to give a shit anymore.

"The usual," Pete said, surreptitiously massaging his aching belly. "Missing kid, turned up next day. Missing husband, probably off in Monte Carlo with his secretary. Visit with the Zimmermans to tell them their kid probably just ran away. They're not buying it. Little Ashley was perfect, life was perfect, she never woulda gone without telling Daddy, she musta been abducted by white slavers."

Rozetti snorted, spewing powdered sugar on the file. "At least they didn't say aliens. Did you break the news that little Ashley is a pothead gettin' it on with every boy in her class and sellin' Mommy's jewelry to buy weed?"

"Nah. Figured you could do it. You're retired any day now, you can spread some cheer before you go."

"Gee, thanks." Rozetti flicked through the sheaf of forms. "Problem with you is, you're too soft. You weren't, you wouldn't be popping Tums like breath mints. What's this?"

"Another express train to nowhere. Maysie, no, Mabel, no, May Williams, housekeeper, reporting her employer missing. Nice woman, actually. Dignified, obviously got a head on her shoulders, probably pretty sharp. Kind of lady you hate to let down. Got no evidence worth diddly-squat, though, just some missing stuff and woman's intuition. She says the husband's violent, maybe. Husband says Mabel Williams is about to get fired anyway, and his wife is alive and well and nursing a sick cousin in Kennebunkport. He's one of those Wall Street freaks. Sounds like a real asshole, for what it's worth, but that ain't evidence, either."

"Batterer, maybe. Get the domestic violence boys to follow up. They got a special mayoral budget, they can do some work."

"Yeah. And I'll give Mr. Asshole a call in a coupla days, see if I can actually verify that poor Mrs. Asshole's alive and well. Make a note on the report, huh? I gotta go to the can."

Rybczinski walked heavily toward the men's room. Maybe a nice quiet spell with the *Daily News* in front of him would quiet the burning. Or one of those liquid antacid things; they all tasted like ground-up chalk, but today he'd drink it gladly. This had to be the mother attack of all time. He looked at himself in the men's-room mirror and took a moment to run his hand over his thick black hair, grimacing at the pain that shot up into his chest as he moved. He was only thirty, for Christ's sake, and he had worse gastric problems than his ninety-year-old grandfather.

What a job, he thought as he closed the stall door painfully behind him and forgot all about May Williams. *What a job.*

As Annie settled into her new life, her fingers began to itch for fabric. The infinite variety of material, soft or crisp, smooth or nubbly, in a million beautiful hues. The sharp *thwick* of scissors snipping out a square, the almost inaudible rustle of thread pulling behind a needle. It had been years since she'd been without a quilt in progress. She felt hungry for the chance to celebrate this strange new life she'd begun to make for herself, to express it in color and shape, to create again. The need was fueled when she found a green Singer sewing machine, decades old but in working order, in the cottage basement.

And the desire to get back to her art had a more practical motive, as well. The problem of money loomed. By January, February at the latest, she'd have run through the small savings she'd brought with her. She needed to work. Work in some way

149

that wouldn't involve Social Security numbers and other traceable information.

She had taken the risk of calling Pleasures on her way to Burnsville, from a rest stop somewhere in New Jersey. Elizabeth Felter had agreed to hold the proceeds of her last quilt, when it sold, until Annie had a usable address. Elizabeth had been a bit puzzled, but willing, and she'd agreed to keep the address confidential once she got it. Annie would have to rent a mailbox at one of those packing centers in some large town, she had thought, Asheville maybe, someplace large and anonymous and far from her little home. It was a risk, but a reasonable one. If she could turn out a quilt or two and watch every penny, she could keep herself going, at least for a while.

She put on her jeans and sweater, tossed her trench coat over her shoulders. She turned the car toward town, parked at the side of the square.

"Thanks," she said politely to the woman behind the fabric store counter a scant twenty minutes later. "I'll be back."

But she wouldn't. She squinted in the sunlight of the sidewalk — so much brighter than the shop's interior, despite the towering thunderheads that drifted in the sky's vivid blue — then turned to walk aimlessly toward the square.

She had been unrealistic, she acknowledged. Unprepared. This wasn't New York, one of the world's great clearinghouses for textiles of all kinds. You couldn't simply take the subway down to the garment district or the Lower East

Side and find incredible fabrics — dupioni silk, iridescent taffeta, and dense ikat and Indonesian batik — at wholesale prices. The Burnsville fabric shop sold nothing but standard things, polyesters and cottons and calicoes — and even those weren't cheap. Six dollars, seven dollars a yard, plus the cost of thread and needles and scissors and batting. It was impossible, even if the material had fired her imagination, which it didn't. The neat prints and gentle colors stirred no vision in her mind.

A sense of flatness and defeat replaced the morning's energy. She turned at the square and stood still, unseeing, in front of the statue of Otway Burns that marked its central point.

Grow up, Annie, she told herself. She was healthy, whole. She wasn't living a terrifying, humiliating lie with Tom. She wasn't being hurt daily, wasn't living every moment in fear. If she wanted to work, she needed to figure out a way to do it, not collapse into a bundle of self-pity at the first setback.

"Annie!"

Annie snapped her attention back to the present at the voice, to see Susie Addamson standing in front of her, laughing.

"Oh, Susie, I'm sorry. I was a million miles away."

"Well, come back." Susie was carrying two laden shopping bags and wearing blue, a soft chambray smock with a touch of embroidery at the collar and cuffs. Her fair skin was rosy, though Annie noticed that there were circles under her eyes.

"You look lovely in that color," Annie said, smiling at her. "Just like a Renaissance Madonna."

"Really?" Susie wrinkled up her nose. "Wonder if they felt as grumpy and tired as I do. Thanks, though. Listen, Annie, I'm having lunch with Meg. She's actually going to take an hour or so off from the café, believe it or not. Why don't you join us? Meg would love it, and I would, too."

Seeing Annie's reluctance, she continued. "Do come, Annie, really. We'd love your company. And," smiling impishly, "you could help me carry these bags across the other half of the square."

Annie laughed. She probably shouldn't agree. But she'd liked Susie so much when they'd met at the party, and her experience at the fabric store had left her at loose ends.

"Now, there's an offer I can't refuse," she said, giving in. "Sold."

They strolled through the square, enjoying the cool wind and the vivid color. The green lawn was dotted with the bright shapes of fallen leaves, like a big emerald quilt stitched with fanciful appliqués. Plantings of yellow chrysanthemums and lavender ornamental kale filled in where the summer flowers had started to wither.

"Oh," Susie moaned, flexing her small shoulders as she walked. "You don't know how good it feels not to have to carry that bag. My back's been aching something fierce lately."

"You shouldn't have been carrying things in the first place," Annie chided gently.

"I know. But one of the older ladies in town offered me all these beautiful baby clothes, so how could I possibly refuse? I should have asked John to come get the bags, I guess, but it feels like the poor man never stops fetching and carrying for me."

"I'd bet he loves it," Annie said, keeping her long stride slow to match Susie's.

"So he says. He'll get plenty more time to prove his devotion before it's over."

"Tell me again — how much longer before you're due?"

"Two months. It doesn't feel like it's that far away, right now. But I'm hoping that's just my imagination. Every day counts, especially with what Ethan refers to as multiple births. I wish he'd just call them twins. Multiple births makes me feel like I'm having a litter."

Meg met them at the door to the café, welcoming Annie like they'd been friends for years. She took Susie's other bag, then shepherded the two women through the café and into a pretty sunroom set off by big French doors and placed at an angle from the main building. The space was a small oasis of silence after the chatter of the restaurant. Annie smiled in pleasure at the marigold-yellow tablecloth and deep cobalt glassware, the curly iron café chairs with their bright Provençal cushions.

153

"Voilà. The only private table at the Cupboard Café. Private, that is, unless Carlos burns down the kitchen or Lizibet has a fight with her boyfriend while she's serving him lunch. I'll get another place setting and tell the gang we've got another guest. Stop it right now, Annie," Meg said, smiling at her. "I'm beginning to know that I'm-a-burden look on your face. Let me warn you that if you apologize for the trouble you're causing or offer to leave, the two of us are going to kill you."

"Don't force us," Susie said, mock stern, as she dropped into a chair. "You don't want these poor infants born in prison, do you?"

"That would be bad," Annie agreed solemnly. "All right. I'll try to accept your kindness graciously. Something I've been told, recently, that I don't do very well."

"That wouldn't be Jed speaking, would it?" Susie cocked one blond brow.

Annie made a rueful face. It wasn't easy to keep secrets in this town, that was for sure. "How did you guess?"

"Oh, just female intuition. Which, in my case, is presumably strengthened by millions of gallons of hormones. It sounded like him, somehow. He's an opinionated one, Jed is. Luckily, he's never really here long enough to start offering advice."

"What in the world does the man do?" *If anything.* Annie was still curious, but right then, Meg came back with the extra glassware and cutlery, and the question got lost in the bustle of lunch.

154

The food, not surprisingly, was delicious: carrot soup dotted with chives, a huge Niçoise salad, and warm, crusty bread. And the company was wonderful, too. Annie kept silent at first, unsure of herself despite the warm welcome. But within what seemed like minutes, it felt impossible to hold back, Meg and Susie included her into the flow of conversation so naturally. Before long, she was giggling with Susie over one of Meg's wisecracks, teasing and exchanging ideas as though she'd known them for years.

Annie glanced at each of the other women in turn as their plates were carried away. Meg, in khaki trousers and a simple white shirt, her short unruly cap of red hair gleaming in the sunshine, her face lively and warm. Susie, blond and flushed and softly pretty, though the dark circles looked even more bruisy in the sunroom's bright light. Neither woman was elegant by New York standards, or sophisticated, or beautiful. Yet their warmth, their genuineness, their lack of pretension, made her feel more at home with them than with any of the socialites she'd known in her old life. She could relax here, be herself. *Ironic,* she thought, *for a woman in hiding.*

"Oh, no." Susie groaned, resting her hands on her belly, as one of the café's waitresses pivoted through the French door with a laden dessert tray. "Not your profiteroles, Meggie. I'm huge already. I'm going to look like a blimp long after the babies come."

"Hush. They're ice cream, and that's calcium,

and you need it. Thanks, Cindy. That woman is a brick," Meg added when the waitress had stepped back into the restaurant. "She's shy, but she's steady. You can't imagine how rare it is to find waitresses that reliable."

"I was thinking she looked tired, today," Susie said.

"I know. There's definitely something going on with her, but I'm almost afraid to ask. It seems like Donna has a cold every week. And Lizibet has boyfriend troubles just about as often. If Cindy falls apart on me, I'm dead."

"Don't believe a word of her complaints, Annie," Susie said. "The staff wouldn't be half so unreliable if Meg didn't encourage them. She's sort of like a cross between — let me think — Dear Abby and . . . Mother Teresa. Always helping the lame ducks, that's our Meggie. And the more eccentric the duck, the better. Truth is, there are plenty of more reliable staff out there, only Meg likes bandaging up her wounded birds too much."

"Hush, girl," Meg said.

"I can believe it," Annie said, laughing with them. "But right now, I can only concentrate on your culinary virtues, Meg. Lunch was delicious."

"Glad you liked it, Annie," Meg said. "And I'm glad you came, too. What's in your bags, Suse? If you'll allow me to change the subject, that is."

"Oh. You'll enjoy this. Baby clothes, from Dottie Barclay. I was telling Annie about them before. You know, Dot used to make almost all of her kids' clothes herself. For Ellen and Jimmy, both. Look."

They passed the tiny clothes around the table, marveling over the intricate smocking and stitchery. Each little garment was different, and intricate, and gorgeous. Each had been wrapped in tissue, stored in lavender; the faint, summery scent of the herb hung in the sunny air.

"What beautiful stitching. They're little works of art, aren't they? Almost no one does handwork like this today," Annie said dreamily, running a finger over the crisp texture of a tiny white piqué dress. The finest of red silk cording rimmed the neck and sleeves, and minuscule pearl buttons ran up the length of the back. "Those buttonholes, and the way that trim is set . . . There are a couple of stores that sell handmade children's clothing like this in Manhattan. They cost an arm and a leg, of course. But still, they're beautiful things. One of the shops was right around the corner from my apartment. I used to stop in when I had a spare minute sometimes, just to look."

Meg and Susie exchanged a glance, and Meg gave a small but decisive shake of her head. Annie was too absorbed in the little clothes to notice.

"It's a rare fabric store that even sells material like this, nowadays," she continued, taking a navy boiled wool jacket with anchor motifs from Meg's hands. "You'd probably have to go to an art weaver to find cloth like that. Or to Scotland or Ireland. Someplace where they still value the old traditions, the old methods."

"It's true," Meg said. "Even twenty years ago, things like this were unusual. Though I'm witness to the fact that Dot's kids were totally ungrateful for her work."

Annie barely heard the words. The thought of a quilt — just half a thought, maybe — was forming in her mind, but she was too replete and relaxed to pursue it, and she was having too much fun with the other women.

Later, she thought, tucking the idea away, as she helped repack the beautiful things.

"Lord," Susie said, looking at her watch. "Can you believe it's almost three o'clock? We've been sitting here yakking almost two hours."

"There's no rush," Meg said.

"I need to get home. John'll kill me if I don't make time for a nap." Susie rose, then pressed a hand to her belly. Suddenly she was swaying, her face gray. She whimpered a little. "Oh," she said faintly. "My back. Hurts . . ."

Instantly, Meg was at one side, Annie the other. Their eyes met as they lowered Susie back into her chair. "I'll call John," Meg said and was gone.

"I'm okay," Susie insisted once she was seated again. "Really. Sorry to make a fuss. It just surprised me, that's all." But her voice was still weak and wavering, and only a hint of the color had come back to her face.

"Sssh," Annie said. "Just relax a minute. It's all right."

It felt natural to sit close, reach one arm around Susie's shoulders, stroke her friend's arm soothingly. Susie accepted the soft touch just as naturally, leaning her head against Annie's shoulder.

"That's so nice." Susie's voice was still shaky. "I'm getting sleepy, even. Must just be all that food."

"Good," Annie said. "Relax."

It was only five minutes before John arrived. His face was sharp with worry. It eased only a little when he saw Susie sitting drowsily at Annie's side.

"We're going to the doctor's. Now. This is the second time it's happened, and that's enough," he said, helping Susie rise.

"No." Susie's eyes teared up, and her voice was fretful. "John, please. I can't stand the thought of sitting in a crowded waiting room right now, I just want to go home and curl up in my own bed. I'll rest. Annie practically sent me to sleep right here. You can call Ethan, and if he wants to see me, I promise I'll go. Just not right now."

"Susie —"

"*Please,* honey."

John gave in, though Annie could see he didn't like it. His face was grim as he supported Susie to the car.

"Do you think she's really all right?" Annie asked Meg as they waved to the departing Cherokee.

"You know, I'm not sure." To Annie, Meg's broad brow looked puckered, her eyes worried. She raked one hand through the curls that shone like fire in the wavery sunshine. "Ethan

Wellman — one of the family up at the farm near your house, actually, the only son who didn't become a farmer — is a fine doctor and a fine man. And John couldn't be more solicitous. She's in the best of hands. Still, pain like that is scary. I wish I knew more about carrying twins or even about ordinary pregnancies. My own was so easy it was almost embarrassing."

"You have . . ."

"A daughter. Tilly. She's twenty-one. I married my high school sweetheart, back when we were both obscenely young. Tilly's off in Raleigh-Durham now, working for a computer firm. I couldn't be prouder."

Annie smiled. "I can tell. But I'll bet you miss her, too."

"I do. Badly. I'd never admit that to Tilly. She needs to be on her own, trying her wings. But with her gone, and Abe, too — my husband died five years ago — the house seems awfully quiet sometimes. I hate to admit it, but Susie was right. I probably do coddle the staff too much, just to have someone to mother."

Over Meg's shoulder, Annie saw the waitress, Cindy, pop an inquiring head out the front door of the café. It was time to let Meg get back to work, she thought. And time to get home.

"Thank you for lunch, Meg," Annie said. "It was wonderful, really — the food, and the company. A real treat."

"I've said it before, Annie. Any time. You're welcome here."

160

"I know, Meg." Annie hesitated, wanting to honor Meg's kindness with candor. "I'm . . . I guess you could say I'm working a lot of things out right now. Feeling my way. I'm not sure where I'm going, what I'm doing. So if I seem reticent, sometimes, it's never personal."

"I understand that. I just want you to understand that no one's prying. Well," she added fairly, "there are biddies in this town who would search your dresser drawers if you turned your back for five minutes. But John and Susie and Jed and I — you're welcome with us, just as you are."

"Thanks," Annie said again.

Impulsively, she reached over, gave Meg a swift hug. Meg returned the embrace, then waved as Annie walked back across the square.

Jennifer Stern wrapped a towel around her hair, carried her cup of Lapsang souchong tea to the end table, and reached for the cashmere throw draped with elegant informality over the arm of her sofa. Soft lamplight shone on the room's carefully arranged furnishings, the few but tasteful accessories. Nothing was expensive — she'd chosen slowly and carefully from sales and closeouts — but all of it was tasteful. And neat. And totally quiet. Not because her roommates were gone, she thought, remembering Tom Mahoney's question during their first date. Because there were no roommates at all.

Never had 'em, she murmured to herself, smiling sardonically. *Never will.* Jennifer Stern was not about to clutter up her life, much less her home, with the constant crises and chatter of other women.

Even at college, where they'd at least been smart, girls her age had never appealed to her much. While her suite mates went to bars or clubs, Jennifer had sat home studying Russian. The former Soviet Union, she'd decided, was definitely going to be a great investment area in the future. While they spent hours dreaming over some gawky boy, she was working on her investment portfolio. It had barely merited the name *portfolio* back then. But now it was a healthy little nest egg. In fact, it had paid for the furniture and the security deposit on this apartment, this haven so mercifully free of interference from her parents or her friends. Not that she was going to let Thomas Mahoney know about that.

She smiled to herself again, a shrewd, ironic smile. Men like Tom were almost too easy. When they saw a pretty girl with a Long Island accent in a clerical job, they stopped observing. It never occurred to them that she might have a bachelor's degree with honors from Yale, an unusual aptitude for figures, and an ambition just as large and urgent as theirs. You didn't even have to lie, she thought, curling her legs more comfortably under her. They saw cute little Jenni, not the real Jennifer, their peer, their equal. They saw only what they wanted to see.

Which was not a mistake that Jennifer Stern

ever intended to make.

She saw Tom Mahoney for exactly what he was. Saw the burly, lower-class bones underneath the exquisite tailoring. Saw the chip on his shoulder and the anger that edged every action, every word. Saw through his story about his wife. Wherever the woman was, she wasn't ministering to some sick cousin. Tom's discomfort when he brought the subject up — the hints of rage and panic that underlay his words — was a mystery. It just wasn't one Jennifer intended to spend any energy solving, at least for now. Although at some point Tom's firm might be interested in the embarrassing marital problems of their star money manager. Thoughtfully, she cached the idea away.

But for now, the status quo was fine. Tom was an ass, but no worse than other men. She had checked him out with care, along with several other possibilities. He was reputed around the Street to have a real flair for choosing stocks, a true gift that almost (if not quite) justified his grandiose notions of his own talent. She could learn from him. Goodness knew he was only too ready to talk. Unknowingly, he'd already given her two great stock tips, and she'd gleaned more about the way an investment manager thought from his conversation that she had in her entire first year at Summerby, Smith and Delinsky.

The four-star restaurants he took her to weren't a hardship either, of course. And the sex would be a bonus, too. She'd staved him off for long enough, now, to make him really hungry and more than a little intrigued. Maybe she'd let him get lucky on their date tomorrow night.

She had no time for the insecure, secretly sentimental young men who usually asked her out. Underneath their hip acts, all they wanted was a wife to cook and clean, entertain their clients, have their kids. Tom was different: a mentor who could get her somewhere and a sexual outlet with no strings attached. The same edge of anger that roughened his conversation intrigued her. She liked her sex a little wild, a little — just a little — rough. A pang of desire spasmed at the thought of their semipublic kiss, the confidence with which he put his hand up her skirt. When the time came, Tom Mahoney was going to be good.

But it wasn't time yet. Not quite. Dismissing Tom as the temporary diversion he was, she reached to her coffee table and opened the leather folder that held her investment portfolio printouts. The volatile stock market — up one day, down the next — called for careful watching. That little health care company Tom had mentioned to her, now; she could use the next market dip to buy another hundred shares at bargain-basement prices. Five years from now, her instinct told her, it would have doubled, maybe tripled, in price. It might go down in the meantime, true, but she could afford to wait it out. And in investing, like in sex, she thought — her lips curling a little with mischief — sometimes you just had to take a calculated risk.

Six

Jed was struggling with his book again when the rain started, a sudden burst of sound against the windows and roof. He clicked off the computer and stood at the front door to call Rooster in from his eternal explorations of the yard, then started the long process of getting the dog's fur dry. Long, because Rooster regarded it not as a necessity but as play. When the worst of the damp was toweled off the shining coat, Jed ruffled the animal's ears one last time and started for the kitchen.

The wet towel, smelling richly of damp dog, needed to go in the wash, and Jed himself was thinking about lunch. It was almost three, but he'd been so preoccupied with the work, he hadn't eaten. That tendency, to get so absorbed neither food nor the clock even existed, worked better than any diet to keep him trim. He glanced through one of the big panes above the window seat as he went, then stopped still, shaking his head in bemusement. As if all of his complicated thoughts over the last few weeks had finally conjured her up, there at the fringe of the woods was Annie Taylor.

Annie Taylor drenched, and Annie Taylor indecisive. He watched as she stood under the trees' dripping cover for a minute. He couldn't see her face through the rain, but he could tell she was struggling with herself. Amused at the indecision visible in her stance even at fifty rain-drenched yards, he rubbed at the light stubble on his chin and waited.

She arrived on his porch even more drenched, if that was possible. And defiant.

"I went for a walk, and suddenly the heavens opened," she announced, pitching her voice over the drumming of the rain and stamping wetness off her feet onto the mat at his doorway. "I'll never be able to make it back up that slippery path in this downpour, so I'm stopping in for some of that neighborly help you were talking about. But if you don't wipe that self-satisfied smirk off your face," she threatened as he led her inside, "I'm leaving again right now. And it'll be your fault if I get double pneumonia and a broken leg on the way home."

It made him laugh aloud, all of it: her words, and the pleasure of her presence, and the ridiculous contradictions of his own mind. One minute he was arranging to flee thousands of miles to get out from under her spell, the next moment he was as pleased to see her as if she was the answer to his prayers. But he'd be gone in another couple of months, he reminded himself. How much could it matter?

"You shouldn't go strolling in the rain, lady,"

166

was all he said, waving her to the Stickley bench at the side of his front hall.

She perched unprotestingly on the leather cushion. Rooster nosed curiously at her thigh. Her hands were blue with cold, and so were her lips. As a wave of shivers hit her, she wrapped her arms around her waist.

"It wasn't raining when I started," she said logically, lifting her damp face to his. "How did it get so cold and so wet so fast?"

He grinned down at her. "Weather changes quick here. Want some help with those shoes?"

"I want a towel to rub my hair dry with and an umbrella so I can walk home."

"An umbrella isn't going to make the path to your house any safer. You admitted it was slippery yourself. And your hair will be soaked again in three minutes. Come on, Annie, be sensible. The worst of it will be over in fifteen or twenty minutes, and I can drive you up the hill then."

Lightning flashed through the door's fanlight, then thunder cracked like a whip outside the house. She stared at him, shaking her head. "You must have paid off some heavenly special effects man, just to make your point."

"I would have, if I could have. Need help taking off those shoes?"

"No." She bent to work at the sopping lace of her little hiking boots, which looked as elegant on her small feet as Cinderella's glass slipper.

"Damn." She straightened again, tossing her

damp, tangled hair back onto her shoulders. "The lace is soaked. Nothing's going to get it untied."

"Hold on a second." Jed made a quick trip to his desk to fetch the scissors there. Back in the hallway, he dropped to his knees, ignoring her protests, and took one of her boots in his hands. In a moment, one lace was cut, and then the other.

"Stop squirming. It's over," he said, rising easily to his feet. "I've even got a spare pair to replace them, if I can remember where. Bathroom's upstairs and to the right. Take a hot shower while I make you some coffee — you're blue right down to your fingernails. Rooster, leave the lady alone. And no arguments from you, woman," he ordered. "Toss your stuff down over the railing. I'll put it in the dryer for you."

"And what exactly am I supposed to wear instead?" she grumbled from halfway up the wide oak stairs.

"Bathrobe. On the hook on the back of the door. Don't worry, it'll cover you from head to foot. You couldn't be more modest in a nun's habit."

Despite waves of resistance he could almost feel, she did as instructed, emerging briefly from the bathroom to toss her clothes down to him, then disappearing again with a firm slam of the door. Jeans, socks, T-shirt and sweater, he noted with amusement as he tossed them into the small but state-of-the-art dryer hidden behind a wall of louvered doors in his kitchen. Just as well. The thought of her upstairs, naked in his shower, was intoxicating enough without handling her underthings. Hell, it had been arousing just to hold the damn woman's feet. Grinning, Jed ground the beans and put on a pot of coffee, made sure Rooster's dishes were filled, then went into the living room to kindle a fire in the big fieldstone hearth.

Upstairs in the bathroom, Annie made a quick grimace at her damp, disheveled reflection, then looked curiously around her. The walls were the soft green of a deep forest, the tile a gleaming white, the floor the same russet terra-cotta tile she remembered from his kitchen. On a brighter day, skylights in the ceiling would flood the room with sun. Through a second door, set near the shower enclosure, she could see a bedroom with the same skylights, the same green walls, a huge oak bed. Everything shone with cleanliness, but a few odds and ends scattered casually around gave evidence of their owner: a razor and shaving brush on a glass shelf below the mirror, a pair of worn leather slippers kicked under the pedestal sink, the promised robe — big and comfortably worn — looped casually over the gleaming brass hook at the back of the door.

On the wall opposite the sink, the room's single decoration, a boldly carved and colored mask, scowled at her. Intrigued, she ran her finger along its artful curves. It was a strange image, at once scary and comical: a male face, half man and half beast, complete with staring eyes and curving horns and bared, fanged teeth. Mexican, Annie wondered, or Asian? Old, certainly, and probably expensive.

Her cold, stiff, soaking jeans had clung to her legs. The dry blue robe was heaven in comparison. She reached an arm behind brass-edged glass doors to turn on the shower, belted the robe's thick folds tightly around her waist, then padded out the doorway to toss her jeans, socks, and sweater onto the landing below. Her bra and underpants were wet, too — the drenching rain had soaked her right through — but she was damned if she was going to have Jed Harper looking at her underwear.

Back in the bathroom, she dropped the robe and stepped gratefully into the full, hot spray. Alma Honeycutt's house wasn't a luxurious place, at least as far as personal comforts went. It wasn't as though she longed for the old days of thick towels and scented soaps. But it was definitely a pleasure to experience them again.

She turned off the shower with regret, rubbed her skin into glowing heat, blotted her hair with a towel, knotted the blue robe securely around her. As she attacked her tangled hair with the tortoiseshell comb she'd found on the vanity, she tried to focus herself for the encounter to come.

Standing, half blind and shivering in the rain, she'd thought she could drop in casually, just to get three minutes' worth of Jed Harper's practical assistance. Instead, here she was, about to have coffee with the man. In his house, his stronghold.

Barely half dressed.

He had a way of slipping around and beyond her cautious boundary lines as if they didn't exist. And the biggest problem of all was that when he was around, they *didn't* exist. Her belief that she could live a solitary, unconnected life, already shaken by Meg and Susie's uncomplicated friendship, evaporated entirely in the face of his laughter, his interest, his warmth. Her distrust — of men and of herself — melted.

Yet she had known him only a few weeks. And she was another man's wife, she added silently, looking down at the hand that had borne her wedding ring. Her skin was so pale that no mark of it showed, but the inner scars were still there and would last for years. Despite the serenity Burnsville had brought her, the thought of confronting Tom still pierced her with fear, and so did the knowledge that the confrontation, when it came, might not be in a time or a place or a manner of her choosing.

Besides, she told herself as she worked at an especially stubborn tangle, who could say if her instinctive trust of Jed Harper was justified? She knew nothing about him, not even what — if anything — he did. Who could guarantee that he was not just another wealthy charmer, used to having his own way and practiced enough to get it? Not with Annie Taylor, who had married Thomas Mahoney until death did them part with no worse misgivings than whether she was really good enough for her husband.

Her hair was as well-combed as she could get it. Wet and hanging down onto the bathrobe's thick plush, contrasting against the cheeks that were so pink from the shower she looked like she was wearing blusher. She reached for the big towel again, turbaned it defiantly around her head. Now *that,* she thought wryly, was a much less inviting look. Annie switched out the bathroom light, gave the belt of the robe one more unnecessary tightening, and went resolutely downstairs.

It was true, as he'd said, that the blue robe swathed her from head to toe. She should have looked funny, draped in yards of blue terry, with her head turbaned in a white towel. But Jed's gut twisted a little at the sight of her, and the feeling definitely wasn't humor. Her normally pale face was flushed pink from the heat, and without the hair to hide it, he could see the precise bone structure of her temples, her ears, the beautiful angle of her jaw, the length of her neck.

Jesus, she was beautiful, he thought for the hundredth time. And desirable. Like an Egyptian goddess, regal and delicate and intensely feminine against the masculine browns and simple textures of his living room. He wanted to pull her down onto one of the deep leather sofas near the fireplace, kiss her, have her. Though the proud tilt of her chin and the stubborn look in her eyes told him, as usual, how far that was from her agenda.

"Sit down," he said neutrally, waving at the pair of couches. "I'll get the coffee."

When he returned, she was perched straight-backed on the corner of one sofa, her spine barely touching the kilim-covered pillow that was set invitingly between the deep back and arm. He set the tray of coffee things down and chose a seat on the other couch, trying to put her at her ease.

"I like that mask — what is it, Burmese? Japanese? — on the wall in your bathroom," she said, a little stiffly, as they sugared their mugs of coffee.

"Thanks. It's from Thailand, actually. I put it there to make sure there was someone even uglier and meaner than I am in the mirror every morning."

"You're not mean," she said, leaning back a little at last. "Irritating, but not mean."

"That's not why, then?" Dangerous waters, but his arousal interfered with caution, and he'd said it before he could help himself.

"Why what?"

"Why you shrink away from me like I might be Jack the Ripper."

"Jed." Annie put her mug down on the Mission oak coffee table, and the sound had a sharp ring of finality to it. "I appreciate your hospitality. But I don't want to talk about this."

"I know that." Suddenly Jed felt angry. "I'm not trying to force you, Annie. No — it's the truth, I'm not. But this big mystery you're creating . . . Can't you see how it just makes whatever the problem is worse? There's no way to handle it. No way to ignore it, no way to dodge around it, no way to act natural. We couldn't stand like ordinary folks in a kitchen together, last week. We can't sit here and talk. Everything's so . . . artificial."

He stopped and shrugged. "I just don't see the point of not getting at least some of these cards on the table, Annie."

"Fine," Annie said defiantly. "Go ahead. Show your own cards, as you put it, if you're so eager."

"Fine," he repeated. It wasn't his damned hand that was the problem. But if she wanted him to get the game started, he would.

"I want to be neighborly with you," he said, choosing his words with care. "You know that. And I like you. I want to be friends."

Knowing he'd be gone so soon gave him freedom to speak his mind, foolish as that possibly was. "But I also want to touch you, Annie," he continued. "I know you don't want to hear that, but it needs to be on the table along with everything else. And it's obvious, anyway, I'd think. You're a beautiful, sensual woman, and I'm a normal man, and I'm very attracted to

174

you. I want to hold you. Kiss you. Make love to you."

The towel she'd turbaned on her head was slipping. She pulled it off, shook out her tangle of hair. It shone blue-black in the ruddy firelight, shadowing her skin. What would it feel like, he wondered, to run his fingers through that hair?

"That's honest. And I appreciate it. But . . . it's obvious that you're a very healthy male animal, Jed." Annie's voice was even and her chin still high, though her cheekbones were suddenly flushed with color once more. "You've wanted women before," she continued. "And will again. So let's not make a big deal out of this."

She had such dignity, he thought, momentarily moved by it. That was as much a part of her appeal as her beauty.

"I have wanted women." His eyes fixed on hers, challenged them. "And when they haven't wanted me right back, I've gone on to the next one. I never had any problem shifting gears."

"And now?"

"Now . . ." He shook his head, feeling the corner of his mouth quirk up. "I'm stuck in first. I don't want anyone else right now. I want you, and I'm damned if I even know why."

"Thanks for the compliment," she said dryly. But she smiled for the first time since she'd walked downstairs, and he smiled back at her, grateful for the moment of ease.

"I didn't mean it like that. I guess I just tend

to take these things more casually, most times. I'm not sure why it's different now."

"Maybe it's just the rare fascination of being refused."

"Don't you believe it. There's been a fair share of women who didn't go for my here-today, gone-tomorrow style."

"That's your style?"

"I never stay in one place for very long, and I probably never will," he said flatly. Reluctantly. It wasn't what he wanted to say. He wanted to promise he'd be there for her. A spectacularly foolish impulse, and a blatant lie.

Annie just nodded. "And what about you?" he said.

She was silent for a moment, her head bent now, her expression thoughtful. The black hair, a sculptor's delight of wave and shimmer, tumbled onto her shoulders. Peeping out from the ample folds of the robe, her hands and feet were narrow, pale, delicate. Jed waited, listening to the logs in the fireplace hiss and crackle, to Rooster's gentle breathing from the hearth.

Finally she wrapped her arms around her waist and lifted her eyes. "My last relationship . . . my *only* true relationship . . . was a disaster." The gaze that met his was both proud and vulnerable. "I came here . . . ran here . . . to get away from it. I'm finished with it, for good. But . . . I'm not sure it's finished with me."

"He hurt you," Jed said, remembering again the scene in his kitchen, her terror, her panic.

"Yes," she said simply. "A lot. In a lot of ways."

"That isn't your fault."

"I don't know, Jed." She held up a hand as he opened his mouth in protest. Her bones were so fine he could almost see the firelight through her skin. "You wanted honesty. That's honest. I don't know. No, I didn't deserve to be hurt, even though I used to think I did. But I have to take some responsibility, anyway. I have to accept the fact that I chose him, and I stayed with him, and until a very short time ago, I let him do what he wanted. I have to figure out what it was in me that made those choices. And then I have to figure out what to do about him and about the rest of my life. That's a big pile of stuff to handle, and I've got no answers at all, yet. The only thing I do know is that I'm not . . . ready."

Everything in him wanted to answer her, comfort her, make it right somehow. But he forced himself to keep silent, letting her have her say.

"I'm not ready." She lifted her gaze to his as she repeated the words. "Not ready to make a decision about the future. Not ready to run straight from one relationship into another. And certainly, even if it didn't seem that way at your party, not ready to be touched."

"I understand that. And I'll respect it. But, Annie . . . sometimes life just isn't very neat, and the timing of things isn't, either. Whether or not you're ready, we've met. I'm more than at-

177

tracted to you. And you're attracted to me, at least a little. Or am I wrong?"

"No." She shrugged. "I am attracted to you, Jed. Very attracted. But . . . I'm sorry, if I led you on at the party. I've had time to think it through since then, and it stops right there. We can be neighbors. And friends, in some nice uncomplicated way, if there is such a thing. Or we can be nothing."

"Friends, then," he said. *Yeah,* he added silently. *Very uncomplicated.*

Her eyebrow quirked upward. "Really?"

Jed shrugged. "Really. I only want you willing. And I'd rather have you as a friend than nothing, Annie. But . . ." He smiled at her, a little ruefully. "You'll let me know if you change your mind. Or if I can ever help you in any way."

"Yes," she said.

He had to be satisfied with that. "All right. Your turn to choose a topic of discussion, then . . . friend."

"Books," she said.

He slouched back in the sofa, letting her lighten the conversation, feeling a pang of regret at the way the new and impersonal subject untensed her shoulders, brought peace back to her eyes.

"My house — Alma's house — has nothing much in the book department but sixth-grade texts and genealogy guides. What I don't know about Southern history and family trees isn't worth knowing, but none of it's great reading for a cold autumn night. You might lend me some books," she said.

He shrugged, amused and frustrated. "Take whatever you want." He watched as she rose to browse the big, crowded bookshelves, tried not to think about how fluid her body was under the big blue robe.

"You like mysteries," she said. "John Harvey — he's good. P. D. James, Christie, Sayers, Hammett, Rex Stout. Poetry . . . I like Auden, too. And travel books. Freya Stark. Jan Morris." Her face lit up as she plucked one from the shelf. "J. M. Bell. God, I loved this book."

Jed slouched even lower in the couch, resisting the urge to squirm. This was what came from being hot and bothered and as randy as a teenager, he thought, and not paying attention. *Damn.* "It's okay. A little simplistic," he managed.

"It is not." Indignation fired her voice as she swung to glare at him. "It's a wonderful book. I'd never even given South America a thought, and suddenly there it was, on the pages, just as if I'd lived my whole life there. He got everything . . . the sights . . . the sounds . . . the smells of the places, even. I felt like I knew the people he talked about, and their homes, and the land. I loved it," she repeated.

Damn, he thought again, not sure whether to groan or laugh. There was no way to tell her, now, without making her feel like a fool. At which point she'd probably bolt, just as she was, up the hill.

"All right, Annie," he said, holding up a

placating hand. "Calm down. Maybe I'm not remembering it right. It's an old one, anyway, he's sure to have grown up since then."

"He didn't need to grow up," she said. It was clear to Jed that she was only partly mollified. "He was perfectly fine from the start. I haven't read the last few, though. I was . . . well, my mind was on other things."

"I'll lend you the latest," Jed said, trying to keep the irony out of his voice. "I've got it some-where."

"Okay. Just don't criticize it." She slid the book back into its place, scanned the shelves again, then turned to face him. "You're not going to tell me that you think Mary Morris is no good, are you?" she asked suspiciously. "Or John McPhee?"

She pleased him, damn it — not just aroused him, *pleased* him, all of him.

"I love them more than life itself, Annie," he said solemnly. Suddenly they were both laughing. They made a pile of books for her, and he gave her back her clothes still warm from the dryer, and he drove her up the hill to her house, letting her go with a casual good-bye.

So, he thought, back in his office, they'd cleared the air, which was good. Except for the little matter of his profession, of course. She'd forgotten the J. M. Bell book, and he'd been glad; it would give him a few hours to figure out what to do about it. Anyway, maybe with that talk behind them, he could get back to normal.

Get on with his life and his book.

Jed sat back down at the computer. And sat. And sat. Despite his best efforts, a rare midday beer, and a string of curses that would have done his daddy proud, he didn't write a decent word the rest of the day.

The view from her porch the next morning was almost the same as it had been her first day in Burnsville, a gorgeous vista of patchy cloud. But so much else had changed in a month, Annie thought, dropping onto one of her rockers to enjoy the morning for a moment.

The weather was colder, for one thing — sharp, with a hint of frost in the air. The changing leaves were in their prime. In a month or so, the view would look dramatically different from the lush landscape she'd arrived to.

The biggest changes, though, were in her heart.

She knew the view like the back of her hand now. Knew the Wellmans, whose farm bordered her yard; Ethan Wellman had stopped in to check on Susie one day while Annie had been visiting, and he had regaled them both with stories of the farm. She knew which chalets were rented out and which were empty. She knew Jed, knew Meg, knew John, knew Susie. She even felt like she knew Alma, whose presence felt so strong in the house.

And best of all, now she knew herself again. Knew what it was like to feel content with who she was. Knew she would survive. Knew what it was like, even, to feel desire again — a gift of Jed Harper's, infinitely more complicated than the loan of his books.

She would never go back to her old life in Manhattan. Maybe Burnsville wasn't the place she'd end up. Living next to Jed, watching him come and go, meeting the scrutiny in those eyes, coping with the dizzying unpredictability of her own reactions — she wasn't sure she could handle it. But she'd resolve that question when the time came.

In the meantime, she would have her peace of mind and her house and her work.

That morning, the hint of a quilt idea that had sped through her mind at lunch with Meg and Susie had returned. Only this time it was clear and urgent.

When a vision for a quilt arose in her mind, it demanded immediate attention and crowded out everything around it. She'd learned, over the years, how fleeting those images were, how easy to lose if you put them aside. Tom had hated that, hated the dreamy look she would get or the quick retreats she'd make to her study to sort through fabrics while the vision was fresh in her mind. But now she was free to explore her vision at will, wherever and whenever she wanted to.

Diving headfirst into the project would be good for her, in fact. Not only because it might bring in some money, but because it would help get her mind off Jed Harper. He was lingering in her thoughts far too much for comfort. The memory of him by the fire the day before — that lean, handsome face with its always-shifting expressions, those beautiful hands, that quicksilver mind — was more disturbing than she wanted to admit. Like the dream of him she still had sometimes, it was erotic, unsettling, and totally impractical in the light of day.

There was a thrift shop, she remembered, turning her thoughts to less shaky ground, at the far edge of Main Street. She dropped her cup back in the kitchen, grabbed her bag, and drove there, hoping that charity stores, at least, would be the same in Burnsville as in a big city. And they were, she decided in satisfaction as she pushed the door open. Ugly fluorescent lighting. Angular chrome racks holding a neat but motley assortment of jackets, pants, children's dresses. Housewares and toys on metal shelving against the walls. A forlorn cluster of drink-scarred end tables and well-worn recliners. And, just as she'd hoped, three big bins of damaged odds and ends, priced at only fifty cents apiece. She sorted exultantly through the jumbled contents, her idea taking form in her mind.

A man's blue chambray work shirt, faded, worn down to white thread at the edges of cuff and collar. A boy's pajama top printed with a pattern of horses, washed so many times the flannel practically gave way under her fingers. An apron, torn but hand-stitched, with a line of pretty embroidery along the pockets. A striped silk tie, so narrow it must have been from the fifties. The silk was badly stained at the bottom, but the top half of the fabric was intact, a black and red pinstripe that would contrast nicely with other, softer colors.

She would make it a crazy quilt, a rhythmic layering of scraps blanket-stitched together in a single-color thread — blue maybe, or rose. She'd find other materials, too. Linen tea towels maybe, scraps of chenille bedspreads, pieces from old curtains. The kind of cotton handkerchiefs her grandmother used to carry. The tattered denim of favorite jeans. Every inch of her quilt would be worn, warm, faded, used, obviously well-loved. Each scrap would remind the viewer of reassurance: the sweetness of hugging a child encased in soft pajama flannel, the pleasure of pulling on a perfectly worn and fitting pair of jeans, the relief of snuggling under an old blanket at night.

It would be as soft and beautiful to touch as it was to look at.

It would be a small collage of memories, bits and pieces of lives.

She would call it *Comfort*.

She couldn't wait to get started. She gathered up her treasures — more than a quarter of a quilt's worth, she figured, and all for eight dollars — and strode to the front of the store.

When she got home with her treasures, she found a pile of fresh-cut logs stacked in the corner of her porch and the book Jed had promised her propped in front of her door.

Her heart warmed, despite herself. Firewood and fine literature. What a contradiction the man was. And what a charmer.

She leaned to pick the book up as she let herself in. Dropping her laden bag on the kitchen counter, she stopped to lift the sprig of Queen Anne's lace he'd tucked between its front pages. The title page was signed, she noticed, and she gave it an automatic glance.

To Annie, the strong black handwriting read. *With gratitude for the nicest, least self-conscious compliment ever paid me.*

It was signed *Jedidiah Marcus Bell Harper.*

J. M. Bell. Annie dropped down into a kitchen chair, her face flooding with color. She couldn't decide whether to laugh or scream. Maybe she should just do both at once.

Of course. The schedule that left him free to play his dulcimer of a morning, yet took him away from the mountains for months at a time. The masks from Thailand and the Navajo rugs, exotic objects grafted on the native rootstock of his house. The house itself, for all its simplicity a luxurious and sophisticated residence. If he was J. M. Bell, he could certainly afford it. And if he was J. M. Bell, no wonder he knocked down her protective fences like they were cardboard. This was a man who could get Mafia dons and drug smugglers, hermits and heads of state to talk to him as though he was their long-lost brother. This was a man who was at home everywhere and nowhere, who moved through the whole world as though it were his own back-yard.

She shook her head, laughing at herself and at the absurdity of the situation. She had fled hundreds of miles for anonymity, just to live next to one of the most visible, most inquisitive minds in the entire literary world. And her hillbilly neighbor Jed Harper, who lived in worn jeans and knew how to fix chimneys, was one of the best travel writers of his generation, author of — what was it, five? six? books and countless *New Yorker* articles. Not to mention the winner of a slew of literary awards, if she remembered right.

And she was a reasonably intelligent woman who'd gushed over his writing like a naive teenager.

The old-fashioned wall phone shrilled. Annie reached for it.

"Don't hang up," Jed's voice said coaxingly into her ear. It made her smile, but some impulse made her drop the receiver smartly down on its hook anyway.

The childish gesture pleased her. She stood next to the phone and waited for it to ring again.

"You've made your point," he said when she picked it up. "My eardrum is still ringing."

"Good." She sat down onto the rickety chair again, frowning. "You deserve it. You lied to me, damn it."

"I didn't lie."

"You omitted, then."

"You're doing a fine job of omitting yourself,

sweetheart, in case you've forgotten. And when exactly was I supposed to tell you? That first time, out on my lawn? When we were arguing about your chimney? After I scared the hell out of you in my kitchen? Or maybe right after I explained to you how I wanted to ravish you? Seems to me a good opportunity to acquaint you with my résumé hasn't arisen."

It astonished her to realize again how few times they'd actually met. It seemed like he'd been confusing and unsettling her for decades.

"It could have. And don't bring logic into this, anyway," she said, listening to his chuckle. "I feel like a total idiot, and it's your fault."

"I know," he said. "I'm sorry, Annie. I mean that. I knew I should tell you right there in my living room. But I'd just put you through one heavy conversation. I thought if I embarrassed you again, you'd bolt half-naked up the hill. Besides, it never occurred to me you'd even have read the stuff."

"I wasn't half-naked," Annie said, concentrating on the essential point.

"On the contrary, darlin'. I wouldn't be wrong about something like that."

Maybe it wasn't a good subject to pursue after all, Annie decided. "Why in the world don't you put your picture on your books? I had pictured you as somewhere about seventy. A grizzled sage with a pipe and bushy eyebrows."

"That's the way I like it. People don't act naturally around celebrities. They smile for the camera, you might say. I tell them that I'm a writer when I need to, whenever it would be unethical or unfair to lie. Other than that, I like to move around like every other ordinary human being."

"You're definitely not ordinary. And I wish you'd stay in one place."

"One . . . ?"

"It's making me seasick, all this motion. One minute you're a fireplace cleaner, and the next minute you're a Pulitzer Prize winner. One minute you're a North Carolina hillbilly, the next you're a world-famous traveler." *One minute you're enraging me, and the next minute you're making me melt.*

"One of the reasons I'm a good travel writer, probably," he said. "A critic once said that I had no fixed identity. He didn't mean it kindly."

Perversely, it made her want to defend him. "That's not true. You have enough identity for ten people," she said. "You should have been a lawyer, though. Or a con man. You're way too slippery. And persuasive."

"I've been told that, too. But at the risk of bringing up all this complicated stuff you don't want to talk about, let me repeat that you're a little hard to pin down, yourself. Anyway . . . friends again, Annie?"

"Friends," she said, still grumpily. "Well, once I get over the shock, I'll look forward to reading your book. But don't expect any more gushing."

"I won't. This time you'll probably rip me to

shreds. Are you all right, Annie? When you're not yelling at me you sound . . . I don't know, a little quiet."

"No. Well, maybe. A good quiet, though. I sew a little — pieces I sold, sell, at a little store in New York. I've got an idea for a project. I'm not sure if it'll even work, but I'm excited about it."

"That's great. I'd like to see it, one day, if you're ever ready. In the meantime, you want to be a real neighbor, you could send some of that inspiration down this way. My writing's as cold as molasses in February."

"You don't need me, J. M. Bell," Annie scoffed, but it was fun to talk to him this way. "Think of your next Pulitzer Prize. That should warm you right up." She could hear him laughing as she hung up the phone.

It was Friday evening, when Cindy worked late at the café and Billy stayed in town to play pool with his buddies. He worked so hard, Cindy never begrudged him his one night out with the boys. Tonight she was sorry that he was occupied, though, and that her girlfriend Lisa was so willing to watch the kids. Moira had been nagging at her for days now, and Cindy had never been happier to have almost no free time. But tonight she'd run plumb out of excuses. Giving Meg Thorn an abstracted wave good-bye and buttoning up her jeans jacket as she went, Cindy half walked, half ran out of the café.

Sure enough, her aunt's car was idling at the curb, its headlights boring into the darkness of the street. When Moira said eight-thirty, she meant eight-thirty sharp. Cindy pulled open the heavy passenger door, slid into the car.

"Finally. Thought I'd have to go in there and pull you out," Moira said as the door slammed shut.

"I'm only five — six — minutes late, Aunt Moira." Cindy dropped her bag on the floor near her feet, pulled her uniform skirt down where it had ridden upward on her thighs, and fought to keep her voice even. It was amazing how Moira could reduce her to childishness with just one snippy little remark. "Donna was out again, and even after the supper rush ended, there were a lot of tables for two waitresses. Meg's busy enough with the cash register and the kitchen without me walking out on her."

Moira laughed, a harsh quick sound. "That Meg Thorn. Thinks she's so perfect, with that big house of hers and her fancy little diner. Her *café*, I guess I should say."

"Come on, Aunt Moira. Meg's nice, not stuck-up at all. And she works real hard."

"That may be. Doesn't make her special. We all work hard, Lucinda. Why should it make her feel so high and mighty just because she gets her hands dirty once in a while? She was so great, she'd be married again by now, rather than rattling around in that house. It's big enough for ten people. But she'd rather spend her time with that so-called friend of hers, Jed Harper. Some friend. No telling what they're up to."

It would have been funny, if the impulse to defend Meg hadn't been so strong. Moira criticizing anyone for their dealings with Jed Harper was surely the pot calling the kettle black. And as for widows, if remarriage was the test of goodness, why wasn't Moira herself hitched up again? The very thought of Moira on a date was ridiculous.

It was tempting to argue, but . . . *Change the subject, kid,* Cindy told herself. The last thing she needed was one of her aunt's crazy diatribes. Especially about Meg, who Cindy adored. Look how brave she was, going on like that after her husband died. The mere thought of Billy gone made Cindy's eyes well up.

"Where we going, Aunt Moira?" she said brightly, chasing the thought away and wishing there was some wood to knock on, just in case. She didn't really believe in the old superstition, but there was no point in taking chances when it was Billy's life at stake. "You sure sounded mysterious when you called me."

"No mystery. Just a little errand."

"Where? For what?" At least they weren't going in the direction of Alma's cottage.

"You'll see." Moira's strong profile looked forbidding in the dim light. Her large, rawboned hands guided the car east, along Highway 19's scattering of gas stations, fast-food places, mills, feed and machine stores. Cindy pulled her jeans jacket more tightly around her, shivering a little — Moira's house and car were as cold as her heart — and prayed they'd get wherever they were going fast.

Not quite soon enough for Cindy's wishes, they finally stopped at a grocery store halfway to Mars Hill. In the whitish glare of the lights the rutted, mostly deserted parking lot looked bleak. Moira pulled the car around the back of the store, to a narrow loading area even grimmer than the front lot. She reached into her big, old-fashioned handbag and slipped a small white tablet under her tongue. "Come on, girl," she said impatiently, as though Cindy was the one holding things up. "You don't think I brought you here to sit there and daydream, do you?"

A pile of banana boxes stood on one side of the doorway Moira led them toward, a neater stack of plastic dairy crates on the other. Despite the cold breeze that eddied around them, the air was rich with the smell of rotting produce. Moira pulled out a set of keys from her bag and tried one, then another, at the big metal door.

Cindy opened her mouth, then shut it again. No point asking. Her cousin Timmy — the son of Cindy's other aunt, Patsy — worked as a meat cutter at this store, she remembered dimly. Moira must have "borrowed" the keys from him, the same way she'd "borrowed" Alma's from Jed Harper.

Cindy's mouth felt suddenly dry. A wave of dismay washed over her, followed by an even stronger wave of fear. There was something really wrong here, something much worse than an eccentric relative, and she'd just kept her eyes closed and walked into the trap.

Billy's gonna kill me, she thought, shivering behind Moira as her aunt fiddled impatiently with the keys.

She followed Moira into the rear of the store on leaden feet, through the produce packing section and into a narrow hallway. Moira seemed to know where she was going despite the dim nighttime lighting. The air was less foul here, but it still smelled cloyingly, sickly, of food past its prime.

"Huh. Just like he said." Moira stepped into the butcher's area and switched on the light there. The air in the cavernous room was frigid. The green white glow of the fluorescent bulbs that hung in tracks from the high ceiling brought out the brownish stains on the floor, the dented metal tables, the high flush of red on Moira's cheekbones, the gleam of the glass doors of the refrigerator cases that lined one wall. Moira stood in front of them, opened one of the doors, and grunted in satisfaction. She bent to lift one of the white plastic containers inside, her body as hard and angular as the stick figures little LuAnne drew in kindergarten. "Timothy didn't forget me. He's a good boy. This'll do fine, just fine," she said.

"Aunt Moira — I don't understand," Cindy

said, halting at the threshold. "What's in there?"

"Just a little present. For the woman in Honey-cutt's house. Little housewarming, you might say." Moira laughed.

There was something horrible about that laugh, Cindy thought. Never soft or harmonious, Moira suddenly sounded manic, gleeful. Mad.

"We'll go deliver it tonight," Moira continued. "Give her a little push to move on. Like she should do. No need for the likes of her in Burnsville. I'm just doing her a favor. She's better off someplace else."

"No." Cindy shook her head, making her little silver-plated earrings jingle and her carroty-red ponytail bounce. "Aunt Moira, I don't know what you're doing, but I can't help. I just can't. This is crazy, and it's cruel. I've seen that Annie Taylor, and she was sweet."

"Huh. Sweet ladies don't need to hide out in little mountain shacks. Sweet ladies don't live by theirselves like she does. Doesn't matter, Lucinda, anyways. I need to get into that house."

"I don't care." Cindy shook her head again, even more forcefully this time. She wasn't going to placate her aunt this time, no matter how angry Moira got. "It's wrong, Aunt Moira."

"Who are you to talk about wrong?" Moira faced her, the eyes behind the ugly glasses hot, the lips thin and set. "A girl who tarts around with a married man? A girl who ripped her own child out of her womb?"

Cindy's pale cheeks flared red as time seemed

194

to slow, to stop. She could feel the burn of the blood rushing to her face, and then the iciness as it leached away again. Her whole body felt cold, suddenly, and a sick, desperate dizziness swam in her head.

"I didn't . . . how did you know?" she faltered. Wrapping her arms around her waist under the stiff hem of the jeans jacket, she willed herself not to faint or cry or throw up. Thank God for the ugly, rubber-soled waitress shoes she'd always hated so much. At least they kept her balanced on the ground. She swallowed once, convulsively, trying to get the sour taste of disgust out of her mouth.

"Never you mind, Lucinda," Moira said, staring her down. "Important thing is, I *do* know. Can't imagine how you thought you'd keep a thing like that to yourself, anyways. People talk, girl. People talk. I learned that with my Arthur. Tongues wagged over him, I can tell you. But I'm no gossip. It's not my place to tell the world your shame if you don't see fit to do it. Didn't want to bring old dirt up at all, only you forced me to."

Don't let her see you're scared. The voice sounded, unbidden, in Cindy's mind. "If you didn't want to bring it up, you didn't have to," she said, as strongly as she could.

"Don't give me your back talk. And don't blame me for the wages of your own sin. 'Twasn't my fault you couldn't keep your skirt down, girl. Or my fault you were hot to trot with any slick-talking man who winked at you. Can I help it if

195

you can't keep your panties on? Can I help it if you make me remind you that families have to stick together? I never told a soul what you did, not your mama or your friends or that husband of yours. And you're going to help me when I need you, just the same, and keep just as quiet. Least you can do. The world doesn't need to know our business."

Moira was off onto a well-known track, and she went on from there. How the McTeague family name shouldn't be soiled. How people didn't appreciate Moira McTeague. The familiar harangue gave Cindy a chance to catch her breath and think, though the thoughts spun crazily in her mind.

Billy would understand, she thought desperately. Billy would forgive her.

Billy would understand the naïveté of a teenage girl, with a body awakening to the first stirrings of sex and a heart yearning for romance. He'd understand how easily a slick, married charmer from the city could work on that body and that heart. He'd understand the eagerness, and then the shame, and then the terror she'd felt when her period didn't come. He'd understand how even the unthinkable would seem welcome after three desperate weeks worrying what her parents and friends and teachers would say, wondering what her life would become with a tiny baby to care for and the stigma of an adulterous affair behind her.

Billy would understand, Cindy thought desperately. Or would he? Would Billy, so forth-right and direct, be able to understand why she'd never told him? How she'd been scared of losing him at first, and then later how irrelevant and far away the whole nightmare seemed to become? Would Billy, who loved his kids so much, be able to understand why Cindy had destroyed an unborn child?

The thoughts still whirled in her head, confused and useless. How could she know what Billy would think? And while she stood in panic, rooted to the spot, Moira had moved on. A second container joined the first on the scuffed surface of the metal table. Cindy trembled to think what was in them. Moira swung one of the containers under her elbow, thrust the other into Cindy's frozen arms.

"You'll be home in an hour, Lucinda. You don't even have to do nothing, just help me carry these. And drive the car up the hill while I do what's needed. What's the harm in that? Stop the conniption, girl. It's nothing. Go on with you now. Out to the car, while I lock up. Get."

Numbly, Cindy went.

Seven

Annie went to bed early these days, pleasantly tired from her work on the quilt. She wanted to read Jed's book, but she knew that even a few pages of a book — any book — would have been enough to put her out. From what she recalled, the writing of J. M. Bell demanded your full attention, just like its author did. The thick black photograph album propped on her lap was a simpler, if guilty, pleasure. She didn't want to invade Alma Honeycutt's privacy, but she was curious — curious about life on the mountain, about Alma herself, about Burnsville, and about the folks she had met there.

Here on the crackling black pages was the cottage in earlier days, with a pair of rockers on the porch and a line of drying wash visible in the backyard. The Wellman farm, behind the cottage, with reedy saplings where full-grown trees stood now. The old stone schoolhouse Annie had passed a few times, with children playing in front of it. She would bet that a little redhead among them was a younger Meg Thorn, though the caption didn't say. There were baby pictures, lovingly arranged, of Alma's son Bobby, and of other children, other families. A Girl Scout troop, some weddings, a big group picnic — she immediately recognized the town square and the facade of the inn in the background. Near the back of the book, in a page of miscellaneous shots, there was even a picture with the terse caption, *"Harpers."* Annie frowned over the picture, finding it hard to believe her eyes.

If the words hadn't told her, she would never have guessed that this painfully skinny boy of thirteen or fourteen, all bones and tension, was Jed. Nor that the couple standing with him were his parents.

The older man was as burly as a wrestler, but with the rolling gut of a man long gone to seed. Bearded, with a cigarette between thick lips, he looked like a bull ready to charge. The woman beside Jed, on the other hand, was pale and washed out, her shoulders stooped, her face set in lines of dissatisfaction. She had Jed's straight hair and fine bones, only something had leached all of the life out of her. The house just visible in the background wasn't Jed's dignified home but a disreputable-looking shanty with plastic-encased windows, a rotting porch, a pile of junk in the patchy yard.

Gently, Annie touched a finger to the image of Jed's face. Standing between two people who didn't look at him or each other, he stood awkwardly, poised on one foot as though he'd like to run away. He was the only one of the three that had mustered a real smile for his neighbor's camera, but the eyes above that familiar grin were bleak and hesitant. Annie's heart ached for him, at the pain and vulnerability the photograph suggested. How hard he must have worked for the warmth, the confidence, the easy intellect, the polished manner she'd always assumed were inborn gifts. How far he'd come from this bitter family stock, this impoverished past. How little was he just the arrogant rich man she'd imagined him to be.

And how easy it was, she chided herself as she turned another page, to make facile assumptions about people. She'd been wrong, or at least oversimplistic, about Jed. She'd been dead wrong about Alma Honeycutt, too. The woman in the album wasn't a stereotypically dowdy small-town schoolteacher but a beauty, a woman who would turn heads and flutter hearts in even the most sophisticated milieu. Tall and rail thin, with beautiful bones and a vivacious expression, she wore her dark hair braided and wrapped on her head like a coronet, in a style that didn't change through all the years the book spanned. Even the fading hues, the stiff poses, and the cumbersome fashions of years gone by couldn't disguise Alma's vivid appeal or the affection she and her thin, balding husband had felt for each other. Annie felt tears prick in her eyes at the tenderness of it: a pair of linked hands here, a laughing glance there, each photo witness to a lifetime of trust and closeness.

No wonder the house had seemed so peaceful,

so happy, right from the start, Annie thought drowsily, leaning to switch off the little lamp. And no wonder she still dreamed, some nights, of dancing, kissing, touching. The spirit of the Honeycutts' cottage was surely a loving one.

Even speculations about supernatural influences weren't compelling enough to keep her awake. Her face cooled by the eddying night air, her body warm under the coverlet, Annie slept.

She dreamed of the man again, the faceless man who danced with her and took her in his arms. Sometimes it was a stranger and sometimes it was Jed Harper, and in the dream there was nothing at all scary about it being Jed Harper who loved and held her. They swayed and kissed and danced as though their bodies were one, moving in total harmony, total accord.

But then, slowly at first, the dream began to change.

The man who held her was no longer Jed. No longer gentle, no longer handsome, no longer courtly. He was a dark and bulky shape: large, powerful, as much animal as human.

His grasp was growing tighter, squeezing the sensitive skin of her waist, pulling her too close. His footsteps were heavy, like big stones dropping onto a polished floor. She tried to pull away, but she couldn't move; she was oddly, frighteningly weak, as though all of her muscles had been paralyzed. The dance floor grew slippery, like glass, and she could find no foothold. She was slipping. The dance became a repugnant, terrifying embrace. And then the floor snapped like cracking glass, and they were falling, and still she could not push him away.

She was sitting upright, her heart racing, before she realized it was no longer a dream. She was awake, but she was hearing the same sounds she'd dreamed of. The thudding footsteps. The heavy, animal movements. The breaking of glass.

Someone was downstairs. In the house, on the porch, she couldn't tell. The footsteps were heavy and deliberate, like Tom's. Only she had never dreamed he could be here this fast; she'd thought she had time. . . . There was no breath in her lungs. Instinctively, for no logical reason except to get as far away from him as she could, she bolted out of bed, into the corner of the room, under the sloping eaves. She crouched there, shaking, arms wrapped around herself in panic.

She couldn't run. The stairs ended only a few feet from the front door, near which the intruder was moving purposefully. But . . . Jed. Jed was close by. She crawled back toward the phone on the bedside table. Some memory she didn't even know she had dialed the recall code on the keypad. Jed had been the last caller, earlier that day. She held the phone with painful, convulsive tightness as she listened to it ring.

"There's someone here," she gasped the moment she heard his sleepy, confused greeting. Heavy steps moved again, on the porch, she thought. "Oh, my God, Jed, he's here." She knew she was whimpering, babbling, but she couldn't stop. "Tom's here. Please, please, help me." Another crash of breaking glass, then a stranger, less definable sound, slurping and liquid.

"Hide," Jed said, his voice firm. "And hold on. I'm coming." Stupidly, Annie tried to answer, then realized that he'd gone. The receiver hung, silent, from her hand.

She dropped it and crouched back in her corner, frozen with fear, half insane with it. She thought her heart would break through the wall of her chest, it was pounding so fast and so loudly. It was as though every blow, every slap, every jolt of terror from Tom was happening here, now, in one short infinitely horrible moment that would somehow never end. She crouched on the cold floor, shaking, arms hugged to her knees, paralyzed with fear, praying for Jed to come.

He'd been reading, in a state so relaxed he was half asleep. Jed dropped the phone, ran barefoot down the steps and through the hall, thought fast. Shotgun from the closet in the study, cartridges, truck keys from the hall table. No time to reassure Rooster or lock the door behind him. No time for a coat or shoes, either.

The truck was cold and he cursed it, pumping the gas pedal hard until the ignition caught. The motor sounded harsh in the stillness of the night, but there was other noise on the mountain. Another engine, he thought, just like his. As the truck swerved up the hill, he saw moving lights on the road at the fork. A drift of clouds had obscured the night's weak moon, and it was too dark to see the vehicle itself; he only knew that it was a car, and it was heading down the mountain, away from Annie's house. He paused for one long moment in indecision at the turn in the road, then floored the gas and raced up the hill.

Annie. That was the most important thing, seeing if Annie was okay. If she wasn't . . . *Christ.* If she wasn't, he thought savagely as he brought the truck to a screeching halt, he'd kill whoever it was with his bare hands.

Her house was unlit, but his vision had adjusted to the darkness. He could see the jagged gleam of broken front windows, and through the shattered glass the hems of curtains moving slightly in the faint wind.

He cursed under his breath as he strode onto her porch. He had Alma's key, but in his rush he'd forgotten to get it from the study drawer where he kept it among a bunch of other little-used odds and ends; he'd have to get in through the window if the door wasn't open. There was a patch of deeper blackness on the darkness of the porch. His heel skidded on wetness at the same time his nose registered a thick, cloying, metallic smell. There was a sharp pain in his foot. He cursed it briefly, but kept going. The front door was firmly locked. He knocked the jagged shards of glass out of one windowframe and angled his body into the house, moving through another wet patch in the darkness for the stairs, not bothering to search for light switches until he got to the upper landing.

The third door in the tiny hallway was the right one. Even with the light flicked on, at first he thought she wasn't there. Then he saw her, crouched in the corner, a trembling fetal shape.

"Annie." He knelt beside her, his own heart pounding in fear. In his arms she was as cold and frozen as a woman made of ice. The only sign of life was a trembling from somewhere deep inside her. She was terrified. But she was unharmed, he guessed. Or at least her body was.

"Annie. Jesus, Annie," he murmured, holding her tight, talking against her hair. "Tell me. Are you all right?"

She nodded once, dumbly, against his shoulder.

"It's all right, baby. They're gone now, it's all right, it's all right. You're safe." She trembled again in his arms, her face hidden by the shining tumble of her hair. He kept his arms around her, stroked her gently and rhythmically, talked to her quietly in an even, steady, half-crooning voice.

It was two minutes, three, before she quieted in his arms. "All right, sweetheart," he said, keeping his tone just as soothing, just as steady. "I'm going to go downstairs, see what's there. Let me tuck you back into bed for a minute."

"No." Terror widened her eyes. Her skin paled, if that was possible. "Please. Let me come. I can't — I don't want to stay here alone. Please, Jed."

205

"All right. But let's get something warm on you." She sat, as unprotesting as a child, as he rummaged in drawers for a sweater and warm socks. He pulled them onto her shaking body gently and led her carefully downstairs.

"Okay, now? Good," he said, smoothing a tangle of black hair from her forehead. "But stay behind me, just in case."

His brow furrowing, Jed noted the broken windows in the tiny dining room, then walked, Annie beside him, across the hall. The living room windows were shattered, too, but the damage hadn't stopped there. Window-side table, armchair, rug — all were roughly spattered with a deep, uneven stain, which spread into black crimson liquid flecks on pillows, lampshades, books.

This was what he'd slipped in, outside. In his fear for Annie, he'd totally forgotten the sticky residue, forgotten even the sharp pain that still twinged in his heel. The thick, cloying smell made him wrinkle his nostrils again. He stood stock-still for a moment, his mind working. It didn't make sense. The big gaping holes of the broken windows, the ugly damage, the door handle loose, but Annie still safe upstairs. It just didn't fit.

Annie reached out a hand to the still-wet tabletop before he could stop her. "Oh," she cried, staring at the bright color on her fingers. "It's blood. God, Jed —"

"Animal blood, Annie." He strode swiftly beside her, wiped the mess from her freezing hands onto his sleeve. "I'm certain of it. And not fresh, either, it feels too cold for that. It's disgusting, but it's okay."

The blood had set her trembling again. Her voice was high with distress, and it shook. "I don't understand. Why would he throw blood on my house?"

He stood in front of her, thumbs hooked into his belt loops, as concern gave way to anger. It was irrational, he knew, a paradoxical aftermath to the swift cycle of fear and then relief, but suddenly her vulnerability filled him with fury. Whatever it was that was going on, she was risking her own life here. And making him a party to it, by keeping him in the dark.

"I can't tell you why he'd throw blood on your house," he said, "until I know who the hell he is."

Her face was ashen. She shook her head. "No."

"You said you were willing to be friends."

She gaped at him. "I am."

"This is friendship?" His voice was rough and angry. He could hear the harshness, but he couldn't control it. "You let me do trivial little things for you, lend you books or clean your chimney, then you come up here and wait for some maniac to kill you? Some maniac whose name you happen to know? You told me your old life wasn't finished, Annie. But you sure as hell didn't hint at anything like this."

He glared at her, hating the beaten look in her eyes, hating whoever it was who'd put it there.

Hating himself for his anger.

"I didn't expect it. Not really. And it's not your problem," she said, her voice helpless. Even that angered him, the futility he heard there. "I couldn't burden you."

"No. Of course not." That surge of fury again. "I'm not burdened, am I? It'll be no burden to wonder who the hell Tom is every night, and wonder when he'll actually show up. It'll be no burden to come up here one day and find you hacked to pieces. Jesus *Christ*, Annie. Can't you understand that I care about you? What part of the word *friendship* don't you understand?"

That brought some fire back into her eyes, a small spot of color into each cheek.

"I've had enough tonight," she flared. "It may be my fault, I may be mishandling this, and if I am, I'm sorry. But I don't need to be lectured. I'm not a half-wit child."

"You're acting like one."

"I'm not. I'm trying to feel my way through a complicated situation. About which you know nothing, Jed. As you yourself just admitted. So stop yelling at me."

"I'm not yelling." But he was. He fisted his hands on his hips, glared down at her, fought for calm. "I'm just . . . yelling. Oh, hell."

There was silence for one long moment before he continued, his voice more reasonable now. "Annie, I'm trying so damned hard to do this your way. To keep you comfortable. To stay on the right side of all of these boundaries. Not to try to help you, protect you. Not to reach out and touch you, please you, comfort you. Not to ask you the hundred questions I've got in my head."

He paused, this time deliberately, to let the words sink in. "But whether it means an argument or not, for me to sit around doing nothing while you get attacked is not one of the options here. I'm sorry, but it's just not."

She shook her head, but kept her eyes on his. "So what do you suggest?"

"I suggest that you come down and spend the rest of the night in my spare room. I suggest that I teach you how to handle a gun and get you either an alarm system or a guard dog. I suggest that we both try to get at least part of a decent night's sleep, and then I suggest that you tell me who the hell Tom is and what the fuck's going on here."

"It's a mess," she said, her voice flat again. "You'll be sorry if you get involved."

"Possibly," he said. "Probably. I'm not a big fan of involvement at the best of times, as anyone who knows me will tell you. I tend to bolt and run when other people's turmoil comes. Always have. Probably always will." He let out a brief laugh. "But whether or not either one of us likes it, I *am* involved. Involved enough to wonder, and worry, and watch whatever this is destroy you. I'm just not involved enough to help. Don't leave me in the middle here, Annie. I know you mean well, but that isn't fair."

It was as though his words were reaching her from miles away, from another country, another galaxy. Even so, she could feel their truth. She *had* involved him. By panicking when he'd touched her before the party. By coming to his house to get out of the rain. By calling him tonight. She'd let his life intertwine with hers. She couldn't even figure out, anymore, why she'd thought she could do otherwise. Even if Jed hadn't been Jed — an irresistible force, as much like a hurricane as a human, she thought, the faintest glimmer of humor flickering amid the exhaustion — his existence would have complicated hers, just as Meg's and Susie's had. How naive she'd been to think that she could live like an island, separate unto herself.

"All right, Jed." The words were faint, and she tried again. "I don't want to admit it, but I know you're right. I'm just not sure I can talk about it. Right now, I mean. I'm just so . . . tired."

"Of course not now. Tomorrow, I said." Suddenly he was standing beside her, warm, steady, solid.

Gently holding her arms to make sure she was steady, he searched her face. "Are you okay to go upstairs and get some things?" He paused. "I'd like to double check the lock on the front door."

"My house . . . we can't just leave it, Jed."

The distress in her voice drove away Jed's puzzlement over that lock. "Yes, we can," he said. "Whoever this was, they're not coming back tonight."

"All that blood . . ." He watched as a wave of distress washed over her again, threatened to drown her in its depths.

"We'll clean it, I promise. Tomorrow. Annie, you're barely standing on your feet, and once this adrenaline rush dies down, I'm not sure I'll be any better. The worst thing that's going to happen to this house tonight is a stray bird flying in through the window or a little bit of dew. Go up and get your toothbrush and some clothes for tomorrow, now, okay?"

Too tired to fight anymore, Annie went. She made it halfway up the stairs before the tears started. They were hot on her face, salty on her lips. Blinded, she put her hand on the banister and stopped, then turned to sit on the cold, smooth surface of one step. She wrapped her arms around her shins, cradled her face on the cleft of her knees, and cried.

"Oh, hell." She could hear Jed's voice above her, and even in the midst of her weeping, she could tell that it was tender, not angry. He rested one hand on her hair for a moment, then angled around her to climb the rest of the stairs. She could hear him rustling in her bedroom, and then he was back beside her, helping her down the stairs and into the truck, into his house, into bed. Despite the fear that still coiled in her belly, she was so drained that she feel asleep before he turned out the light.

The next morning dawned gray and dull and

211

faded, as though the sky had been put through the wash too many times. Annie awoke with a pounding head and a sense of confusion. This large, comfortable room with its old oak furniture, deep cobalt drapes and quilt, braided rug, tall windows . . . she blinked in the pale light, confused.

Jed's house. Jed's spare room, she realized, images of the previous night coming back to her in a rush.

She didn't have her watch. The bedside clock said eleven, which seemed impossible. Tentatively, she swung her feet out of bed and stood. She felt stiff but steady. The feeling of being basically intact reassured her. In the bureau's oval mirror, though, she looked like she'd been in a brawl.

Purple circles under red-rimmed eyes. Skin as white as ice and not much warmer. The delicate pink of her cotton nightgown added another note of discordance. It belonged on some dewy blond innocent, not on an exhausted, black-haired waif, she thought. Not on a woman who'd chosen a battering husband and run away like a thief and ended up with blood all over the supposed haven she'd run to. Her empty stomach churned a little at the thought.

Her toothbrush, her hairbrush, and a lipstick sat atop a neat pile of her clothes on an armchair in one corner of the room. She couldn't remember bringing them, either. Ignoring them, she peeked through an open door into a small guest bath.

Ten minutes under the hot shower spray did wonders to ease the stiffness in every limb, if not to improve her looks. She did her best with brush and lipstick, then walked warily downstairs. The delicious scent of coffee brewing led her to the kitchen. As she walked over its threshold, Rooster padded over to meet her, his wet, black nose nudging her hand, his plumy tail waving in greeting.

"Hi, Rooster," Annie said, running her hand over the dog's ears. "Good morning, Jed."

"Mornin', Annie," he answered. "There's coffee there, and some breakfast things. Help yourself."

The kitchen looked warm and comfortably rumpled despite the bleak, grayish light from the windows. A sheaf of newspapers were folded messily on the window seat, a deep blue sweater tossed beside them. One of Rooster's chew bones lay abandoned near the sink. Rooster himself sniffed happily at Annie's knees, then settled himself at her feet, muzzle on his paws. On the big table, a pottery bowl piled with fruit sat next to a basket of rolls and muffins.

Jed was sitting in one of the Windsor chairs, a sheaf of marked-up manuscript pages in front of him. Unlike Annie herself, he seemed untouched by the night's alarms. He looked as handsome as ever, the bronzy hair gleaming, the blue eyes inscrutable. She made her coffee and lightened it with cream, conscious of his gaze on her back.

"Jed," she began. "My house —"

"It's fine. I checked this morning, before you

213

woke up. There's time enough for that," he said calmly. He pushed the laden bread basket toward her. "Drink up and eat some breakfast. You look like you need it."

"Thanks," she said, wrinkling her nose at his bluntness, but somehow the comment put some ease between them. He rose to refill his own mug, and they sat in silence as she ate. Only when she'd finished her pastry and poured a second cup of coffee did he speak.

"All right. I don't want to rush you. But I reckon now's as good a time as any, Annie," he said.

She'd known the moment was coming — had to come — yet she still felt unprepared.

Unbidden, the image of him from Alma's photograph album flashed in her mind. Jed vulnerable. Jed unsure. Jed, like Annie herself, fighting the fierce undertow of a difficult past. The thought helped her, steadied her. She curled her fingers more tightly around her mug, hoping for courage.

She might not want to tell this story. But if she had to, she wanted to make him understand. "All right," she echoed.

"Good." His eyes didn't leave her face.

"I lived in New York. In the city, on the Upper East Side. That's where I grew up. My dad died when I was little, so it was just my mom and me." She stared at nothing, trying to make it make sense. "I wanted to be an artist, but my mom hated the idea. She was . . . bitter, I guess.

214

Sort of twisted, angry about her own life. She'd never gotten the things she wanted, the security, the glamour. And she wanted them for me. Even when they weren't what I wanted for myself."

She couldn't sit still. She rose and went to the window, her back to him.

"I majored in art in college," she continued, "but I took computer and finance courses, too, and then signed up for art school. When I graduated, I took a job on Wall Street, just to make some money to help pay back my student loans. That's where I met Tom."

They were coming to the bad part. "I . . . I can't really explain it, Jed. How it could happen. The day I left — the day I ran away — I tried to figure it out, and I couldn't. I couldn't understand how it was that I was full of dreams one minute and hopeless the next."

She shook her head. "I was naive, I guess, and eager to please, and maybe my mother had gotten me used to feeling that I never quite did enough. Then Tom came along — he was a broker, older than me, who took the office next door to my boss's — and, well, he just dazzled me. Tom's good at courtship. Even when things got so bad, later on, he had a way of sending the perfect bouquet of flowers, or making a charming little phone call, or choosing just the right gift to persuade me that everything was fine. My mother was so pleased. We got married when I was twenty-eight. He paid for it all, a huge ceremony, a reception at his club, a designer gown, the works. My girlfriends couldn't believe it was me in that fancy gown, and I think they were right; it was a kind of dress-up costume that didn't really fit who I was. But it was one of the few times I could remember that my mother ever seemed totally happy."

Somewhere in the house a door banged sharply. Annie flinched at the sound, twisted in its direction.

"Shit," Jed said. "Cleaning lady. In the midst of all the ruckus, I forgot she was coming, Annie. Hold on, this'll just take a minute." He rose, moved to Annie's side, rested one hand briefly on her shoulder. "Moira?" he called. "In here."

To Annie, the woman who responded looked as tall and angular as one of the wind-blasted trees on the mountain. Her graying hair was pulled tightly back into a small bun, her posture was ramrod straight, and her eyes were indistinct behind thick bifocal glasses. She advanced into the kitchen stiffly, like a marionette worked by an unskilled puppeteer. Annie shivered a little. Not a woman she'd like to have in her own home, she thought. And nothing like warm, sensible May Williams.

Jed, however, seemed utterly at ease. "Moira," he said smoothly, not moving his hand from Annie's shoulder, "this is Annie Taylor, who rents Alma's cottage these days. Annie, Moira McTeague. Moira's one of the town's real old-timers, Annie. The McTeagues have been here since — what, Moira? The turn of the century?"

Moira nodded once at Annie, but there was neither warmth nor welcome in that deliberate acknowledgment. She said nothing, but turned her eyes to Jed. "Those stairs need cleaning. And the rugs, too."

"Whatever you think, Moira. We'll be out of your way in a half hour or so."

Moira nodded sharply but didn't speak again. Annie glanced doubtfully at Jed as her heavy footsteps receded, raising one brow. "Is my being here a problem? She definitely doesn't look happy."

"Oh, Moira never looks happy. She wasn't exactly the life of the party to start, and when her husband absconded with the church offering and then killed himself, she really got grim. They were desperately middle-class folks, painfully respectable, and he left her with nothing — no money, no reputation. I've never had the heart to let her go, even though she's as sharp as a hen sucking lemons."

"She seems so . . . intense, the way she looked at me. Us."

"Don't worry about it. I don't." Jed refilled her coffee, dropped back into his chair, stretched his legs in front of him. "Finish the story, Annie," he said, lacing his long fingers over one knee. "So you married this Tom. Were you happy? To start with, at least?"

"Happy? You know, I have no idea. I didn't think about it that way. Not really. That sounds so foolish, doesn't it? But . . . I thought about

217

whether I was . . . acceptable, I guess. And in the beginning I was. I think he liked, well, creating me. Can you understand that?"

"Yes," Jed said grimly. "Don't stop."

"He made it all sound so reasonable. He liked to choose my clothes — but then, he was so much more sophisticated than I was. He liked to plan our social life — but entertaining was so important to his business. He controlled the money, but then, he made so much more than I did. It seemed so silly to fight him when I could make him happy just by going along. I didn't notice that I was losing all my control, my independence."

"And then it got worse."

"He got angry." Annie's voice was low, somber. She rose, restless again, painfully aware of Jed's strong presence, his steady attention. At the window seat she stopped, sat on one of the deep cushions, swung her legs up onto the seat. Tucking her chin down, she hugged her arms around her knees.

There was no point putting it off. "He'd go into a rage if I didn't manage a dinner party just right," she said, her voice flat. "Or if I forgot to restock the wine, or if I was less elegantly turned out than someone else's wife, or if I smiled too much at this man or didn't smile enough at that one. He'd scream and break things. But then he always apologized and made some lovely gesture, and there was peace for a while. I wanted that peace so much, so very much. So each time I persuaded myself that it was the last, that I could do things well enough to avoid the scene next time. It never worked, of course. Something would always set him off again. And eventually . . . he started pushing me. Hitting me. When he drank, he got more violent, less inhibited. My mother just told me to try harder. She seemed to think it was my fault, and by then I'd lost so much confidence that her criticism didn't even seem strange to me. I didn't fight back, I just tried even more desperately to do everything right."

There was the worst pain of it said aloud, the most terrible shame: how hard she had tried to please him.

"That's what I meant, the other day, when we talked in your living room. I can't blame Tom alone," Annie said wearily. "For years he hit me, and I let him. I came back for more, even though I knew better somewhere inside. I can never forget that."

She realized that Jed had moved to her side. He sat on the window seat beside her. She could feel the warmth of him, smell his clean male scent. He put one hand on her bare feet, then reached for his abandoned sweater and tucked it around them. She hadn't even noticed how cold she had grown.

"But you left, Annie."

She felt the tears begin, but she made no move to stop them. Closing her eyes, she let the past envelop her.

Yet another dinner at yet another fancy restaurant. Too much rich food and too much liquor. By eleven the men's faces were flushed, their voices loud, their jokes increasingly crude. Jim Perry's girlfriend had bottle-blond hair and a deep cleavage, amply displayed by a low neckline. Annie could see Tom glancing at her breasts, his face avid and greedy. She was used to it by now. She even welcomed it a little, though she could see Jim Perry's growing anger. Flushed with desire for little Tiffany, Annie was sure, Tom would leave her alone.

But he didn't. What had happened then was brutal and terrifying and blessedly short.

Annie had never thought she'd tell anyone about that night. But she told Jed now, skipping the details but making no attempt to hide the ugly truth.

"That had never happened before," she finished, her voice barely audible. "When I looked at myself in the mirror the next morning, I knew I had to leave — that if I didn't, I would die, somehow. Kill myself, or let him kill me, or just die of exhaustion. It was like I finally came to my senses, and also like I'd made my plans all along, without even knowing it. I did what I could to start with enough money and enough time. And I ran."

She couldn't look at him. The shame was too great, and the fear. Could someone like Jed, so confident and powerful, ever understand how weak a frightened woman could become? Could the warmth of his friendship, much less the desire in his eyes, survive the ugly story?

But his hand was on her shoulder, stroking her gently. When he spoke, his voice sounded tender. "You have a lot of courage."

"No. Not much. Not enough."

"More than enough. Annie, look at me."

"I can't."

"You can. Look at me."

Gentle as it was, the command held power. And she knew him by now, knew how persistent he could be. Reluctantly, she raised her eyes, aching from the tears, to his. She searched his face, knowing she had to find out. But even in her fear she could find no judgment there, no disgust, no contempt.

"This isn't the time for me to tell my story, darlin'," he said softly, his hand still touching her arm. "But my daddy beat the shit out of my mama sometimes, and sometimes he walloped me. We never knew when it would happen or why. So I know all about it. The fear. The anger. The hope that you can avoid the next battle. The desire to please someone who's never going to be pleased, no matter how hard you try. It's painful. I know that. No one should ever have to endure what you've been through. But I'm telling you, Annie, it's no shame."

"I expected you to be disgusted."

"No." He shook his head, his expression sure. "Not disgusted. Well, not with you, though I'd sure like to have a little talk with this Tom. But it's a lot of unfinished business, princess."

She nodded. "I know. I need to resolve it somehow. But my instinct was just to let it lie for a little bit. Does that make sense? Just to let myself heal before I tackled it. I thought I had a little time. I never expected him to find me so fast."

"This wasn't him."

"It must have been. Jed, who else?"

He shook his head. "No. You're too close to it, and too frightened. If you look at it objectively, it just can't be him. For starters, where the hell would he get animal blood in a strange town? That's what it is, Annie, and there's a lot of it. Besides, why would he want to? And why would he just run away without even going upstairs?"

"He saw you coming."

"No. I saw the car at the fork. It was already leaving, probably by the time you hung up the phone. If it was your husband, what purpose would all this have served? Acting like some teenage vandal, but not even trying to confront you? He'd know a stunt like that would only make you more cautious. It might even make you run for the second time and risk him losing you again. I don't know the man, Annie, but my gut tells me he's smarter than that."

"Oh . . ." He was right. But news she would have thought would be welcome was no consolation. Annie's eyes welled with tears yet again. She hadn't known she could cry this much. She knuckled the moisture away, impatient with her weakness. "You're right. I can't think how I didn't see it. But, Jed . . . I don't know which is worse. Thinking that it was Tom or thinking that someone here — someone in Burnsville — wants to hurt me."

"I understand." He reached out for her, stroked a stray lock of hair off her forehead. She felt no sensation of fear at his touch — hadn't, she realized, even last night.

"We don't know that they're trying to hurt you," Jed said softly, pulling his hand reluctantly away from her hair. "Only to scare you."

Annie shook her head a little, unconvinced. "There were two of them," she said suddenly.

"Two? Why do you say that?"

"I don't know. It just came to me. And it feels right." Annie closed her eyes and concentrated. The fear, the footsteps, the other sounds of the night . . . She probed the memories she hadn't consciously stored. "The car," she said triumphantly. "The car was running while he — she — was on the porch. And it started moving the minute the door slammed. I remember hearing it start to roll on the gravel, right away. I don't think it would have started to move so fast if there hadn't been a driver, waiting to go."

Jed looked unconvinced. "Maybe. You said she. Do you think it could be a woman?"

"No. Not really. I was just being precise. I didn't see whoever it was, so I don't know. The steps were heavy, Jed. Loud, forceful. I can't imagine a woman walking like that. Or a woman throwing blood on some other woman's furniture. You're shaking your head."

"Yeah. I'd love to think you're right, but I'm not so sure that bizarre behavior is limited to one sex. It doesn't matter, though, at least for now. Finish that coffee, okay? The alarm people are coming at one, so we need to head back up to your house."

She blinked at him. "The alarm people?"

"You need something to protect you. A gun, for sure. Either a guard dog, too, or a good security system. And I want to call the police."

As usual, he was miles ahead of her, and she was fighting a rear-guard action. She tried to marshal her thoughts. "I'm not going to call the police, Jed. I'm not here under my own legal name, and I don't want to set down any information that can trace me, anywhere, in any record. It's unlikely they can do much, anyway. I can't get a dog, either. I don't even know where I'll be a month from now. I can barely take care of my own life, much less an animal's. And assuming I could learn to shoot, I'm not convinced I could ever fire at a human being. Even Tom. So having a gun would be useless."

"That's all crap, Annie."

"It's not, Jed. Could *you* kill someone? I remember that you told me that you were pretty nonviolent yourself, or words to that effect."

The look he aimed at her was level, challenging. "I don't have a husband that beat the shit out of me."

"And if you did, you'd shoot him?"

224

"It wouldn't be my first choice. But if I needed to, yes. In fact, my trigger finger's itchy, and I've never even met the bastard. Don't expect me to feel peaceful right now, Annie. Not after that story. And not after last night."

"All right, Jed. I can understand that." And she did. But there were other issues to be faced. Things that were important to her. Things she didn't want him to barrel over, no matter how logical it seemed. "I want to make my own decisions, Jed. That's how I got into trouble in the first place, letting someone else control my life for me. I've got enough problems without jumping straight from the frying pan into the fire."

She could feel the sudden tension in the big body that sat so close to hers and the cool blue eyes looked suddenly hot. "I'm not your Tom," he said.

"I didn't say you were, Jed. If I thought you were even vaguely similar, I wouldn't be sitting here. But that's not the point, as I just said."

"All right. I can respect that. So what are you going to do to protect yourself?"

"I'm not sure yet." She faced him squarely.

"Right. Which is why it became my decision. Someone has to face the facts, here. And the facts are that whether it's your Tom or someone else tossing blood through your windows, you may not be safe in that house alone. The risk is here now, not tomorrow, not next week. I'm not prepared to take that risk, not when I can do something about it. And if the couple of hundred bucks an alarm system costs me bugs your conscience, so be it."

"It's more than a couple of hundred."

"That's correct. More like a thousand. I make ten times that for one magazine article, Annie. Look at it as an investment in my own rest, not your safety, if you want. Because I'm sure as hell not going to be able to sleep nights worrying about you up there all alone, being raped or maimed or murdered."

"You're so damned stubborn."

"So are you. If you weren't, you'd look at this rationally, and you'd give in gracefully. A minute ago you were blaming yourself for not fighting back when your husband hurt you, Annie. Think about that, and ask yourself why you're not fighting back now."

"Oh." She shook her head, the black hair bouncing. "You're exasperating. And you're right, which is even worse. I know I should be grateful, but it just makes me angry."

"I don't need you grateful," he said. "I just need you safe."

"All right," she said. "I give up."

"Good. Maybe this is a good time to ask you something else, then. Annie . . . you're exhausted and still upset. Let me take you away for the day, once we get the few practicalities you'll let me help with handled. Just a drive, and lunch or dinner, in Asheville, maybe. Something easy. I know you don't like my being protective, but I think you could use a little break. And maybe the truth is that I could, too. Will you?"

It surprised her, how strong the pang of longing was.

A day with Jed. New sights. A chance to relax after the harrowing fear of last night. A chance to be normal, average, ordinary. Well, as ordinary as being with an extraordinary man could be. It sounded so good.

It sounded delicious.

And she could ask him to stop on the way so that she could check the mailbox she'd rented in Asheville, the practical side of her mind said virtuously, as though that were an excuse.

She shook her head a little at Jed, smiling ruefully. "I'd like to go. Thank you. But I think you've broken my pride."

"No," he said. "Your false pride, maybe."

"I wonder. When do you want to go? Tomorrow? That's fine. But safe or not, I'm going back to my house for now."

"Fine. I'm coming with you."

Annie shook her head. "I never imagined otherwise," she said.

Eight

The great writer and his floozy finally left and took that dirty mongrel with them.

Good riddance, Moira McTeague thought as the truck roared away up the drive.

The great writer. She always called him that, in her mind. Burnsville's only author. Its most famous son. The little bookstore on Main put his picture in the window every time one of his books came out. It said something about Burnsville, that Jed Harper was the best man it could find to celebrate. He couldn't even dress for the honor. The larger-than-life picture the bookstore always used showed him in worn and faded blue jeans no decent man would wear beyond his own back garden, and a grin so wide you'd think he had done something great.

Young Jed Harper. Some kind of hero. Moira snorted in derision as she scrubbed at the oak steps with oil soap, shifting the heavy bucket past one riser and then another with a thump. How hard could it be to write a good story if you had the time and the money to go roaming all over the world, amid filth and foreigners and who knew what else? Making a book about your

own home, about decent folks, about the hard-
ships that came to upstanding people, even
when they weren't wandering around looking
for them — now, *that* would have taken some
skill.

But Mr. High and Mighty Jed Harper didn't
want to write about Burnsville. Oh, no. Because
then he'd have to tell the world the truth about
himself. That the great writer's daddy had been a
nasty drunk. That his mama was half a drunk
herself, and a layabout, and she would have been
a slut, too, except that she was too afraid of her
husband's fists to stray. That the great writer
himself had been a scrawny, grimy boy with a
sharp mouth who had more than flirted with
trouble before snooty bleeding hearts like Alma
Honeycutt and Emmylou Thorn took him under
their wings. Where Jed Harper was only too
happy to go. He was a shrewd one, she had to
give him that.

The stairs were done. Moira stopped in the
powder room to take her blood pressure medi-
cine. It was a trial, poor health, when you had to
work. The great writer didn't care that her veins
throbbed or her heart pounded, not him. But
what couldn't be cured had to be endured.

The floors were next. More oil soap, diluted
into the bucket, scrubbed with the grain, and
then the old electric floor buffer for the polish
coat. The old way, the traditional way, not those
lazy plastic polishes. The floors would look
beautiful when Moira was finished. Like a pic-

ture in one of those highfalutin magazines. But it never occurred to the great Jed Harper that keeping his fancy floors dustless and polished took hours of work, hours of strain on Moira's aching knees and knuckles, hours of damp that Moira's arthritic joints could ill afford. All that wasted time and effort, when he could have a nice dark carpet like everyone else.

The jabbing, darting rhythm of mopping established, Moira's thoughts ran back to their familiar track. Fine wood floors. Those fancy little windows in the ceiling, skylights or whatever they called them. Rugs and masks and books from all over the world, ugly things most folks would have paid a pretty price to get rid of. What a laugh. White trash, the Harpers always were. Sure, young Jed Harper made something of himself. But blood told. No amount of fancy argument would ever persuade Moira different. Trailer trash was trailer trash, even when you put it in a palace. And good stock was good stock, no matter what befell it.

What did the likes of Jed Harper know about that? About families like hers, good, respectable families, English and Scots in their background, who'd come to these hills and struggled for generations to make an honest living? What did Jed Harper care about people like Moira herself, who'd done her duty as a woman only to see three pregnancies end in pain and mess and humiliation, only to be forced to watch women no better than they should be parade around with their babies? What did Jed Harper care about Moira? What had he cared about her husband, Arthur, who'd slaved his entire life only to end up as the town joke, the town laughingstock?

Moira bundled up the Navajo area rugs as she went, carried them to the back stoop to beat against the railing. Her footfalls sounded heavy in the empty house. Most of the workingwomen in town wore those running shoes today, but Moira didn't hold with them. She wore proper shoes, laced and sturdy, good for your bones and suitable to her work.

It had been years, but the townspeople still talked about Arthur, Moira knew. Small-town scandals didn't die quickly, especially not juicy ones like that. *Arthur McTeague. Carried on with Alma Honeycutt. Ran away with the church collection. Who'd have thought such a timid little rabbit could be a thief? Guess the scaredy-cat part of him came out in the end, though. Couldn't face the music, had to kill himself before the trial came.*

That's what they said, to this day. But they were wrong — oh, how they were wrong. They thought they knew what she felt, Jed Harper and little Meggie Thorn and the townspeople that treated her with such condescending tolerance. But they didn't.

Meantimes, though, working for the great writer had its advantages. Like the key to Alma Honeycutt's cottage, which Moira was going to get into, come hell or high water.

And like today's gift, the glimpse of that

Taylor woman. On the small back porch, Moira beat the dust out of a rug with her broom and laughed to herself.

Annie Taylor was perfect for Alma Honeycutt's cottage. She had the same stuck-up look that Alma did. Not that she had anything to be stuck up about. Skinny as a rail, she was, and a slut to boot. Moira hadn't been born yesterday. She could recognize the heavy-lidded look in the woman's eyes. The possessiveness of Jed Harper's hand on that scrawny shoulder, too. Whores like Alma and Annie Taylor knew how to get men. They spread their legs, and it was easy. Not like respectable women, who had to work for what they got.

Huh. The great writer was bold as brass, not even ashamed of having someone respectable walk in on them. But the slut was. There had been shame and confusion in her eyes. And before Moira finished with her, there would be fear as well. Annie Taylor would be cowering, and she'd hightail it out of that cottage so Moira could do what she needed to do. Alma Honeycutt and Annie Taylor. Two birds with one stone. *Waste not, want not,* Moira thought, and stomped off to clean the kitchen.

Huge and disheveled, the man hunkered over the tiny café table like Godzilla over the streets of a miniature city. The contrast with the Sunday-morning church crowd in the café couldn't have been greater. His weather-beaten skin was several shades darker than his crew cut or the blond stubble that crusted his cheeks. Meg could barely make out his face, which was cradled in his hands. He looked like a very large, old-fashioned tramp . . . or maybe not. His suede safari jacket had been expensive about a century ago, she decided, and the camera slung like an afterthought around his neck probably cost a fortune.

Donna was out again, and Meg was filling in. She really had to stop feeling so sorry for the girl. And Cindy looked awful; maybe she was coming down with the same virus Donna had. Meg walked toward the blond giant. "May I get you something?" she said, standing at his side.

"No. I just thought I'd come by and sit a spell. What the bloody hell do you think?" he growled.

Meg smiled down at him, amused. "I have absolutely no preconceptions," she said mildly.

That made him look up. One blond brow lifted, and bloodshot brown eyes met hers in a withering stare. "Coffee, woman," he said in a throttled whisper, returning his head to his hands. "Hot. Strong. Now. And keep your voice down."

Meg gathered up the restaurant's biggest mug and a whole carafe of coffee. The stranger's head was still propped in his splayed fingers, his face invisible again. She set the mug gently down on the table, then leaned over to tap, equally gently, at his shoulder. "When the stomach acid recedes a little, give me a call, and we'll get you some breakfast," she said. She got a only muffled groan in return.

Back near the entrance to the café, she bumped into Jed, who gave her a kiss on the cheek. "You look tired," she said.

"A little. Didn't get much sleep last night. I'll tell you about it some other time. I'll be fine. Can I order one of those lunch boxes you make, Meggie, on such short notice? Something nice?"

"Hmmm. Gonna tell me why?"

"Yeah. Later, maybe. Please?"

"Of course. Tell Carlos what you want." Meg scowled as she spied a quivering black nose at the door. "Harper, get that cur out of here."

"He's not a cur. Rooster is an animal with a pedigree."

"I don't care if he came over on the *Mayflower*. I don't care whether he *steered* the *Mayflower*. Tie him up outside, Jed. I've got the church volunteers' luncheon in less than two hours, and Donna is sick again, and there's a man who's either a drunk or a psychopath sitting over in the corner. I don't need the health department coming down on me, too."

"Oh, Jesus. Great timing," Jed said, half under his breath, sighting the hulking blond giant in the corner.

His book was stuck, there was a blood-tossing nutcase loose in Burnsville, and for the first time he had something like a date with Annie Taylor, which was either bliss or insanity, he wasn't quite sure which. And now here was

234

Sven Rasmussen, just in case things weren't complicated enough.

What the hell had happened to his peaceful, orderly life?

Ignoring Meg's protests, he gestured Rooster over, bent to tie the dog to the leg of the wrought-iron plant stand near the door. "Just one minute, Meggie, I promise, then I'll bring him right outside. And by the way, would you keep him for me until tomorrow morning? I'm driving to Asheville. Not sure when I'll be back."

Meg stuck her hands on her hips and glared in exasperation. He had to pull out his best half-sheepish, half-pleading, aw-shucks grin before she gave up.

"I'll be glad to watch him, you know that. But at my house, not here. I want him out of here in five minutes, Jed Harper, absolutely no more," she warned. "And if you're going to talk to that human hangover in the corner, I'd suggest you speak softly and carry a big roll of antacids. That is not a happy man."

"Let him take the consequences of his actions," Jed answered cheerfully. Meg watched as he strode over to the corner table. Tired or not, she could have sworn he was putting an extra bounce in his step. The cutlery on the tables nearby rattled with each exuberantly heavy footfall, and the leather bomber jacket he tossed onto an empty chair knocked it over with a resounding crash. Jed gave the blond man an almighty clap on the back.

"Sven Rasmussen. Well, look at that. Fancy meetin' you here," he boomed.

"Jesus *Christ*," the man named Sven growled. "Put a bloody lid on it, Harper."

"I'm glad to see you, too, pal." Jed dropped into a chair and grinned brilliantly at his friend. "Welcome to Burnsville. It's going to fix you right up. You can't stay at my house, I'm needin' my privacy these days, but I've got a million plans for us. Thought we'd start with a nice drive on the Blue Ridge Parkway. Great views, cool air, terrific winding roads with sickening hairpin turns over thousand-foot cliffs. Just the thing to clean the cobwebs out of your brain . . . and clean out most of the contents of your stomach, too."

"Fuck you, you bastard," Sven moaned, lifting his face to Jed's. "I never intended to stay at your bloody house. Who the hell wants to have you in their face around the friggin' clock? And stop yelling, for Christ's sake. Get me some aspirin."

"Hey Meg, friend of my youth, light of my life," Jed called, twisting in his chair. "Could I get a couple of aspirin for Mr. Cheerful here?"

Meg reached into the cubby next to the register, sorted through its contents, and tossed a small plastic bottle of painkillers toward them. Jed reached to catch it, graceful and sure.

"Glad to oblige," she said, propping her elbows on the counter. "And I'll be glad to get that lunch box you were talking about, too.

Once you get your dog out of my restaurant."

"Shrew," he grumbled, reaching over to swat her rear as he headed back for the door.

"Brat," she said, swatting him back. "Here's the key to the house; let Rooster in, and I'll pop over to walk him a little later. Meanwhile, do you think your poor friend is ready for breakfast?"

"Oh, I think so. I'll be back in a minute to say good-bye to him." Jed bent to untie the dog, looking over his shoulder to wink at her, his face bright with amusement. "In the meantime, go ask him what he wants, Meggie, by all means. Offer him something good and rich like eggs Benedict, and do it nice and loud."

Even in the middle of a sunny October Sunday, the back room at Frascati's was as dark as a cave. Waiters took orders *sotto voce,* busboys cleared tables so carefully that barely a glass clinked, patrons chatted softly in the deliberate gloom. Tom liked the civilized hush of the place and the hotel it was part of, the dark, paneled walls, the dim glow from the red-shaded sconces, the way the high backs of the leather-upholstered banquettes hid one table from the next. He liked the way it awed Jenni Stern, too. Even on the weekends, when most of its clientele fled the city for their country houses, it still took clout to reserve a table at Frascati's . . . a decent table, at least. Jenni appeared to be suitably impressed by the big, secluded booth, the way the obsequious waiter knew Tom's name, the folded bill that passed almost imperceptibly between Tom and the maitre'd.

Taking advantage of the dim light and the ample cover afforded by the booth's generous tablecloth, Tom slid his hand onto Jenni's thigh, keeping it there as he answered her questions about the latest movements in his portfolio. She wiggled when she felt his fingers tracing the lace tops of the stockings he liked her to wear, and she parted her thighs just a little even as she gave him an arch, warning glance.

She'd come through later, at the anonymous suite he'd rented at one of the city's residential hotels to avoid the issue of her goddamned roommates. So let her play coy now, Tom thought. It was no skin off his ass.

She was a hot one in bed, with a boundless appetite for sex and a total lack of inhibition that drove him wild. She liked dirty words and hard screwing and surprising him with sexual treats. Just last week she'd waved him toward the sofa, stepped up onto the coffee table, and given him a strip show lewder than anything he'd ever seen — and he'd been at plenty of bachelor parties where the action got pretty hot. He had a sudden memory of her gleaming body, her big tits bouncing free as she pulled off her red lace bra, her bare ass swinging and pumping, the neat little triangle of dark fur between her legs practically pushing into his face.

He couldn't get enough of her that night. He

hadn't gotten back to Park Avenue until almost three, an hour that inspired a sly wink from the doorman. He'd have to make sure his Christmas tips to the building staff were even bigger than usual. It was worth a few extra bucks to keep things smooth, with the kind of fucking he was getting. Hell, his marriage would have been a hell of a lot calmer if Annabel had been even half as eager to please. Tom thanked the fates once more for the fact that his wife hadn't returned. When he thought about his rage that first night, about how close he'd come to actually looking for her, he could hardly believe it. Jesus, he'd have missed the best fucking time of his life.

The best fucking time, very literally. The thought of it made him randy even now. He moved his hand off Jenni's leg, used it to guide her hand toward his crotch, then moved it back under her skirt. She didn't miss a beat, just rubbed the backs of her fingers lightly along the growing bulge in his khaki slacks. Jesus, it felt good. He pushed against her hand as the waiter appeared at their table. *Shit,* he thought. *Perfect timing.* He twitched free as he gave their order, asked for new drinks, replied impatiently that they didn't want bread.

"And what about Edsco?" Jenni asked him, looking at him with those big eyes. "Is the chairman of the board going to be dumped, like you told me?"

She was a pretty damned good conversationalist, especially for a broad who was still almost

239

a kid. She loved hearing about his stock picks, his buys, his sells, his dealings with clients. And he loved telling her. Reliving the highlights of his work week with Jenni as his rapt and glowing audience had become a necessity, a pleasure almost as addictive as the frantic screwing she practically begged him for thereafter.

In fact — encouraged by her wide eyes, her avid attention, her flattering memory for every detail he shared — he probably said too much. It was lucky that she didn't have a clue about how sensitive some of the crap he told her was. If she'd had a brain in her head or a dollar in her pocket, he could have gotten into a shitload of trouble. She didn't think that way, though. Chicks like her just wanted the glamour, the vicarious excitement, the taste of power.

Tom sensed a presence at the end of the booth, interrupting his thought. Goddamn waiter was a moron. Tom chose Frascati's because it was discreet, for God's sake. This fool better not expect a tip if he kept hovering around like a friggin' nanny. He twisted to glance over at the man, frowning.

Christ. His heart practically stopped, and the heat in his groin instantly disappeared. What the hell was McNaughten doing in town?

"Stretch," he managed, struggling to keep his voice smooth. Thank God for that stupid waiter; otherwise, Stretch would have caught them with Jenni's hand on his dick. This way, at least he could save the situation. He forced himself to smile, his thoughts racing almost as fast as his heart. "What keeps you in town? I would have thought you'd be with the family in Tuxedo, beautiful weekend like this."

"My granddaughter was baptized at St. James's today," Stretch said, his voice cool. "We're all gathering for a small luncheon at the hotel, so I stopped by to check the final arrangements."

"Congratulations. Stretch. Meet Jennifer Stern," Tom continued, trying to keep the conversation going. "Jenni, this is Stretch McNaughten. I'm sure you've heard of him, Jenni. Stretch is a legend on the Street. Stretch, Jenni's from Summerby, Smith and Delinsky. She's looking to be a broker. I'm telling her a little about the business."

"I'm pleased to meet you, Mr. McNaughten," Jenni chimed in perfectly, as though they'd rehearsed the exchange in advance. "Anyone who loves Wall Street as much as I do knows your history. The Sunny Breads deal is a classic of takeover history. And, of course, Finch McNaughten is always talked about as one of the best houses on the Street."

Tom blinked at the command she had of the old bastard's background. He must have told her about McNaughten's business coups, though he didn't remember doing it. If anything, maybe she was overdoing things. He felt a touch of irritation at the rapt way she was looking at the man. But that was the least of his problems, and at least she was smoothing over the awkward moment.

McNaughten wasn't pleased with him, he could certainly tell that.

Stretch nodded at Jenni and turned his attention back to Tom. "Thomas. How is your wife? Miller tells me that she's been away. An illness in the family, I believe?"

"That's right." As usual, the bastard seemed to know everything. "Her cousin, in Maine. Annabel and Bunny" — the name came out of nowhere — "are very close, and Annabel was anxious to go and lend a hand. I miss her, of course. And it's played merry hell with some of our social obligations. But we've always felt that family comes first."

That might have been laying it on too thick, Tom thought as the words left his mouth. But to his relief, Stretch didn't comment.

"Yes," the old man said. "I've always believed that, myself. Did you happen to ask Annabel about donating a quilt for the auction, Thomas?"

Fuck. With all that had happened over the past month, he'd totally forgotten McNaughten's request. An incredibly stupid mistake, he had to admit. He didn't need anything to tick the old bastard off, especially since Jim Perry, at SafeCo, was barely returning his calls.

"I did, Stretch," he improvised. "She was right in the middle of a project when she left, and she's not sure she can finish anything suitable in time, given that we're not sure when she'll be back. But I'll check with her again."

"Please. Dora is anxious to finalize the inventory so that the catalogue can be printed. And you know, of course, how generous the other staff have been. You let me know in a few days, won't you?"

"Sure will, Stretch. I'll follow up with her this weekend. If she can't contribute, we'll make another suitable donation, of course."

"Dora is quite taken with the idea of one of Annabel's quilts," Stretch said calmly, with the air of a man used to being obeyed. "And, of course, we'd like to see Annabel at the event as well, so she can be acknowledged."

With a frosty nod to Tom and an only slightly warmer one to Jenni, he strode away. As always, Tom thought as he watched the tweed-jacketed figure leave the restaurant, McNaughten looked like he had a poker up his ass. Tom sagged back against the banquette, relieved to see him finally gone.

Jenni turned to Tom, wide-eyed. "I didn't know your wife's cousin was still sick," she said. "Is it very bad?"

"No," Tom said, resenting the need to keep the story up. Why couldn't the little bitch just let it go? "Well, yeah, I guess so. A car accident."

"That's awful," Jenni said.

Despite the warm sympathy of the words, Tom could have sworn her eyes held a hint of mockery. And the mood of the lunch was spoiled, anyway. He tossed a sheaf of bills onto the white tablecloth and gestured to Jenni with a quick jerk of his head. "Let's go."

"But I haven't finished," she said.

"I don't give a damn," he snapped. "Let's go, I said."

The city was almost blindingly bright after the dimness of the restaurant. Tom strode off of the side street and up Madison Avenue, half oblivious to Jenni struggling to keep up at his side. Resentment consumed him, lengthening his strides, shortening his breath.

He worked his ass off to make a goddamned living. Wasn't that enough, without having to deal with all this aggravation? What the fuck did people want from him, anyway? He tightened his lips as the anger drummed in his chest. He wasn't even sure who was pissing him off the worst. Stretch, who had no right butting into his business? Jenni, with her ass-kissing eagerness? Or Annabel, who had put him into this position in the first place? What a loser she'd turned out to be. He should have left her in the gutter where he'd found her.

It was enough. Enough. And now he had to pull one of her goddamn quilts out of thin air or face the wrath of dowdy little Dora McNaughten, the power behind the throne.

He crossed Sixty-ninth Street against the light, without waiting to see if Jenni was with him. And then he came abreast of Pleasures.

Where one of Annabel's freaking quilts hung in the window.

He couldn't believe his eyes. He hadn't even thought about the shop, not for weeks. Maybe

244

this wasn't one of Annabel's rags after all. Christ knew, he was no expert. But he'd seen enough of her crap over the years to know more or less what they looked like, and if it fooled him, it would fool Stretch. He came to an abrupt halt near the shop's gleaming glass door.

"I've got an errand to do here," he told Jenni curtly.

"I can come —" she began.

"No. Look, just let me take care of this. Here." He could see rebellion, even resentment, in her eyes. He didn't give a good goddamn; he treated her right, and she could fucking well accommodate him for once. He pulled out his wallet, handed her four twenties. "Buy yourself something sexy somewhere and meet me back here in a half hour." Stubbornness battled with greed on her face. Greed won out, as he'd guessed it would. With a shake of her auburn mane, Jenni flounced off. Tom pushed the heavy door open and stepped inside.

Aside from the uniformed guard at the door, only a single attendant was visible in the colorful shop, a blond girl fiddling with some papers at the sales desk. Young, he diagnosed, and none too experienced. An idea began to form in his mind. He hoped the owner wasn't lurking in the back. What was her name? He searched his memory. Annabel had mentioned it at some point, he just hadn't paid attention. Falk? Felton? Something like that. The blond girl offered him help in a high, eager voice, but he smiled and declined. No use looking anxious. This should be just another ordinary transaction.

He circled the room, touching a glass vase here, a hooked rug there. After a reasonable time had passed, he paused at the front to reach into the show window for the corner of the quilt. Annabel Taylor, the label read simply. Bingo. He'd always insisted that she use her maiden name for her so-called art. It was bad enough that people in the firm knew about it, without clients finding out. The price handwritten on the back of the tag was insane, of course. What kind of fools paid over a grand for a fucking blanket? But he, Tom, would have paid double — even triple — and gotten every penny's worth from the purchase.

He could donate it to Dora's goddamned auction, he thought, grinning at the irony of it. And it could be the key to tracking pathetic little Annabel down. He might not want her back, but he certainly wanted a chance to give her what she deserved. It wasn't even as though he'd have to lose Jenni if Annabel returned. After this asinine little runaway stunt, she'd damn well be living by his rules. Although he was beginning to suspect that Jenni, for all the pleasure she gave him, could be a pain in the ass, too.

Tom brought his mind back to the task at hand. Now more than ever, it was important not to look anxious, or eager, or even especially focused on Annabel's work. He worked his way back through the rest of the shop's wares slowly, making sure the girl at the counter saw how widely he browsed.

Eventually he chose an absurdly overpriced serving platter, carried it to the sales desk, and asked the girl to wrap it for him. He could give it to Jenni, butter her up a little more. "Oh, and I'd like the piece in the window as well," he added. "The Annabel Taylor quilt."

The girl's eyes widened as she smiled. It would be the biggest single sale they'd made in days, and she, Courtney, had done it! She didn't need to admit to her boss how little work it had involved. Or how incredibly handsome the customer had been. Her hands trembled a little as she swathed the platter in tissue. "It's a beautiful quilt. All of her work is wonderful," she said, a little breathlessly, conscious of his eyes on her face. *God, he was handsome,* she thought again, *with those sexy brown eyes and that tough expression.*

"Yes. I have several of her works. They're marvelous things," he said. "In fact, I need to ask Ms. Taylor's permission to donate one of them to a charity auction my firm's putting on. Good publicity for her, you know, much as I hate to part with the piece. I'd spoken about it to Mrs. — Felker? Isn't that the owner's name?"

"Felter. Right," the girl agreed eagerly. "Elizabeth Felter."

"Of course. Well, Mrs. Felter already gave me the information, but Ms. Taylor seems to have moved since then, and there's no forwarding address. Could you check your files for me? I'd be very grateful — what is your name? Courtney? How lovely. I'm sure a charming young woman like yourself wouldn't mind helping out, would you?"

The girl hesitated, unsure of herself. Automatically, her fingers riffled through the Rolodex beside the register. Annabel Taylor. There was the card, with an old address crossed out and a new one written in. She thought for a moment, frantically. Could she really be sure her boss had already given out the information? Her training had been too hurried, she thought in confusion. She'd replaced a girl who just hadn't shown up one day. There hadn't been time for a thorough orientation, and Mrs. Felter was so busy the two of them barely saw each other.

She thought she remembered something about keeping the vendor information confidential. It didn't seem right, somehow, giving out an artist's address. But she didn't want to offend such a wealthy customer, and she sensed that this man wouldn't take kindly to the word no. What if Mrs. Felter got angry at her for alienating a big spender like this one? Besides, it was only a mailbox, she noticed. What harm could that do?

Caught in the dilemma, she didn't see Tom's eyes flick toward the Rolodex card. "It's in North Carolina, as I recall, isn't that right?" he prompted.

"Yes." The girl smiled in relief. If he knew

that already, his story must be true. "Box 5568, in Asheville," she said eagerly, and read off the mailing center name and zip code.

His breath quickened with triumph. *Got you, bitch,* he thought.

"Now, about the quilt. I'll have to have it taken down from the window and packed. Can we deliver it to you?" the salesgirl continued, as though she hadn't just given Tom the best gift of his life.

Tom paid for the purchase with his credit card, made arrangements for delivery of the quilt, accepted the gift bag in which the girl had nestled the platter. He was glad to see that she didn't seem to know of any connection between Thomas Mahoney and Annabel Taylor. That would have been sticky. But he could have handled it, Tom thought. He could handle just about anything.

Outside the shop, he turned his wrist to check his watch. Jenni should be back in five minutes or so. He couldn't wait to see her. Hopefully, she'd found something sexy in one of the fancy lingerie stores that dotted the avenue. If not, maybe he'd blow a little more money, pick something for her. Red, he thought. She looked fucking sexy in red. The wrath he'd felt earlier had vanished. Suddenly, he was in a very good mood.

Annie had put on her jeans and her pink cotton sweater. The clothes were a practical choice for an unseasonably warm, Indian summer day. They gave her pockets to put her key and money and lipstick in, and they let her wear comfortable shoes.

So why, when she heard the engine of Jed's truck rumble from down the hill, was she suddenly racing upstairs, tugging off the jeans, reaching for the vintage dress she'd brought from New York, searching her drawers for her single small handbag?

For the same reason she'd let Jed talk her into this trip to Asheville in the first place, she thought, beginning on the row of the little pearl buttons that ran the length of the dress.

Because telling him her story had freed something in her, completed a process that had started the day of his birthday party. For the first time with Jed Harper, she had nothing to hide.

Because she wanted to plumb a little of the mystery of this man who made her laugh, made her cry, made her furious, and made her feel so blazingly alive.

Because, she admitted silently to herself, Jed had reminded her how good it could feel to be a woman. How good it could feel to be desired by a man. How precious it could feel to desire a man back.

She couldn't hide it from herself. She did desire him, and powerfully so. She thought of him, missed him, dreamed of him. For the last twenty-four hours, he had barely been off of her mind, a sweet, teasing, powerfully sensual presence that countered the darkness and fear of the attack on her house.

And she wanted to savor the feeling a little, however foolish that might be.

The last stubborn button was finally fastened. Despite the worn spots on Alma Honeycutt's wavy mirror — and the echo of Tom's endless criticisms — she decided that she looked fine. The soft dusty roses of the dress, set off by the paler pink of the sweater she'd draped over her shoulders, brought out the blush in her cheeks, the faint rose of the lip gloss she'd put on earlier, and the darkness of her hair. Annie paused in front of the bureau, suddenly struck by the contrast. Last month she'd been standing in front of a mirror miles away, only half alive. And now, her hair was glossy again, her slender frame a few crucial pounds heavier, her face glowing with health.

She should have felt nervous, frightened, she knew. But even with the problem of Tom still unresolved, even with the thought of the vandalism still scaring her, she felt whole and peaceful and able to handle whatever came. Annie stood still for a moment, giving a quick blessing for her new life, however tenuous it was.

From beyond her window she heard the truck stop, the door slam, and Jed's quick, firm, decisive steps sound on her porch. There was no time for reflection now. And this wasn't a day for thought. As long as she was taking the risk of letting herself get closer to Jed Harper, she might as well enjoy it. Her mouth curled into a smile as she ran lightly down the stairs. She might as well have fun.

And fun it was. As the truck nosed its way along the deserted, sun-kissed roads, she found that his mood was as light as hers. He pulled over after an hour or so, and they ate a wonderful lunch of cold chicken and salad from Meg's café under the shade of a tree. Back in the truck again, they sang along with oldies and silly country songs, voices equally bad and equally loud. In between, Jed told her about the history of the small towns they drove through, gave her the names of the farms and factories they passed, helped her identify the birds that flew, arcing and graceful, over their heads.

She liked the knowledge he had of this land, the affection that warmed his voice, and most of all, his courtesy. He never lectured, never showed off, never interrupted her, never tried to control the conversation. What a pleasure it was not to have to worry about every small thing you said. Not to have to be on, or amusing, or clever. Not to have to struggle to keep up your end of a dialogue with someone whom, when you did, accused you of talking too much. The moments of silence, with Jed, felt as natural as speech.

As they drove, she glanced over at him, acutely aware of his large, masculine presence beside her. Like her, he'd felt some need to dress for the occasion. He wore the familiar jeans and boots, but instead of his usual work shirt he wore a black crewneck knit, some kind of thick silk. She glimpsed a tweed jacket tossed nonchalantly on the narrow space behind their seats. The homespun roughness and strong color of blue denim had always seemed perfect for him, but the simple sophistication of black suited him, too. It brought out the elegance of his body, the refined strength of his profile, the rich gleam of his hair.

His movements were elegant, too. He drove well, confidently, the strong hands light on the gear stick, the long, lean thighs tensing and untensing as he worked the gas and clutch and brake. For a single moment, as she watched the corded muscles of his forearm move, she could have sworn he noticed her glance. The blue eyes lingered curiously on her face for several long seconds. To her gratitude, he said nothing, just let the moment pass.

The open spaces of small town and field had just given way to the density of city when he stopped at a red light and looked over at her, his eyes — so vividly, electrically blue — unusually tentative. "We'll stop at that mailbox you told me about next. What do you want to do then, Annie? The city is worth a look, if you want. Or we could go to the Biltmore House. It's ridiculously grand and not a little pretentious, and it'll be full of the usual tourists. But you might like it, Annie. It's part of the history here, just like the little struggling towns. And it's magical, in its way."

She smiled back at him. "How did you know I was longing for something magical? I'd love to, Jed."

Annie couldn't remember, later, the business of entrance and payment at the grand old house, just the silly face Jed made as he waved her hand away from her bag. None of the mundane things registered, the people milling in the lobby, the signs for cafés and rest rooms, the drone of a tour guide, the Lucite barriers and velvet ropes, even the fact that the entrance fee was more than she would have spent on food for a week. It was as if there really *was* something magical about the place, some small, temporary spell that blurred the practical details into insubstantial shadows and left only the pleasure in high relief.

They wandered through the opulent rooms, library and study and winter garden, bedroom after bedroom after bedroom full of ornaments and paintings and fascinating furniture, gardens glowing with rare plants. Annie's artistic eye delighted in the rich play of color and pattern. Her hands itched to caress the stiff brocades, the delicate glassware, the smooth patina of the silver, the gorgeously delicate fronds of the orchids. And here, as in the truck, Jed was a wonderful companion.

He was aware of everything and everyone, and full of small bits of history. He had a magpie's mind, he had said, sardonically. And a hawk's eye, Annie had added silently. No wonder he was such a wonderful writer. He noticed the funny heraldic emblem on the flags on the parapet. The bald baby cocooned in a snuggli on her mother's back, watching him, sleepy and goggle-eyed. The elderly guard standing in the corner of the library. He asked perfect strangers questions, and two minutes later they were chatting to him like they were long-lost cousins. Yet he seemed to know by instinct when just to walk beside her, in silence, as she took things in. He got her jokes, grasped her thoughts so clearly. And she was constantly aware of his solicitude. Always he took care of her, just as he had at his party. Keeping her close by his side. Buying her a cookie at one of the courtyard cafés even before she realized she was hungry. Making sure her feet were secure on the narrow stairs in the servant's quarters.

After an hour or so, they turned, in silent agreement, toward the relative solitude of one of the terrazzo balconies. As wide as an ordinary room, it was dotted with rattan sofas and jardinieres. Elbows propped on the parapet, they gazed out onto the acres of sun-dappled farm and woodland beyond the great mansion.

"I'm glad we came," Annie said. She felt acutely conscious of his arm brushing hers, his clean masculine scent. The awareness made her feel a bit shy. "Glad you brought me."

"I'm glad, too. And happy that you liked it."

"I did. All of that color and texture are a treat after a month spent in my plain little house.

Though it all reminds me, too, how much work it is to be rich."

He looked down at her. She could sense his curiosity, and sense him reining it in. "It felt like work?"

"Yes. Not the money, I suppose. Just the way we used it, Tom used it. As a kind of . . . weapon. To prove a social point, to keep up with the people he worked with. What we bought, what we wore, where we went — it was all scrutinized. And the funny thing is that we weren't even very wealthy by this standard. We were . . . comfortable, people like us called it. As though you needed foreign cars, and fancy clubs, and eight-room apartments with doormen to be comfortable."

He looked down at her. "You look unhappy, talking about it. My damn nosiness again. I shouldn't have asked."

"It's all right, Jed." She touched his arm as lightly as he'd touched hers earlier. Even so, she could feel the warm, strong muscle beneath the tight silky weave of his shirt. "Really. I don't mind. And I'm not unhappy. It's just . . . they're complicated memories. Bittersweet. Not for a wonderful day like this."

"I understand. Should we head for town, like we came to do?"

She glanced up at him, a smile in her eyes. Suddenly she felt free and playful. "Is that what we came to do?" she asked.

His white teeth gleamed against the tan of his

skin when he laughed. "Hell, no. Good point. What, then, milady?"

"Food," Annie said firmly. "I know it's barely time for dinner, and I know I had a gigantic picnic *and* a cookie a little while ago. But I'm ravenous."

Eyes dancing, he made a sketchy bow of acquiescence. "Your wish is my command. I know just the place, if you can wait for twenty minutes or so. Thirty, if you want to stop at that mailbox."

"You've got thirty minutes exactly, no more. Hurry."

They strode off to the car park, laughing. But they were silent in the truck, a companionable quiet they both let alone. Annie slid her shoes off her tired feet and let her head fall back against the high back of the seat. She gathered three pieces of junk mail from her rented mailbox, barely registering the fact that there had been no check from Pleasures. She felt pleasantly tired, dreamy, replete — happy to let Jed choose and navigate, content to muse on the sights and sounds of the day. *Cinderella near the end of the ball,* she thought, smiling to herself. But the spell would last for a few more hours yet.

She came back to earth as Jed pulled up at the immense doorway of a huge stone building. The Grove Park Inn, its sign said. The opulence of the awning, the bustle of the porters, and the line of Mercedes and BMWs waiting at the curb overwhelmed her a little. She glanced up at him only to find his gaze already on her face. Those blue, blue eyes, she thought in confusion . . . half the eyes of a mischievous boy, half the eyes of a compelling, dangerously attractive man.

"I'm damned if I'll eat fast food just to salvage that pride, Annie," he said.

She shook her head at him, but she was too hungry — and the scene before her was too intriguing — to argue the point yet again. Instead, she turned her attention to the lobby of the inn. It was huge but beautiful, with everything from the high ceiling to the vast stone fireplaces — with stones, here and there, carved with sayings from the inn's famous writer guests — perfectly scaled. The light from glass-and-metal lanterns was warm, the furniture welcoming and well made in the solid, rectilinear Arts and Crafts style. Accents of polished leather and hammered copper shone softly against wood and stone, and the bustle of arrivals and departures was muted in the high-ceilinged space.

Jed guided Annie through the busy room to a broad, flagstone porch set with a series of large, white-draped tables. Beyond the sturdy columns that supported the roof lay the grounds of the hotel and, beyond them, what seemed like an endless vista of autumn-hued hills. The sun was just beginning to set, turning the cloud tops pink. Annie caught her breath at the colors, the way the rosy light flooded the endless blanket of trees. "It's gorgeous, Jed."

"I thought you'd like it. The inn was built in 1915 or thereabouts, I think. The story goes that those big fireplace stones were hand-carried up the mountain, though it might not be true. The hotel runs a good convention business now, but they've managed not to screw up the place's charm."

A maitre'd seated them at a table right at the edge of the terrace. Annie thought she saw a folded bill change hands, but she was enjoying herself too much to feel guilty about how much money Jed was spending on what was supposed to be a simple day out. Jed ordered them both wine and then waved at her menu, a folder just as overscaled as the rest of the place. "Let me warn you, princess. If you worry for a single damn minute about the prices," he said, "you'll end up wearing your drink."

She made a face at him, taking in the way the silly threat made his eyes dance with light and his perfectly shaped mouth curl with amusement. "I'll order the most expensive dish here. And the most expensive appetizer, and the most expensive dessert," she promised lightly.

When she'd chosen — and it wasn't easy, selecting among so many mouthwatering enticements after weeks of eating the simplest of fare — she leaned back in her chair. "So. You asked about me. But you're the wealthy one," she said.

He nodded. His hair shone in the deepening light, which threw half of his face into shadow. He leaned back in his chair, turned his wineglass with the lazy ease so characteristic of his every gesture.

"I guess so," he said to her. "Still seems odd, though. If you'd told my pappy his kid would make a fortune running around the world and writing about it, he'd have told you you were crazier than a coot. And spit some chewing tobacco on your shoes to punctuate the thought, probably."

"I gathered you didn't come from money."

"Jesus, no. My family was dirt poor. White trash poor, you could say. Three, four generations of folks who never quite made ends meet. And who wasted whatever money they did have distracting themselves with booze and bets and honky-tonks."

"That's sad, Jed."

"It is," he said. His expression was unreadable to Annie, bleak and a little distant for the first time that day. "The tragedy of the mountains. Life here is just too hard, sometimes. There are folks that draw strength from it. Meg, she's one. And Alma Honeycutt, actually. You'd like her. But some people . . . it just twists the heart out of them. They never quite have a chance."

"But you love this place. This land."

"Do I?" He shrugged, paused as the waiter delivered their appetizers. "I guess so. But it's love hard won, to say the least. For most of my life, I hated my town, and my house, and my folks above all. Sounds ugly, but it's the honest truth. I hated them, and I was afraid of them, and I looked up at that damn moon and prayed with everything I had not to grow up like them. And I left for the first time, when I was seventeen, to change my life as much as I could. To make sure I never would be like them, or live like them, or think like them."

"Where did you go?"

"University of North Carolina. Got myself a scholarship, mostly thanks to Alma's intervention. Chapel Hill was a damn sight better than Burnsville, but I wasn't the college kind. Too restless, probably. And kids my own age talked about their cars, their high schools, their respectable parents. What was I supposed to say? That my daddy could put away shots or trap skunk faster than anyone west of Winston-Salem? That my mama barely knew how to turn on the stove? Besides, there was always some crisis at home. My mama would call, seemed like almost every week. She was sick. She was out of money. Or my daddy was drunk, or in jail. Or the porch had collapsed or the truck had broken down. . . . I'd go home, fix whatever needed fixing, but after a while, I finally had to face the fact that I could never do enough. Not all that different from your situation, in a way. I finished up the year and headed north. Sent my folks an envelope of money — every extra dime I'd earned from waiting tables — but I didn't tell them where I was going."

"Which was . . ."

"Manhattan."

Annie shook her head, intrigued. "I'd never have pictured you in New York."

"I didn't take to it much. But I waited some more tables, and then I got a job at the *Times*. Figured out that people got paid for bumming around and writing. Met Dana, my agent. That was the beginning."

"And then you wrote the South America book that you don't even like anymore. And your parents?"

He shook his head, his face bleak. "They're gone, now, been gone for ten years. My pa died of cirrhosis, my mother of uterine cancer. I'd gotten back in touch with them by then, but she never would go to a doctor — hid it from me and everyone else until it was way too late. What a waste. Ethan did his best, but by the time she went to see him, the only thing he could really do was give her morphine for the pain. A waste, Annie, such a waste."

"I'm sorry, Jed. It's painful."

"Yeah." He sipped from his wineglass, cocked an eyebrow at her. "Some special occasion. Seems to me I'm going on and on, and not very cheerfully, to say the least. Look at you, you're almost finished with your food. But for what it's worth, that's my life, lady. No family, no solid job, no commitments. The story of the proverbial rolling stone."

"No. You have gathered some moss, Jed. Your house. Rooster. Your friends. Whether you like it or not, you do come home."

"Well, it's where my roots are. Those memories of my parents, they're part of my roots, too. I don't enjoy them, but I don't want to forget them, either. I can't afford to. Even the bad things — the disgust, the anger — are part of the fire in my belly. Part of what drives me to travel. Part of what drives me to write. Like I told you last week, I'm no stranger to shame."

She shook her head at him. "It's not deserved, in your case. I chose Tom, Jed, and I was an adult — chronologically, at least — when I did it. You're not responsible for who your parents were or where you started. Beyond that, I think you should be proud. All of your choices — they've been good ones."

"Have they?" he asked. "Have I even made choices, where my personal life's concerned? Or have I just run away from them? I'm not sure right now." He grimaced. "The only thing I'm sure of is that it's foolish to talk like this here, in this gorgeous place, with a beautiful and fascinating woman sitting lookin' into my eyes."

It was odd to see him struggling with himself, this man who usually seemed so easy, so confident. This new perspective on the raw, vulnerable boy she'd glimpsed in Alma's album moved her. She felt honored by it, as well. Jed Harper didn't share confidences like this often, she'd have bet on that.

One of his hands was resting on the table, strong and honey-brown against the white cloth that now bled crimson with sunset light.

"Pretend I'm not doing this," she said. It was meant to be playful, but it came out breathless. She was embarrassed at her emotion, but not enough to stop. She reached her hand across the snowy cloth and put it on top of his, sliding her fingers between his fingers, then just holding on.

He said nothing, but the grim expression melted into something else, something she couldn't define. After a long moment, he turned his palm upward so that it was clasped against hers, with the hollows of their hands together. Then he leaned down to kiss the inside of her wrist, letting his warm mouth linger on that cool, sensitive skin.

Her body shook a little when his lips touched her. It was as electrifying as it was unexpected, the desire that hit her, like a sudden crack of lightning on a still, velvety night.

She'd wanted to comfort him, she thought in confusion. But his touch — their touch — wasn't soothing. And suddenly it wasn't his need she was conscious of, but her own.

The waiter reappeared with their check. Annie didn't care who saw them touching, but she pulled her hand gently away. Jed let it go with a glancing look and obvious reluctance.

When the business of payment was over, he rose and helped her out of her chair. He touched her elbow, steering her back toward the lobby. Instinctively, without thought, she took his arm and walked him in the other direction, to the place where the tables ended and the broad terrace met the bulk of the main building. The sun had finally dipped below the tree line, and the unlit corner was velvety with darkness. The murmurs of the other diners twenty feet beyond, the clinking of glassware and cutlery, seemed as far away as the moon.

Jed was close beside her. Masculine and irresistible and essential. She stopped, turned, put her arms around him, lifted her face to his.

He paused for a moment, as though he was waiting for her to change her mind. Then he leaned to kiss her. His mouth was warm, the taste of him tangy with the good flavors of the food and wine. His lips searched her mouth, her chin, her jaw as though he were memorizing her by touch. She had never been kissed like this, so searchingly, so completely, with such a perfect balance between tenderness and passion. It was urgent, his kiss, but there was no greed in it, and no violence. His hunger spawned a hunger of her own. She had never been so fearless. She was afraid of nothing, except that he would stop.

Feeling had replaced thought, need had overwhelmed caution. She angled her head to meet the kiss more deeply, opened her mouth hungrily against his. Her arms slipped upward, clasped his neck; her fingers cupped the back of his head, tangled in the thick, silky hair. He made a quick, low growl in his throat before pulling her against him harder, until her breasts pressed against his chest and one leg slid between his blue-jeaned thighs. They swayed together. Annie felt as though they were floating, barely anchored to earth.

Time didn't exist, or manners, or anyone else in the world. Nothing but this man and the desire she felt for him. The desire they felt for each other. It was Jed who broke the embrace, lifting his mouth from hers, guiding her head until it was cradled against his shoulder. She could feel him take a long, steadying breath. She leaned against his body for a moment, breathless herself. She could feel his heart pounding, its racing beat rivaling hers. Her body trembled a little. From weakness, she thought dazedly, or maybe just from need.

"Let's go home," he said against her hair. "Now. To bed. Jesus, I need you."

All she could do was nod.

Nine

They drove home in silence. The world seemed to shrink down to the warm, dim cab of the truck. The dark, empty roads passed by them in a flash. Annie nestled next to Jed, his arm around her shoulder, her hand on his thigh. The dreaminess she'd felt earlier had returned, only this time it was a sensual dreaming. It was as though her mind — all her worries, all her fears, all her need for limits and caution, all of her insecurities — had gone to sleep, leaving only languor and delicious anticipation in her body and a sense of inevitability in her heart.

It was needless — foolish — to pretend anymore. She had been falling in love with Jed Harper for weeks. Since the night they'd danced in the shadows of his porch, maybe. Since she'd sat across from him in his firelit living room. Or maybe right from the start, since that first day when she'd stood warily in the woods and watched his hands move so swiftly over his dulcimer, listened to the sweet, haunting sound.

And now? Now she had fallen so far she had come to rest on solid ground. She loved him; it was that simple, that final. Infuriating and exciting, elusive and solid, he was as necessary to her as food, as drink. The problems of the past, the uncertainty of the future made no difference.

She wasn't even sure what he felt was love, and she sensed that speaking the words would trouble him, even if it was. Somehow, oddly, she didn't care. He wanted her. Little else mattered. Not the fact that she had her own tangled life to work out. Not the fact that Jed would be gone again, and probably soon. She knew, by now, that she could survive — even thrive — on her own. That she would never go back to Tom, no matter what happened. The knowledge gave her power, gave her freedom . . . the freedom to love Jed Harper, come what may.

The drive seemed to take only a moment. Jed had left a light on in his house. The warm, yellow glow beckoned them in from the cool night. In the hallway, a small parchment-shaded lamp shone golden on the wood floor, making deep shadows in the corners. The air inside was cool, fragrant with the lingering scent of wood smoke and lemon oil. The house was so still, so silent, she could hear an owl call outside. "Rooster?" she asked.

That made him smile. "At Meg's. Forget him," he ordered gently, gathering her into his arms.

His mouth searched hers, nipped gently at her lips, licked her jaw. They tasted each other, by turns playful and voracious. It was as good as their first kiss, she thought, dazed by the pleasure of it. Or better, because there would be no interruption here. She reached up to pull his head even more closely against hers and arched her body against his. She murmured softly, deep in her throat, when his hands slid down to cup her hips.

Without speaking, they pulled apart, turned arm in arm toward the stairs. Up in the big master bedroom, another small lamp shone, illuminating glowing oak dressers and a king-sized bed. Jed paused in the doorway, surprising her.

In the dim, gentle light, his face looked set and troubled. "Annie . . ."

His eyes searched her face. He shrugged restlessly and stopped, then began again. "I should have said this before. I want you, Annie. God, I want you. It would half kill me to bring you home now. But I'm not going to lie. You have to know . . . I'm leaving soon, just after New Year's. A long trip, and not the last of them. No matter what happens between us . . . I'm just not going to be here."

"You're a good man, Jed." She stepped to hold him again, smiled a little at his puzzled look. "An honorable one. To tell me and to let me make my choice, knowing the facts," she said softly. "But I knew already. I never expected otherwise, not since I found out who you were. You can't write books like that at home. And even if you could, Jed, I have my own journeys to make. How could I ask for commitment? Just . . . make love to me now. While you're here."

When she lifted her face to his this time, he kissed her mouth possessively, like a lost prince reclaiming his rightful domain.

They held each other, swaying. Explored with their hands, their mouths, their eyes. Celebrated with their eyes and their voices. They gave and they took from each other, and it felt to Annie like a dance, with two partners perfectly, impossibly attuned. There was no leader, no follower, just their mutual need.

Hungry for the touch of skin against skin, she reached for the first of her tiny pearl buttons, but he brushed her hand gently away.

"Let me," he said against her hair. These were the hands that played the thready strings of the dulcimer so gently, she remembered, smiling. His strong fingers worked the tiny pearl orbs easily, one after the next. He made a quick sound of pleasure as he slid the dress from her shoulders, a sound more eloquent than any compliment she'd ever received.

She hadn't worn a bra underneath the loose, soft dress. His hands were the color of honey against her ivory shoulders; they seemed to heat her skin as they moved to touch her collarbones, cup her breasts, stroke the pink nipples that tensed under his touch. She swung her head in helpless pleasure, and the languid ache turned urgent within her.

Slipping off her panty hose, she twisted once, let the dress fall to her ankles, stepped away from the pool of rosy fabric. Self-consciously, she reached for him again.

"Let me look," he said softly. His hand traced her small, high breasts, her narrow waist, the gentle curve of her belly and hip. Brushed the tangle of black curls between her legs so lightly that the caress was over before the jolt of pleasure fully hit.

"My God," he said, "you're perfect. Like you were made just for me."

She believed him, somehow. And for the first time in her life, she believed in herself, trusted the tender prettiness of her own body. Trusted its responsiveness, of which she could have no lingering doubt, not when she felt half crazy with need. He bent to kiss her breasts, and she held his head tightly against her, wanting him to hurry, wanting him never to stop.

Breaking away, moving more quickly now but as gracefully as always, he pulled down the bed's coverlet, guided her onto the cool sheets. He kept his eyes on hers as he pulled off his sweater, bent his head to unfasten his belt, shrugged off his jeans.

She drew in a breath of delight at the sight of him. Lean and strong, his rangy body as elegant naked as it was clothed and yet compellingly male, he was a classical statue come to life. Her body ached to feel that silky, honey-colored skin against hers, feel the rough kiss of the hair on his arms and legs, feel the weight and strength of him claim her. "Jed," she breathed, holding out her arms.

"Annie." His voice was as breathless as hers. But she could hear the familiar current of laughter in it, too, and it warmed her heart. "I feel like a teenager. I just want to consume you. But . . . I don't want to scare you."

"You won't. You couldn't." It was the truth. "Hurry now," she said, holding his eyes with hers. "You can be gentle later."

Suddenly they were moving together, fitting together. When he entered her, she arched against him in delight, in perfect fulfillment. They moved against each other, their rhythms raced, settled, crested. Arms tight around her, he turned onto his back, pulled her on top of him. For one fleeting moment, shyness stilled her, but then she looked down at him — the blue eyes vivid with desire, the handsome face showing nothing but wonder and heat — and she knew there was no room for shyness here, no room for "her" or for "him," room only for pleasure and union. She braced her palms against his chest, feeling the small male nipples harden against them, and anchored her knees on either side of those narrow hips. Arching her back in delight, she moved in and around and against him, watching his face, feeling her pleasure begin to peak, watching the urgency in his eyes grow until it seemed to consume them both. "Jed," she breathed, "now." His hands tightened on her breasts, and he moaned sharply, tensing every muscle as the climax hit him. Feeling his release, Annie surrendered, too, to a wave of sensation so overwhelming it took her breath — and her thought, and her reason — entirely away.

They lay facing each other, finally sated. He pulled the coverlet around them and reached a lazy hand to push the soft tangle of hair from her face. She smiled at him, deliciously sleepy.

"Do you remember fairy tales?" he asked, running a finger over her lips. She kissed it before it slid away to trace her jaw, her collarbones. "You look like Briar Rose. White skin, blue black hair, rosy lips. Beautiful."

"I'm glad I'm not a fairy tale princess; good mattresses and down comforters are so wonderful," she said drowsily. "But . . . I think I finally know exactly what happened when the prince kissed Sleeping Beauty awake." She heard him laugh in his throat, and then she heard nothing at all.

She fell asleep so suddenly, like a child. So close to his on the pillow, her sleeping face looked innocent and peaceful. Lovemaking had flushed her cheeks; his kisses had ripened her mouth, made her lips rosy and full. Her black hair, glossy and wild, streamed over the pillowcases, and the arm she'd curled around his chest was heartbreakingly delicate. *Briar Rose,* he thought again. *Sleeping Beauty.* Her body was so lovely, and her face. But beyond that, even, she had some kind of radiance he didn't even understand, a beauty that came all the way from within, from some secret source of tenderness and delicacy and femininity. Jed reached to brush the lightest of kisses on her forehead, then gently disentangled himself from Annie and the bedclothes. She made a soft, mewing sound of protest but didn't wake.

Taking care to move quietly, he turned off the light and padded downstairs to lock up the house. It seemed oddly quiet, almost eerie, without Rooster's presence. Back in the bedroom, he lowered himself into the Mission armchair near the window. His body felt relaxed and pleasantly tired, but his mind was electrically awake. The light from the three-quarters moon touched the bedroom with a silvery glow, highlighting the gleam of Annie's hair and the pale shapes of her arm and shoulder. Jed took a deliberate sip of the water he'd brought upstairs with him and stared broodingly at the bed.

He had gotten what he wanted. And unlike most things he'd wanted in his life, it was even better than he'd dreamed.

There were no words for it, only silly old clichés that just happened, in this case, to be true. She was fire and ice. Delicacy and strength. Woman and girl. Her own separate being, and his.

He had enjoyed good sex before. Often. But he had never felt like this, as though the lovemaking were something he and his woman were inventing on the spot, as though they were moving and thinking in perfect accord, as though every sensation was brand-new. He had never looked forward to the morning after or felt his brain crackle with all the things he wanted to tell her, show her, do with her. He'd never felt so intense, but he'd never felt so easy about it, either. This was what things between men and women must have been like in the Garden of Eden, he thought, before millions of complications had come along to screw things up.

And he had two months to savor it.

Not so long ago, that would have seemed like eternity.

But no longer. Now it was precious, a tiny window of time. Two months to make love to Annie Taylor, to talk to Annie Taylor, and probably to fight with Annie Taylor; two months to explore Annie Taylor to his heart's content before he headed out of town and got back to his real life. But somehow the knowledge wasn't enough to satisfy him. He sipped his water and watched Annie dream and felt the sharp, metallic foretaste of loss.

Annie woke late, to the dazzle of sun from the window. The expanse of bed beside her was empty, but the now-familiar blue robe was draped on the opposite pillow.

Down in the kitchen, coffee bubbled aromatically in the coffeemaker. Jed was stretched out amid the cushions of the window seat, newspaper in hand. He didn't seem to hear her barefoot approach as he paged intently through the newsprint, eyes lighting on something of interest here and there. He was wearing jeans — this pair even more worn than usual, she noted — and apparently nothing else. The sight of his smooth brown chest brought back memories of the night before: the feeling of her breasts against his muscle, the taste of his nipples under her tongue. He looked up suddenly, and his face shone with joy at the sight of her.

It flustered her, the pleasure she saw, the pleasure she felt.

"I feel shy," she admitted as she stepped onto the rough tile floor. "Do you?"

"Hell, no," he answered, dropping the paper and holding out his arms. "Come here."

Annie went. She was lowering herself onto the edge of the window seat beside him when he pulled her onto his lap. Laughing, she let herself be settled on his thighs, let her mouth be claimed by his.

"Mm. Toothpaste," he murmured against her cheek. "A famous aphrodisiac."

"I borrowed your toothbrush. And your comb."

"Anything you want. *Mi casa es su casa,*" Jed said and kissed her again. A longer kiss this time, deliberate, exploratory. When she pulled her face away, she could see that the look in his eyes was the one that had grown so familiar to her already, that stubborn, wild, mischievous look that always signaled that Jed Harper wanted something. Before, it had usually made her mad. Now, sitting on his lap with the big blue robe gaping open, her body still blissfully tender from last night's love-making, it stirred something urgent and primal deep within her.

"We're acting like teenagers," she murmured.

"You complainin'?"

"Mmmm," she said and shivered a little with pleasure. "No, I don't think so."

Supple and catlike as always, he bent to kiss her neck, then her collarbone, then the upper curve of one breast. His mouth was so warm, his touch so sure — gentle but strong, sensitive but confident. His hand slid under the hem of the robe, stroking her thigh. Instinctively, driven by no conscious message from her mind, her back arched to press her breast against his mouth, her legs opened just a little to his caressing hand. His warm lips tugged at her nipple at the same moment his fingers grazed her inner thigh. She made a little sound, half gasp, half laugh of pleasure.

"Still feelin' shy?" he asked, his voice muffled against her breast.

"Hell, no," she said, and she pulled his head upward so she could kiss his mouth again.

For a poky little dot with barely enough people to be called a town, in the middle of some bumps barely tall enough to qualify as mountains, Sven Rasmussen thought later that afternoon, Burnsville wasn't half bad.

There was the fact that it was totally different

from his apartment in Manhattan, which had been depressing the living hell out of him lately. The place was full of crap Ellie had never bothered to clean out — unlike his bank account, which she'd cleaned out quite efficiently. Typical Ellie. Why the hell he'd decided to marry a duplicitous, gold-digging, anorexic model in the first place, he'd never quite figured out; he only knew he wasn't going to make the same error twice. He also knew he needed to get rid of her shit and move on with his life, but for some reason he couldn't seem to muster the energy to actually do it. Night after night, he'd found himself giving it a try, then heading out to a bar instead. It was funny how just being in a new place tamed the demons. He'd gone more than twenty-four hours without once craving a drink, although that might have been the memory of yesterday morning's lethal hangover rather than the influence of clean country life.

Then there was Wray House, the bed-and-breakfast where he'd booked a room. With its antique furniture and secluded garden, it might have been a little — well, a lot — more elegant than his usual style, but it had a bed a big man could really stretch out in, a TV so that he could check in with CNN, and a pair of solicitous but delightfully self-effacing innkeepers.

There was the Cupboard Café, where he was having a belated lunch. It was the kind of restaurant Sven approved of: good food, good service, and no pretensions at all. Meg Whateverhernamewas was an added bonus. Solidly built and not even tall, she wasn't really his type — his former type, he amended hastily. But there was something appealing about her anyway.

And then, of course, there was the chance to drive his good old pal Jed Harper a little crazy. An opportunity, he thought as he stared across the busy restaurant in astonishment, that Harper was handing him on a platter.

Jed and a slender, black-haired woman had just pushed through the café's big front door and were standing, backs to him, talking with Meg Whoever at the cashier's desk. Harper had one arm draped around the woman's shoulder, a possessive gesture the likes of which Sven had never once seen his cool, self-contained friend make before. And from the way she leaned ever so slightly against him and kept her arm snaked around his waist, Sven guessed that the woman was as smitten as Jed was.

Well, well, well. He waved away a red-haired waitress with a pot of coffee in her hand and scrutinized the couple as they were seated. No wonder his pal Harper, that legendary loner, hadn't really wanted him in town. Didn't want the spectacle of his surrender to a woman witnessed, no doubt. Because old Jed had it bad, that was for sure.

Sven grinned to himself, threw a handful of bills down on the small table, and walked jauntily up to their table, where he installed himself — ignoring Jed's irritated glare and the woman's confused frown — in an empty chair.

"So, Harper," he said, leaning back and making it clear he was staying put awhile. "This must be the woman you weren't telling me about."

"Sven Rasmussen," Jed said, still glaring at him. "Meet Annie Taylor. Sven's the climber I told you about, Annie, here in town for a few days. I'm sure he's got a lot to do — he's probably got to run." Sven could have sworn his usually imperturbable friend was gritting his teeth.

"Oh, I've got time for another coffee," Sven said, ignoring him. "Pleased to meet you, Annie. Known Jed long?"

"Oh, long enough," Annie said. Seated between the two men, she tried to suppress a smile at the tension that crackled between them. Elegant Jed and big, battle-scarred Sven were like a tiger and a rhinoceros, she thought fancifully, fighting for dominance around a water hole. Despite his burly size and his rough-hewn bones, Sven Rasmussen looked as playfully troublesome as a spoiled child. As for Jed, she suspected he wasn't much liking the experience of finding their brand-new intimacy subjected to his friend's merciless gaze. She gave his knee a reassuring squeeze, then turned her attention back to Sven.

A few months before, she thought in passing, she might have felt intimidated by Sven's cool stare, his macho attitude, or even just his writing credits, which were almost as illustrious as Jed's. But no longer. These days, she was feeling like anyone's equal, and she might as well make that clear. Sven Rasmussen, she suspected, could be a bully when he chose.

"So. What's your verdict?" she asked him, her voice as mild and pleasant as if she were offering him afternoon tea.

Sven raised his eyebrows, feigning innocence.

"Your verdict. Your judgment. You're obviously scrutinizing me, checking me out," she said. "You might as well share your conclusions."

"Let's see," Sven said, unfazed. "Pretty but a little fragile."

Annie could almost feel Jed bristling at both the words and the challenging tone. He opened his mouth to speak, but she gave him a quick shake of her head. "Brawn isn't the only measure of endurance," she said to Sven, still smiling. "I suspect I could survive — have survived — things that would make you crumble. And I don't say that in ignorance. I've read *Upon K2*, so I know you can take a lot."

"Ah. A fan. What did you think of it?" he said, challenging her.

"It wasn't as good as your Everest book, reviews or no reviews," she answered coolly.

To her surprise, Sven Rasmussen threw back his head and laughed, a genuinely good-hearted, unguarded laugh that made her understand why Jed made this man his friend. "You're right. It was the toughest goddamn climb I ever made, but I always thought the book sucked. And I stand corrected," he said. "You're tougher than you look. Burnsville seems to have its share of feisty broads," he added, glancing across the room.

"I'm glad we meet with your approval," Annie said dryly, but then she grinned. "Welcome to Burnsville, Mr. Rasmussen."

"Thank you, Miss — sorry, Miz — Taylor," Sven said.

"Now that you two are bonded," Jed said, "Rasmussen, could you give me a break? You know perfectly well I'm gonna entertain you, and show you the sights, and do all that Southern hospitality jazz. But I got up this morning, and for the first time in forty years the only damn-fool thing I was wantin' to do was sit around in public and make a total ass of myself over a woman. Could you just go away and let me do it?"

Laughing, Sven went.

She hadn't called him in days, Goddamn it.
Well, Jed corrected himself, in one day. He'd said good-bye to her last night after some love-making that was even better than their first few times, if that was even possible. She'd told him that she didn't want to get too used to staying at his house, that she needed to stay independent, that she couldn't afford to feel as though the vandalism had scared her away from her own cottage. He'd wanted to protest but knew that if he pushed her too hard, he'd just drive her away.

So he'd given in, and she'd given him a sweet

kiss good-bye. He'd gone back to bed and felt lonely for her, and woken this morning feeling lonelier. And then she hadn't called all day. He'd ignored that fact during his writing hours, then had given in and called her at two. There was no answer then, or at three, or at five. By now, he'd gone from feeling mushy and sentimental to feeling pissed off, even though he knew that his irritation was mostly wounded male pride. And he couldn't even enjoy his anger when some protective part of him was worried that something was wrong.

He stood on her porch in the cool evening air, foot tapping, waiting for her to answer the bell. Rooster, by his side, had picked up some of his master's irritation. He sat alert, ears pricked, poised for action.

It took Annie forever to answer the door, Jed thought, adding that to his catalogue of grievances. When she did, she blinked at Jed as though he was a stranger.

"Oh," she said. "It's you," reaching up to give him what he judged to be a deflatingly absent-minded kiss.

Jed stared down at her. The fact that she was clearly alive and well made him tense with irritation. The vague tone with which she said "you" didn't help. She would have welcomed an encyclopedia salesman with as much enthusiasm, he thought unfairly.

"I thought you were dead," he said.

"Why?" She pivoted toward the living room,

as dreamy as if she hadn't so much as noticed his accusing tone. "Come on in," she continued over her shoulder, sounding as if she didn't give a damn about whether he came in, went home, or dropped dead. "That sunset is hurting my eyes."

The cottage — Annie's neat, feminine, much-cared-for cottage — looked neglected, even untidy. A book — one of his own books, Jed noticed — was lying facedown on the rug, near an abandoned teacup. A vase of dying flowers stood on the edge of the dining room table. The rest of the table's surface was littered with cloth. Pinned to the long, windowless wall was a huge square of fabric, eight or ten feet wide.

Jed stared at it, and his indignation faded.

It was a mosaic of gentle patterns, what seemed like a hundred prints and dots and checks in a variety of soft colors. The pieces of fabric had myriad sizes and configurations; their curves broke upon each other, he thought as he stared, a little like the rippling of waves. But somehow, underneath the apparent randomness, there was order and structure. The delicate yet strong hues and shapes worked together like a symphony, all in harmony, yet each piece as distinct as a note of music. Jed wasn't much on the visual arts, usually. The mask Annie had liked and his few hand-woven rugs, that was about it for him. But even a man with no appreciation for aesthetics couldn't look at this big fabric square and not feel something . . . some comfort, some longing, or some drift of memory he could barely name.

"Annie." He paused. "You said you . . . 'did some sewing,' I think is how you put it."

"Did I?" She rocked back and forth on her bare heels, looking at her work. Her voice was soft, her eyes dreamy. She was somewhere else, he could see that, somewhere inward, somewhere where only she and the big square of fabric on the wall existed.

And she, like the house, was a mess. Her hair was mussed. Her jeans were wrinkled, scattered with snippets of fuzz and thread. She looked tired and worn and utterly desirable to him as she stood there, barely aware that he existed.

"Well, I don't know what to call it. Them. Quilts, I guess," she said finally, as though his comment had traveled several light-years to reach her. "But I don't work to a pattern, and I don't use repeated blocks. They're not used like quilts, either. People buy them as hangings. As art."

"So I see." Jed said. The remnants of his frustration warred with fascination in his mind. This was Annie, his damned woman, who he'd thought of about twenty times today and who obviously hadn't thought about him once. But this was also a specialist, an expert, an artist, absorbed in her complex work. It intrigued him, as the work — the process — of all craftspeople did. And it humbled him, too. Despite her comments that day on the phone, he'd never given what she called her sewing a thought. It had never occurred to him, for one moment, that she might be an artist, someone with a real gift and a complex craft of her own. Someone not all that different, in that regard, from Jed himself.

"You mentioned that you sold them, I'm remembering. Where, again?"

"A shop called Pleasures. In Manhattan," Annie said, still focused on the big square of fabric. "They still have a piece unsold, last I knew, but Elizabeth is always willing to take more. I just have to figure out that bottom corner. I can't get it right. It's that piece of denim, I think. It's too heavy. . . . " She reached over, tugged the deep blue patch an infinitesimal distance to the left. "I'll have to work it out. I'd like to get this piece off. I'll need the money this winter."

"It must be hard, giving them up," he said, instead of offering her a loan as he'd have liked to do.

"It is, always. You get attached, so many hours of work, so much thought and planning and dreaming. They're like a child, in a way. It's always a pang to let them go." She paused, reached out one slender hand to caress a strip of eyelet.

"This one will be especially hard; it seems to have so many stories in it," she went on. "There's a scrap from one of Meg's kitchen towels, and some snippets from the baby clothes people gave Susie, and parts of an old tablecloth that was torn up in the cleaning basket, here. It'll feel hard, sending them away."

"I could buy it."

"Absolutely not."

"I knew you'd say that."

"You know me pretty well, Jed," she said. She blinked, as though just waking up, and looked at him, really looked at him, for the first time that day.

"No," he said honestly, gazing back. "But I do know you well enough to see that you want to be left to yourself."

"Just for another few hours or so," she said. "Jed . . . I'm sorry." Swiftly she moved to stand in front of him. Rested her hands on his chest. Searched his face. "I never called you. I didn't even think — the piece really came together in my mind, and I unplugged the phone so I wouldn't lose it. It's been so long since I've been able to work, I just got carried away."

"It's okay, darlin'," he said. Only a few minutes before he'd half wanted her to suffer. Now he just wanted to smooth the consternation off her face, remove the fear from her eyes. He smiled down at her. "It's okay."

"You're not angry?"

He reached to smooth a strand of black hair back off her forehead. "I was," he admitted. "A half hour ago, my big male ego was fit to be tied. I couldn't believe you weren't calling me every hour on the hour, making a fuss over me, telling me I was the best damn lover you'd ever had."

He made a quick, wry face at himself. "But I

can't blame you for something I do myself, Annie. I'm no different when a book really takes hold of me. I disappear for hours — hell, days, maybe weeks. I've just never experienced it from the other end. And now that I have, I understand why folks didn't much like it."

Annie looked up at him, warmed by his honesty. He was so fair, this man. And so unpredictable. And so sexy. The hunger she'd stifled all day while she assembled the big quilt stirred again within her. She stood on tiptoe, twisted her arms more closely around his neck, raised her face to his. The kiss started out gentle, a series of small, playful gestures, then held, deepened, intensified.

"Forget it, lady," he teased when he released her mouth. "Don't ignore me all day, then expect me to get all hot and bothered the minute you remember who I am."

She leaned against him, letting her breasts press softly against his chest, her knee nudge between his thigh. "Sure you won't change your mind?"

He'd have liked to. As uncertain as she was about her own sexual power, Annie could tell. His heart was pounding and his jaw was taut and his body was hard against hers. But Jed Harper didn't miss much, and he'd seen the way her eyes strayed toward the quilt even as she melted in his arms.

"I'm not going to compete with some damn scraps of fabric." The gentle, playful tone belied the tough words. She could see the pride in his eyes and the understanding, as well as the desire. He gave her one last kiss. "I'll have dinner with you," he said. "And make love to you. And sleep with you. Tonight, when you've had a few more hours to work this out of your system. In your house, if you want. How about that?"

"Definitely an offer I can't refuse."

"Good." Jed called Rooster back from his exploration of the kitchen and walked with Annie to the door, their arms intertwined. Annie blinked again in the last vivid rays of the sunset, waited on the porch while Jed herded Rooster back into the truck cab, started to wave good-bye.

The ignition was firing when a thought struck her. "Jed," she called. He twisted in the driver's seat, leaned back out the window, squinted back at her, just as he had on the day he'd come to clean her chimney.

"Jed . . . You are the best lover I ever had," she yelled over the sound of the engine.

She could see his eyes dance and hear his laughter as he turned and started down the hill.

It remained unseasonably balmy, as though the warmth inside her warded off the world's chill, Annie thought fancifully one day. But slowly, autumn leached the color from the mountains, stripping first one then the next oak, birch, or maple bare.

The stark shapes of the leafless trees stood in haunting contrast to the dense stands of evergreen that ringed the hills. The birds searched harder for food, squirrels cached away nuts and acorns against the long freeze. The sky seemed even more blazingly blue some days, now that it was set against a grayer landscape; at other times it seemed to pick up the subtle toning-down of the world, repainting itself in soft, dull, watercolor tints.

Just as Annie's artist's eye had gloried in the vivid blaze of summer, she observed the land around Burnsville with fascination, intrigued by the hundred tiny changes in the texture, color, and life rhythm around her. The approach of winter had a sadness to it and some discomfort. Some days were too chilly for her trench coat; she shopped with care in her beloved thrift shop for a warmer wool one. Alma Honeycutt's old radiators hissed like teakettles until Jed came up and helped her bleed them.

But Jed was warmth and love and revelation, a friend and a lover, a strong presence and yet not a dominating one. Just as they had that day in Asheville, they seemed to move naturally in tandem, sometimes touching and sometimes not, sometimes together and sometimes alone. It astonished her how natural the rhythm felt, how comfortable and easy an exciting man's companionship could seem.

Her world seemed to alternate like a patch-work pattern: her house and then his, the re-laxed companionship of time with friends and the blazing intensity of their time alone. Annie sensed them both treading a bit warily, trying not to trespass on each other's private space, like cats carefully circling around a shared new territory. It wasn't a bad feeling, she thought — and how odd and invigorating to be part of the process, rather than a passive recipient of someone else's decisions.

She avoided interrupting Jed's writing days and waved him cheerfully off for evenings out with Sven, who had intertwined himself in the life of the town with astonishing ease. Jed, similarly careful, asked her out on dates, made no plans without consulting her, even accepted ungrudgingly — though with that familiar wry smile — the nights she decided to spend alone.

In the meantime, there were a million things to experience, to enjoy, to try, to discover about him, and she savored them all. He fell asleep immediately and woke just as fast, to a mental alarm clock he could set at will. He slept motionlessly — the legacy, he said, of years on bunks, in hammocks, in sleeping bags — and yet, even asleep, he moved toward her warmth as naturally as if they had been sleeping together for decades. He was capable of eating like a horse or of going for nearly a day without food if his mind happened to be focused on something else. He could set her blood boiling in a minute; the high-handed hardheadedness she'd fumed over from the start hadn't disappeared. At the same time, he was the most considerate of men, a man who ran her a bubble bath when she was tired, brought her sprays of evergreen for her mantelpiece, asked her how she felt and what she wanted — wonderful signs of not just affection but awareness.

He was as independent as a cat, and yet, like a cat, he was overwhelmingly sensual. She wasn't sure which pleased her more, the inventiveness and sensitivity with which he touched her body or the pleasure with which he accepted her own hesitant touch. His unforced delight in her caresses warmed and heartened her.

And what a body his was to explore. His skin rippled like silk over the hardness of his bone and muscle, over a frame that was as lean and economical as a lion's. Except for those neon-blue eyes, he seemed to be touched with gold all over, in the honeyed warmth of his skin and the gilt shimmer of the hair on his arms and legs, as though a bit of the sun glowed unquenchably within him. He smelled of soap and light, and he tasted delicious, she discovered as she sampled the flavors of him, first shyly and then with increasing boldness.

He was a revelation, she echoed in her mind. Or was she herself the surprise?

Suddenly, she was a woman of needs and desires again. A woman who climbed on his lap and claimed his mouth with hers, who woke him in the middle of the night for lovemaking, who said without fear that she wanted Chinese food or a night at the movies. Suddenly she was a woman of opinions again, too. She found herself taking silly positions for the pure pleasure of debate, savoring the freedom to be as arbitrary as she chose. Jed gave as good as he got, and though they often didn't agree, they never bored or hurt each other. She would glance at the clock, sometimes, and find to her astonishment that an hour or more had gone by while they talked. He teased her about her stubbornness, but she knew as well as he did that they were equally matched: equally able to laugh, equally able to persist, equally able to give in or forgive.

Nature might be dying outside. But inside her own tiny cottage and Jed's larger, more opulent home, Annie felt the world blossom.

Ten

The hospital looked bandbox-new, as neat and modern as the ambulance that had sped Annie and Susie there. The walls of the emergency waiting room glowed an incongruously cheerful pink. Paper turkeys and Thanksgiving garlands were taped amid No Smoking signs and notices about insurance coverage. Annie perched on one of the molded plastic chairs but then rose again, pacing the hallway, shivering with fear and memory.

Since the day of her lunch with Annie and Meg, Susie had been confined to bed, a precaution against the premature birth that could be so dangerous for twins. Knowing that her own schedule was more flexible than John's, Meg's, or even Jed's, and aware that Susie must feel bored and lonely even with family in town, Annie had stopped by for a tentative visit and then, assured of her welcome, for several more. Today they had sat in the master bedroom, laughing over the funny gifts friends had already begun to send for the unborn babies. Now, only half an hour later, Susie struggled desperately somewhere upstairs in the hospital, and Annie waited numbly for Jed. The nurses had no answers. No news yet, they said crisply; and besides, was she family?

The sight of Jed's tall form swinging through the emergency room doors was a beacon of hope and comfort.

"Oh, Jed," Annie said, reaching for him. He held her tight for a moment, then tilted her face up to his.

"It's all right, sweetheart. How's Susie?" he asked, still holding her, making a small private island amid the bustle of nurses and visitors around them. How familiar, how essential his touch and his comfort had already grown, she thought fleetingly.

"She's in the operating room, I think. It's hard to get answers," she said. "John's over in the surgery waiting room, and Susie's parents should be here any minute."

"Good. Come on, let's go on up there."

"I wasn't sure . . . Will it be all right, Jed? My coming? You're family, practically. But I'm a stranger."

"You're not a stranger to Susie. Or to me, lady," he said. "But if you're feeling shy, you can get me a cup of coffee from that machine. I'll be back in five minutes, and we'll see."

He was back in three and shepherded her into the hospital cafeteria for what he said he hoped would be a more drinkable brew. "No news yet," he told her over their steaming cups and uninspired institutional pastries. "They're still working, and John was told it could be a while. He asked where you were, told me how much you helped."

"I didn't do anything." Across the teal-blue laminate table from him, Annie's eyes widened at the memory. "It was so *awful,* Jed. We were so scared. She started to hurt all of a sudden, and I helped walk her to the bathroom — she's allowed to get up just for that. I'd barely moved away from the door when I heard her scream. She could feel the cord, she said, and she knew — we both knew — that it must be tangled around the babies somehow. And then the pain got so bad, so fast."

Annie could feel the coolness of tears pooling in her eyes. Impatiently, she used the back of her hand to wipe them away. "I need a tissue, damn it. Or a napkin. Thanks. Oh, Jed, I felt so damned helpless. God. John and Susie and those babies, all that hope and love —"

"Sssh." He reached out, took both of her fluttering hands in his. "We need to have faith right now. We don't have any choice. You did everything you could do, Susie's doing everything she can do. Ethan and the other doctors here are good, too. They're no hicks. They'll do all they can."

He held her hands, coaxed her to drink her coffee, made her talk about everything and nothing for five minutes until she was calm.

"All right, princess," he said. "Come back into the waiting room with me, meet her family. No, don't shake your head. Annie, everyone will be confused, even insulted, if you don't come. They don't think like you're thinking. *We* don't think like that, haven't I been telling you that for months now? The family knows you're Susie's friend and appreciates that. John, too. Besides, they know me. And I need you. Come with me now."

His eyes were steady and vivid, a lighthouse's bright beam in a storm. And maybe he was right, maybe this wasn't time to quibble about her own foolish shyness. She let him pull her within the warm circle of his arm, walk her to the cheerful yellow waiting room. John reached out to hug her and whisper a thanks in her ear. Susie's parents, both as fair and sturdy as their daughter, greeted her with warmth. Jed kept his arm around her, nestling her against him while they waited.

It was a long, long wait. Jed, Annie, John, and Ron and Cecilia Fields talked quietly, eddied in and out of the room for bathroom or coffee breaks, or just sat in quiet companionship. Susie's sister Fran arrived like a whirlwind, a slimmer, trendier, taller version of Susie. Meg walked in an hour later with a huge basket of rolls and cookies, a bag of disposable cups, and three large thermoses of coffee: "Real coffee, not that hospital swill," she said, "and just let them tell me it's against the rules." Even Sven Rasmussen came by, a Sven so subdued Annie could hardly believe it was the same feisty, belligerent man she'd grown so used to.

Jed seemed so calm, Annie noticed, so re-laxed. But somehow he was the one who told a silly little story about Susie's girlhood just in time to stop the spill of tears that were gathering in Mrs. Fields's eyes. And he was the one who noticed the angry motions of John's wringing hands and beckoned him out for some private man-to-man solace. As always, he seemed almost uncannily aware of her, always there to squeeze his arm more tightly around her when the terrible anxiousness hit her, to pour her a warm cup of coffee when she grew cold.

They'd gone through all of the rolls, all of the coffee, and more faith than any of them thought they had when Ethan Wellman, plump and wrapped in a very creased gown, peeked through the waiting-room door. "Everybody's fine, gang," he said. "*Everybody.* You better get in there, Papa. You've got two little boys to meet. Five pounds plus, each — pretty good, considering. On monitors, not totally out of the woods for now, but I think they're going to be fine." Annie could never say for sure, since her own vision was blurred with happy weeping, but she could have sworn that Ethan had tears in his eyes just like everyone else.

Suddenly the small room was a kaleidoscope of noise and movement. John disappeared like lightning, Fran rushed off for the pay phones, and Sven did an ebullient version of a war whoop that involved lifting Meg right off the floor. Cecilia Fields stood in front of Jed and Annie, her face suddenly ten years younger.

"The doctors won't let anyone but John, Ron, and me see her for an hour or two. She's still groggy from the anesthesia. We'll all be going back to the house, though, and Meg and I are going to rustle up some food. Will you two come along? It's the least we can do to repay you."

"Thanks, Cecilia." Jed smiled down at Susie's petite mom. "I appreciate it. But I think I'll take Annie home. It's been a long day."

"It surely has." Cecilia reached out and touched Annie's forehead. "You go get some rest, honey. And thanks for being there with our girl." Shyly, Annie kissed the woman's soft, gardenia-scented cheek, promising to visit soon.

A half hour later, she was in her own house, her own familiar bed. Jed insisted, against her protests, that she sit and let him serve her. He brought up a tray laden with food that made her laugh: ice cream and cookies along with her favorite herb tea.

"I'm not the invalid," she said, letting him settle the tray over her knees.

"Thank God," he said.

She'd been teasing, but his voice was hard. Her spoon halted in midair as she glanced at him, concerned. He'd prowled over to the window and stood there rocking back and forth on his heels. His back was to her, his lean body springy with tension.

"Jed . . . what is it?"

"Nothing. I don't know." Lightning quick, he

was back at her side, the wry, familiar grin back in place. "Don't mind me, lady. It's just the aftershock, I guess. Nothing to worry about. Finish your treats, and see if you can nap."

"Could you sleep, yourself?"

"I don't think so, darlin'. I was fired up about this latest chapter anyway, and I've got so much adrenaline still rushing through me I can't keep still. Think I'll take Rooster for a run, see if I can get back to the book again. We'll go by John's tonight, or the hospital, if they'll let us. Okay?"

"Okay." She looked at him, still wondering. But if there was one thing she'd learned about Jed Harper, it was that if there was something he wasn't ready to do or say, you couldn't force him.

"I'll come down to your house when I wake up, then," she said.

"Yeah. Interrupt me if I'm still working, okay? I've really done enough for today, I'll be ready to take a break." And with that she had to be content.

The gleaming office door of Friedman & Associates closed behind Thomas Mahoney, and Liz Friedman let out a sigh of relief.

A jerk, she concluded, taking off the glasses she wore to make herself look at least marginally like an authority figure. She swung her neatly trousered legs around to face her computer and started to type the session up. She'd have loved to delegate the menial task of reporting to a secretary. Unfortunately, the revenues of Friedman & Associates didn't yet run to even a part-time temp. In fact, the only Associates the firm had were her boyfriend Eddie, her kid brother Ben, and her mother, who'd gotten the rosewood office furnishings at cost through her sales job at Macy's.

"Client: Thomas Mahoney," she typed in hunt and peck style. *Jerk*, but she didn't write that. *A potentially profitable jerk*, she amended. A boon to her still-struggling business. But a jerk nonetheless.

Thomas Mahoney had come to her on the recommendation of the secretary of security unit at Finch McNaughten, for which Liz sometimes handled employee background checks. Mahoney had told her that his wife had run away with a lover, and that he needed her new home address traced in order to finalize the divorce. He had handed her a wedding photo, read her off a mailbox number in North Carolina, and ordered her to start there, speaking in the condescending tone a four-star general might use to dress down the worst screwup in boot camp.

Most clients lied about something. She'd learned to have a nose for it, even after only a year in the business. Liz didn't swallow this lover story for a minute, especially when Mahoney proved either unwilling or unable to divulge a single piece of information about the guy. No name, no job, no address, not even hair or eye color. "Who is he, the Invisible Man?" Liz had asked.

He ignored that. "Concentrate on Annabel," he'd said curtly. When she'd explained that a post office box number alone was going to be a time-consuming and expensive clue to follow, he'd just repeated the words, simultaneously scanning what little of her body he could see behind the double armor of the big, solid desk and her conservative navy pantsuit. If she was married to a hostile creep like that, she decided, she'd be running, too.

It wasn't her job to question either the likability or the motives of her clients, though, and the guy seemed to be well connected at Finch McNaughten. F. M. was far too important an account for Liz to lose. She would do the job appropriately, but she didn't have to rush. She could work nice and slowly for a jerk like Thomas Mahoney. She'd check out the mailing center in Asheville, fly down there for some personal scrutiny. Maybe one of the clerks could be persuaded to give out some info in return for a surreptitious bribe. Failing that, she'd have to hire a local to sit outside in a car and piss into a milk carton until Annabel Mahoney stopped by for her mail and could be followed home.

Liz finished the report, printed it out, and put it into a folder. She stapled the photo of Mrs. Mahoney onto the inside front and endorsed the nice-sized retainer check Thomas Mahoney had given her. It could go to the bank that afternoon, when Ben got out of school, on his way to pick up her tickets to Jamaica. Gee — when she'd told Mr. Mahoney his lead would take a while to get results on, she must have forgotten to tell him that she couldn't even start until she and Eddie got back from their ten-day vacation. At this rate, she wouldn't find Annabel Mahoney until the woman started picking up her Social Security checks.

"Golly, Annabel," she said aloud to the picture, "now, isn't that a shame?"

Jed holed himself up in his office, played his dulcimer with something approaching fury, went on long treks with Sven, polished the truck to glittering brightness, and said he was fine.

Which, very clearly, he wasn't.

Oh, Annie thought, he was good to her, and tender, and passionate. This wasn't Tom's angry, punishing withdrawal. But he didn't quite meet her eyes. And since the day at the hospital, the ease that had been his most obvious characteristic had gone. The lazy cat had been replaced by a brooding tiger, ready to strike. Annie could see the tension in his shoulders and face, hear it in his voice.

She wasn't sure whether to be amused, concerned, or irritated, but a strong instinct kept her silent. Whatever it was, he hadn't asked for her help. He had to work it out for himself.

Four days had gone by since the babies' birth.

They'd visited the Addamsons twice, meeting what seemed like half of Burnsville at the little house. But they'd stayed home tonight, in his house, cooked a huge pot of pasta, made up a fire.

Now, the dinner eaten and the dishes cleared, they'd moved to the living room. Rooster dozed by the fire, his russet fur gilded in the flickering light. Annie sat cross-legged on the floor by the dog's side, her back against the sofa, sorting through scraps for the pair of crib quilts she planned for the babies. Only Jed seemed oblivious to the peacefulness of the night and the room. He would settle near her on the couch only to rise again. Hole up in the study for fifteen minutes, then wander out again, irritated. Prowl around the room as if he were searching for something or running away from something — she couldn't quite tell which.

"Harper." Annie reached out a hand, patted the sofa beside her. "Sit. You're making me dizzy, pacing around like that."

He slid a book out of its place on the shelf. He'd picked up twenty books, this past week, and left them lying here or there with only three pages read.

"I'm restless," he said, not looking at her, sliding the book back into place.

"I can see that. I could see it days ago. And I've been trying not to intrude on it. But now I think you should tell me what's on your mind."

"I can't believe you even have to ask."

She lifted her chin at the unfamiliar sharpness

of his tone. "I'm sorry. But I do."

"Yeah. Well . . . am I the only person that whole mess scared the shit out of?"

"Mess?"

"Yeah. Mess. Susie, in trouble. Susie, half dead. And two babies at risk, too. Maybe still at risk, for all we know, since they're still on the monitors."

"We were all scared, Jed. You know that. You saw it."

"And now you've all forgotten it. John's going around beaming like he found the cure for cancer. You're making baby quilts. Even Susie. The woman nearly had her belly torn out of her, nearly lost the babies she'd carried for months. But now she looks like a Madonna again, like nothing ever happened."

She shook her head at him, baffled by the fury in his tone. "None of us have forgotten it, I don't think. Or could, even if we wanted to. But we've moved on, yes."

"She could have died, damn it. In agony and terror. Right in front of you." He pivoted to face her now, eyes hard, jaw clenched.

"Yes. And she could have been hit by a bus while she was crossing Main Street any time in the past thirty years."

"That's not the point."

"Isn't it? Isn't that what you're saying, that she took a risk, getting pregnant? Why is that different from the risks we all take every day of our lives?"

"I don't know, Annie. But it is. If something happened to Susie — if she were hit by a bus, like you said — John would be devastated. But if she died carrying his babies, died, maybe, *along* with his babies . . . Christ. Don't you see it would kill him?"

"Yes. It might. But would you have him live his whole life lonely, just to avoid that chance?"

"Alone isn't necessarily lonely."

"No. I've had the chance to test that for myself this fall. And God knows I've tested it in reverse, too. I've been lonely enough to die when there was someone right beside me. But what kind of a life is it, if you're so afraid of loss you can't ever attach yourself to anyone?"

"You callin' me a coward?"

His voice was sharp again. Pained, she thought, more than hostile. Yet she felt her chin lift, her backbone straighten.

"Don't twist my words or make this personal. I'm not talking about you, Jed, not necessarily. I'm just saying that for most people, it's worth taking some risks — enduring some messiness — for love."

"Bully for most people. But this *is* personal for me. I hate it, Annie. The whole thing — the whole thought of it — makes me feel caged. I had enough life-or-death scares when I was little. Enough of wonderin' if my father was dead out there somewhere when he'd disappear for days. Enough of my mama crying, enough of bein' tangled up in other people's lives. Enough

306

of seeing things go wrong and knowing I couldn't fix them."

"I can understand that. At least I think so, though I think that what you felt was chaos — even abuse — and not the kind of ordinary messiness I'm talking about. What I can't understand is why you're angry at me. If you feel a cage, it's not of my making," she said.

"No? Ten people must have made some comment to me this past week." His voice shifted in perfect mimicry. "Gettin' serious, Jed? What about Annie, Jed? It's your turn, Jed. What about some babies of your own, Jed?"

"Ten people, maybe," Annie said. "But not me."

He folded his arms in front of him, gave his head a quick, sharp shake, let out a quick laugh. "You tellin' me you're not serious about this, lady?"

"No." She stared back at him, her gaze just as level. She was damned if he was going to bait her out of her dignity.

"I've never said that. Or pretended, for one minute, that I'm not going to miss you when you go. But I'm also not sitting around knitting baby booties and expecting you to change, and it angers me to hear you assume I am. This is your battle, Jed, with your own feelings. I'll accept them, whatever they are. I'll even help you with them, if you let me. But they're still your fears."

"This isn't about my fears. It's about our situation."

"It's not. And if you can't see the difference between the two, my heart goes out to you."

"I don't want your damned pity."

"You don't have it. I save my compassion — my pity, if you want to call it that — for people with real troubles, not problems of their own making."

She rose from the floor to face him, letting the scraps of cheerful fabric fall like confetti at her feet. Her anger gathered steam as she spoke.

"I said that I wasn't calling you a coward before," she continued. "But the truth is that maybe I am. If you don't want a family or kids of your own, then make your decision and leave it at that. If you don't want to take any risks or any responsibility — if you want your life to be neat and separate and predictable — then live without love and be done with it. If you want me, even for now, then take the risk that one of us or both of us will get hurt. I'll support you either way, Jed. I'll have to make my choices in the end, and you've got a right to yours, too. But there's one thing I'm not going to let you do. I'm not going to let you take your fears and call them by Annabel Taylor's name."

Her only answers were one last blazing blue glare, the sound of booted footsteps, and the slamming of a door.

The sound of Jed's steps woke Rooster, who padded to the kitchen door after him. Jed gave the dog a reassuring pat, waved him into the yard one last time. Now he stood, leaning on the rail of the back stoop, staring unseeingly at the black line of the woods and the crystalline night sky, waiting for the angry pounding of his heart-beat to slow again. It was too cold to stand out-side without a coat on. But the chill felt good to him, cooled him down, focused his mind.

He was wrong, and he knew it.

It wasn't her fault. Whatever the hell he was feeling, wherever his famous detachment had gone, it wasn't her fault.

Her footfall sounded behind him, light and delicate.

"I'm going, Jed," she said as he turned. "Not angrily, don't think that. But maybe we both need to be alone right now."

He blew out a sigh. Shook his head, turned toward her, held out his arms. She looked at him, searching his face in the dim moonlight.

"I'm sorry, Annie," he said.

Still gazing at him, she stepped into his em-brace.

"I'm lousy at this," he said against her hair. "But . . . I just care a hell of a lot about you." It was less than he could have said and more than he'd ever said before. It made him feel foolish, and it made him feel relieved.

"I know you do," she said.

"How can you tell? I sure as hell didn't show it tonight."

"Yes, you did." *You wouldn't be so angry at me if you didn't care. Care more than you wanted to.*

But she didn't say the words aloud. They wouldn't soothe him, and neither would the intensity of what she herself felt. She just let him hold her instead, let her own stillness cradle and soothe him.

She stood with him, unmoving, until she felt a shiver run through his body. He wasn't even wearing a sweater, she realized, just his thin denim shirt. She pulled away a little, put her hands against his chest, looked up at him. In the moonlight he looked as insubstantial as a ghost; only the warmth of his body against hers proved him human.

"Jed," she said gently, bringing up a hand to trace his cheek with her finger. "I'm not going to pretend it isn't going to be hard on me when you go. I'm going to hurt, and I'm going to cry, and I'm going to miss you more than you can imagine. But when I said I accepted you the way you are, I meant it. And you're not the only one leaving. Who knows where I'll be in six weeks or six months? I've got business of my own to take care of, you know."

"I do know. That's one of the things eating me, Annie. Thinking about Susie, hurting, vulnerable . . . How can I pretend you're not exactly the same? You've got a thief or a vandal or who the hell knows what attacking your house, and I haven't been able to do a damn thing but get you an alarm and try to find out where a person gets blood around here. Hell, I couldn't even persuade you to call the cops, and I'm still worryin' over that. You've got a husband who's probably murderous by now, and I can't do anything about that, either. I feel like a total shit. Knowing that I'm going to be thousands of miles away when you deal with all of this, or it deals with you. Walking away just when you need me."

"You won't be gone."

His baffled look was comical, and she smiled, keeping her hand against his face. "You've taught me about myself, Jed. About what it's like to be with a good man, a loving man, a peaceful man. About what I deserve. That's not going to leave me. Everyone in Burnsville has taught me, for that matter. Even Susie and the babies . . . It affected me differently than it did you. You saw risk and loss and disaster. I saw people surviving pain and helping each other through it. It's all changed me. Strengthened me."

He shook his head, but gently now. "I'm glad. And honored, I guess, if you say I played a part in it. But some nice memories and a few good friends aren't strong weapons against a violent man."

"Maybe not. But they're more than I had before. I'll handle Tom, Jed. Carefully. Self-protectively. I'll even get help when I need it; I promise. Another thing you've taught me."

"All right." He sighed, leaned down, put a kiss on her lips. "Annie, don't go home."

"I changed my mind. I'm not going anywhere.

Except upstairs. To your bed. To your arms. Jed, we have so little time left. Let's try — let's both try — to live in the moment, not in the future. To make sure we don't back each other into corners. To just *be*. That's what I need, just as much as you."

Silently, Jed nodded. Unconvinced, he held her close.

To everyone's surprise, not least that of Sven himself, Sven Rasmussen took to the routine of Burnsville like a horse takes to hay. He'd hit town less like a visitor than like a burly blond hurricane, Meg Thorn thought, leaving almost no one unaware of his presence. And yet, only a few scant weeks later, he seemed to have been there for years.

He was already a familiar figure around the town square, and he'd made the Cupboard Café his unofficial headquarters, despite — or maybe, given his obvious relish for a good fight, because of — Meg's firm refusal to bend to his will. Like a boisterous, oversized child, he expected constant attention, meals at odd hours, carafes of coffee so strong Meg was afraid it would eat right through the pot. Unruffled by his coaxing or his sulks, Meg said no and offered him whatever she felt was good for him instead.

He groused that she was hard, uncaring, and stubborn. She said calmly that he was childish, selfish, and spoiled. Both of them enjoyed the fight. Enough that somehow he'd started to stop at Meg's house for dinner some nights. Meg wasn't quite sure how it happened, this new routine. Certainly he'd never done anything so gracious as invite her for a date. He just seemed to arrive around seven, like a stray cat that turns up at mealtimes looking for scraps.

And after one of the dinners they'd ended up, with just as little fuss or formality, in Meg's bed. Her own willingness astonished Meg, and so had the fact that aggressive, inconsiderate, and unpolished Sven Rasmussen was a generous and very appreciative lover. More pleasurable for her, in fact, than Abe had been. Or maybe it was true, what all those women's magazines said, that women reached their sexual prime far later than men. Whatever it was, the pleasure it gave her made Meg feel a little guilty and more than a little foolish. Self-consciousness made her keep the news to herself. But she didn't feel guilty, foolish, or self-conscious enough to stop sharing her bed with Sven Rasmussen. In fact, without ever discussing it aloud, they both seemed to take for granted that he would move his few things out of Wray House and come to stay with her.

He should have been a nuisance, with his unpredictable appearances and his argumentative moods. But somehow he wasn't. Opinionated and even obnoxious he might be, but Meg had rarely met anyone so devoid of malice, and despite its force, his personality was so unselfconscious that she found herself accepting him as naturally as if he'd been just another fact of life. And others did the same, she noticed with secret amusement. Lizibet blushed at his outrageous compliments. Carlos made him special burgers loaded with salsa and cheese. Improbable as it seemed, he'd even struck up a firm friendship with gentle, feminine Susie. Watching them together on the nights she'd dropped by with food, Meg was reminded of a huge sheepdog guarding the gentlest of ewes.

Yes. Considering his truculent manner, Meg decided, Sven Rasmussen's welcome in Burnsville had been surprisingly warm indeed. What he thought of the town in return, she wasn't sure. Sven certainly wasn't the type to show gratitude for the welcome people gave him. But whether he admitted it or not, his stay had clearly done him good. His color was better, and the dark circles had slowly faded from under the belligerent brown eyes. He hiked Mount Mitchell and walked everywhere in town, though he protested loudly. He still talked like a carouser, but it was common knowledge that he'd been seen at the Elks clubhouse for AA. Now, if she could just persuade him to cut out some of that coffee.

As for Meg herself, she hadn't felt so burstingly alive in years.

She pulled her gloves off her hands and slid them into her pocket. A light dusting of snow had been followed by a quick thaw, and the air was less cold than cool. The dampness and sudden warmth made the world smell almost springlike. Jed, Annie, Meg and Sven had decided to hike for an hour along the creek bed before a big Saturday brunch, cooked by the men. Or, Jed had amended in the face of hoots of derision from Annie and Meg, by the man. Sven couldn't be counted on to do much more than flip on the coffeemaker or complain. At least Jed could turn out some passable flapjacks.

Sven and Annie lagged behind, picking their way carefully across the uneven, rocky terrain and arguing playfully about the movie they'd all gone to see the night before. The two voices, Sven's gruff and Annie's soft and crisp, carried easily in the clear air. Jed smiled at the contrast in their tones, Sven's so unabashedly contemptuous of director, screenwriter, and stars alike; Annie so reasoned and fair.

Jed glanced sideways at Meg as he walked beside her. She was wearing a familiar red parka and Nordic cap, and yet she looked different to him. Serene, but somehow secretive. A kind of cat-with-the-cream expression.

It had been impossible not to notice the way Sven gravitated to Meg, and it was difficult to figure out exactly what her reaction was. She was calm and cheerful as always, yet she didn't send him away the way Jed expected. Despite his own habit of detachment, concern nagged at him like a sore tooth. Maybe it was because he'd been the one to introduce Sven to Burnsville and, more to the point, Burnsville to Sven. Having been the one who presented Pandora

315

with the box, he felt oddly responsible for it.

"It feels good to walk, doesn't it?" Meg said, unaware of his thoughts. "I needed to use up some of my energy. I think I'm still jumping from all the excitement this fall. Annie arriving, all the excitement of little Matthew and Nathaniel, Sven, the attack at Annie's house, not to mention all of the usual drama at the café. It's like we're all living in a soap opera all of a sudden."

"Yeah. Lots of surprises," Jed said, seeing an opening. "Like that nice Meg Thorn, for example. Great lady, stable, sensible, pillar of the community for years. And then suddenly it looks like she's carryin' on with some crazy mountaineer."

"Carrying on?"

"Well, I went to meet the man for breakfast the other day," Jed said. "Couldn't help noticing that he wasn't in his room at eight A.M. And that when he finally showed up, he strolled up from the big white house on the corner."

"And? You congratulating me, Jed?" Meg's voice was dry.

"I'd like to. But I don't know, Meggie. Sven's a good man, but he's not what I'd pick for you. It worries me some."

"Does it now," Meg said, raising an eyebrow. "And why would that be?"

"Why else? Because I don't want to see you hurt."

"Really?" The dryness in her tone, Jed saw, had turned to irritation. She turned her head to look up at him as they walked, fixed him with a stare. "Because you don't want to see me hurt? Or because you don't want to see me at all?"

He looked down at her, flummoxed by her heat. "Meaning?"

"What do you see when you look at me, Jed? Seriously. Not a woman, that's for sure. None of you really see that. A nice little granny, maybe. A sister. Or a nun, that's the most accurate of all."

He'd never heard her talk so forcefully. Well, not since junior high, at least. He remembered, belatedly, that though young Meg Thorn had been hard to anger, she'd been ferocious once the tinder was touched to flame.

"Sister Meg, so calm and charitable," she continued. "Sister Meg, with her nice little café and her nice little friends and her nice big house and all her good works. Did you ever wonder if that nice little life was enough for *me?* Did you ever wonder if I was lonely sometimes, or if I might want a little more excitement, or even if I might want some sex one or two more times before I just shrivel up and die?"

"For God's sake, Meg. I never gave it a thought," Jed said.

"Exactly. You didn't think about it. Well, maybe you should have. At least if you're going to go butting into my business."

"Get a sex life if you want one, Margaret," Jed growled. "But don't tell me you couldn't have one with a more . . . well . . . dependable character than Sven."

"Maybe I could. But maybe all of those dependable characters left me cold. Maybe this is the sex life I want. And maybe I don't even see what makes him quite so undependable."

They had stopped short by now. They stood, face-to-face, under a huge, leafless oak. Jed tucked his hands farther in his jacket pockets, stared down at Meg's angry face.

"Look, Meg. Let's leave aside the little things for now, like the fact that the guy lives for a good argument or that he's just getting over a bout of drinking that would put a lesser man in his grave. The truth is that Sven is a man who writes about climbing. Period. That's what he does, that's all he does. And by this point in his career, he's used up the bunny hills. He's on Everest, he's on K2, he's on Annapurna. And the odds are that one of these days he isn't going to come back. And, let me repeat, I don't want you getting hurt."

"Abe was an insurance salesman, Jed," Meg said. Her voice was quieter now, as though she, too, was conscious of Annie and Sven catching up behind them. Still, her eyes stormed at him silently. "Abe came home every night, ate the same meal every morning. But he still died of a heart attack in five minutes flat, so fast I couldn't even say good-bye to him, and he still broke my heart. If Sven Rasmussen falls off Mount Everest tomorrow, I'll deal with it. But in the meantime, I'm alive, really alive again for the first time in years. I'm not stopping it for anyone, and certainly not for someone who's the worst case of the pot calling the kettle black I ever saw."

"The situations aren't the same."

"Aren't they? Granted, Sven doesn't have your money, or your big, solid house, or your orderly routine. But if I'm in such danger with him, why is Annie so damned safe with you? Why do you have permission that Sven doesn't? Aren't you going to do exactly the same thing with her? Leave her? Go get sick or killed on her? Break her heart?"

The words pierced him like an arrow. And stung. And he couldn't even argue with them, because they echoed the same thoughts he'd been trying so hard to suppress. But he tried. "I'm not going to fall off some fucking mountain, for Christ's sake, Meg."

"No? How do you know? Do you think I — we — haven't read your books? What about that earthquake in Bogotá? What about the cocaine smuggler and that Russian mob boss, Jed? How dare you pretend that you're immune to danger or risk? And let's say, just for the sake of argument, that you were," she fumed. "Let's say you do come home safe. What then? Another month or two or three of romantic bliss for Annie before you hare off to hell and back again? Another bout of heartbreak, another bout of hope? She's in love with you, Jed, passionately, head over heels. And if you think you're not going to hurt her terribly, then you're seeing as little of her as you did of me."

"I've had that exact same argument with her, Meg," he said, his voice quiet. "And she insists that she'll be fine."

"Well, I'm telling you that *I'll* be fine, too," Meg said.

"I hate to be possessive, but I just saw some lady having a passionate discussion with my man," Annie said lightly, catching up to them. "What gives?"

"Nothing new," Jed drawled. "Just another debate with the original love 'em and leave 'em guy." He could hear the cynicism in his tone, but it was too late to take the careless words back.

Annie was wearing a rosy wool turtleneck sweater he'd bought her, a scarf from Alma's cottage, and one of Jed's outgrown parkas. Despite the mismatched clothing, Jed thought she looked elegant and completely desirable. Her normally pale cheeks were flushed with exercise, her expression sure and loving, her eyes alight. He watched the gaiety die out of them as he avoided her gaze, replaced by puzzlement and the beginnings of hurt.

"C'mere, Rasmussen," Meg said. She was always tactful, even when she was pissed as hell. She tugged at Sven's arm. "I want to show you the oak the famous Mr. Harper and I climbed thirty years ago. The one I should have pushed him off of."

"Does it have a goddamned john in it?" Sven

asked grumpily, following her. "Or maybe a coffeemaker? I don't care if I am supposed to be a climber. This before-breakfast hiking is crap."

His voice and Meg's answering chime died away as Jed strode forward. Hunching his shoulders against his tension and the wind, he let the rhythm of his strides engulf him.

"Hey," Annie said from beside him. He always forgot that her stride was almost as long as his own. "Stop running away. What is it?"

He glanced down at her beautiful, trusting face and relented. "Nothing."

"Oh, no. Haven't we just been through that?"

Smiling at himself, he slung his arm around her shoulders as they walked. "Yeah, we have. And we've been through a hell of an argument, too, same kind I just had with Meg. Now all I have to do is go pick a fight with Susie, and I'll be three for three. One fight each with all my best girls."

"You don't have to have a fight with Susie," Annie said. "Because John is taking care of her, and she's safe now."

"You're unnerving me a little, Annie Taylor. How the hell would you know what we fought about?"

"You're a fake, Harper," she said. "You con everybody into thinking you're a marvel of detachment, when inside you're a medieval knight quivering with chivalry and protectiveness."

"You may be right. But I think I liked it better when I didn't give a damn," he said ruefully.

"Come on, I'd better make amends with Meg. And then," he added, "your medieval knight will make his women pancakes."

The second time was worse.
Much worse.
Because Cindy was sick with shame, and growing sicker. The awareness of what Moira knew and the fear of what she might say twisted in her gut every day, every night. She could barely meet Meg's eyes, much less Billy's. Only with the children was she at peace: the children who didn't care what ugliness was in her past, the children whose birth and mothering were the best things she'd ever done in her whole life.

The rest of her days passed in a blur of anxiousness and indecision. A hundred times she braced herself to tell Billy, call Annie Taylor on the phone, put an end to the whole awful mess. And a hundred times she stood, paralyzed, letting the quiet moment with Billy go by or watching her own hand fall, defeated, from the telephone. Knowing she just didn't have the courage to act when it could mean giving up everything she loved. Dreaming foolish fantasies that fate would somehow solve the problem for her: that Moira would never come home from her visit with cousin Daniel, that her aunt would abandon this ridiculous quest, that her own disgusting secret would somehow disappear.

It was worse this time because she was sick with guilt, too. Annie Taylor had been in the café several times. Sometimes she sat laughing over coffee with Meg, sometimes she just ate lunch alone in the dappled sunlight of the far corner table. She always smiled at Cindy, asked how she was, left a good tip. A nice woman, just as Cindy had told Moira. A nice woman Cindy was helping to damage and terrify and disgust, all because Cindy was terrified of her crazy aunt and the things her crazy aunt's vengeful words could do.

It was worse because this time, Moira made her help and not just drive. Her aunt had shoved half of the packages they picked up at the same empty supermarket right into Cindy's arms — white parcels that felt squishy and sickening inside their stiff white butcher-paper wrappings. "Never you mind what's in them," Moira said, but Cindy could guess. The very feel of them in her arms sickened her. The thought of entrails, viscera, and blood made her want to retch.

In the car, fueled by her shame and repulsion, Cindy had refused to help, to go on the journey at all. Moira had thrust her face close. Her breath was acrid and her eyes wild behind the glasses, her voice a throttled hiss. The litany of curses and threats that poured from her aunt's lips was terrifying, even more vile than the time before. And Cindy was aware, suddenly, of the strength in her aunt's rawboned, country-woman's body — of the physical, not just emotional, danger.

I'll do it this time, Cindy had vowed, tears

tracking silently down her cheeks, a leaden sense of hopelessness settling into her very bones. *But never again. I swear, no matter what she does, I'll never do this again.*

And she never would. She guessed that Moira wouldn't, either. Because in the weeks since their last visit, the house had been wired with an alarm.

Moira hadn't so much as checked, just sailed up onto the porch as though she were Queen Elizabeth dropping in on a peasant. She must have known that Annie Taylor wasn't there, Cindy had thought as she followed, numb and leaden, behind her aunt's heavy, decisive strides.

The alarm started a minute after Moira slipped the key she'd taken from Jed Harper into the lock. The shrill blare of the bell seemed to surround them, seemed to echo off every angle of the hill behind the house. It was as though the screaming sound of it was everywhere — so loud, Cindy thought ridiculously, that they must be hearing it all the way up in heaven. It stopped Moira for only a moment. The older woman dropped the key, ripped the parcel she held open, stepped inside, and flung the contents violently into the house. Somehow Moira's calm was scarier than the head-numbing clamor, the dreadful smell of raw meat, or even the thought of being discovered.

Cindy dropped her own unopened packages on the porch and bolted.

It took only seconds to reach the car, but by

the time she got there, she was crying, panting with big gasping openmouthed sobs, moaning in terror. She wrestled with the car door, thrust herself into the driver's seat, turned the key that had been left in the ignition in panic.

It didn't catch, and she twisted it savagely again, jabbing her foot on the gas pedal, so desperate to get away she barely noticed Moira beside her, standing beside the still-open door. Out of the corner of one eye, Cindy saw lights springing on in Jed Harper's house down the hill. Her aunt reached down and shoved Cindy away from the driver's seat. The skirt of Cindy's waitress uniform stuck against the plush car seat, but her aunt kept pushing, shoving, until Cindy was forced to the side, half sitting, half lying across the passenger seat. The engine roared to life just as Moira swung the door shut.

For all of her imperturbability up on the porch, Moira drove like a demon, flooring the accelerator and taking the curves wide. As she tried to right herself, Cindy glimpsed vehicle lights in the rearview mirror. Jed Harper's truck, probably. She froze, afraid that it would follow them, but they were far down the road already and after one brief moment, the headlights were lost in the darkness. The car seemed to veer crazily; it took Cindy a moment to realize that it was because Moira's hands were slippery on the wheel. Slippery with blood, the sweet stench of which filled the car like poison. Helplessly, Cindy felt her stomach begin to spasm. She tried to calm the awful panic, steady the violent sickness, but she couldn't. She leaned forward, propped her hand against the dashboard, and began to retch.

"Don't you dirty my car, Lucinda," Moira said savagely.

Head hanging over her knees, losing the delicious dinner she'd eaten on break at the café, the taste of tears and bile sharp in her mouth, Cindy felt a bubble of hysterical laughter rising in her throat. *Don't dirty the car,* she thought wildly. The car that smelled of flesh and woundedness and death, the car with blood smeared all over its steering wheel and gearshift, the car of a crazy woman who was ruining all of their lives for some mysterious quest, or maybe for nothing at all. It was too much. More like a bad horror movie than real life. The bubble of laughter burst in between her gasping breaths. Despite Moira's cursing, she laughed and retched and cried the whole way home.

Eleven

They were already in bed, lying curled closely to-gether, when the alarm sounded. Annie, long used to New York's endless car alarms and ambulances, just nestled her head more firmly into the crook of Jed's shoulder at the shrill, faint noise. But Jed raised his head, then swung his body out from under the warm comforter, ignoring her murmur of protest.

"Sorry, princess," he said grimly. "But that's your alarm. Your house."

Annie rose, too, shivering as the cool air hit her naked body. Rooster, who'd been asleep on the rug near the bedside, stood quivering with alertness by her side, his soft fur brushing against her bare leg.

"I'm coming, too," she said, heading for her clothes. Sensing her anxiety, Rooster began to whimper.

"Annie —" Jed lifted his head to gaze at her, opened his mouth to speak. After a moment of indecision and one long hard look, he gave in. "All right. But hurry. Grab your keys, will you? The one Alma gave me is somewhere in my desk, but we don't have time to look for it.

Hurry," he said again and was gone.

Annie shrugged on her clothes and ran to the truck only seconds after he did. He had just started the engine when she noticed the gun, a dull gleam of metal in the dim light. She wrapped her arms around her freezing body and looked at his set profile.

"The safety's on, but it's loaded. Be careful," he said before she could speak.

"This is yours?"

"Ordered it a while back, after the first . . . incident. And your story about Tom. Been meanin' to trade it for the shotgun I put in your kitchen and try to talk you into learning to shoot. Again. But we've been together —" He squinted into the night beyond the windshield, jerked his head toward the road. "Damn. There's a car down there, but it may be too far ahead of us to catch. This isn't the right vehicle to do high-speed car chases in. Hang on."

Annie obeyed, grasping the edge of her seat as he swung the truck down the mountain road. It seemed as though they were gaining on the other car, but the headlights swung in and out of sight. When they reached the bottom of the hill and Highway 19, Jed blew out a breath in frustration. There were several cars on the road, going both east and west, but no way of telling which was the one they'd seen. He pulled the gearshift into reverse, began to turn the truck around. "I was afraid of this. Did you get a look at it?"

"No. The glimpses were so brief, and it looked so average. Dark. A sedan, midsize. I'm sorry, Jed. I know that's no help."

"I can't do any better. Not our fault; they just had too much of a head start. Well, let's see what the damage is this time."

They drove back up the hill in silence. As they approached the cottage, the sound of the alarm intensified to a painful shriek. Jed swung the truck to a stop on her gravel driveway, put out a restraining hand. "Stay here," he said, pitching his voice to be heard above the bell's squealing. "No, Annie, don't fight with me this time. Just tell me the alarm code and let me take a look. I'll come get you in a minute or so, I promise."

Annie saw the steel in his face and decided it would be useless to fight. And in truth, after the sickening surprise of the blood last time, she wasn't entirely sorry to let him be the pioneer. She reached out to touch his arm. "Be careful," she said, and told him the code.

"Don't worry." He threw her a small, tight smile over his shoulder as he reached for the gun and slid out of the truck. "I will."

Jed walked fast up the steps of Alma's cottage, listening hard. The fact that a car had driven away was no guarantee that someone wasn't lurking.

On the old wooden floor of the porch, something small and shiny glinted, catching his eye. He pulled his small penlight out of his pocket and squatted. A key, golden-bright, almost new.

He frowned at it as something nagged in his mind. When the thought wouldn't form, he left it to simmer. He rose, stepped carefully over the key, and walked into the house.

He was just over the threshold when he heard a vehicle screech to a halt behind the truck. Tension clenched in his belly. Pulling the gun from his pocket and bracing his back against the door, he turned to face the driveway. Just Ethan Wellman's old Saab, he realized, just as Ethan's unmistakably rounded form emerged into the moonlight. Good; at least the alarm had raised some troops. He took a moment to press the code into the keypad that rested next to the door, returning the world to silence. Ethan was already at the truck, reassuring Annie. Jed turned his back on them and went inside.

"No one here," he said, shutting the living room door behind him as they stepped into the house. He caught Ethan's eye over Annie's shoulder. "Call the police station," he said. "No buts this time, lady. Ethan, the phone's in the kitchen." Then he took a stiff Annie in his arms, gave her a quick, hard hug.

"Is it awful?" she asked.

"No. Really, princess," he said, trying to sound casual and yet not patronizing, and not sure he was managing it. "It's a little disgusting, I'll give it that. But mostly just foolish. Nothing a chef wouldn't take in stride. In fact, you could cook a decent French dinner from what's there. Sweetbreads, tripe, the works."

"Tripe . . ." She shivered. "Well, I never did like organ meats." He could hear her trying to match the lightness of his tone, and he spared a quick thought of gratitude for her courage. "I want to see it for myself," she added.

"Why? There's nothing there to give you any information, I promise you that. It's your home, someplace you love. Why put this vision of it in your mind? Especially when Ethan here can help me clean up, right, Ethan?"

"Sure." Ethan materialized at their side after a side trip into the living room, a reassuringly sane, ordinary presence in the nightmare. "The cops should be here in a minute or two, then we can tidy up the mess. Come show me where the coffeemaker is, Annie. I think we could all use some."

"You guys are ganging up on me. But even it doesn't make sense, it's my house, and I need to look at it anyway." For the moment, though, she followed Ethan to the kitchen. Jed stood alone in the hallway, his mind puzzling over the key once more.

Ethan could watch over Annie for a bit. "I need to get something at my house. Back in a couple of minutes," he called over his shoulder. Annie emerged onto the porch as he turned on the truck again, but he just waved her back.

"Wait for me," he called. "And don't let the police step on that key. On the floor of the porch. Watch out for it." Ignoring the puzzled look that was visible even in the weird low light of the porch's little lantern, he pulled off down the road.

The door to the double-wide wasn't locked, thank goodness. She wasn't sure she could have managed the key. Cindy stepped inside quietly, hoping that Billy would be asleep in front of the TV. The set was off, though, and most of the lights were dimmed. She stopped in the kitchen to wash her hands. She'd never even opened the packages she held, just dropped them on the porch, but it felt as though they had tainted her anyway, seeped into her very pores.

She washed her hands again and dried them with the rough kitchen towel. In front of a little mirror she stopped, almost mechanically, to straighten her hair. Now that the explosion of feeling and flight at Annie Taylor's house was over she felt drained, numb, oddly disconnected. It was as though she were watching herself from very far away. She looked awful, she thought, tucking the last stray strand of russet hair in place. And she deserved to.

She tiptoed past the children's room, peeking her head in by habit to make sure that they were okay. LuAnne was tangled in her Pocahontas comforter, upside down and half on top of the rumpled covers as usual. Little Billy was asleep, too, under the Michael Jordan poster that was one of his most cherished possessions. They were fine, thank God. One thing right in her world.

The door to the master bedroom was closed.

Inside, the room was dim, the familiar shapes of hand-me-down bed and dresser reduced to blurred rectangles. As her eyes adjusted to the darkness, she realized that Billy was sitting up in bed. Cindy's stomach clenched. Billy awake, Billy sitting was a bad sign; he was always tired at night.

"Hi, honey," she said brightly, hoping her voice didn't sound as false to him as it did to her. "What're you doing?"

"Waitin' for my wife," he said. "Who's late, as usual."

"It's only, what, eleven? Not that late, baby," she hedged.

"Late enough," he said. "Have a good time, Lucinda? With Moira?"

"Well . . . you know Aunt Moira," she said, her back still to him. "She's not exactly fun. But it was okay."

"You're right about that. Moira sure ain't fun. Makes it all the stranger, you stayin' out with her so late, twice in a row, no less."

"Billy —"

"Then there's the funny look on your face," he said as though she hadn't spoken. His arms were crossed on his bare chest, his hair wet. She could see the little cowlick at the back, the one that always melted her heart. He looked straight ahead as he spoke, not at her. His broad-boned, solid, usually open face was impassive. Cindy waited, helpless, clasping her hands together as he spoke.

"Been there for a while now," he said. "That funny look. Kind of shifty. Not lookin' me straight in the eyes. Not wantin' to talk. Not even really wantin' to have sex. A million miles away all the time. Someplace else. Someplace better, I guess."

"Billy," she said again, desperately.

She had to tell him. She just had to. Because she was going to lose him anyway if she didn't. And because she couldn't stand to see the hurt in him, the pain he was trying to hide. It had never occurred to her that he'd think she was cheating. Now that she knew, she wasn't going to let him suffer. Wasn't going to let him think that he wasn't good enough for her, when it was really Cindy failing him.

He rose from the bed, stood a few feet away from where she stood rooted near the dresser. He should have looked silly, a stocky blond man with cowlicky hair and baggy old pajama pants, but instead he looked dignified, full of strength.

"I love you," he said. "Always have, always will. But I'm not sittin' around while you cheat on me."

"Honey." The dam inside her burst, just as it had in the car only fifteen minutes before. The tears started as she stepped toward him. Weeping, she slid onto her knees, put her arms around his thighs, cradled her head against his muscular belly. He stood stiffly, but at least he didn't push her away. "Billy. Oh, God, I'm in such trouble, I don't know how to tell you."

The whole story poured out then, everything and at breakneck speed, Dr. Andrews and the baby she'd aborted, Moira and the vandalism of Annie Taylor's house, her fear of exposure, of losing Billy and the kids. Somehow, as she talked, they moved into the kitchen. Somehow Billy made her a cup of tea — too strong, and in LuAnne's dumb Smurf mug. Somehow she got through the story, all of the horrible secrets purged and brought into the light. It seemed to take hours, though the light-up hands of her watch seemed to hang forever at ten-fifty-five.

The words were finally exhausted. Cindy stared down at the mug of untouched tea and braced herself to look into Billy's eyes. Her whole future hung in the balance of what those eyes would show. Slowly, she looked up.

His face was set and stern. "You shoulda told me sooner," he said. "You should have, girl."

"I know. I did wrong, I know it. I'll do anything to make it up to you. Just don't hate me," she said. "I couldn't stand it, Billy. Please."

He stared at her, clearly shocked. "Hate you? I'm not mad at you, Cin. Christ, don't you know me well enough to know that?"

"But — Dr. Andrews." Her voice caught. "The baby."

"You were only a baby yourself, girl. No different than Lu will be, not too long from now. You think I'm gonna hate her if she makes a mistake when some slick-talking man comes around? Now, this doctor, I'd like to settle a score with him, that's for sure."

"Maybe it's just as well I've got no idea where in tarnation he went."

"Maybe. But we sure as hell know where Moira McTeague can be found."

"Billy . . . no."

"Don't be tellin' me no. The woman's a menace. I been tellin' your family that for years, you and your mama, too, and you never would listen. I shut up back then, 'cause she ain't my kin and so it ain't really my business, but you're all gonna listen now. Moira McTeague wants to run around the county in the middle of the night tossin' blood on people's houses, that's her business. She wants to get my wife involved, though, wants to drive *my damned wife* halfway crazy, she's gonna have to deal with me."

How had she forgotten how strong Billy was? Cindy wondered. How sure of his own mind, his own values. How protective of his whole family, which did, after all, include her. How had she managed to let a crazy woman convince her that this man was her enemy, not her friend? She felt herself going limp with exhaustion and relief. "She'll tell everybody, though. I bet you she will, just for spite."

He snorted. "Moira ain't gonna be tellin' people squat. Don't you worry about that. I gotta get dressed. Call Lisa, ask her if we can stick the kids on her couch for an hour, and get the phone book out."

"The phone book?" But he was gone. That

was Billy, too. Not romantic, not sentimental. But once he made up his mind to a thing, you'd better get out of the way.

She rose and walked over to the drawer in which they kept the white pages.

"Sorry." She heard his voice from behind her. "Forgot somethin'."

Billy Byrne came back into the kitchen pulling a sweatshirt over his head, reached down to tilt his wife's chin upward, gave her a brief, hard kiss, and disappeared again.

Ten minutes after he'd left Annie's house, Jed was back, bringing the truck to a stop on the grass, out of the way of the black-and-white squad car that now stood behind the Saab.

"Tommy," he said to the officer who stood at the living room door, with Annie and Ethan only a few steps away from him. Jed had gone to high school with Tommy Straub before Tommy had gotten married, had a couple of kids, and grown a soft beer belly. A typical small-town cop, but fair and shrewd. They could have done worse. Beyond him, another blue-clad form bent as flashbulbs popped.

With the door open, the odor of meat and blood had eddied toward where they stood. Knowing it must distress her, Jed slid one arm around Annie's shoulders, hugged her to his side. "So," he said to Tommy. "What do you think?"

"Kids, probably. Miz Taylor — Annie, yeah, sorry — here confirms that nothing was taken.

Stuff was just tossed around. Not much more to say, Jed. Unless you know more than Annie here does."

"I do, unfortunately. I think I know who this is, though I sure as hell don't know why," Jed said. "Did you see that key, Tommy? On the porch?"

"Yeah," Tommy Straub said. "Not yours, I'm guessing. And I gather not Annie's."

"Not Annie's," Jed said. "But mine, yes." The three faces around him all registered the same surprise.

"The minute I saw it, I wondered," he continued. "It looked brand-new, like a copy. It wasn't Annie's key, the one she got from John; she'd just given that to me. So whose? I figured at first it was from another tenant, an earlier one. But it seemed damned unlikely. Before Annie, the place was barely rented. Then I remembered that I had a newish copy of the key myself, the one Alma gave me last spring so that I could check on the place if I noticed anything amiss when I was going up and down the mountain. When I went down the hill to look for that key in my desk drawer, it wasn't there."

"The cleaning lady," Annie said immediately.

"Christ, that was quick. Yeah, good old Moira McTeague. She's the only one who's in and out of my house except Annie, myself, Meg, John, and Susie. And I never stay in a room she's cleaning. Truth to tell, I basically ignore her. She'd have ample chance to look for it if she wanted."

"Come on, Jed," Tommy Straub said robustly. "This sounds like one of those mystery novels all of a sudden. You're going to be telling me it was Miss Scarlett with the knife in the library in a minute. You could have just lost it, for cripe's sake."

"Ordinarily, I'd say you were right. But not this time. No one else could have gone through my desk. I'm only sorry I forgot to check for the key the first time this happened."

Tommy fixed him with a baleful look, which he then swept over Annie as well. "And just five minutes ago I'm being told nothing like this ever happened before and nobody knows nothin.' Never trust a pretty lady, that's what they tell you in the Academy. Come on, folks, let's get real here. What first time?"

"We didn't report it. Come on, Tommy, we'll tell you about it later," Jed said calmly. "Point is, Alma gave me the key. And Moira could have taken it any time."

"Right. She could have. But there's no proof she did, and no obvious reason why in hell she would. Lived here all her life and never threw any blood and guts around yet. Far as I know, she's a respectable woman. Unless there's something else you've decided to cover up."

"No," Annie chimed in. "There's nothing, really. I'm sorry, Officer Straub. Jed's just being kind. It was my decision not to report the first incident. My reasons had nothing to do with Burnsville, and, for the record, Jed disagreed with me wholeheartedly. We can certainly tell you about it, if it helps. As far as Mrs. McTeague goes, I know it's not evidence, but something was clearly off the day I met her. It was at Jed's house, in fact, the day after the first vandalism. She was there to clean the house. I asked Jed at the time if something was wrong. She seemed so — I don't know — odd, to me."

"You did," Jed said. "My mistake. I never paid her any heed. It just seemed like ordinary sour Moira to me. And I had other things on my mind that morning."

"Exactly," Tommy said, breaking in to their exchange. "Ordinary Moira McTeague. No law against bein' morose, that I know of at least. This earlier incident have any links to Moira?" Tommy Straub asked.

"No," Annie said. "Jed, do you see any? I don't think so."

"You're right then, ma'am," the policeman said at the shake of Jed's head. "Harsh looks aren't evidence. And speaking of harsh looks, don't give me the evil eye, Harper. This ain't some Third World country, and I'm not rousting some perfectly respectable old biddy in the middle of the night on the evidence of one lost key and one dubious look, especially not for a misdemeanor. Hell, maybe she looked at you funny because she didn't like the brand of window spray you left her. I'll run this by the chief, maybe interview the lady in the morning, but that's the best I can do."

"You'd better do a good job at it, Tommy," Jed stared the shorter man down. "I mean it. If I'm blowing smoke, fine and good. But just in case I'm not, you'd better put the fear of God into her. Because I'm not letting her hurt Annie, here, and I don't want to hear about how it's just a friggin' misdemeanor. This crap is going to stop."

"You done in there, O'Malley? Yeah, I'll meet you at the car," Tommy yelled over his shoulder. "All right, Jedidiah, calm down. I'll do what I can, I told you that. Meanwhile," he added, a sly grin stealing over his face, "when's the wedding?"

"Wedding?"

"Hell, Harper, you're a legend in five counties for not giving a good goddamn about anything, anyplace, or anyone. If you're practically beating me with a two-by-four to protect the lady's life, you must be pretty damn serious." And with that parting shot, Tommy Straub and O'Malley clumped heavily out of the house.

There was a moment of silence, then Annie dissolved into laughter, sliding down against the wall she'd been standing near and collapsing in giggles onto the floor.

"Uh . . . Think I'll go clean up some entrails," Ethan Wellman told them, his own mouth twitching with amusement.

Jed stood in front of Annie, disbelieving. "You're some woman," he said, shaking his head and hooking his thumbs through his belt loops. Despite himself, he found himself grinning down at her. "You've got a maniac husband, let me remind you. And a crazy lady vandalizing your house, and guts all over your livin' room couch, and a lover who's so busy not getting involved he doesn't even notice that it's his own damned cleaning lady who's *putting* the guts on your livin' room couch. And here you are, sitting on the floor, looking like you're fifteen and giggling your head off."

"I know. It's nuts. I'm sorry." But the laughter still trembled in her voice. "It was just — the look on your face when Officer Straub said that, after that fight we had. . . . I'm sorry. I'll stop. It's probably just aftershock, too. I know there's a lot to find out, still, but it's such a relief just knowing who it is."

"Even with no proof? You'll have trouble convincing Tommy."

"I don't need proof. I just know. I knew the minute you told me that key was yours. And I don't need Tommy. At least not yet. Help me up," she said, stretching out a hand. "I'm going to have a little talk with Moira McTeague myself."

"Annie —"

"You can come along if it makes you feel better," she said sweetly, smiling at him. "As long as you don't open your mouth. You can even bring that gun in your pocket. But I'm tired of fighting shadows. I'm going to find out why she's doing this, and I'm going to try to make her stop. And if I can't, well, *then* I'll argue with Tommy Straub."

"Christ. Words fail me, and that hasn't happened since I was three. I'm not sure whether you're brave or whether you're nuts, but I'm not crazy about the sound of it either way. Could we please talk about this before you make up your mind? Preferably in the morning, when both of us can think?"

"I don't need to think. And as for you," she said, giving him a slightly tired smile, "forget thinking. You're not only the lover who didn't know Moira was crazy, you're the guy who practically handed her the key." She nodded her head toward the living room. "But if you're feeling protective again, you could certainly come help me and Ethan get the guts off of my couch."

The phone rang just as she finished speaking, its old-fashioned bell sounding loud in the stillness of the house. Annie started to get it, but as if by instinct Ethan must have picked up the living room handset first.

"Phone for you, Annie," he said, appearing at the living room door. "He says it's William Byrne."

Jennifer Stern arrived for her appointment at Finch McNaughten a judicious ten minutes early. Just enough extra time to check her makeup in the ladies' room, make sure the nine-block walk from her office hadn't mussed her makeup or hair, and get settled before the receptionist let Stretch McNaughten know she was here. No point arriving at such an important meeting rushed or looking less than perfect. Not when so much depended on the outcome.

It seemed to Jenni that the reception area of Finch McNaughten almost breathed power and money. The paneled walls were polished to brilliance and accented with old maritime paintings and Oriental rugs. The soft-voiced receptionist had patrician features and sported a designer suit. Even the women's room had the restrained gleam of capital carefully but not ostentatiously spent. Jenni noted with approval the polished mahogany of the mirrored console, the vase of fresh lilies, the pile of cloth hand towels. Details like that counted. Those small things, she thought with satisfaction, were the signs of real wealth — wealth that was more than just display, that showed even behind the scenes.

She turned her attention to the reflection in the immaculate, artfully lit mirror. She looked fine, but she repowdered her nose, refreshed her lipstick, and smoothed her hair anyway. Her suit was neatly and unrevealingly cut but made in a vivid persimmon-red fabric. Stretch McNaughten was too smart, Jenni had guessed, not to smell a rat if she showed up in anything too blatantly conservative. The earrings were expensive but clearly costume jewelry. On impulse, she took her comb out of her bag again, loosened the sweep of her bangs just a little. With the faint hint of girlish tendrils framing her face, the effect was perfect, complete. Jenni dropped her cosmetics neatly into the small handbag, clicked the gilt clasp shut, and returned to the reception area where she waited, poised and patient, until McNaughten was ready to see her.

"Jennifer. Sit down." The reception area had merely been spacious. Stretch McNaughten's office was huge, with a sweeping view of the South Street harbor and furnishings that made it feel more like a gentleman's club than a place of business. Within this overscaled, austere habitat Jenni thought that Stretch seemed larger and even more imposing than he had that day at Frascati's.

"May Eleanor get you some coffee? Or some sparkling water?" he asked.

"No, thank you." Jenni settled herself carefully in the club chair he pointed her to, making sure her skirt hadn't risen too high. She waited for McNaughten to sit and for the secretary to close the office door behind her before she began.

"Mr. McNaughten . . ." She paused, bit her lip. She didn't need to fake the hint of nerves necessary to make her story work. Despite all of her forethought and planning, the larger-than-life quality of both the room and the man were intimidating. But then, wasn't this what she was searching for? Jenni asked herself silently. True power? True wealth? The big leagues? She took a deep breath and went on.

"I know it must have seemed odd, me asking you for an appointment like this. But I've made a fool of myself," she said. "And . . . gotten in over my head. Under the circumstances, I felt it was best to come straight to the top."

Stretch McNaughten leaned back in his chair and templed his fingers, then nodded for her to continue.

Jenni took a breath and began the story she had so carefully rehearsed. It was the tale of a young, ambitious, slightly naive girl overwhelmed by the charm and power of a successful man. Though much was omitted — the true extent of her sexual relationship with Tom, the true quantity of information he had given her, any of the profits she had made — none of it was an actual lie, either. She'd planned her words carefully to avoid outright falsehoods, less out of ethics than to avoid getting caught.

"I know that it's all horribly foolish and reckless, Mr. McNaughten," she finished. "And I know there's no excuse. I never should have let him tell me so much. I know it compromises your firm terribly. But my career means everything to me. I've wanted to be on Wall Street since I was a little girl. I've been trying so hard to make my way up the ladder, and I guess Tom just seemed like a step to the next level, the key to some inner circle where I always wanted to be. I can't justify it; I just got carried away."

The recitation had soothed her jitters, given her confidence. Jenni watched Stretch's face, trying to gauge the reaction forming behind those stern, hooded eyes.

He wouldn't like the mess, the sexual intrigue,

the disloyalty, the indiscretion. But he would be anxious to keep Tom's foolish, unethical behavior quiet. And while Stretch McNaughten might be immune to the blatant sexual charms that worked on the likes of Tom Mahoney, Jenni had wagered that such a traditional man wouldn't be truly able to blame a woman. Her whole strategy depended on his inability to resist a damsel in distress.

There was a pause when she stopped speaking. *A deliberate man,* Jenni thought, *weighing his options.*

"Thomas's behavior was unseemly, but it is not your concern," he said finally. "My partners and I will deal with it in our own way and in our own time. I can assure you of that, just as I'm sure I can assume that your . . . disclosure will go no further."

"Of course not, Mr. McNaughten. You have my word on that."

He gave her a sharp look, but he didn't ask her, as she'd feared he would, what her word was worth. "In the meantime," he said, "a passion such as yours for the world of finance certainly should not go unrewarded. If you'll send me a copy of your résumé, we'll see if Finch McNaughten might not have a more suitable position for you than your current job. Once Thomas Mahoney is handled, of course. Though here again, I would rely on your utmost discretion. One lapse, shall we say, is permissible in an intelligent but naive young person. But a second is not."

"Again, Mr. McNaughten, you have my word." And he did. Why would she want to scheme and plot for a foothold in power if he would hand it to her on a platter?

Objective number one was accomplished. Now it was time for the kill, Jenni thought. To take care of her own, small, private pleasure. She hadn't liked the way Tom had snapped at her, after their lunch at Frascati's. No, she hadn't liked his tone one bit.

Nervously, she wet her lips. "Mr. McNaughten, I wonder if I could get your guidance on one final issue. I'm reluctant to bother you about this, but I think you should be aware. You see, it's about Tom Mahoney's wife. I've been worrying. . . . Is there anyone who can verify that she's actually still alive?"

Moira McTeague set the small bottles in a line along the polished laminate surface of the bathroom counter. Prevacid. Ambien. Hytrin. Elavil. Clonapin. There had to be twenty or more of them, in various degrees of fullness. It was too bad the translucent brown bottles were so many different sizes, Moira thought, and that the labels were so many different colors and types. So untidy. Still, she did the best she could to organize them.

Neatness counted, she thought virtuously, her thin lips twisting in a smile. Why, she could have acted immediately, the moment that disgusting, hypocritical little visitation turned away from her door, walked so self-importantly down her brick front path. But she hadn't, unlike some of the modern flibbertigibbets she could mention. She had scoured, scrubbed, polished the house. Cleaned out her closets and drawers. Tossed away all of the extra papers, and made sure the crucial documents, her will and insurance policy and birth certificate, were easy to locate in the old wooden desk. Emptied the refrigerator and kitchen cabinets. No one would ever be able to say that Moira McTeague wasn't a wonderful housekeeper. Yes, even at the end, neatness counted.

She always saved the odds and ends of prescriptions. Waste not, want not; that was always her way. It wasn't her fault if no one appreciated virtues like that anymore. The world would have been a much better place if people took care of these little things.

The bright jar of applesauce looked garish in the bathroom's fluorescent light. She had done some looking-up, in those weeks after Arthur had disgraced them. Compazine reduced the nausea, and applesauce helped mask the bitterness of the pills, helped keep them down. That was what all those choice-in-dying brochures she'd sent for said.

Choice in dying. That was a laugh. What choice had Arthur have? Oh, he'd wanted to fight. Wanted to let the trial go forward, trust to the mercy of the court, go serve his time if he had to. What kind of a choice was that? To drag Moira and her family even further through the mud? To make them even more of a public laughingstock? To throw every dime they'd worked for into the hands of bloodsucking lawyers? You'd better believe she'd had a serious talk with Arthur. A talk about responsibility, about family, about pride. It was easy enough to persuade him, in the end. He never did have any backbone. And of course he felt guilty about Alma Honeycutt; he knew that he owed her something. It was the least that he could do. "If you think it's best, dear," he'd said, his face defeated and colorless. He'd eaten his applesauce nicely, without leaving a drop.

And now it was just the same, Moira thought, beginning to crush the pills to powder under the bowl of a spoon. They had all looked so caring and virtuous, the little deputation that had come to see her. Hypocrites. Liars. Lucinda and that Billy Byrne. Moira never had thought that boy was good enough for the McTeagues. Jed Harper, Annie Taylor, Tommy Straub.

What a laugh. A baby-killer, her blockhead husband, a slut and her paramour, an officer of the so-called law who'd never have been able to solve the case if that weak little Cindy hadn't told them all about it. Stupid, the lot of them, and not one of them any better than they should be. Who were they to judge Moira McTeague? Not that they admitted to judging her. Oh, no. They wanted to *help* her. Get her counseling. Someone to talk to. A program. A facility. Avoid prosecution. When all the while they knew she would no more wash her dirty linen in front of some so-called doctor than she'd strip naked in town square. Hypocrites. Liars.

Some of the pills weren't easy to crush, but the task was finally done. It was good to have such strong hands, even if people thought they were ugly. Moira poured some applesauce into a bowl — part of the Lenox set she'd gotten from her mother — and stirred the white powder neatly into it.

She would be the victor in the end. Because she never had told them why she wanted to get into Alma Honeycutt's house, and she never would. They would always wonder. And they would all be sorry. They would know that they'd driven an old woman to her death with their *programs* and their *counselors*. They would know that her blood was on their heads, and they would have to live with the guilt, the shame, the sin.

The powder disappeared into the applesauce. Moira washed up the spoon, placed it tidily on the edge of the bathroom sink. The applesauce tasted fine. The store brands were just as good as those fancy kinds: If she'd told Cindy and her mother that once, she'd told them a million times. Soft and sweet, the fruit took only a minute to eat. Moira McTeague rinsed the bowl, applied a coat of the deep crimson lipstick that was the only cosmetic she ever wore, flicked off the bathroom switch — it was wasteful to leave the lights blazing, like so many folks did today — and lay neatly on her bed to die.

Twelve

It was almost ten at night, but Jed was still working.
His book had finally come together, he'd told
Annie two weeks before. Since then she would
wake before dawn to discover he'd already clos-
eted himself away in the study, come back from
a walk with Rooster to hearing him pacing behind the closed study door, or glance at him
while they were eating dinner only to find that
his attention was half a world away. One night,
with a slight shyness that touched her, he'd
given her the first section of his first draft to
read; she savored each page with wonder and
fascination, intrigued to see the man she knew
so well at home move through such an exotic
setting, amazed at the ease and range of his
mind.

Tonight she had eaten dinner with Sven and
Meg, enjoying every minute of their playful
sparring, then driven her car carefully back up
the road to Jed's. The front door was unlocked,
and he'd left a note greeting her under the lamp
on his hall table. As she deposited her coat on
the hall tree, she could hear the furious sound of
his strong tapping from his study. Rooster

trotted drowsily out of the kitchen to greet her. She smiled. Jed must be deep into his work indeed, if even his constant canine companion had been exiled from his side.

She made herself tea, then padded quietly back through the house. Its strong shapes and simple textures looked warm and inviting after the sharp cold of the night. Here and there signs of her presence lightened the masculine space: the green pottery vase she'd filled with yellow roses on the mantel, an antique Nine Patch quilt she'd persuaded him to buy, bringing life and color to a long dining room wall, one of her sweaters draped across the back of a kitchen chair, her basket of fabric at the end of the sofa where she always sat. He had his own equivalents at her house, too, small signs of the rich and comfortable intertwining of their lives.

The living room was chilly. She switched on a pair of parchment-shaded lamps, lit a match to the logs he must have laid earlier, hauled the basket of fabric onto the cushion next to her place on the couch. Legs tucked into a warm wool throw, Rooster sleeping heavily at the other end of the sofa, she sorted idly through the scraps and waited contentedly for Jed to appear.

Since their fight three weeks before, things had been easy between them. He had exorcised his demons, it seemed, at least for now. It seemed to her that the playful battles between them grew fewer, replaced by the unspoken tenderness of two people storing up memories.

Oddly, despite her constant awareness of their limited time together, his disappearance into his work didn't feel lonely to her. She finished her *Comfort* quilt, lost for a day or two in her own intense concentration. It was beautiful, she thought, perhaps the best thing she'd ever made. Regretfully she went about the tasks of having it photographed and packing it off for Pleasures. She had checked the mailbox in Asheville the week before and discovered a check, written in Elizabeth Felter's precise hand, for the last quilt she'd had in the shop's inventory. Even with that payment, Annie worried that her hoard of cash was getting low; she simply couldn't afford to keep the new quilt. After it was gone, she spent her days finishing the crib blankets for little Matthew and Nathaniel, musing about a new project, enjoying the knowledge that Jed was working only a few hundred yards down the hill or a few feet down the hall. In the evenings, when and if he broke for the day, they visited friends, went out to dinner, sat and read together near the fire. He played his dulcimer as she listened, she stitched while he watched, and they talked endlessly of their childhoods and their work and their lives and nothing at all.

Nothing marred the pleasure of it except the knowledge that it was coming to an end.

The trees had long since lost their last leaves, the Burnsville fire department long since hung Christmas lights and wreaths and swags on every lamppost in town. They'd had no deep snows, much to the dismay of the ski-conscious Chamber of Commerce. But winter was still beautiful on the mountain. The bare branches of the trees had a stark, aching purity, and they often awoke to the dazzling glimmer of frost, a glittering spectacle that took Annie's breath away.

She had promised herself that she would live in the moment. And for the most part, she'd made the promise good. Yet sometimes the smallest signs of the passing of time could fill her eyes with tears. The parade of tiny opening doors on the Advent calendar she'd bought herself. The growth of John and Susie's twins — Matthew and Nathaniel were thriving now, growing by leaps and bounds. The deepening connections she felt with her new friends, her new town. Good things, happy things. But also omens, portents, reminders of how soon Jed would be gone.

Trying to push the thought away, she reached into the pile of scraps for an old camisole she'd found at a local antique shop. The fabric felt almost alive under her fingers, the silk as liquid as batter, the lace as scratchy as a terrier's coat. She sorted through the heap of cloth again, loving the way the pieces gleamed in the soft light. Deep yellow and pale pink, bright white and ivory, the colors of spring in the dead of winter. She bent her head to the sensual delight of sorting them, choosing just the right pieces to express her new vision.

Hearing a noise Annie's dull human ears couldn't detect, Rooster woke, stiffened, then raced for the study door, a ruddy blur of motion. Annie smiled at the yipping sounds of welcome, the thudding of paws against the wooden door, then Jed's laughter as the dog danced around him. He came into the living room with Rooster capering at his heels and eyes that mirrored the warmth in her own.

"Evenin', lady," he said, bending to brush a kiss on her mouth. "No. Don't move." He strode to the other couch, dropped onto it with the grace of a cat. His bulky ivory fisherman's sweater suited him just like everything he wore, she thought. His face looked tired but content, and he folded his arms lazily behind his neck, propped his bare feet on the arm of the sofa nearest the fire.

He smiled at her questioning expression. "I'll come sit by you in a minute, but for now I just want to look at you. Pretty as the proverbial picture you are, sittin' there like some nineteenth-century lady with your sewing on your lap. Although," he said, brows knitting, "isn't the sewing supposed to be calico, or feed sacks, or something? That looks more like lingerie."

"It is."

"Ah. Darning? No, women don't darn lingerie anymore, or do they? A new artwork, maybe? What's this one going to be about?"

"You're like the Elephant's Child. Did you ever read those stories?" she said, smiling back at him. "A million questions. This one's going to be about sex, actually, since you ask."

He shook his head, laughing. "This I have to see. You're a marvel, Annie Taylor," he said. "And you're turning me on, if you don't mind me being crude. Are we sleeping here tonight or up at your place?"

"Here," she decided. "I can't drag you out into the cold or subject you to that cramped little bed after you've been sitting at a desk all day. I'm too warm now to move, myself."

"I'd expected you to want to spend more nights there. Now that the problem of Moira's been . . . well, let's just say resolved. You're not still troubled by it, are you?"

"I don't know," she said pensively. "Maybe. It's silly, maybe, but I wish I'd gotten a chance to talk to her alone before all of us stormed in on her together. It really doesn't feel resolved to me. Oh, I'm thrilled that I don't have to worry about those horrible break-ins anymore. But I feel guilty, I guess. She died so alone; she must have been so troubled. And Jed, I needed to know *why*. To finish the story, somehow. Without that, the house still doesn't feel at peace. Does that sound ungrateful?"

"No. I don't think so. Though you're kinder than I am. When I think of the terror she put you through, what I feel sure as hell ain't guilt. And it's going to be well nigh impossible to figure out what she had in that crazy mind, now she's gone."

"I know." How good it felt just to talk to him at the end of the day, even when the subject was troubling. She felt as though they'd been doing it for years, felt an ease she'd never felt in even the best days with Tom. "Cindy asked her mother and her aunts and uncles, and no one had any idea. I had another thought, though. I asked John to call Alma Honeycutt for me, to see if she and I could talk."

"For . . . ?"

She liked the way he didn't dismiss her thought. His expression considered what she'd said, didn't condemn it.

"I'm not sure, exactly," she said, feeling a little foolish despite his openness. "Maybe it was something to do with the house itself and not with me. Maybe Alma herself had some trouble with Moira, something that none of us know."

"It's possible. I wouldn't have thought of it, in all honesty, but it's possible. And it can't hurt. You'll enjoy Alma, too. If I'm gone by the time you talk with her" — he seemed to hesitate for a moment, then went on — "give her my regards, and tell her that I'm still the same crappy speller I always was."

"I will." She tucked the scraps of fabric she'd chosen carefully aside, swung her feet up onto the coffee table. "I asked John to recommend a lawyer, too. Just someone to talk to. It won't help with New York State law, but it will be a start, a way to get myself focused. My marriage — it's another loose end. Another shadow I'm tired of fighting. I'm ready to fight Tom now, for real."

"I'm glad." His tone was simple. "But . . . you in touch with him, him knowing where you are . . . it's not a very comfortable thought."

"I know. But it's time, Jed. More than time. It's as though I've been bewitched, all this fall. I came down here exhausted and fearful and bruised. I couldn't even imagine wanting anything more than peace, than safety. And suddenly it was like a fairy godmother had waved her wand over me. I didn't just get peace and safety, I got the first real home I've ever had. The best artworks I've ever done. A sense of myself again and my own strength. Friendship. And warmth. And love. The miracle — the joy — of love."

She stopped, but he didn't react to the word. "But I was thinking about it today, and I realized that it isn't enough. Because the clock is going to strike twelve, the beautiful soap bubble is going to break . . . the dream's going to end. No, not just because you're leaving or because Tom's going to come after me sooner or later or because Alma Honeycutt's going to make a decision about her house at some point. Because it just isn't real. I'm not real, anymore. I can't take a job. I can't file taxes. I can't open a checking account. I'm down at the post office twice a week just getting money orders. I can't visit the gallery where I sell my work; Pleasures is in New York, way too close to Tom. I can't talk to my mother — and no matter how difficult she is, she *is* my mother. I can't tell my new friends the whole truth. I can't even let old ones, people like May Williams, so much as know that I'm all right. *I'm* the shadow I'm fighting, not Tom. And all of a sudden, I don't like it at all."

"What will you do?"

"I'm not sure yet. Find out from the lawyer what I need to do to get a legal separation, how I can protect myself, to start. After that, just take it step by step."

He seemed to go still, somehow, and he didn't meet her eyes. "Will you stay in Burnsville?"

She took a deep breath. "No."

"You said it's your home."

"I know. But I can't, Jed," she said gently. "It's not safe, for one thing, not once Tom knows where I am. I've been incredibly lucky so far, but it won't last. Once I'm going through a divorce from him, I'm better off somewhere else, some anonymous big building in some anonymous city, maybe, with a doorman and lots of people around. And Jed . . . I couldn't stay here, even if Tom wasn't a factor. I've thought about it, a lot. Thought about whether I could be here and watch you come and go so close to me. Live like this, so warm, so intimate, so intertwined for a few months, then just wave good-bye. And the truth is that I can't do it. I would always be adjusting, just like I am right now — bracing myself for you to leave, longing for you to come home, worrying about where you were and whether you were well. I would end up angry or needy or clingy, rather than loving. It would just . . . break my spirit. And break my heart. After Tom, I can never let that happen to me again."

Jed moved restlessly on the couch, grimacing. "Meg told me the same thing, the day we argued, the day we all took that walk. She said it would hurt you. And I understood. I understand now. But Annie . . . it's selfish, I know that. And unreasonable. But I just don't want to lose you."

"I know. I feel that way, too." It felt odd, she thought as she gazed at his troubled face. Being the sure one, the certain one, the strong one for once. "But it's the best way."

He rose fluidly to his feet. She expected him to come and sit beside her. Instead, he prowled to the hearth, propped one elbow on the stone ledge of the mantel. His attention had shifted, she diagnosed, and she waited. He flexed his hand, stared down at the fire.

"Jed, tell me," she asked when no words were forthcoming.

"I talked to Dana today," he said, his eyes on the ruddy, charred logs. "About my schedule."

"And?"

"There are some things I need to handle in New York before I get on the road. Some meetings with my editor, a reading I should do, basic business stuff. And my publicist has scheduled an interview for the Monday after Christmas. I'll have to leave that Sunday. Earlier than I planned."

Ten days away. Only ten days. She thought she was prepared for it, but it still hit her like a blow. She steadied her breath. "It's going to be just as difficult whenever it happens. It's good to know for sure, Jed. Or . . . not good, but necessary."

He did come to her now, sitting next to her on the leather sofa, close by her side. She twisted to face him, slid her arms around his back, felt the texture of his cheek where it leaned against hers. It was getting cold in the room again; the fire was dying. The embers crackled gently behind her. She could feel tension in the broad shoulders, a tightness under the thick, nubbly texture of the wool. He gazed downward again, the blue gleam masked by the thick sweep of his lashes.

"I love you, Jed Harper," she said softly.

The moment seemed endless, liquid, pregnant, both sweet and uneasy at the same time. She kept her arms still where they crossed his shoulder blades, just holding him, sensing him struggling to speak.

He shook his head gently against hers. "And I love you, Annie Taylor," he said, his voice rough.

Words he had never said before, words he was reluctant to say even now; that she knew for sure. She hugged him tighter for one brief moment, her eyes filled with tears. She blinked them away before they could spill onto her cheeks, before he could see or feel them.

There would be plenty of time for tears once she no longer held him in her arms.

"All right, then, love. Come upstairs and show me," she said against his hair.

Detective Joseph Conway, senior investigator for the NYPD Domestic Violence Unit, pursed his lips as he stared down at the report in his hand. In the last twenty-four hours, two calls, one from a Mabel Williams and one from a Jennifer Stern, had come in on the possible disappearance of the wife of a Wall Street investment manager. And a routine check showed that the same possibility had been already reported two full months before, by the same Mabel Williams.

Follow-up . . . Conway pushed his bifocal glasses up farther onto his nose and scanned the page the police network printer spat out. Nothing. No confirming call, no confirming visit, no results. He frowned, squinting at the name at the bottom of the report. Well, that explained it. Rybczinski was the poor kid who had a heart attack. Twenty, thirty years old or something, and keeled over right in the men's room of the One Nine. The news of it was so chilling to your average NYPD cop that it even percolated from the precinct into the more rarefied atmosphere of the Domestic Violence Unit. Conway had made the mistake of telling Linda, and he'd spent the last six weeks eating fish and broccoli instead of steak in consequence.

Rybczinski was still out on disability, Conway seemed to remember someone telling him. Rozetti had retired. And someone had just tidied the report away without ever seeing if — he checked the report's tiny boxes again — Mrs. Annabel Mahoney had ever been seen again.

It happened all the time: loose ends, untied strings, stuff that slipped between the cracks. It wasn't even surprising, given the huge volume of suspected crime reports in a city this size, the reality of limited budgets, the strain on all the cops. But it made Conway wince in anger anyway and think of his beloved Linda waiting for him at home. Such a good woman, such a joy in his life. Her ex had been a batterer, too, and it was a miracle that she'd survived.

Plus, even if he didn't get personal about it, this was the kind of needless sloppiness that risked lives. And the kind of carelessness that gave the department a black eye: made people think cops didn't give a damn about violence against women and kids, opened them all up to accusations of not just incompetence but also insensitivity. Conway was a stickler about thoroughness, propriety. That was one of the reasons they'd tipped him to head the mayor's special unit. The Professor, they called him, teasing him about his immaculate tweed jackets and gold-rimmed glasses and precise way with words. They'd picked him in part for the good image he brought to the special squad, the impression of crisp, careful professionalism. That, and the fact that he was a damned good cop.

He was also a realist. He knew that if there had been a chance for the department to protect

Annabel Mahoney, it had probably passed in October, while Rybczinski had been gasping for breath in the john and Rozetti had been signing out to go collect his pension checks. Or maybe even before, before Mabel Williams had even realized her employer was gone. Conway looked at the small photograph of Annabel Taylor clipped to the report. Well, at least Rybczinski and Rozetti had gotten that far. A pretty woman, with the same long, black hair as his Linda and an expressionless face above a fancy dress. Unless she had fled or come back on her own, she could be dead by now. But still, Conway decided, the NYPD owed her something. He squinted at the report again and reached for the phone.

Meg and Sven ate roast chicken with pureed sweet potatoes and wild rice at the round kitchen table, listening to the wind whip the bare branches outside in the yard.

"Delicious. A man could get used to that. *I* could get used to that," Sven said, pushing his plate away. "Not that you should get ideas, mind you," he told Meg belligerently. "I might stop by to visit you now and then. But I'll always leave again."

"I know that," Meg said calmly. She rose to clear the plates, his as immaculate as if it had been washed.

"And I know I'll never leave with you," she went on, setting mugs on the table. "Not to go off to some godforsaken pinnacle in the middle of nowhere, and not to live with a billion other fools in New York."

"Huh. Never even liked the place, for your information. Plus," he said, "as long as we're getting this crap straight. I'm not going to have some sickly-sweet ceremony. Or a ring. On my finger, or through my nose. This is between us."

"I wouldn't have it any other way." She looked at him through her lashes as she poured the coffee. He had the stubborn, defiant expression of a little boy underneath the lines of sun and hard living, the ever-present deep blond stubble. The contrast, the unlikeliness of him, made her grin.

"One marriage was enough," she said, baiting him a little. "One husband. I have no need to replace him. He was a saint. Unlike you."

"Damn straight. Let's see. . . . What else? I'll probably drink sometimes," Sven said. Though he hadn't, Meg thought, since he'd been in Burnsville.

"And brawl," he insisted, as though it were a point of pride to be bad. "And disappear to write my books and do dangerous climbs and just generally act like my usual bloody macho asshole self," he continued. "You're going to put up with that?"

"I'm curious," she said. "Are you making some kind of proposal, or are you just picking a fight?"

He looked at her, then burst out laughing.

"Nothing fusses you, does it, woman?" he said. "You're unflappable. Both, then. I'm doing both."

"Fine. Then the answer is yes to the one, whatever it is you're proposing. And go to hell, to the other."

He laughed again, a loud, ebullient sound, full of vigor and life. "Unflappable," he repeated. "You're one in a million, I'll tell you. Get over here, then."

Meg went. She had no doubt that he'd do exactly as he'd said. Come and go. Argue. Take advantage of her shining house, her good cooking, her almost infinite patience. Irritate the hell out of her, despite her supposed unflappability.

And she would enjoy every minute of it. She would savor the zest he infused into her life when he was there, the energy, the physical heat, the trustworthiness he hid under his gruff manner. She'd savor the peace he'd leave when he disappeared, until life got too neat and tidy and she started to miss him again. And if he fell off a mountain sometime, as Jed had predicted he might, well, she'd pick herself up and go on if she had to. After all, she'd done it before.

Meg pushed Sven's arm aside and sat across his lap, then looked up to glimpse their reflection in the rain-soaked kitchen window. A sensible woman in an oxford shirt and chino pants, perched on a disheveled giant's thighs. Neither of them slim, neither of them young. It looked ridiculous. And she didn't give a damn. Meg

Thorn tightened her arms around Sven Rasmussen's solid shoulders and gave thanks for the late, sweet, utterly improbable gift of love.

Two days before Christmas, Jed finished his book.
He punched Print on his keyboard, leaned back in his chair, watched the first pages of the manuscript begin to spit soundlessly into the laser printer's tray. The house itself was soundless, so quiet it was almost eerie. No wind at all outside and no movement inside. Annie had gone into town hours before to do some last-minute Christmas shopping, stop in on Susie and the kids. Rooster was gone, too. Annie had offered to drop him off for his monthly grooming. Sven and Meg, Susie and John were all staying tactfully away, in deference to the furious concentration he always accorded the end stages of a book. There wasn't even any Moira McTeague to clump up and down the stairs and make him feel guilty about not liking wall-to-wall carpet or polyester bed linens.

Cotton sheets and all, his damned house felt about as welcome as a morgue, he thought suddenly.

Jesus, Harper. What the hell put that into your head? he wondered. Maybe the memory of poor old Moira was making him morbid. Even so, it was a ridiculous thought. He had a sudden vision of his homecoming three months before. The utter silence of the house hadn't felt deadly to him then. He had savored it, drunk it up like a thirsty man gulps pure spring water.

He stared at the growing pile of printed pages, tried to feel excited about putting Hong Kong to bed. Seventy-eight thousand words, vivid and staccato, as dense and jazzy as the place itself. Not his longest book, not even close, but surely his fastest, even after that first long, stalled struggle. Oh, there was minor tinkering to do, and minor revision. But it was done, the shape made whole, the threads all woven into a single strand. He knew that, instinctively, though he didn't know whether the result was a decent read, as he hoped, or a confusing jumble, as he feared.

He never knew, at this stage. It wasn't until a book was edited, proofed, fact-checked, and set in type that he began to get some distance on it. Right at the end, on days like this, he felt like he imagined a woman must feel a minute after giving birth. Proud. Elated. And so drained she could barely tell whether the baby had ten fingers and ten toes.

Of course, it wasn't his first baby, so to speak. After six literary kids, maybe you got a little blasé.

That thought shocked him, too. Since when was he blasé after almost a year of planning and research, writing and rewriting came together on the page?

It wasn't the book that was the problem, or the past, and he knew it.

It was him, and the future.

He was leaving in four days. He didn't want to go. At the same time, he wanted to run as fast as his boots could take him, without even saying good-bye.

He needed to finish packing. He didn't like to do it while Annie was around. Not that she made a fuss — she'd been perfect about it, not clingy at all. It just felt like a betrayal, somehow, when she was staying behind.

He needed to go pick up the last of her Christmas presents, too. The fabric shop had promised the shipment would come in today. He was looking forward to seeing her face.

Here's your present, Annie. Glad you like it. Merry Christmas. 'Bye.

He shook his head in frustration. In the blur of motion, his computer monitor caught his eye. At this angle, the light from his halogen desk lamp turned the deep green screen into a mirror. His own face looked back at him, dim, oddly colored from the screen saver, visibly torn, intense.

For the first time since he could remember, he didn't like the man he saw.

But he was damned if he knew how to be anyone else.

He rose abruptly, sending his chair sliding on its casters until it crashed against the edge of his desk. The printer hiccuped but went on printing. Jed strode out of his office, leaving the pages of his latest work to pile up without him.

Fired.

Or, as the bastards at Finch McNaughten would put it, terminated.

Let go.

Freed to pursue other opportunities.

Given a special holiday bonus. You had to love a firm that fired a nine-year employee three days before Christmas.

Released with a golden parachute. Or at least a glittering one. Six months' salary. His stock options purchased at market value. His retirement fund ready to be rolled over.

It was a generous severance under the circumstances, the mousy little so-called outplacement manager had implied. But why the hell, Tom thought as he stood outside the firm's front door, should dumping him come cheap? What was six months' salary compared to an office, a job, a secretary, a future, status in the only fucking world that had ever mattered to him? What was any amount of money when you'd been quietly but unceremoniously canned by the same firm you'd given your life's blood to, slaved for, sweated over? When your chances of getting an equivalent job were zero? When yet another bitch had tricked you again?

Because it sure the hell wasn't coincidence that Jenni Stern had stopped returning his calls last week, and this week he was fired from Finch McNaughten on charges of not just mishandling accounts but also leaking inside information. The companies that bastard McNaughten had cited — well, Jenni was the only one he'd told. Jenni, with her hot body and her conniving little mind.

Goddamned bitches. Goddamn sluts. His mother, Annabel, her mother, Jenni — each one was worse than the last. The rage built in him as he took the elevator downward, pushed through the building's revolving doors, headed north toward the Stock Exchange. Even on a chilly winter afternoon, the narrow streets and sidewalks of the financial district, built in the days before automobiles, were crowded with office workers, tourists, vendors, and messengers. Tom shouldered his way through the throng as though it didn't exist, ignoring the trail of muttered curses and dark looks he left in his wake.

"Fucking bitch," he said aloud as he turned west on Wall Street. In fact, he decided, they weren't all the same. In fact, it was Annabel who was the worst bitch of all. If it hadn't been for her, none of this would have happened. He wouldn't have fucked with Jenni, he wouldn't be out on his ass like some fool, some loser. And then there was the latest one, his stupid private detective. What did he expect, when Finch McNaughten had recommended her? She probably spent more time doing her fucking nails than working. Well, he was paying enough for her time. She'd better produce some results, and fast.

He stopped at a pay phone, pulled out his Palm Pilot, punched in the phone and credit card numbers.

"Yes. Actually, I do have the information you asked for," Liz Friedman said coolly.

"This one's taken, slant-eyes," Tom said over his shoulder. "That's just great," he said into the static-filled receiver. "You couldn't have fucking called me?"

"I just received it yesterday afternoon. I was going to call later today."

Christ, Tom thought, *some customer service.* But it didn't matter. Nothing mattered, except where Annabel was and when he could have the satisfaction of punching the living shit out of her. "No, I don't have a pencil," he said. "But don't you worry. I'm not going to forget."

He dropped the phone down onto the hook with a flourish, triumph mingling with the anger in his veins. Some dipshit town in the back of beyond. Why didn't she just lay herself out on a platter?

What a stupid, pathetic woman. You could almost feel sorry for a person as stupid as that. Only you wanted her to learn her lesson, didn't you? You wanted her to get the appropriate punishment for her mistakes. After all, this was a world in which people did get punished. Look at Tom himself. He was being punished, wasn't he, and he hadn't done a frigging thing wrong. Except to have a little fun for once. Now, there was a Goddamn sin. And to piss off that asshole Jim Perry somehow. SafeCo had pulled its whole $200 million account from Finch McNaughten's management last week. Well, it happened. But naturally, McNaughten had to find somebody to blame.

He found himself at West Street, a broad band of highway bounded on one side by the Hudson River and on the other by a straggling line of bars, warehouses, and dives. Hookers prowled West Street, and gay prostitutes, and drug dealers of all kinds, even in the bitter December wind. This was what he had come to, Tom thought, heading off to nowhere, standing in the frigid cold with a bunch of riffraff. He turned northward, walking fast, hunching his shoulders against the cold until the black velvet collar of his Chesterfield coat hit his chin. He saw a yellow cab coming toward him along West Street and he stuck out his arm, but the cabbie sped on by as though he were invisible. And the next one did the same, empty taxis, idiots zooming by like his money wasn't good enough for them. Like he was invisible. *I'm not fucking invisible,* he wanted to scream. *I'm someone, Goddamn it!* Beginning to shake, burning with rage so intense he thought it might blow up the universe, Tom turned to try again.

"Mr. Thomas Mahoney?" the man in the tweed jacket said. "I'm Detective Conway. Joseph Conway, NYPD Domestic Violence Unit. May I speak with you for a moment?"

Tom's stomach lurched for about the fiftieth time that day. Jesus, would the nightmare ever end? Instinctively, he reached up to smooth his hair, then remembered he'd stopped at the Racquet Club to shower after that ridiculous walk downtown. He looked fine, like any professional coming home after a long day at the office. He'd only gone to the club to make sure that the neighbors and building staff wouldn't notice how windblown and disheveled he looked. He'd never imagined that a fucking NYPD dick would be sitting right in his lobby, right underneath the huge natural Christmas wreath the co-op board hung above the lobby fireplace each year.

Dan, the fat-faced doorman, was looking with open curiosity their way. How could he not? Detective Whateverhisnamewas must have identified himself. That was the rule. Visitors had to be announced. There was no such thing as privacy at 1051 Park Avenue.

"Could we make an appointment for another time, Detective? It's been a long day." He tried to keep his voice cool and make it less a question than a statement. Christ knew it was no lie.

All through the cab ride to the club, the shower, the cab ride home, the shaking that had started on West Street hadn't stopped. Tom kept his hands in the pocket of his coat, hoping it didn't show. Jesus, he had to pull himself together. Instead, he had a sudden, insane desire to tell the detective that he'd just been fired, walked for miles, felt like screaming aloud like a crazy person. Say it all really loud, give the guy a little taste of the fury that kept burning within him, bubbling within him, not letting him relax for a second. Vent a little. Spill his guts. That would wipe the calm, pleasant, long-suffering look off the fucker's face. And Dan's face, and the face of nosy Mrs. Falk from the third floor, who was standing by the elevator with her yappy little poodles. He'd like to see their expressions, actually. See what they'd do when the volcano really blew. He stifled the wild impulse with difficulty.

"I'd prefer to talk now," the detective said, still pleasant. "It will only take a few moments. But it's a matter that's been pending for quite a while. In your apartment, perhaps. If you don't mind, of course."

I'd prefer. A few moments. If you don't mind. Prissy bastard. Where did he think he was, Harvard Law? Tom did mind. But he didn't have a choice. This wasn't the guy that had called him a few months earlier, that had been a kid with some Polack name. This one, with his tight-ass little tiepin and skeptical face, wouldn't be fobbed off with some fairy tale about car accidents and beloved cousins. He'd better get it together, Tom told himself again. He gestured toward the elevator, and led the detective upstairs.

Thirteen

"Wake up, princess," a voice said from above her head.

"Mmm?" Annie was deliciously drowsy. They had gone to a candlelit carol service the night before, and then made love when they got home. It had an extra edge to it now, their love-making, an intensity compounded of fear and love and longing and the shadow of the sadness to come. It was delicious and exhausting. All she wanted to do was curl up into Jed's arms, close out the world, and go back to sleep.

"Oh, no you don't. Good little girls wake up bright and early on Christmas morning. Especially little girls that have to be over at their friends' house for brunch in an hour and a half," he said.

Moaning a little, she turned toward his laughing voice only to bump into something hard and knobby. A gift-wrapped present, she saw, blinking and sitting up, propping her hands against the mattress. One of many, big and small, strewn across the coverlet and vividly bright in the clear morning light. Jed, sitting in his jeans and flannel shirt on the edge of the bed, grinned at her like a boy. She shook her head in pleasure and disbelief.

"I haven't seen so many presents in one place since I was a little girl. In fact, I'm not sure I ever had this many, even then. Morning, Santa," she said, holding out her arms.

"Mornin'." He leaned over the gift-strewn bed to kiss her. His mouth was warm, with a faint taste of cream. "I brought your coffee. It's on the nightstand."

"Mmm. Just what I was needing. Is that snow I see falling outside, or am I dreaming?"

"No. Real snow, right on cue. Not a blizzard, exactly, but enough to do the job."

She braved the chill to go to the window, savor the magical scene outside. The fat white flakes fell thickly from the gray white sky, softening the angles of tree branches, turning the world into a black-and-white photograph, a Steichen or an Adams. "It's so perfect it almost doesn't look real. There'll be kids celebrating all over town."

"And driving their moms crazy," he said, coming to stand behind her and wrap her in his robe, "and tramping snow into the house, and running their sleds into trees."

"You're a cynic. Or — I guess I can't call you that. Jed . . . so many presents. You only have one thing to unwrap."

"Doesn't matter. These are little. Silly."

Little, but not silly. She exclaimed over a monogrammed robe the same shade of blue terry as his. A fat, round teapot for her kitchen, and four matching cups and saucers. A long wool challis dress with a high neck and sleeves. A ribboned twig basket of fragrant imported bath oils and soaps. A cashmere shawl, soft and supple and the same robin's-egg blue as the cottage walls. Four pairs of lace-topped stockings. A delicate antique pendant and earrings set with opals — the gray of her eyes, he said. And, hiding at the foot of the bed, a gleaming sewing machine, just like the one she'd abandoned in New York.

"I think it's the model you told me about," he said, "but you can return it if I got it wrong."

She vaguely remembered his questions weeks before — queries about how she worked, where, on what, that she'd assumed were the product only of his endlessly inquisitive mind. He must have heard her cursing, too, over Alma's old Singer. How wonderful it would be to have something so fast and responsive to work on again, and something so familiar. She kissed his cheek, reached for his hand. "It is the same, and that's perfect. Nothing new to learn, no new gimmicks I don't need. Thank you, Jed."

"It's not very romantic, I reckon. But I wanted to get something that would help."

"Taking my sewing seriously is one of the most romantic things you could do for me. It's not that, that's making me quiet." She tightened her hold on his hand, blinked furiously. "I'm just trying not to cry. As usual, lately."

"Oh, God. Well, try hard, sweetheart. Because if you get all sentimental, we're both going to fall apart."

She laughed a little through the teariness, then distracted herself by going to get his gift. As he pulled open the glossy red wrapping on the huge box, she watched his beautiful hands, his fascinating face. The lump stayed in her throat, no matter how hard she swallowed. He pulled her gift out of the box, held the four-foot square of fabric high.

She waited, suddenly self-conscious. She'd had no spare cash to buy him something special, and anyway, she'd realized, there was little that he needed. So she had fallen back on her imagination, on her art. And on her beloved thrift shop, of course, not to mention a few expensive side trips to the antique shop next door. "It's a hanging. For your office wall. You said it looked bare," she said, a bit uncertainly. "And you said you'd like something I made. It's us. The piece, I mean. You and me."

"I know. Couldn't miss it. You," he said, smiling, tracing a finger over an arc of shell-pink antique lace, a scattering of pearl buttons she'd appliquéed on top, an arabesque of pale blue cording. "And me," he finished, sliding his hand onto a square of blue denim. Denim and lace, sturdy cotton and delicate silk, deep blues and pastels, masculine rectangles and feminine curves, all curling together, overlapping, intertwining, until the utterly different pieces could never be pulled apart. "Is this the same one you told me was going to be about sex?"

"The same. Only I changed my mind. While I worked on it," she said, looking at his face, "I realized it was actually about love."

She did cry then, tears spilling soundlessly down her cheeks even as she squeezed her eyes tight shut to try to contain them. As she dropped her face into her hands, she could feel him pushing the litter of boxes and gift wrap aside, taking her in his arms. His strong body seemed to envelop hers; she clung to him, his solidity, his warmth. They sat motionless, holding each other close. A small, loving island, Annie thought, amid the great shifting vastness of the world.

But they were due in the world, and soon. She dried her eyes, put on the gorgeous deep rose challis dress, and drove with Jed to John and Susie's. The rest of the day seemed blurred to her, unnatural, unreal. Part of her seemed to hover over each scene of joy and closeness, more like a historian than a participant: storing away images into some mental photograph album, collecting impressions to remember in the harder times to come.

An image of Jed in his black wool turtleneck and jeans, his blue eyes crinkling with laughter and sheepishness, one twin baby cradled in each arm.

A picture of Sven winking at Meg over the table, and the loving glance Meg threw him in return.

An image, glimpsed from the hallway, of Susie, gone off by herself to the kitchen to nurse, her rosy face bent over Matthew's tiny, blue-blanketed form. And John, standing beside her with a softly whimpering Nathaniel, resting his hand on her shining blond head.

A picture of Jed and Sven on their way to the café to pick up the wine Meg had forgotten to bring, a huge rumpled Mutt and a tall elegant Jeff, moving together in perfect amity.

A vision of the ordinary Burnsville street outside John and Susie's living room bay window. Just middle-sized houses with warm yellow light pooling from the windows, a dotting of Christmas wreaths and light strings, the movement of cars bringing people to and from their Christmas celebrations. Nothing wealthy, nothing exotic or rare, and yet somehow special, touched with grace.

And a picture of the whole group of them standing near John's piano, singing and making music. Jed, and John on the banjo, and Dottie Barclay's daughter Ellen on the fiddle, playing reels and carols and ballads. How hard it was to believe that she had never heard their music before September. How much her life had changed in three short months. Jed looked up from his dulcimer, threw her a quick, questioning glance.

She turned blindly away, hoping that no one would notice. In the empty kitchen she leaned her head back against the cool smoothness of the refrigerator and tried to get herself under control.

"Annie." Susie appeared beside her, slim again now, but no less warm or maternal. "You okay?"

"Yes." Annie touched her hand to Susie's. "No. Oh, Susie. I keep crying, like a fool. I promised myself that I'd be strong."

"You are strong. But you're also human. Letting him go like this — I couldn't do it. I wouldn't be crying, I'd be yelling his head off. Heck, I've been tempted to yell his head off, and he's not even mine."

"He's not mine, either. He's not anyone's. And he made that clear from the start." Annie found a holly-printed cocktail napkin, used it as a tissue. If she didn't stop crying, her eyes would be as pink as her dress. "It's not his fault, Susie. He couldn't be content if he stayed; he'd snarl like a tiger in a too-small cage, and I'd be hurt, and he'd be guilty. It's better this way, it really is. But . . . every moment is so precious. I keep telling myself there'll be plenty of time for sadness after he's gone."

"True. But it's an easier truth to tell yourself than it is to live."

"Ain't *that* the truth," Annie said, and then someone, Annie didn't even know who, called to them to join the party again.

Sunday's dawn was opulent red clouds bleeding against the dull gray sky, a beautiful backdrop for loss.

Jed had been up in the night, but he was

sleeping soundly now, his long legs bent to fit into Alma's double bed. His face was as smooth as a boy's against the pillow, though his eyelids twitched a little as he dreamed.

Her house was icy. Annie wrapped herself quietly in her new robe, pulled on thick wool socks. Downstairs, she adjusted the thermostat, put on the water for tea.

Jed had finished packing the morning before, then brought all of her gifts and her new sewing machine up the mountain. They'd spent the day together quietly, saying little, doing less. In bed on Saturday night she'd held him tightly, but he seemed to understand that she couldn't bring herself to make love. He seemed like a stranger again; his handsome face looked still and shuttered to her, and she wondered if she seemed just as inscrutable to him. But she didn't ask.

She held the warmth of her teacup in the curve of her hands, wandered out of the kitchen. In the hallway, his jacket was gone from the closet. In the bedroom, the drawers no longer held extra socks and underwear or his favorite flannel shirt. The book he was reading was gone from her sofa, the notes he'd been sorting through gone as well. She had packed his things up the week before, searching out everything except his toothbrush and spare razor, bringing them to his house quietly, when he was out at the post office arranging to have his mail held. If he noticed that the shirt was back in his closet or the book on his desk, he didn't comment. He, too, seemed to be treading warily, walking on eggs. The only signs of him left in her home, ironically, were the guns she disliked so much: the shotgun, propped in the corner near the kitchen door, and the smaller gun cached safely in a drawer. She had insisted she could never use them, but getting him to take them home was an argument she hadn't won.

Rooster was already at Meg's; he knew the sights of Jed's departures, and they distressed him, Jed said. His house was emptied of food, immaculate, ready to close up. She had the key and his encouragement to use the place if she wanted, but she knew she'd never be able to set a foot inside. He'd sent several boxes of books and supplies off in advance, arranged to let John and Susie drive him to the airport and return his truck from their house. It cut their time together short by hours, but Annie was glad. She didn't want to say good-bye to him amid the impersonal maze of airport corridors, the Sunday-morning bustle of vacations ended, the heart-breaking clamor of greetings and arrivals.

She could hear him moving now, his footsteps firm and sure. When he came downstairs, he moved gracefully and economically as always, easy in himself, at home with the task of departure.

The truck was outside. He went out to slide his duffel bag and laptop on the seat and came back into her hallway smelling of winter, his strong cheekbones flushed with cold. He reached into his leather jacket, checked for his wallet and ticket. How well she knew the glowing tumble of his hair, the fluid movement he used to check his watch for the time. How little she knew his thoughts.

"You have Dana's number in New York, and she can always reach me, within a few days at least," he said, coming to stand in front of her. "And I'll call you once I get settled."

"No," Annie said quickly, reaching out to touch a finger on his lips. "No, Jed. We never made any promises. Let's not start now."

"I wasn't intending to. I'd like to call you, Annie. I want to. I need to. Need to hear your voice, know how you're doing, find out if you're all right. You told me you wouldn't be here when I got back. But you didn't say we couldn't be in touch."

"When you talk about it, the traveling, the writing . . . it's the freedom that makes your eyes glow," she said, shaking her head at his attempt to speak. "That excitement I love in you, in your books . . . It's all about letting a new place consume you, letting it take you where and when it will, becoming whoever you need to be to learn its secrets. I think it's one of the reasons your writing is so wonderful, that ability to be totally wholehearted about where you are in the moment. Your attention has never been divided, and it shouldn't be. In all the times we've talked about your trips, I've never once heard you mention missing your house or Burnsville or your friends here. You don't even say you miss Rooster."

She reached a hand to touch his cheek, smiled a little into his somber eyes. "This has been so good, this thing between us. Something we're both pleased with and proud of. Let's finish it cleanly. I don't want to picture you somewhere feeling guilty because you haven't gotten to a phone. And I don't want to become the kind of woman that sits around at home, feeling resentful that a man doesn't call when she wants him to. Meg or John will know where I am when I leave here. But please, Jed, let's just let it go."

She could see he still wanted to argue. "Please. You need to let me do this my way."

"Annie. . . . " His jaw clenched and unclenched, and he shook his head in frustration. "You sandbagged me with this. Let me assume we'd have some kind of connection, at least. Waited until the last minute to tell me we wouldn't, when you knew I couldn't fight."

"Yes," Annie said. "You're right, Jed. I know it's not fair. But I did."

He stared at her, hurting and knowing he had no right to. Wanting to speak and not knowing what to say.

His fairy tale princess, he thought, looking at the soft fall of her black hair, her gorgeous mouth, the eyes that were so pearly and pretty and now so sure. She looked beautiful and tired and somehow bruised. It came to him that this leave-taking was battering her, pummeling her with loss, just as her damned husband had pummeled her with his fists.

Everything in him wanted to argue her point, to insist that he'd call, to make arrangements to meet her here or somewhere else when the trip was done. But that would be a worse pummeling than good-bye, and he knew it. Newfoundland was vast and largely empty; that had been its entire appeal. As she had guessed, he couldn't guarantee when he'd reach a phone or when he'd want to use it. He couldn't tell when he'd be back to civilization or what kind of mood he'd been in when he got there. And making empty promises would only make them both feel worse in the end.

He shook his head again, but gently this time, and held her once more in his arms. The way her head nestled against his shoulder, the fresh scent of her hair in his nostrils, the sweet curve of her arms around his back . . . it was as though she'd been designed just to fit against his body. And the way she rested against him . . . so soft, but she never clung. Right now he wished — selfishly, stupidly — that she *would* cling, that she'd show some evidence that she was dying inside, like he was. It was ridiculous, it was insane, but right now he felt like all he needed was that single excuse, that single plea, to call the whole damned trip off. But that *was* ridiculous. He blinked the thought fiercely away.

He had just managed to calm his face when she leaned back to look at him. "It's time, Jed," she said.

He nodded slowly. "Take care of yourself, Annie Taylor," he answered.

"You, too . . . J. M. Bell."

He sensed that they were both looking for words, but there was nothing left to say. He took one last searching look at her face — so calm and resolute it was, that gorgeous face, without a single hint of tears.

If he didn't go right now, he wouldn't be able to. She walked with him to the porch, then stopped by her doorway, in between the pair of empty rockers that moved a little in the wind. He stepped down the stairs and into the truck, started the engine, and drove carefully down the hill.

All too quickly the taillights of the truck were lost, and then even the sound of the engine. He was gone, and he might never have been there, so empty the mountain looked. Numbly, Annie walked inside, shut the door behind her, lowered herself onto one of the kitchen chairs.

It had taken every ounce of will, every reserve of strength she had not to break down. But she'd meant what she'd told him. She'd wanted to end it cleanly, without guilt or manipulation or expectations that would only muddy things. She'd wanted him to understand that she loved him — honored him — as he was, free and unfettered and belonging to no woman. She'd wanted him to remember Annie Taylor strong and loving and proud.

But she couldn't have managed it a single moment longer. Already she could feel her body shaking with the aftermath of her efforts at stillness, with the tension and the grief and all the nights of little sleep. She felt boneless, as empty as though someone had scooped out her mind and heart and innards, leaving only a trembling shell behind. It was a luxury, suddenly, the chance to indulge this weakness. Like a dessert that she'd been saving until all the healthy vegetables had been eaten. Alone in her kitchen, Jed Harper's shotgun propped silently in the corner, proud Annie Taylor bent her head, wrapped her arms around her knees, and cried as if her heart would break.

The little chalet was furnished in a style Tom had immediately dubbed dipshit country: rows of little china ducks, walls edged with stenciled leaves, ugly throw pillows with blue and maroon fringes. It was tacky, and everything in it was cheap: the showerhead that gave only a trickle of water, the too-soft mattress, the wall-to-wall carpeting that was dotted with stains. No wonder the idiots who had leased it in the first place had canceled. He'd rented the place for two weeks from a big realtor in Asheville, and it looked like just what it was: some middle-class fool's idea of rental property, a ski chalet used by ten or twenty or thirty groups of vacationers a year, each one as anonymous as the next. With the Eddie Bauer parka and Orvis gear he'd bought before leaving

New York, he had no trouble looking the part. He'd chosen bright colors: a royal blue parka, a red hat, iridescent ski goggles, and he'd consciously broadened his voice back into the old New Jersey harshness. Between the northern accent and the ski gear, he'd bet a grand that the bored young girl at the realtor's office wouldn't even remember his face.

It was Sunday night. The rage he'd felt last week had gone, leaving only a sense of focus. He'd never felt sharper in his life, more on top of things. He'd always had a good mind for planning, and no general could have strategized a campaign more brilliantly. Even this tacky A-frame was a base camp even more perfect than he'd ever have dreamed. It wasn't the interior, he thought, enjoying the black humor of it. It was the view.

Tom had watched them for three days now, his bitch of a wife and her hillbilly stud, watched them since he'd arrived the day before Christmas. Watched the way they moved between the big log house and the crappy little cottage he figured must be hers. Three months, and the cunt was already shacking up. It hadn't taken little Miss Prissy Annabel long to spread her legs, had it? The thought made the rage return for a minute, but he pushed it aside. He didn't have time to be pissed off. And besides, as far as he was concerned, the slut could fuck the army if she wanted to. She might as well enjoy herself, he thought, his lips curling. For the time being.

Still, the hillbilly had been a problem, back and forth all the time, always hovering somewhere around the place except when they both went out together. Until the past day or so, that was. Tom had been afraid to believe his eyes when he saw the fool start packing the truck, closing up the shutters of his house. It was too good to be true, the possibility that he was leaving the place for good. Just this morning, Tom had squinted through his expensive new binoculars in disbelief. Sure enough, the man was swinging a couple of bags into the truck. From the hell-bent way he drove off and the stricken pause before Annabel went inside, he figured the good-bye seemed pretty final. "Congratulations, bitch," he said aloud. "Looks like you blew another one, didn't you?"

He'd kept the binoculars to his eyes off and on for hours, ignoring the tremor that still moved in his hands, but there was no motion from the cottage. What a perfect time for the breakup, right now when Tom had arrived to settle his old scores. Obviously, he thought, some things were just meant to be.

He put the binoculars down, sighing a little with regret. He'd have liked to take care of his business right now. But haste made waste, and he'd done his planning too carefully to ruin it. He'd wait until tomorrow, until she left the house. Without the hillbilly hanging around, he could scope out the lay of the land, arrange for a little surprise for his beloved Annabel. In the meantime, he'd check his equipment. He wanted his visit with his wife to be just perfect; he didn't want to arrive on her doorstep and find he'd left something essential behind. He'd laid out his gear on the fake-oak dining table. Now he ran his hands along it, enjoying the heft and weight of each piece. As any good hunter could tell you, catalogs sold items far more useful than hats.

All the city's Christmas finery was still in place. Huge, opulent displays in every elegant shop-window. Sparkling fairy lights twined around the lampposts, the trees, the apartment-building awnings. Evergreen branches, topiary, and garlands were everywhere, and enough red ribbon to wrap gifts for the entire world.

An old yellow cab with a garrulous driver and no shock absorbers to speak of drove Jed bumpily through Central Park. Though he didn't love Manhattan, Jed loved the park, a huge and astonishing rectangle of wilderness in the midst of the city's man-made density. Today it was in its full winter glory. There'd been snows here recently, and good ones, he guessed, blanketing the rolling, varied terrain with pristine white. And then a sleet storm, encasing everything, even the tiniest twig, in a sheath of diamond-bright ice, making even the smallest tree a miracle of gleaming lace. At the Wollman Rink, skaters circled vigorously in riotously bright winter gear; at Sheep Meadow, cross-country skiers slid soundlessly along the gentle slopes. The sun was setting gorgeously over the old skyline of the city's West Side, silhouetting the varied and eccentric spires of the buildings and bathing the glitter of the park with brilliant orange red.

God, how he wished Annie were beside him, sharing her city with him. The thought came to him before he could stop it, even though he'd promised himself sternly to leave Annie and Burnsville and everything but the forthcoming trip behind. How she'd love the brilliance of this, the contrast between the fire and the ice, the solid geometry of the buildings and the free-form tangle of the trees. And God, how he'd love to have her at his side, bring her up to Dana's apartment, where he was due for a Sunday dinner. Watch her flush a little at Allan's certain admiration, hug little Olivia onto her lap, talk books with Dana, just enjoy the shabby, unselfconscious comfort of the big old apartment. He stepped out of the cab, took a deep breath of air so cold it seared his lungs, and pushed the longing fiercely away.

Upstairs in Dana's apartment, everything was comfortable confusion. Olivia, at ten already leggy and beautiful, danced over for a kiss, then raced back and forth celebrating the presents he'd just bought at F. A. O. Schwartz. Dana greeted him with a rib-crushing hug, Allan with a grin and the offer of a drink. The household's two cats regarded him curiously from a wide windowsill. The signs of Christmas were still here, too, a huge wreath over the fireplace, a tree garlanded with popcorn strands and home-made ornaments and still surrounded by toys.

"Forgive the ghosts of Christmas past," Dana said as she waved the girl off to get washed and led him to one of the living room's big, shabby, comfortable armchairs. "Livy is resisting the thought of having to put a single piece of her loot away. Speaking of which, don't let her over-whelm you with her Spice Girls mania. If you don't watch it, she'll tell you more about Sporty Spice than you ever wanted to know. You know you always have our permission to cut it short."

"Amen to that," Allan said, handing Jed a glass of wine. "I, myself, am looking forward to the end of the Spice Girls craze, except when I face the fact that the next pop band du jour will prob-ably involve men with green hair and screeching guitars. Cheers, Jed. Welcome to New York."

"Thanks, Allan. Glad to be here," Jed re-sponded, trying to persuade himself it was true.

Dinner — a big, hearty pasta fragrant with olives and garlic — was over, and Allan was putting Olivia to bed. Dana shooed away Jed's offers to help clean up and waved him toward the living room. He swung his booted feet onto the coffee table — blessedly, Dana's was that kind of a home — and leaned his head against the sofa back, wishing he felt as relaxed as the apartment.

In what seemed like only a moment or two, Dana reappeared with a tray of coffee. After lowering it onto the coffee table, she put one hand briefly on Jed's shoulder. "You're preoccupied, friend," she said.

"Sorry. I was trying not to be obvious."

"You weren't. Not to the others, anyway. In fact, Olivia was fully persuaded you were fascinated by the horrifying departure of Ginger Spice. But to me, you just look like you're a million miles away."

"I guess so." But whether he was back in Burnsville or already in Newfoundland, he wasn't sure.

"You're missing your lady," Dana guessed.

"I am," he said. "And I'm not liking it much."

"It's no fun."

Jed raised one eyebrow at her, and she smiled.

"You've been thinking I'm immune to romantic ups and downs?" she asked. "You just didn't know me in the days Allan and I were first dating. We put each other through merry hell there for a while. If it wasn't one of us getting cold feet, it was the other. Sometimes I think it's a miracle we were able to forgive each other when we finally wised up."

"Yeah. I know what you mean. But Annie and I . . . the logistics are much more complicated than that."

"Are they?" Dana threw him a shrewd glance.

Jed shrugged, overcome by a sudden feeling of restlessness. "I don't know," he said. "I don't know that I even have the balls to find out. It scares me, Dana. I'm not sure I could write, or think, or even observe things, with a woman by my side all the time."

"But what makes you think it would be like that? I can't see you falling in love with a dependent woman, or a conventional woman, or a woman who would cling."

It was true. Images of Annie flashed into his mind. Annie, refusing his offers of help and money. Flashing fire when he made decisions without consulting her. Having the courage to start a whole new life alone when the old one wasn't right. Working on her quilts so hard she forgot that time existed, just like he did. Bidding him good-bye with love and dignity and not a single hint of resentment.

Dana spoke into his silence. "Jed . . . I'm not going to ruin our good relationship by starting to push advice on you at this late date. Just . . . don't make things too black and white. You've decided that either you have to be the great solitary genius or the housebound husband tied to a woman's apron strings. But you don't. Marriage doesn't have to be like that — marriage *isn't* like that. It's always a compromise, a matter of two people finding a balance that gives them both enough comfort and enough space. And that's the end of the lecture for today."

The restlessness in him had grown. It was almost intolerable now. He reached for her hand, kissed the back of it quickly, let it go. "I appreciate it, Dana. No, really. I just feel antsy. I need to be walking. Thinking. Would you mind?"

"Of course not." She rose, tugged his jacket from the hall tree, walked with him to the door. "But you promise you're not leaving mad?"

"What does Livy say? Cross my heart. Cross my heart, Dana, I'm not leaving mad. I'm leaving feeling lucky to have you, as an agent and as a friend. Plus," he added, smiling, "you're a darned good cook. So don't worry. Just say good-bye to Allan for me, okay?" He reached down to envelop her in a hug, grateful, as he'd said, to have her in his life.

And grateful, despite it, to be alone and moving again. His body felt electric with anxious energy, and the city that greeted him outside Dana's building matched it. Even at ten on a freezing December Sunday night, the city was jazzy and thrumming. Bright yellow cabs cruising for passengers, neon signs and vivid shopwindows alight all night, a scattering of New York's astonishingly varied population passing by him this way and that. Without conscious decision, he ignored the beckoning cabdrivers and headed south, striding fast to generate some warmth, hearing his boot heels click sharply on the pavement. It was cold, close to zero he gauged, but his fleece-lined leather bomber jacket was thick, and his gloves and boots had taken him through far more biting chills than this. As he walked, the restaurants of the Upper West Side gave way to the office towers of Midtown, lit but silent and empty on the weekend. He moved without thought, without intention, driven by some kind of animal instinct, feeling as rootless as the cold wind that stung his cheeks and brought water to his eyes.

He'd veered eastward, somehow. On a tiny side street in the Village he passed McSorley's, one of the oldest ale houses in the city and one of the few that had survived intact. Impulsively, he swung inside, ordered a shot of Jack Daniel's at the dark, age-scarred bar, tossed it down. The liquor burned his throat, left a fiery trail through his gullet. He ordered another, took it to one of the worn leather banquettes that ran along the back of the dim, beer-scented, half-empty barroom. Sitting, he took a more moderate sip of the second drink. The alcohol soothed him a little, continued the calming effect that the walking had begun.

Only it wasn't walking, he thought, propping one booted foot against the rung of a teetery wooden chair.

It was running.

He was almost alone in the bar, but he could hear a babble of voices around him. Meg's voice, telling him about risk. Annie's voice, telling him about fear.

His own voice, telling her he loved her.

Loved her, he thought now, yes. But he hadn't trusted her. He hadn't trusted anyone.

Other figures joined the chorus now, his mother and his father, in all their failure and their pain. It was as though his mother's nagging, discontented, dependent voice had followed him his whole life, superimposing itself on every woman he'd ever met or even imagined. And as though his father's angry, powerful bellow dogged him, too, an image of the caged, resentful man he'd always feared he'd become.

And even when Annie Taylor came into his life — Annie, who loved him with an independent heart and let him go with open arms, Annie whose voice was warmth and honesty and reason, Annie who needed him now — he hadn't been able to still their echoes in his heart.

Well, it was time to do it now. Because if he didn't, it would finally, irrevocably be too late.

"Another shot, sir?" the bartender asked when he went to settle his tab.

"That's enough," Jed said, and he meant it.

Fourteen

Annie had the dream again on Sunday night, the dream of herself and Jed dancing, the dream that shimmered with sensuality and tenderness and now, with loss.

Which was just too damned bad.

She didn't have time for dreams right now, Annie thought as she showered and dressed. She'd given Sunday over to mourning, and she knew she'd cry many times more. But for Monday, she'd made plans. To keep herself busy. To distract her aching heart. And to get on with her life. With Jed gone, the magic spell was truly over. It was time to face reality again.

The lawyer John sent her to had in turn recommended a woman attorney in Asheville, a nationally recognized expert on cases involving domestic violence. Annie had made an appointment for that afternoon, the first slot she could get. She knew she'd have to handle the actual divorce in New York. But the chance just to consult with someone who dealt with her situation all of the time — who knew how to protect and advise women just like her — would be worth every penny of the cost.

She was looking forward to it, even leaden with tiredness and with her eyes still red from her weeping. Just as she was looking forward to her visitor this morning.

The thought no sooner entered her mind when the doorbell rang. Feeling unaccountably nervous, as though she were back in the same fifth grade Alma Honeycutt had once taught, Annie brushed the hair off her forehead one more time and straightened her sweater.

When she opened the door, she blinked hard in surprise. The woman on her porch had on a hot-pink down coat, a teal blue track suit, and a pair of dangly earrings in the shape of tropical birds. Even the cane that rested by one leg was bright. Only the hair was as Annie expected, gray now but still wrapped in a coronet of braids high on her head.

Taking a look at her astonished face, Alma Honeycutt hooted with laughter.

"Tell the truth, child," she said. "You were expecting a schoolmarm in sensible shoes. Or maybe a pioneer woman in faded calicos and an apron."

"Not exactly, but close," Annie said, smiling back. Alma's forthrightness put her immediately at her ease. "Sit down, Mrs. Honeycutt. I feel strange, offering you a seat in your own house. You're right about the clothes. I took a peek at your albums. There was one dress — a dark print with a white collar? I guess I always pictured you in that."

"Alma. Please. Hundreds and hundreds of schoolchildren had to call me Mrs. Honeycutt; no need to add you to the list." Alma sat, handing Annie a laden white paper bag. "I brought pastries from the café. That little Meggie Thorn runs a fine kitchen, unlikely as it seems. Oh, I remember that dress. I wore it for years, to every blessed PTA meeting and church social and Elks dinner they had. Everything I owned back then was some sensible, practical dark color. Maybe that's why I've taken such a fancy to bright colors now. My Bobby says I make his eyes hurt. But he was always a conservative boy."

"The bright colors suit you. And your hair is right, though. Just like in the pictures," Annie said, lifting the teapot she'd set out, ready. It felt odd, playing hostess to another woman in that woman's own house. But Alma's lined, composed face showed no discomfort. "Tea?" Annie asked. "And a cinnamon roll?"

"Yes, thank you. No, no milk. Oh, my braids will never change, not as long as I'm in my right mind and have a say in it. I've worn these braids since I was a little girl, and I'll wear them as long as I can manage for myself." The bright, dark eyes surveyed the living room. "John said you'd done nice things here. I agree. I was never house proud, I'm afraid. Always wanted to be out and around. And I was terrible at throwing things away, as you may have noticed. The thought of sorting through all of those boxes isn't a pleasant one, but I'll have to do it one of these days."

"I won't be in your way much longer. John probably told you that I think I'll be leaving at the end of next month?" The very words pained Annie. It was too much, she thought for the hundredth time. Losing Jed, losing this beloved little house, losing the life in Burnsville she'd come to cherish. But as she'd told him, staying simply didn't make sense.

"I'm in no rush," Alma Honeycutt said. "You take your time, child. Between you and me and the lamppost — and don't you dare tell a soul here, they'd never forgive me for being so blunt about it — I'd never dream of coming back again. Oh, John probably told you, I went down to Tampa with a rebellious heart. And I thought this visit might make me homesick. No, indeed. These winters, this cold — I've had a bellyful of them. Now that I'm walking well again, I'll find myself some little condo, get out of Bobby and Judy's hair."

"Will you sell the place?" Again the thought hurt, illogical as that was.

"Someday, maybe. You just take your time, child," Alma repeated. "Meanwhile, John said you had something to ask me."

"Yes." Annie told the story of Moira McTeague. "It sounds silly, I know. But I was wondering if you might understand why she would want to damage the house or why she would want to get in."

"I heard about her death," Alma said. "Terrible thing. Yes, of course I know why she'd want to get into this house. Or at least I can guess. Evidence, that's why."

"Evidence? What kind?"

"Goodness knows. Love letters, maybe, or diaries, or handkerchiefs stained with my lipstick and Artie's Old Spice, all cached away somewhere in what she well knew to be my very crowded attic. Who knows what silly notions were in that poor woman's addled mind? Little Artie McTeague — Moira's husband Arthur — was sweet on me for years, even after I married Teddy and he married Moira," the older woman said. "Oh, it was nothing. Just a high school romance to start, and then the foolish dreaming of a poor, weak man wed to a harsh, unloving woman. It made Artie feel good to have someone to admire, I thought, and what harm did it do me to be kind to the poor man in return? I was head over heels in love with Teddy, and everyone knew it. Even Artie."

"When I spoke to her, Cindy mentioned something about that," Annie said slowly, remembering. "But how could there be evidence of something that never happened?"

"There couldn't. But Moira . . . she had three, four miscarriages, and they brought out something troubled in her. Something twisted, some kind of obsession. She'd make awful comments about young girls who seemed too popular, or women who divorced. The woman seemed to have a nose for every scandal in town, and she read scandal into all sorts of things that were nothing of the sort. She simply wouldn't believe that Artie's little smiles didn't mean a thing. And it got worse, if anything, after he died. She made comments about it to me for years, asked questions, tried to trap me into some kind of confession. I suppose I never quite took it seriously," Alma finished. "I surely never guessed how much it obsessed her. I'm sorry, my dear, to let you in for something so frightening."

"No one could have known," Annie said. "And it doesn't matter anymore; I'm just glad to know the end of the story. It's a sad one, though. And it seems so wasteful. So unnecessary."

"It is that. Did you know," Alma asked, "that the name Moira means *bitter?*"

"I didn't," Annie said. "How awful, to name a daughter that. No matter how appropriate it turns out to be."

"And did you know," Alma went on, her dark eyes dancing, "that Jedidiah means *prince?*"

"Really," Annie said dryly, pleased that she could even smile over it. "At the moment, I would have thought it meant *man who leaves town.*"

Alma burst out laughing again, with that already familiar, exuberant hoot. "He always had itchy feet, that boy. John told me about the two of you, and I was pleased for him, thought he was settling down. High time, too. What's he waiting for, his first stroke? Now here he is, off again, and you're here alone, with teary eyes. Well, at least he'll be back."

Startled and amused by Alma's perception, Annie took a sip of her tea. "I'll be gone by then, I expect. I'm so grateful for your latitude about the house, but I have things to handle in my own life, in other places. I asked him not to keep in touch, not to get in touch when he comes back. It just wouldn't work. You must know that, Alma, if you've known him for so long. He couldn't be the writer he is and be tied down."

"Now that," Alma said roundly, "is bull."

Teacup poised in midair, Annie gaped at her, astonished.

"I'm sorry, child, and I hope you don't mind an old biddy you barely know meddling. It's one of the great glories of getting old. You can stick your nose in everybody's business, and no one can really argue. In this case, though, I happen to be right. Don't forget, I've known the boy his whole life. Jed Harper's nonsense about freedom is just that. He's scared, that's all, and he always has been scared. Oh, I'm not criticizing him. He's done very well with the cards the Lord dealt him. Goodness knows it was a terrible hand. But the fact that his parents had miserable lives, miserable characters, a miserable marriage, and a miserable home doesn't have to shape the rest of his life. Of course he needs to travel. A hundred years ago, maybe he'd have to go alone, but today women travel almost everywhere. You can't tell me you couldn't go with him, at least part of the time. And in the meantime there are planes and trains and hotels and faxes and phones, and even an old withered-up granny like me uses E-mail. If Jed Harper's persuaded himself he can't do his job and make some kind of home life for himself at the same time, he's a blind fool. And if you're letting him get away with it, child, well, I'm afraid you're being a fool, too."

"I honestly never thought of it that way." Annie shook her head. "But Mrs. Honeycutt — sorry, Alma — it's not that simple."

"Annie, it's never simple. If you get a wanderer like Jed Harper, well, you want to kill him when he doesn't come home. If you get a nice comfortable homebody like my Ted, you want to kill him when he *does* come home. You long for him to go away and leave you in peace sometimes. If you get an Artie McTeague he's too weak, and if you get Dottie Barclay's husband Sam he's too strong. No matter what, you have to fight it out. You do what you need to do, my dear. No matter how opinionated I sound, I do understand that I don't know you or your history or your heart or even what it is that young Jed Harper really wants, when he's honest with himself. But there's one thing you shouldn't do, Annie, and about this I'm sure. Don't let Jed Harper dress up his fears in fancy clothes. And don't you do it, either, even out of love for him. Because there'll be nothing worse than having to look back ten or twenty years from now and knowing that you never even tried to fight for what you want."

The words echoed in Annie's ears as she hugged Alma good-bye, changed her clothes, drove to Asheville for her appointment.

Maybe, she thought, because they had a familiar ring.

"You can't take your fear and call it by Annie Taylor's name," she'd told Jed angrily, weeks before.

But was it possible that she was taking her own fears and calling them by his?

Was it possible that it was easier to face this heartache now than to let herself hope, much less fight, for the love she'd found? Was it possible that what she called respect for him would only cheat them both in the long run?

She hadn't fought for what she wanted with Tom, she'd just clung on too hard. Was she not fighting for what she wanted with Jed by letting go too easily?

It was as though Alma had taken the kaleidoscope of Annie's life, with the hundreds of images and memories and impressions that made up her relationship with Jed and Tom and her own self, and given it a strong, decisive twist. The pattern she'd thought she'd seen in all of the colorful fragments had vanished, and the new pattern wouldn't quite form.

She drove the winding roads away from Burnsville slowly, her mind filled with doubt.

After many calls and many arguments, Jed had found himself a flight home at noon. Cost a fortune, his ticket did, and it was worth every single penny. The journalist he'd antagonized and editors he'd pissed off were another price to pay, but that was worth it, too, and he'd take the time to soothe all the feathers he'd ruffled once he'd gotten home and talked to Annie. That was the important thing now. Everything else could wait. But he wasn't going to leave Annie all alone, thinking he was still the same unforgivably stupid shit he'd been at this time yesterday, for a moment longer than he had to.

Jed zipped up his duffel bag, glanced at his watch, scribbled his name on the express checkout receipt he'd had the hotel make up last night, after he'd gotten home from his endless walk to McSorley's. If he left right now, he'd just make it. The roads to the airport would be crammed with traffic on a postholiday Monday morning, but even if it meant cutting it close, there was something he had to buy on the way.

Annie drove back up the mountain three hours after she'd driven down it. Tired to the bone but at peace for the first time in days.

It had been a remarkable day, of remarkable women. Alma Honeycutt, funny and shrewd and living very much in the present. The ghost of Moira McTeague, laid to rest now — a telling vision, perhaps, of what happened when you couldn't let go of the past. Lillian Doherty, the lawyer, a stocky, gray-haired fount of information, contacts, reassurance, strategies. She should have found Lillian Doherty three months ago, Annie thought ruefully as she turned off Highway 19 onto the mountain road. Should have taken Tom on at once, rather than hidden in fear. But sometimes, perhaps, the pieces of the kaleidoscope just took time to settle, to find their proper place.

She pulled up in front of the cottage at the very end of twilight, almost too weary to get out of the car. How she hated these short winter days and looked forward to the spring, when the glowing light would linger, sweet and golden, on the hillside, as it had done when she'd first arrived in town. Only she wasn't going to be here in Burnsville, she reminded herself. Or so, at least, she had thought. Now . . . she just didn't know. Anything was possible. She found her mouth curling into a smile as she walked to the house and let herself in.

She had forgotten to set the alarm, she thought guiltily. She'd been so preoccupied when she left, and with Moira gone, the urgency had seemed to lessen a little. Foolish, with Tom still out there and the cottage so isolated; she'd make sure to arm it starting tomorrow.

She had left a single light on in the living room. The lamplight glowed softly on the wood she'd polished, the curtains she'd starched, the pillow covers and tablecloths she'd made to replace the ones that Moira McTeague had ruined. A pleasing glass jar stood on her mantelpiece, filled with sprays of holly and bittersweet berries from the shrubs on the border of Wellman's farm. The cashmere shawl Jed had given her was draped over the arm of the couch, ready to warm her when she needed it. Even without the comforting additions of his things, his books and papers and slippers, it was a cozy room and somehow a loving one. Together, she decided, she and Alma Honeycutt had done a good job with her home.

Tea, first, she thought drowsily, and then a bath, with one of the scented oils Jed had given her. And then to bed, nice and early. Tomorrow was going to be another busy day. She walked into the kitchen, stepped into the darkness, turned on the burner under the kettle with one hand while she reached for the light switch with the other.

"Hello, Annabel," Tom said from behind her.

It was almost funny, how little surprise she felt.
It was as though something in her heart had known since the beginning that this day was going to come.

He stood not ten feet away from her, his back against the refrigerator. At first glance he looked like a sportsman or skier, dashingly vivid in a blue pocket- and flap-covered parka. But as she looked at him closely, cracks started to show in the gleaming facade, hints of unkemptness and disorder. One of his hands was in his pocket, but the other shook with a small but ever-present palsy. His corduroy pants were creased. His red-rimmed, curiously empty eyes moved constantly, and his chin was covered with a blue black stubble that stood out against his pallid skin like the mark of some disease. He looked volatile, dirty, and brutish.

He was so ugly. The foolish, incongruous thought came to her unbidden. It wasn't his physical form, or even his lack of grooming. It was the rage in him, the coldness, the hatred. All of the ugliness that her own insecurity had blinded her to for so long.

Instinct told her to keep things as calm, as ordinary as she could. "Would you like some tea, Tom?"

His grooming might have changed, but the quick contemptuous laugh hadn't. "Sure, Annabel," he said. "I chased you halfway across the country for some fucking tea, made in some crappy little shanty kitchen. A real gourmet treat. Maybe we could have some scones while we're at it, right, bitch? Maybe we could wear white gloves and make nice little chitchat. Jesus, you're a stupid broad."

The forgotten kettle shrilled. Moving slowly, letting him see there was no trickery, she reached behind her to turn it off.

There was wildness in his voice as well as rage. He was hovering right on the edge of self-control, she thought. And yet she didn't feel afraid. Not consciously, anyway. Everything in her felt still and very focused. Keeping her gaze calm, she tried to assess her options. There were knives in the kitchen drawers, but no way to reach for them. Both of the guns were loaded, but they were behind him, and she couldn't imagine that he'd move. If she'd taken either the guns or Jed seriously, she would have placed them better, farther apart. Now, faced with the actual need for them, she had no doubt that she could shoot Tom, or at least try to, if they were accessible.

But there had to be some way to distract him. Some way to reach something, anything, she could use as a weapon. Or some way to run.

"Is there something I can do for you, then, Tom?" she asked.

Oddly, the simple question threw him. Clearly he had come to find her with no conscious intention at all. But even as the thought formed in her mind, she could see his expression changing. The dark brown eyes grew sly, the ugly face looked knowing.

"You know, now that you ask me, there's not that much you can do, anymore, Annabel," he said, as though he were actually considering the question. "Three months ago, sure, you could have done something. You could have shown some fucking gratitude, you could have done your job, you could have been a decent wife. But no, you couldn't do that. Did you know I lost my job, bitch? No, of course, you were too busy fucking your corn-fed hillbilly dick to care about that. Yeah. Spent my whole career slaving for the bastards, make them and their clients — make that goddamned Jim Perry — millions, and they walk me out of there on five minutes' notice with a security guard on each side of me, right in front of every secretary and receptionist in the place. Like I'm a fucking felon. All because of you, because you decide to run off to God knows where, stir a load of shit up. It's too bad, Annabel, but no. You can't get my job back for me anymore. Or my reputation. Or my future. Or my fucking life."

He was breathing hard now, almost panting. A distinct rim of white showed around the dark irises, and the trembling in his hand was worse. He moved it into one of his pockets as though to hide the shaking. She had never heard him talk like this. Usually terse, he was voluble now, the words spilling out as though he couldn't stop them. There was something odd about it, something weak. This wasn't the strong, driven man who had raped her that evening three months before. Something had broken in him, and that was good. Because she was going to need every advantage she could get.

"No. There's nothing *important* you can do for me. Just a little luxury, you might say. You can give me the pleasure of letting me beat the shit out of you, Annabel," he said. "I'll give you what you deserve, and then you can give me a nice wild screwing, just like the one you gave me the last time I saw you. I liked that. I mean, it's a Goddamn shame you need this kind of foreplay before you'll give your husband what he needs. But hell." He pulled his hand out of the parka, and in it was a gleaming black-handled knife.

"Whatever turns you on."

The fear surged into her now, bursting like flood tides through a broken dam. The knife was terrifying, unthinkable, and yet it made the danger real. And even if it was an empty threat, the memory of that unspeakable night had done what Tom's mere presence couldn't. She couldn't bear it, she thought. Couldn't go through it again, the pain, the shame, the horrible violation. The healing Jed had brought to her, the sensual rebirth she'd felt at his touch, only made the agony of terror worse. She would die if Tom touched her now. She could feel her heart pounding, her already dry mouth getting parched. Her stomach roiled with nausea, and her knees felt weak.

And Tom could see it. She could tell. He could see that the balance had shifted, that he'd regained the advantage again. He ran his thumb gently over the base of the blade, enjoying his power. He didn't speak now, though his breathing sounded as heavily as before. He just stood and savored the pain in her eyes.

Help. Dear God, she thought. Please, she needed help.

And, by some miracle, it came.

A car. On the hill.

Tom ignored it, just as she might have three months before. In the city, the sound of an engine was unremarkable. But not on the mountain, where the houses were so few and far between. There was only one road that would bring a car that close. The road that led to Jed's

416

house, now closed up, and then curved on up to her own.

Ethan, maybe. Or Meg or Susie, dropping by. The sound of the car came closer. Only it wasn't a car, she thought with disbelief, keeping her eyes locked on Tom's. It was a truck. Jed's truck. The old, purring engine was unmistakable, even to her. It couldn't be Jed's truck, which was probably still at John and Susie's house after the trip to the airport. It couldn't be Jed. Jed, who was in New York. Jed, who had left with such grim finality only the day before.

But somehow she knew it was.

It might help her, or it might hurt. It could be even more dangerous. But the knowledge that he was back gave her infinite courage. She stared into Tom's face.

And smiled.

"You don't have to persuade me, Thomas," she said, continuing to smile at him and opening her eyes wide. Deliberately she made her voice sensual, husky. And drew it out, giving Jed time to arrive. "Come on. I've had wonderful sex since I saw you last time. You could tell that, though, couldn't you? Come on, let's see. Let's see if you can do better."

It had been a guess, and a wild one, but it had been right. The sudden provocation in her tone unnerved him. And so did the confidence. He was used to her timid, self-doubting, afraid. He wanted her that way. Needed her that way. In a second or two, he'd figure out that she was just

417

manipulating him. But for now, he simply didn't know what to do.

Now, Jed, she prayed.

With no conscious intention, adrenaline surging through her and every muscle tensed, she threw herself at Tom's torso, aiming her shoulders at his ribs.

He didn't want to scare her, but he hadn't been able to wait through the ringing of the bell. So he let himself in the unlocked door and called out to her, like a schoolkid coming home to an eager mom.

He registered all three sounds at once, a crashing, a low male grunt, her soft-voiced cry. And ran blindly toward the noise, dropping the huge shopping bag he held in his hand onto the hallway rug.

They were on the floor in the kitchen, moving frantically together, Annie and a man who could only be Tom. Jed sighted the shotgun in the corner and grabbed it by the stock. Not aiming it, they were rolling together too closely for that, just holding it like a club. As he paused, she drew a leg back and kneed Tom in the groin. The man let out an anguished wail and arched his body backward in agony. It was all the space Jed needed.

With one hand he reached for her shoulder, pulled her head and upper body swiftly out of the way. And with the other, he swung the gleaming butt of the shotgun with measured force against Thomas Mahoney's skull.

The strong body went still.

"Oh, my God," Annie said, staggering to her feet on the other side of Tom's inert form. She brought one hand up and pressed it against her heart. "Is he dead?"

"Part of me wishes I could say he was. But I don't think so." Jed squatted down, held Tom's wrist, shook his head. "No. Find me something to tie his hands with, would you? I reckon he'll live to make your life miserable again."

She fished in a kitchen drawer for the clothesline she remembered seeing there. It was lucky Alma was a pack rat after all. "Remind me to tell you about the lawyer I met today," she said, and suddenly she smiled.

Somehow he'd imagined tears from her, and apologies from him, and long earnest explanations. Instead they were standing over the body of an unconscious man and grinning at each other like fools. Either it was just relief, or they were out of their minds.

Whatever you could say about their future together, he thought as he gazed at her gorgeous, disheveled form, it sure as hell wasn't going to be boring.

"The scary thing is," she said, still smiling, "that we timed that just great."

"Yeah. Well, we've had a chance to hone our instincts in the last few months, I guess. Speakin' of which, I guess we'd better call Tommy Straub," he said. "Tell him that Annie Taylor, the single-handed source of the only crime wave in all of Burnsville's history, has done it again."

Now her smile widened, filled with triumph and welcome. "He'll be thrilled. I won't mention that you flew back home from New York after only twenty-four hours, though. He might think you were serious about me."

"He'd be right. You know, you're lookin' pretty damn cocky, lady," Jed said. "I'm wonderin'. Is it just kicking Tom in the balls, or did you know I was going to come back to get you?"

"I didn't know you were coming back," Annie said, answering the important question. She stepped around her husband to take the love of her life in her arms. "I knew I was going there. To get you."

Epilogue

"Come here," she told him three nights later. "I have something to show you."

"Where?" He was sitting at the kitchen table fiddling with the Canada itinerary, trying to juggle some dates and places to make a less punishing trip. Stretched onto the wall above his head, adjacent to the window seat, was Annie's *Comfort* quilt, which Jed had gone to Pleasures to buy the morning he'd left New York. He hoped he'd get a marital discount next time, he'd told her. But he just couldn't let it go.

"Outside," she said.

"Lady, it's about twenty degrees out there. I'd think you'd be staying warm while you still could," he said, but he shrugged into the jacket she handed him and walked with her onto his back stoop.

Out in his front hallway rested a stack of suitcases, her bags now along with his. They were flying to New York together the next morning, so that Jed could make up the meetings he'd canceled so abruptly and Annie could begin the long process of her divorce. Lillian Doherty had recommended a New York attorney, another woman, another specialist. After the paperwork was started, Annie and Jed would travel together to Newfoundland to start the first leg of his trip.

She'd leave him there at some point, but they weren't quite sure when. They had filed a restraining order against Tom, who in any case was still under the weather from the concussion Jed had given him — Tommy Straub had said a few choice words about that. But he'd be free on bail while both the divorce and the charges against him were pending. Jed wasn't taking any chances; he'd already done that, and he wasn't going to push his luck. It was unlikely that even Tom would be crazy enough to try to track them through the wilds of Canada in January. Annie might freeze to death there, he'd told her, but aside from that, she'd be safe.

She stood against the railing, her back to the house. Jed slid his arms around her waist, and she leaned back against his body, resting against his warmth, feeling his cheek against her hair. "There, up the hill," she pointed. "Look."

It was a bright night, cold and sharp and cloudless. The cottage was clearly visible in the crystalline air, a small fieldstone form, sturdy enough to stand there for decades more. They had decided to keep the place, use it as Annie's studio, and buy it when Alma sold. In the front window, behind the ivory blur of a lace curtain, a light glowed soft and yellow into the night.

"Do you remember the story I told you the

night of your party?" she asked. "The one about the house across the street from me, with the little lamp in its window?" Feeling him nod, she went on. "I found a little lamp just like it today, down at the antique shop right off the square. I bought it and I put it in the window, where you can see it when you come home from your trips. So that you'll always know there's something to come home to — that I'm waiting for you, and thinking about you, and wanting to make sure you're safe."

His arms tightened around her. "I could definitely get used to that. Although, you know, I'm thinking about taking a couple of months off, after Newfoundland. Not forever. Just enough to try that book about the mountains that Dana's been mentioning for years. Well, maybe. Still makes me a little nervous, now that I hear myself sayin' it aloud. We'll see."

She nodded but didn't speak. "Look, I've got something to show you, too," he added, pivoting her gently in the other direction. "There. Harper's Moon."

Annie tilted her head to look up at the huge yellow orb, then turned to gaze back at him. "I don't know," she said, gently teasing. "Remember, I share this mountain, too. Maybe the moon wants to be Taylor's Moon, now."

"Awful possessive all of a sudden, aren't you?"

"Oh, yes. I am that."

"I could compromise," he said, kissing the top of her head. She could hear his voice warming with laughter, a sound she knew she would hear a million times over the years. And feel her body warming from his touch, despite the piercing cold of the night. "Harper-Taylor's Moon," he said.

"Ugh," she said promptly. "It sounds like a law firm."

"Right. I know," he said, turning her to face him and kissing her again, this time on her mouth. The warmth in her kindled, began to turn to heat. He paused, and when he spoke again, his voice sounded elaborately, suspiciously casual.

"We can compromise and just name the damn thing after our first baby," he said. "Will that work for you?"

Tears stung at her eyes at exactly the same moment she felt a smile of wonder and love and gratitude fill her face.

"Oh, that will work," she said, reaching up to kiss him again. "It'll work for me just fine."